THE HIGHLAND OUTLAW

THE HIGHLAND OUTLAW

HEATHER McCOLLUM

Entangled Publishing, LLC
2614 South Timberline Road
Suite 105, PMB 159
Fort Collins, CO 80525
rights@entangledpublishing.com

Amara is an imprint of Entangled Publishing, LLC.

Edited by Alethea Spiridon
Cover design by Bree Archer
Cover photography from The Killion Group
vishstudio/Shutterstock
nutriaaa and akv_lv/DepositPhotos
solarseven and nicolamargaret/GettyImages

Manufactured in the United States of America

First Edition October 2019

To my sweet Kyrra (who is still too young to read this book). Your love for animals inspired the relationship between Alana and her wolfhound, Robert. A heart that respects, protects, and loves animals is golden. May you always have a golden heart and a sweet bundle of fur in your lap.

– Love Forever, Mom

Foreign Words used in *The Highland Outlaw*
(Scots-Gaelic and French)

Beinn Nibheis – Ben Nevis or Nevis Mountain

Sgian dubh – Black-handled knife

Mo chreach – My rage

Deamhan Die! – Die Devil!

Dia mhath – Good God

Gu buaidh no bàs! – To victory or death!

Falbh! – Go!

Mattucashlass – Short dagger

Ionnsaigh! – Attack!

Bòidheach – Beautiful

Tiugainn – Let's go

la petite fille – the little girl (French)

trois bébés – three babies (French)

Màthair – Mother

Mousquet – Musket (French)

To Laird Shaw Sinclair, 7th Earl of Caithness

The infant who journeys under the protection of this letter is of strong health yet might succumb to an assassin's poison. Therefore, she must be taken to safety shielded by the fierce Sinclair clan. Take the child to the ruins of St. Andrews Castle, where a ship will ferry her over to France to be raised in secret until such time as she can be claimed.

In return for your service, Castle Girnigoe and the lands historically kept by the Sinclair Clan will be retaken from Edgar Campbell of Glenorchy to be returned to Clan Sinclair. The child must arrive, alive, to the ship before the winter snows blanket the Highlands.

May God in his ultimate wisdom and power guide you and see that you protect this very important child.

20 October 1685

Chapter One

"Ooooo…" Cici MacInnes whispered, her eyes round as if lusting after a honey tart. "With this fine weather, the men will be tossing off their tunics along with tossing those cabers." She bounced up and down on her toes and hurried to keep up with Alana Campbell.

"Evelyn would tell you to behave," Alana said but smiled over her friend's excitement. "That we are here merely to promote the school, not to ogle the men."

"Fortunate for us then that Evelyn is traveling with Scarlet and Nathaniel back to England right now to ready Hollings Estate for lease," Kirstin MacGregor, Alana's best friend, said next to her.

Martha Campbell giggled. "So we can ogle all we want." She linked arms with Cici.

"Very well," Alana said. "But no getting carried off, wed,

or with child." They all burst out laughing as they nodded their agreement of the pact.

Together, the small group of Highland Roses School students strode across the meadow filled with representatives from various clans, their wolfhound jogging along beside them. It was the last day of October, and Samhain would begin when the sun sank below the line of mountains. The more senior students had traveled to the annual Samhain festival at the base of *Beinn Nibheis*, the tallest mountain in the grand, sweeping Grampian Mountains. Men, women, and children moved about in clusters as the clans competed, their tents set up by clan to ring the meadow in a colorful display of kinship pride.

Alana, sister of Grey Campbell, the chief of the Campbells of Breadalbane, glanced across the meadow to the men who walked along the line of stout tree trunks. Some of the cabers weighed over one hundred eighty pounds and stood to twenty-two feet high. Izzy Campbell, the youngest of their group at twelve years old, jabbed her finger toward the far end of the field. Izzy was mute, an affliction that had struck her when her parents died several years ago. Alana followed the girl's motion to see a cluster of dogs across the trampled field. "I see them," Alana said, smiling down at the girl. "I think Robert will beat them all in the competition. Don't you?"

Izzy nodded vigorously, her hand patting the head of the large wolfhound who stared up with bright brown eyes. Shaggy gray, strong, and possessing the most playful expression, Robert made a wonderful companion, even though he still didn't follow commands well when he became flustered and excited. He was also huge, standing well over Alana's head when on his back paws, which deterred villains who might not have heard that the Highland Rose students were always armed and ready for defensive attack.

Cici whistled low. "Look at him," she said, brushing her red hair back from her pretty round face to tuck behind her ears. She jutted out her chin toward the far field. "He is a brawn fellow and so tall." Her assessment ended with a dramatic sigh.

The group of men opened a path to allow the warrior to enter the field where three other men dropped a long, thick caber. He was broad and towering, the muscles obvious in his bare arms where dark lines formed a picture on his tan skin. He wore a kilt and a sleeveless tunic with the autumn sun covering the scene with golden warmth. Alana caught the toe of her boot in her skirt and stumbled to a pause in her stride.

With large biceps and powerful legs, the man squatted low to lift under the caber's end. Alana's breath stuck as he heaved the soaring tree upward, taking several power-filled steps forward to build the momentum of his toss. His shoulders bunched as he threw his strength into lifting the end of the tall caber so that it flew upward toward the blue sky. His deep yell from the effort reached across the field, sounding very much like a war cry. Alana realized that all six of them had stopped in their tracks to watch as the tall caber flew over, landing in a perfectly straight toss.

"'Tis a horse's head painted on his arm," Martha said, her words breathless.

Robert circled the Roses as if guarding them, his rope leash dragging untended behind him to get caught on their skirts. The warrior turned, his arms reaching overhead where he grabbed his elbows in a stretch as he strode effortlessly back to the cheering men. "Och," Alana murmured. "Who is he?"

Kirstin tsked where she had stopped next to her. She bent her face closer to Alana, lowering her voice. "They are Sinclairs, so do not even look. All Sinclairs are tricksters, liars, and scoundrels."

"The enemy then," Lucy Kellington said just behind them, her sharp English accent still fresh since she'd come to Scotland only six months prior.

"Aye," Kirstin said. "To Campbells anyway. He is likely the chief who won the lairdship when his horrible uncle died almost ten years ago. I heard his name is Shaw, Shaw Sinclair. Don't know why they are this far south unless they are here to cause trouble."

"Trouble?" Alana asked. There had always been whispers about the mighty Sinclairs from the north, their ancestors being godlike warriors with unnatural abilities to guide horses. But she thought that they were now virtually powerless, a penniless and landless clan. What type of trouble could they cause?

Kirstin propped her hands on her hips. "Kerrick told me that even though Campbells took their clan castle, Girnigoe, fairly to pay a debt incurred by the old laird, once he died, his nephew has been trying to steal it back ever since. There was a battle about five years ago to regain the castle, but the Sinclairs lost. You know the one at Altimarlach, Alana."

Alana nodded, remembering her father and Donald Campbell sending troops to defend their Campbell cousin's won castle in the northernmost edge of Scotland. Even Grey fought to defend the legally won bargain.

"Why must all the men I have to stay away from be so... enticingly brawny?" Cici asked, a prominent pout on her lips.

"Perhaps he is coming south to attack Campbells to win his clan castle back," Martha said in a hushed voice filled with drama.

Alana had once suffered the loss of her clan's castle when Finlarig Castle was taken by the English crown because of lies that the Campbells were plotting against the king. She rubbed her arms as the smoke from a cook fire brought back the terror-filled memories of the cruel fire, a constant nightmare she tried to block.

"Why would they attack Campbells in the south when there are plenty of them up on Sinclair land in the north to attack?" Kirstin said, wry irritation in her voice as she frowned at Martha.

"Whatever his presence here means," Alana said, glancing first at Martha and Izzy, then sliding her gaze to fix meaningfully on Cici, "we shall stay well away from the Sinclairs while we are here."

Hopefully they would listen to her. When they made plans to attend the festival, her brother had put Alana in charge. But then Kerrick volunteered to come. Instead of acting like their escort, he acted as if he were their leader, and the other students had started to ignore Alana's guidance. Back at Finlarig Castle, Alana sort of…blended in, especially with such strong women like Evelyn and Scarlet Worthington in charge of the school. There was nothing special about Alana, so she'd been looking for a chance to stand out a bit more and prove herself.

She stood even straighter and cleared her throat, raising her voice over the girls' continued chatter. "We are here to represent the Highland Roses School." She started them walking again toward the knife-throwing area of competition. "Talk to the ladies you meet. Tell them how important it is to be able to read. Right, Izzy?" She looked at the girl, who nodded vigorously. Izzy had read an important message when an English officer abducted her last year. The knowledge she'd gained from the letter had saved their clan in the end.

Martha picked up her steps to move slightly ahead, glancing back with a determined smile. "And how every student learns to defend herself. I think that is the most important skill taught at the school."

Alana nodded, keeping her gaze on the targets far at the end of the throwing field. "Although being able to read, especially all those books in the school library, brings us knowledge which can defend us nearly as well as a *sgian dubh*."

Kirstin smiled wryly. "Evelyn would be so proud of ye," she teased.

"Oh yes, I love the books," Cici said. "Especially that art book." She couldn't contain her laughter, and Kirstin joined in before sucking her lips inward to stop. Alana shook her head but smiled. It was a festival, after all, and a perfect place to be silly.

"Tarts and fresh-squeezed apple cider," called a woman from a tent as they passed.

Izzy jumped up and down. "I will take her," Cici said, grabbing her hand. Since Izzy's sister, Cat, had journeyed with the group traveling down to the Worthingtons' English estate, they all took turns looking after the girl. Izzy had become best friends with the young English orphan, Mouse, who had returned with Cat from England last winter. But she and her friend, Michaela, had remained at the school with some other students and Mistress Jane, the new housekeeper. Slowly, but surely, the school was growing.

"Meet us at the dagger throwing then," Alana said, and the two of them ran off, Cici just as excited as Izzy to get a tart and cider.

Alana breathed in the crisp air, glancing at the snow-topped mountain range rising behind the forest. The gorse and heather had darkened on the meadow, and trees of gold, red, and orange encircled the fair, adding to the festive atmosphere. Samhain would start at sundown with huge bonfires and people dressed in costumes to frighten away the evil spirits. Many feared that ghosts walked the world when the boundary between spirit and human worlds thinned on Samhain. Alana would set a place for both her father and mother at the meal tonight, in their memories. So much had changed in the two short years since they had been killed at a Covenanter meeting outside Stirling.

Alana scanned the contest area and couldn't help but notice the large Sinclair warrior who had obviously won the caber toss. He frowned as he spoke with some of his men, one of them gesturing toward the tents with a jabbing finger. Something had them out of sorts.

No matter. She turned her gaze. The Sinclairs were no concern of hers or her students. She rested her palm on Robert's shaggy back as they marched forward past the stacked wood for the bonfires to the far side of the field. The dog circled around her happily and licked her hand.

"Very well," she said, wiping her hand on her skirt. "I love you, too." Of all the dogs that she'd raised back at the school, Robert was the largest and the friendliest. No matter how many times the Campbell warriors asked, she wouldn't give him up to them to train for war.

Alana stopped before a table covered with polished knives and daggers of every length and weight. She smiled at the man in charge of the competition, an older warrior who wore an impressive scar slashed across one cheek up to his eye. "We would like to enter the contest," Alana said, her voice strong.

The handful of men standing at the table turned to look at her, but Alana ignored them, keeping her gaze centered on the one in charge. "Myself, Alana Campbell, and my two friends, Kirstin MacGregor and Martha Campbell."

The man stared at her from under bushy gray eyebrows that curled in wild swirls. His lined mouth quirked to the side.

When he didn't say anything, she cleared her throat. "I am the sister of Grey Campbell, the chief of the Campbells of Breadalbane. We are students and instructors at the Highland Roses School in Killin."

No one moved, and Alana kept her strong stare despite

the heavy thump of her heart. The man rubbed his chin and squinted his eye where the scar crossed it. "'Tis a competition for men. Not meant for lasses or children." His voice was a gruff bark, but Alana imagined that he was Killin's always-ornery blacksmith, Craig, with his lethal frown but kind heart.

She made a signal for Robert to sit, his head reaching up to her chest. She inhaled fully. "I request to see the rule book then, where it says that one must possess a jack in order to throw a dagger."

Several of the men listening chuckled, and she heard one spit. Women were definitely the cleaner of the sexes. But she'd grown up around warriors, and she was used to their annoyances.

"'Tis not written down," the old man said. He tapped his gray, shaggy head. "The rules are right up here, and they say no lasses compete."

Alana heard more people gathering behind her to watch the disagreement and had to signal Robert to sit again, although his large head kept sweeping left and right to take in whoever might become an enemy. Alana kept her focus on the bad-tempered rule keeper. She wasn't a screaming shrew nor was she strong enough to force her way into the competition. She needed a new tactic.

Her frown turned into a condescending smile, and she tipped her head. "You are afraid then? Afraid a lass might beat the mighty warriors here." She swept her hand out to indicate the other men lined up to compete. Her breath stuttered when she saw that the Sinclair warriors had come over, including the tall caber toss winner. She let her gaze slide away to rake along the gathered men on her other side. "So, you are all afraid that a couple of lasses might beat you in the dagger toss?" She laughed lightly, playing the part that Scarlet had taught her back at the school. She looked at

Martha and Kirstin. "'Tis too bad that Scotland is made up of warriors who are frightened of women."

The men around them frowned, some of them grumbling a "bloody hell" or "damn not." Although no one threatened them outright, the tone and tension were enough to make Robert stand, a low growl drawing up from his barrel chest. Cici and Izzy nudged through the crowd, along with Lucy, who strode with Kerrick Campbell next to her. He shouldered his way forward, and Alana held up a hand to stop him from trying to come to the rescue. Lucy frowned, stopping next to Martha, and whispered in her ear, giving her fiercest stare outward.

Alana let her gaze settle across the Highlanders who had shaken their heads at her. "'Tis no wonder the English have been known to rout—"

"Let the lass throw a knife before some undisciplined bastard cuts out her tongue." The large Sinclair's voice came like a deep rumble of thunder through the mountains. Restrained power and authority in each word.

He stood with his legs braced apart as if in battle, his muscled arms crossed over his chest. His beard was trimmed close to a strong jaw under a straight nose. Here and there a scar stood out against his tanned skin, and sharp black lines of a tattoo cut across his upper arm to form the head and neck of a primitive-looking horse with an expression as fierce as the man.

She raised her gaze to meet his. "The undisciplined bastard would end up in an early grave," she said. Pride filled her as she saw the other Highland Roses students form a circle, their backs to each other as they looked outward at the gathered crowd, Robert's growl the only sound in the stiff hush. Each Rose held a dagger in her hand and a vicious scowl on her face, even cheerful Cici.

Sinclair kept his frown, but his eyes widened the slightest

amount, making him look…intrigued. With his bearded jaw, straight nose, and eyes just a shade lighter than a stormy sky, Alana was struck by his beauty as he radiated raw power and intimidation. Even the white scar at his hairline enhanced his rugged good looks. *Damn. He's a Sinclair.*

She tore her gaze away to meet the squint of the old warrior in charge. She balanced her own *sgian dubh* in her grasp, feeling its weight like she did before throwing. "Shall we draw blood and shame from these men, or will you let these feeble lasses give it a try?"

The old man cursed low, glancing toward the Sinclair warrior. The old man's bushy brows lifted, and Alana knew she'd won. "Wouldn't want to taint Samhain with blood," he said. "Liable to bring all types of demons and spirits here." He scratched his head, making his hair stand on end. "But only two entries from each clan. 'Tis the rule for the men as well." His gnarled hand swept along the blades. "Ye can choose one of mine or use your own, lass."

The crowd backed up, and the ladies, Kerrick, and Robert seemed to relax. Although, Alana knew they remained alert as their self-defense instructors at the school had taught them. She looked to Robert. "Stay," she commanded and made the signal for him to sit. With her heart still thumping, Alana stepped forward to the throwing line burnt into the dry grass. Everyone was watching her, including the bloody handsome Sinclair and his small army of rough Highlanders. *Blast.* She was nervous.

She took a deep inhale, focusing her gaze on the target beyond. She would throw from the side, bringing the blade point to fly forward toward the center circle on the hay bale. Just like in training where she'd practiced hundreds of times. It had become her most lethal skill.

One of the other Sinclairs next to the chief snorted. A younger man in their group leapt about like an idiot in her periphery. Was the man already drunk on whisky or trying to distract her?

"I bet a shilling she doesn't even make it to the target," said a Sinclair with a tattoo of a hollow-eyed skull on his forehead near his temple. Several men laughed, either at his words or his kinsman's antics. Others yelled out that they'd take the bet.

Alana looked back down the field. Her eyes narrowed as she focused, ignoring them, but their taunts brought a flush to her cheeks. They were waiting for her to fail. The responsibility to represent not only the Highland Roses School but all of womankind was a heavy burden to carry. Anger that women had to endure such unfairness hardened her stance.

She heard Robert growl and hoped Kerrick would hold the braided rope she'd tied around the dog's neck earlier. Kerrick was the only one in their group strong enough to keep Robert back when the huge dog became riled.

Alana took a deep breath. The Sinclair chief stepped up next to her but still gave her plenty of room to throw. She raised her arm, her focus returning to the red painted circle in the distance. In her periphery, she saw the other Sinclair jig around, his knees rising high. Men laughed and several of the Roses shushed them.

"The enemy don't stay quiet, lasses," the skull-tattooed man said.

"Aye, they are right bloody loud when throwing knives," another called and more laughed.

Breathe in. Breathe out. Alana focused. All she heard was the exchange of her breath. She raised her front foot, gathering momentum to lunge forward.

"*Stad!*" Kerrick yelled as she whipped the knife around.

The large shaggy bulk of Robert barreled into Alana's leg as the dog ran in a tight circle around her, his leash cutting under her skirt to wrap around her boots. The *sgian dubh* teetered in the air, landing with a soft *whump* in the grass at the base of the target. Chuckles erupted, and the fool turned a few sideways somersaults between her and the target, his arms and legs out like a scarecrow.

Alana closed her eyes for a moment before finding the courage to turn around to meet the crowd. "I lost hold of the dog," Kerrick called over the talking and laughing men, some demanding their money for the bets they'd won. "A re-throw is in order."

"No re-throws," the old warrior said and pointed at Martha who had her dagger out to throw, Kirstin nodding to her to take her turn.

Robert ducked his head under Alana's hand, lifting it as his sweet brown eyes peered up at her. Alana sighed, curling her fingers into his coarse curls, petting him as they walked away from the throw line together. "Will you retrieve my *sgian dubh* when you pull yours from the target?" she asked Martha.

"Ye can have my turn," Martha said.

Alana shook her head, giving her a small smile. "Do your best." Alana stepped through the clustered men, none of them willing to risk Robert's bite to get too close. She forced a pleasant expression onto her tight face for several ladies standing nearby. "The Highland Roses School teaches ladies everything from reading and sewing to throwing knives and defending themselves." Her words came out rather weak after her bumbled throw. One smiled, and one whispered to another. They moved around to the side to watch Martha throw.

Alana filled her cheeks with her inhale and exhaled long, blinking to rid her eyes of the ache of disappointment. A Highland Rose would never shed a tear for failing, but that didn't mean she felt no sting from it.

"Ye should not have pet the beast after he knocked ye."

Alana turned, her heart skipping into a faster pace. Shaw Sinclair stood parallel to her, his arms crossed before a broad chest as he watched the contest over the heads of the crowd. He was all muscle and strength, as if he were chiseled from tanned granite. A "Warrior in Repose" it would say under his picture in the school's art book. *Damn*. He made her insides flutter and flip.

He glanced her way, those intense eyes staring directly at her. "And your friend just hit the target."

Chapter Two

It took a full exchange of breath before the warrior's words sank in. Alana was caught between relief over Martha's success and annoyance over the man's unwanted advice and her ridiculous reaction to his ruggedness. He was an enemy to the Campbells, not some handsome warrior in her brother's ranks. Although, most of her brother's warriors either still thought of her as a little freckled girl or didn't dare come near her for fear her brother, the chief, would geld them.

She pinched the pads of her fingers together and tipped her hand in the air. Robert sat next to her at the silent signal. "He was trying to protect me with all the tension and yelling about. He encircles me to keep me safe."

"Aye," Sinclair said. "But the dog must learn that ye are the pack leader and not make decisions on his own. He must obey what ye say or signal. If ye reward him after he has disobeyed, he learns that he should disobey when he thinks it is warranted." Sinclair held her gaze with those deep gray eyes of his. "He will begin to worry that he is pack leader and disobey more, trying to assert his supremacy."

Look away, she chided herself. Alana crossed her own arms and tilted her head to regard the man, focusing on another little scar that sat just over his eyebrow. "Is that how you treat your men?" She drew in a fuller breath when he looked back outward toward the target.

"They each know their positions within the unit," he said.

She wondered what position the hopping man played. Idiot? Jester? Second-in-command? "Should I have beaten the dog?" she asked, her hand rising to rest on Robert's head. "Or tied him to a caber so that he choked himself trying to reach me?"

Without a word, the man turned away from her, presenting his back but without moving away. The reprimand in the silent withdrawal was loud and clear. It was like the snub that Evelyn said ladies threw at one another at the English court. Even without a single utterance, the rejection left Alana feeling cold. Robert let out a little whine as he watched. The dog stood, and Alana had to make the hand movement twice before he would sit again.

Shaw turned back around. "Like that," he said. "A pack animal understands exile. When he misbehaves, he should be ignored and exiled from the pack by ye to learn he must adhere to your orders as the leader."

Without another word, the man's gaze slid down from her face to her breasts. Like a swath of wild fire across a brittle-dry moor, Alana felt the path, and a flush heated her cheeks. Was he inspecting her womanly form? Bad-mannered, leering rogue!

His assessing gaze traveled back up to her eyes. He nodded without a word and stalked away from the crowd toward the Sinclair tents, leaving Alana openmouthed with shock and a bit breathless. The wind tugged at the close-cropped waves of his dark hair, and his kilt fit snugly around narrow hips. The strength in his calves was obvious through his bleached woolen socks that rose above the edges of his boots. His straight back tapered down from broad, muscular shoulders, and his bared arms in the sleeveless tunic were tanned and chiseled. *Damn*. She was inspecting *his* form.

"Did ye see?" Martha asked, running up to her. She handed Alana's *sgian dubh* back to her.

Alana smiled, glad to have something to pull her attention. "Not over top of everyone, but I heard you hit it square."

"Not exactly in the middle like ye can do," Martha said and frowned at Robert as he stood, wagging his thick tail and panting at the Roses and Kerrick who followed Martha.

"Sorry, Alana," Kerrick said. "That horse of a dog ripped his way free. They should have let ye throw again."

She waved his suggestion off. "Martha proved that women can throw daggers as well as men." The woman beamed with the praise.

"So, the huge Highlander who said you should throw and not lose your tongue…was he not the Sinclair chief?" Lucy Kellington asked, her English accent making several men nearby frown.

"Shaw Sinclair, the chief of the Sinclairs in the north of Scotland," Kerrick said, confirming Kirstin's gossip. "And someone ye should all stay far away from." He frowned, his hard gaze moving from woman to woman as if he were twenty years older and had sired each of them. "The Campbells and Sinclairs are enemies. Our cousins to the north bought their castle, and when the Sinclairs battled for it back, they lost."

"Against him?" Martha asked, looking around as if trying to find the Sinclair chief.

"I guess not all the Sinclairs are built like him," Kirstin said. "And the northern Campbells likely have muskets as they are considered wealthy."

"Losing one's castle seems to be a reoccurring incident in

Scotland," Lucy said, referring to Finlarig Castle where the Highland Roses School was started.

Cici laughed but covered her mouth when Alana frowned.

"But Scots do not set the castle on fire and throw people inside to die," Kirstin said, making the smiles on Lucy and Cici's faces fade. Alana swallowed past the tightening in her throat at Kirstin's reminder and purposely didn't look to her friend. She could feel Kirstin's watchful gaze on her. The nightmares were bad enough. Alana didn't need anyone trying to talk with her about it if they saw her upset from the memories. The incident was in the past, the ugly burns on her feet healed, and fires no longer worried her. Alana's lips pinched as she realized the largeness of the lie.

• • •

"Bloody foking hell," Alistair called, the skull tattoo at his temple likely making him look frightening if the infant knew what it represented. He lifted the tiny thing high in the air over his dark head. She howled with disapproval.

"Puke on him, little one," Rabbie said to the bairn.

Alistair frowned at him. "There ain't nothing in her to foking puke up."

"Give her to me," Logan said. "She is wet through her clothes."

"And stop swearing around her," Rabbie added, jingling a little bell over her face. He was the youngest of the circle of devoted Sinclair warriors and clean shaven. "Ye will scare the wee lass." But the bairn was still too young to notice much except that her belly was empty.

"Try the cow's milk again, with the soaked rag," Shaw said, worry stiffening his shoulders more than the day after a fierce battle. "I will keep looking for a wet nurse here at the festival."

Logan grabbed his arm. The most sensitive of his men, he often acted like the conscience of the group. He stared hard at Shaw. "Ye do not plan to take a mother to feed the bairn, do ye? Her own bairn will perish."

Shaw stared back with intensity. "Ye have seen me battle. Ye have seen me spare life after life when warranted. Ye doubt my honor toward the weak? That I would steal away a mother?" This small group of men had grown up with him, making them unafraid to question his plans. They were friends, and he trusted their judgement, otherwise he wouldn't let them touch the infant that meant the difference between life and death for so many.

Logan ran a hand up through his thick hair, glancing away. "Nay, but the wee lass…" He glanced to where Mungo jumped around in his usual dance, trying to catch the bairn's attention for a moment. Logan looked back at his chief. "She is important, and she must have milk."

Shaw met his look. "If I must abduct a mother, I will bring her bairn, too." It didn't sound like a mercy, even though it was.

Logan nodded, and Shaw pushed out of their tent, ready to continue his search for a woman with heavy, milk-filled breasts. He weaved between the two propped tarps that Logan and Rabbie had set up as tents for them. He'd left most of his men back in the north squatting on the lands around Girnigoe Castle, the rightful home of the northern Sinclairs. Only his four most loyal men had he brought with him on this crucial mission to save their clan before winter set in.

The sun was already lowering behind the mountain range, the time when Samhain officially began, ending at sundown the next day. He should set out food and drink in his tent for Reagan in case her spirit walked the earth tonight. He shook his head. The dead returned home on Samhain, and he and his family had no home. Reagan would have nowhere to go.

Shaw slid between several tents set up by the different attending clans, some of them small and propped up as if children had put them together, others sturdy and large enough to house a battalion. A woman stepped out of a yellow canvas tent, pulling closed a deep blue cloak under her chin and wearing a mask. She giggled and ran away, obviously on her way to the celebration fires. A small group of children wearing masks skipped around, begging for soul cakes at each tent although most were already vacant.

Mo chreach. How was he going to find food for the bairn? The wet nurse, who had traveled with the child from England, had succumbed to fever along the way. The desperate couriers delivered the wee thing this morning, hungry and filthy. It was a wonder that the child still breathed. But he'd be damned, figuratively and literally, if he let it die under his watch.

His gaze scanned the women, sliding over those who were too old or too young. He'd come to the festival in order to meet the couriers and had spent the day out among the competitors and their women in hopes of finding a substitute wet nurse, but he hadn't spotted a single suckling baby. The new mothers had either stayed home from the festival or were hidden away nursing their bairns in privacy.

Rounding the corner of two wide tents, Shaw stopped. The large hound belonging to the Campbell lass stood there. He had a leash around his thick neck, but it wasn't tied to anything. The end looked ragged and damp as if he'd bitten through it. He was watching the giggling children and trotted off in their direction.

"Robert? Where are you?" a melodic voice came from inside the tent, and a woman swept the flap aside to step out into the twilight. "Oh," she said, standing straight. It was the Campbell woman from earlier, the one with the long, wavy brown hair with golden streaks. She held a mask, but what caught his immediate attention was the form-fitting trousers she wore with a man's tunic sewn to fit her. Was this her dress for Samhain? And who was Robert?

Shaw glanced down at her hands and spotted a thin circle of silver on one of her fingers. Was Robert her husband? Shaw frowned, his gut tightening in annoyance.

"Hello," she said. "Are you looking for something or do you just like to slink around the tents at night, frightening women and children?"

Her perturbed tone loosened his frown. "I...am looking for someone."

"I am the only one here at present. Just me and my untrained beast who has a very large set of teeth." She glanced behind him briefly, probably looking for the dog.

"Ye have no bairn then?" he asked, frustration welling up further inside him. "One ye have recently given birth to?"

The woman's eyes widened, her jaw falling slightly open. Clamping her mouth shut, she planted hands on her sloped hips and glared at him. "Do I *look* like I just birthed a bairn?" she asked, her words coming through clenched teeth.

Shaw let his gaze roam the generous curves of her body, which were quite evident in the tight-fitting clothing. The ring on her finger indicated that she was likely wed or promised, but the only evidence of a birth was the fullness of her breasts. He nodded toward them. "Yer...yer bosom is full."

The twilight was making it harder to see, hiding the green he'd studied earlier in her large, dark-lashed eyes. But he'd have been blind to miss the surprise in her face. She didn't say anything. "So ye have no bairn and are not currently producing milk?" he asked just to make sure.

"Is this something you ask every woman you encounter?" Wide eyes with pinched brows gave her a shocked look.

"Presently? Aye."

"Good God," she cursed. "You do not go around asking a woman if she has just had a babe unless you see her nursing one. That is like asking a lady if she is with child, which you do not do unless she is writhing on the ground screaming 'I am having a babe'," she yelled, her hands gesturing wildly. "You will get yourself punched or stabbed." She ended her lecture by crossing arms over her lovely, full bosom.

He frowned and glanced away, but there was no one else to see. "Do ye know of any wet nurses at the festival?" he asked, looking back at her. "Or nursing mothers?" She looked astonished and shook her head again. Speechless.

He exhaled in a huff. "Happy Samhain," he said and turned.

• • •

Alana stared after the retreating form of Shaw Sinclair and untangled her arms, letting her hands slide down to her stomach. Was it more rounded than usual? Had he seen it sticking out in the trousers but didn't want to offend, so he said it was her breasts that looked full? It was true that she had an ample bosom, but no one had ever mentioned it to her before. She'd been eating a lot of Evelyn's tarts back at school. The honey apple ones should be a constant offering up in Heaven. She had no resistance against their sweet aroma.

"Blast it," she grumbled and ducked back into the tent to step into her regular skirts and stays. She cinched her stays a bit tighter, glad to have the laces in the front, so she could tie them herself. She left the wool trousers on underneath to keep warm in the lowering temperatures and made sure she could still access the *sgian dubh* sheathed in a leather pocket sewn into her boot.

Robert trotted back to her when she emerged, his leash wet and frayed from where he'd chewed through it. She frowned, shaking her head. "Are you trying to be in charge?" If she exiled him now, he'd have no idea why since he'd misbehaved earlier before Shaw had shown up. Instead she hugged him, inhaling the smell of fresh grass on his fur.

"Let us find the others," she said. The dog kept pace easily as Alana hurried between the forest of tents to meet the Highland Roses and Kerrick at the bonfire in the center of the meadow. Darkness was descending rapidly, and the music had begun. Each Highland Rose wore a rose hair spike in her hair, and some of the ladies wore their training trousers, so Alana easily picked them out despite the masks that they'd made to cover all but their eyes and mouths.

"What happened to your trousers?" Kirstin said as Alana stepped up, her words snapping like an accusation.

"I was…cold," Alana said, and lifted the edge of her petticoat to show that she still wore them. "The petticoat is another layer to keep me warm." Izzy ran over, wearing a mask painted with the white face of a skull. She held her arms out, palms up as if asking why.

"When out with people, ye should all be in skirts," Kerrick said, making Alana regret her change. The blasted man never wanted them to wear their training trousers where others could see. He didn't seem to mind when they were practicing their self-defense moves inside the classroom at the school.

"With the bonfire, ye will be plenty warm," Kirstin said, frowning.

"I am putting on my petticoat, too," Martha said, grabbing Cici's arm. "Come with me."

"I have been feeling a bit…exposed here," Cici whispered. "People keep looking at me."

"Since when do ye worry about people looking at ye?" Kirstin asked but turned to follow them back toward the tents, Izzy running with them. Only Kerrick and Lucy, who hadn't worn the training trousers, remained.

Kerrick held Lucy's arm. "Makes my job easier to protect

ye all when ye are wearing more clothes," he said.

"Your job of protecting us?" Alana asked, her brows high as she blinked in wry amusement. "Because you know that we are all armed. Even Lucy here." She nodded to Lucy's head where she could see the steel hair spike, its point as deadly as an awl.

"That is correct," Lucy said, her accent light and reprimanding. "We Roses are quite lethal on our own, and the skirts often get in the way." Lucy slid her hand from Kerrick's arm and frowned as she lifted the edge of her petticoat to show that she wore them, too.

Kerrick looked like he was going to apologize, anything to get in Lucy's good thoughts again, but an elderly man hobbled over, using a gnarled tree branch for a cane.

"Ye be Campbells here?" he asked, flipping his rough-cut mask up onto his balding head. He squinted in the splashes of firelight, studying their faces.

The wind shifted, and the smoke billowed toward them. "Aye," Kerrick said and coughed into his fist.

"From Finlarig in Killin?" the man asked.

"Aye," Kerrick answered, trying to edge them out of the path of the woodsmoke.

The man bobbed his head. "I was in Edinburgh just a fortnight ago. There are still some covenanter prisoners there, kept and forgotten. Met a lady. She said she was a Campbell from Finlarig Castle in Killin, said her husband was killed and she was taken."

Alana yanked her mask from her face, the sting from the smoke in her eyes forgotten. "What was her name?" Alana's stomach clenched, her heartbeat taking flight as her mouth hung open, waiting for his next words.

His gaze moved to Alana, and his eyes widened. "Ye look like her," he mumbled. He rubbed his chin. "Said it was the name of a flower." He glanced upward as if recalling which flower. "Rose? Nay. Viola…?"

"Violet," Alana said, the word breathless.

"Aye," he said, nodding. "Violet Campbell from Finlarig."

Alana grabbed onto Kerrick's arm as she felt dizzy, her nails digging in. "My mother." She held her hand up so that the firelight reflected off the thin silver circlet that ringed her finger, her mother's wedding ring. "My mother is still alive." She turned to look into Kerrick's grim face. "I am going to get her."

Kerrick shook his head. "Not alone, ye aren't. We need to tell your brother, send for troops if she is in prison there."

Alana released his arm, turning back to the elderly man. "Exactly where in Edinburgh did ye see her? Was she sick, hurt?"

He scrubbed his chin. "I was working up at the castle when I saw her working in a garden on the premises, said she had been a prisoner for nearly two years and her family did not know. Told her that if I heard of Campbells from her area, I would let them know she was there."

Alana reached forward and squeezed the man's bony hand. "Was she well?"

"She was working in the garden, so, aye, she seemed well enough, though…she…"

"Go on," Alana said, the dread in her gut hardening into a heavy boulder.

"Well, the lady I met, she was blind. Was your mother blind before?"

Alana shook her head, feeling the worry press at the backs of her eyes, making her want to cry. "No, she was not," she murmured. She met the old man's gaze. "Thank ye for bringing us news."

"The lady is a strong one," he said, nodding, his mask falling over his eyes so that he had to push it back up. "Working out there with the others without complaint. I don't think they guard her as much, seeing as she lost her sight. She gave me a few potatoes meant for the commanders' suppers. A true lady, your mother."

"She is," Alana said, remembering the strong convictions her mother always held, one of them being that no one should go hungry. She reached into her pocket where she kept a few coins and pressed a shiny shilling into the old man's palm. "Thank you, kind sir. The Campbells of Finlarig Castle are indebted to you." He nodded and used his staff to hobble off.

Alana turned back to Kerrick. "We must go get her now. Leave tonight."

He was already shaking his head. Blast the man. *I should kick him.*

"I will send word to Grey," he said. "He will gather Campbell troops to ride to Edinburgh."

"Grey is in England. It will take weeks to reach him, and more weeks to wait for his return with troops. Send all the words you want, but we should go now."

"Lady Campbell is locked up in Edinburgh Castle, Alana," Kerrick said. Lucy stood beside him, her fingers flat against her mouth over wide eyes as she listened. "We need troops or at least the chief to petition for her release," he said.

"I will petition in his absence as the chief's sister and daughter of the captive," Alana replied. "And if the petition is refused, we go in quietly and sneak her out, a group of women perhaps, an unexpected army of warriors."

Alana glanced at Lucy, but the woman just stood without comment, although she looked frightened. She'd only been a Rose for six months. No doubt this mission sounded dangerous to her.

Kerrick scratched at his scalp as if Alana's words were bringing on hives. "Let us think on it tonight, Alana, and form a plan tomorrow. But I will send word to Finlarig and then on to Hollings Estate where Grey is right now."

Alana grabbed Kerrick's arm. "She is family, Kerrick. Grey would agree that we must risk all for family."

Kerrick met her gaze with serious eyes. "We have a new family that we need to also protect." He glanced toward Lucy and then nodded to the other Roses who were hurrying back toward the fires, now clothed in heavy, burdensome skirts.

"Violet Campbell is family by blood, Kerrick," Alana said, her words spoken through stacked teeth.

"Aye," he answered. "But does that make her more important than the lives of your students?"

"Violet Campbell is family," Alana emphasized.

"The Roses are family, too."

Damn him. He was asking her to choose between her family by blood and her family of Roses. She gave the man a fierce frown.

"What has happened?" Kirstin asked, sounding breathless as they came up, her gaze volleying back and forth between her and Kerrick.

"A man came up who has seen Alana's mother still alive," Lucy said. "She is a prisoner in Edinburgh."

Alana let Lucy describe everything as her mind raced forward. *I will go now.* She would not even wait for the Samhain dancing to start. If Kerrick was worried about the Roses, she would just go alone—well, with Robert and her Highland pony, Rainy.

She watched the old man lean on the thick stick. He worked his way slowly over the tufts of grass to the other side of the fire where someone handed him an ale. Off to the right, a movement far from the circle of firelight caught her gaze. Narrowing her eyes, she studied the large form in the shadows. It was Shaw Sinclair. He stood by himself, and he was...swaying. She could see him dipping low, bending his knees. It wasn't even to the drumbeats being pounded out to call people to dance.

"Alana," Kerrick said, drawing her attention. "We will get your mother back. She has survived this long, and she is a strong woman."

"She *was* a strong woman," Alana said without looking at him. "We do not know that now. The man said she is blind."

"My chief commanded me to protect the Roses while at this festival. Letting ye all go to Edinburgh to storm the castle is definitely not protecting ye."

Alana turned to stare at him, breathing in even exchanges while her mind churned with possible plans. But she wasn't a fool. If she left on her own, how many nights sleeping outside would it take to reach her mother? Three nights? Four perhaps? She glanced upward at the night sky where only a few stars peeked through the growing cloud cover. She'd learned the basics of navigating by the night sky, but not enough to bring them to Edinburgh.

"Robert is wandering again," Lucy said, coming next to her. She leaned closer. "And I am sorry about your mother. Well...I mean...I am happy that she is not dead like you thought, but I am sorry she is imprisoned and blind."

"Thank you," Alana said, her gaze scanning the crowd opposite them where her large dog was licking a giggling child who was likely coated in something sweet. Robert would eat whatever he could find. If she was going to ride to Edinburgh, she didn't need a vomiting dog as a companion. "Excuse me," she said, heading after him. "Robert," she called.

Dodging masked revelers, Alana weaved through to the outside of the circle. Up by the dark tree line she spotted the large Highland warrior again, who was still oddly swaying. "Robert." She glanced over to see him eating something that a child was feeding him while two young girls helped each other climb onto his broad back. The boy held up his hands to show him it was all gone. *Good Lord, don't let him get a bellyache.* "Robert," she yelled, but he trotted off in the opposite direction after several other children holding soul cakes, the two little girls laughing while clinging to his back.

Alana rubbed a hand down her face. Could she convince the Highland Roses to travel to Edinburgh with her in the morning? Should she even ask them or just go alone? Lord help her. What should she do?

She dropped her hand and looked back to the woods. Shaw Sinclair still lowered and straightened in the shadows. Was he...dancing? With one last glance at Robert who was headed back toward the Roses, she gathered her full skirt and trudged toward the Sinclair chief.

The crisp leaves that had already fallen crunched under her boots. He glanced over his shoulder at her as she neared but did not halt his deep knee-bending. She stopped some ways back, definitely out of snatching range. She had one *sgian dubh* strapped under her skirt and her rose hair spike holding a small bun on top of her head in case he tried anything villainous. "Are you drunk, or do you just fancy odd dancing?" she called to him.

Waaa. Hiccup. The sound of a distraught newborn answered for him. Alana rushed forward. "You have a babe?" She dodged around to his front to get a better look. He cradled a wrapped infant on one of his forearms, pressing what looked like a rag to its mouth as it fretted, twisting its face away. "What are you doing to it?" She tried to take the baby from his arms, but he turned away, so she couldn't reach it.

"Feeding it," he said, dipping low again and straightening, although his jostling of the tiny thing wasn't helping in any way. "Rather, I am *trying* to feed it. She will not take the milk."

She? It was a girl. "This is why you need a wet nurse," she whispered. She grabbed his arm to stop him, so she could peer down at the pinched features of the hungry child. "Where is her mother?" Alana's fingers curled into the sleeve of Shaw's shirt as the poor thing cried against the dripping cloth that Shaw dipped to her lips.

"Far away."

"Far away? Did you steal her?"

Shaw cut a glare at her. "Do I look like a man who would willingly spend the night trying to woo a wee bairn into staying alive by drinking this damn milk?"

"Not without good reason," she said, touching the rag. "It is cold."

"Aye, now it is. It was deliciously warm when it came from the cow."

"And she does not have a wet nurse?" Alana stared up into Shaw's pinched face. There was a story here, but she doubted he would tell her since he wouldn't even let her touch the child.

"The wet nurse died on her way to Scotland. The bairn arrived just this morning, hungry and filthy."

Alana gasped softly. "She will die if she is not properly cared for."

Shaw's gaze snapped to Alana, and she took a slight step backward from such intensity. "Ye know how to care for bairns." It wasn't a question.

"Well, I know not to force a dirty, cold rag into one's mouth."

He huffed, his one hand shooting out in frustration to throw the rag away into the dark woods. "How do I feed it then?"

"Come," Alana said, tugging his sleeve. "Bring her to my tent. I can make a warm pap of milk and bread. It will stop her belly from pinching, so she can drink more."

"Is Robert there?" he asked.

She glanced over her shoulder at the giant man who frowned on the fringe of woods. "Robert is out being ridden by some generous lasses."

Shaw choked, coughing, which made the baby cry more

at being jiggled. "Your husband is being ridden by generous lasses?"

"Husband? No. My hound, the one you said I should exile for misbehaving." She shook her head and tugged him down the slope into the meadow, though they stuck to the edge away from people. Her helping a baby in the arms of a Sinclair was sure to cause Kirstin and Kerrick to spout lectures all night long.

"Your dog's name is Robert?" Shaw asked.

"Yes, for the French explorer, Robert de La Salle."

His long strides brought him up even with her in the deepening darkness. On the edge of the woods, the firelight didn't reach them. "I am Shaw Sinclair. What is your name?"

"Alana," she said. "Alana Campbell." Would her family name make him slice her through? Surely not with an infant against his chest.

"Alana," he repeated, and a slight shiver ran through her at the sound of her name sliding upon his tongue. His accent was northern, and his dialect tumbled around the syllables in her name like the burbling of water over rocks. The ridiculous heat she'd felt before threatened to rise again within her. She wrapped her shawl tighter around her shoulders as if warding it off. "Ye are not wed then?" He repositioned the baby against his shoulder and threw a short blanket over her. To hide the baby or keep her warm? Probably both.

"Not wed," Alana said and felt him grasp her cool fingers, raising her hand so that the distant firelight caught on the silver of her mother's wedding ring.

"Yet ye wear a promise ring?"

Alana's gut pinched again, her wild plans to save her mother flying forefront in her mind. "Yes," she said softly as she led them back toward her tent, bypassing the small group of Campbells talking in a tight circle near the fires. "It is a promise ring. A promise to my mother."

Chapter Three

Shaw's head brushed the ceiling of the large tent erected for the Campbell women. He'd seen only one man with them, a young warrior who hadn't the strength to hold her dog. Did he sleep inside with the women? Shaw shut his mouth before the question tumbled out, for there were more important matters at hand.

Alana moved about the shadow-filled space with a bowl of milk that she'd quickly warmed in the coals of their fire outside. Shaw had signaled Logan and Alistair as he'd followed the Campbell lass back to her tent, but they would stay hidden, listening. His men had been keeping watch for any English soldiers throughout the day. The courier had said that the bastard, Major Dixon, was hot on the trail of the wee bairn.

Alana mashed up bits of bread in the milk-filled bowl until the bread was so small that it would dissolve on the bairn's tongue. "Do you have a pap boat or vessel for the babe?" she asked but waved the question off, obviously knowing the answer if he had been trying to make the bairn suck milk off a rag.

She squatted down before a trunk, the bowl by her side, and rummaged around inside. Her back slightly bent over her task, the bottom half of her hair that was in a braid fell over one shoulder while the rest of it was coiled up on top of her head. It was beautiful, dark golden hair; he remembered it being full of shine from the afternoon sun. He could see the soft, pale bit of skin at her nape over the edge of her bodice and looked away. There were much more important details on which to focus. Not the soft neck of a Sinclair enemy. *An enemy who right now is possibly your savior.*

The bairn cried, a long, weak sound. He brought the feather-light bundle around to look in its face. Large eyes squeezed closed. It was the look of hunger and hopelessness. "I need to feed it now," he said, beginning the deep knee-bends again.

"The babe is a *she*, not an it," Alana said, spinning around with a white glove in her hand. "It is leather and will hold the pap and milk." She drew a dagger from her boot and poked a hole in the tip of one digit, then filled the glove with the warm mixture from the bowl. "Stop throwing her up and down."

"I am rocking her. Logan said bairns like to be rocked. It soothes them."

The lass raised an eyebrow. "You are thrusting her up and down, not rocking her."

Shaw stopped. With the bairn held pressed against him, he dropped his chest forward and then lifted back up, rocking the bairn forward and back instead of up and down. Was there some magical dance that mothers knew to calm bairns? A secret they kept to themselves? He frowned as the bairn still fussed.

The lass huffed, shaking her head. "Stop. Just...hold her against ye," she said.

"I am." But the bairn still gave a low wail.

"Let her hear your heartbeat, her ear against your warm chest," she said, indicating his tunic.

"Ye want me to take off my shirt?"

"Skin-to-skin contact is good for a babe, especially one so fresh to the world. It is warm and soft like the mother. The heartbeat reminds her of being inside her womb, safe and warm. She needs to calm down to eat."

She frowned when he didn't move. "Here, I will hold her." She tried to take the bairn again, but he just turned, setting the well-wrapped bundle on the table while he threw his shirt up over his head, whipping it off. "I do not think my skin is very soft," he murmured as he settled the infant against his hard, naked chest.

Alana paused behind him, and he wondered if she would mention the wide swath of scars across his back. After a moment, she came around to his front, her voice higher as if she forced a lightness into it. "She will get used to the feel of her father, too." Alana held the glove, pinched closed at the wrist. "Cradle her now in your arm." She held the poked digit so that milk wouldn't flow out and released a drop of warm milk to brush against the bairn's open lips. "Is that pigment, on your arm, permanent?"

"Aye, and I am not her father," he said. The little face turned toward the digit, and Alana released the end, so the milk would flow gently from the tiny hole. The bairn sucked the glove into her mouth, greedily working the full digit as if it were a mother's nipple. Shaw inhaled, and relief uncoiled the knot in his gut as he watched the newborn feed, anxious for the chance to live.

"Shaw Sinclair," Alana said, her voice soft, and he raised his gaze. "Did you steal this babe?"

He certainly didn't need to answer her. She'd asked once before, and he thought he'd deflected it. His mission was a secret, to keep the bairn safe in order to regain what his weak uncle had lost. Girnigoe Castle and the honor and survival of the Sinclair clan were at stake.

Shaw met Alana's piercing stare. "Nay. The infant was given to me for safekeeping as she journeys to St. Andrews. I will sacrifice my life to keep her alive. She is my responsibility."

Alana's features softened, and she stepped closer as if drawn by his determination. "You are very noble to be protecting a babe that is not even yours." Her empty hand rested on his bare arm, the warmth of it penetrating the thick layers of muscle there.

She smelled of some sort of flower, and her skin looked soft all over. If he weren't completely entrenched in this plan to save his clan, and didn't have a bairn suckling hungrily between them, he'd be tempted to draw her in and kiss those lush, expressive lips. He didn't give a damn that she was a Campbell since she came from the south, although she was distantly related to the devil, Edgar Campbell.

Alana. Her name even drew him. She had changed out of the trousers he'd seen her in earlier. A shame, for the skirts covered much of her form, although the stays lifted her ample breasts high, their soft roundness sitting above the lace edge of her smock.

"But unless you suddenly start producing milk," she said, "you cannot take care of the babe. She needs constant warmth and feeding to survive, and a rough Highland warrior is not equipped to do so on his own. Your men will have to help you. Keep the milk fresh and warm. You can make more pap or a mix of mashed grain with broth, which is called panada, but you need to find a true bottle. The glove will become tainted and could make her ill if you cannot keep it clean."

Alana released his arm while continuing to rattle off directions. She spoke quickly, her instructions unclear, as if she spoke in a language he only halfway understood. The boulder of worry reformed in his gut. *Bloody hell.* He was a warrior, not a nursemaid. He had no experience or knowledge in the ways of bairns. He'd only ever held animal newborns before, never a human one. And this one must live.

He glanced between the little face, so intent on sucking from the pricked hole, and the woman as she held the makeshift bottle. "Ye will help me," he said, making her pause in her list of required provisions.

"I...I will help you find a bottle, although I have not seen anyone bring their babes to the festival, only older children. And if they did bring their babes, the mother would be nursing them, so there would be no need for a bottle." She huffed, blowing a loose strand of her hair upward. It looked soft, like her skin, silky, and he itched to slide his finger down it. With a silent sigh, the worry in his gut turned into remorse.

"Maybe we could find a hollowed drinking horn," she said. "My grandmother had one she fed to babes who lost their mothers in the birthing. Or a leather flask, which you will have to wash every day. I can write down the ingredients to make her meals. You can read?"

"Aye," he said, watching her carefully. The woman could write. She was beautiful and intelligent.

"I will cut up a blanket for you to use for her breech cloths. You must change the cloths whenever you can tell she has fouled them." The woman was talking without pause. "Just wash the dirty ones out in the streams you come across and hang them overnight to dry." He picked up a hint of worry in the quickness of her words. Aye, the lass was intelligent enough to grasp her jeopardy in standing alone with a warrior who she realized required her help in keeping the bairn alive. Alone and without anyone knowing her current whereabouts. Not even her giant dog named after a French explorer.

He met her gaze over the bairn's slack face, its lips relaxing in sleep, letting the nipple release, a drop of milk left on its lip. "Ye, Alana Campbell, will help me keep this very important bairn alive."

Alana's mouth dropped open, and she backed away. "I will do what I can here in the camp."

He shook his head slowly, stalking forward, holding her gaze. "Ye will journey with me to keep her safe."

Alana shook her head, pulling the *sgian dubh* she'd replaced in the holster on her boot and dropped the nearly empty glove. He wouldn't risk the bairn, grabbing Alana, but then again, he didn't have to. Without a sound, Logan stepped into the tent, followed by Alistair and Rabbie.

"My apologies, lass," Shaw said, and she whirled around to confront the Sinclair warriors. "But right now, ye are this bairn's best chance to survive the journey."

• • •

Alana held out her hand before the three huge men who had entered the tent like a silent fog. "Stop," she said, holding her ridiculously small knife before her. Even if she was able to hit one of them with it, the others would grab her. "Do not touch me."

"If ye stay quiet and walk with us, no one will touch ye," said the man she recognized from the dagger-throwing field. He had a tattooed skull on one side of his forehead, his thick accent smooth and even as if confronting a fearful dog.

Alana spun back to face Shaw Sinclair. With the baby nestled against his naked chest, sleeping like the world around Alana weren't falling apart, the man looked gentle and caring. But he wasn't. No, the man was the Sinclair chief, a hardened warrior, and her enemy. How could she have been so stupid as to bring him into her tent without knowing his circumstances? Without signaling to anyone where she was going? The child's need for food had numbed her self-protective instincts.

"How dare you," she spat, her self-loathing at her stupidity adding to the fury in her tone. She should scream for help. But then the one with a skull on his own damned skull would throw a hand over her mouth. She wouldn't be able to talk Shaw out of this. And God only knew where skull-man's hand had been.

"I was helping you, and this is how a Sinclair repays help? No wonder it is known that Sinclairs are tricksters."

One of the other men behind her cursed, and she glanced over her shoulder. "That's right," she said, her lips curled in a snarl. "Never trust a Sinclair." She nodded, her brows raised high. "It is a well-known saying."

She turned back to Shaw. "I will help the babe as much as I can, but I am not going with you." She had an important mission at present, to save her mother.

Shaw kept his gaze on Alana even as one of the others walked around behind him, sliding the little girl from him. Without the child nestled trustingly against him, Shaw Sinclair looked fierce, beyond fierce to downright lethal with his mountainous half-naked frame and intense stare, the power evident in the muscles of his taut stomach and impressive biceps.

"Once the bairn reaches St. Andrews and is handed off to our contact there, we will escort ye back to Campbell land," he said. "And on my mother's soul, no harm will come to ye from us."

She held her knife steady. "So says a Sinclair."

"Who the hell says that Sinclairs are liars?" the youngest-looking of the group demanded as he held the sleeping baby, a frown etched on his smooth face. "'Tis not true. They are the liars."

"Rabbie," Shaw said, the warning obvious, and the lad pinched his lips tight.

Another man ducked his head inside. It was the thin man

who had hopped about at the knife-throwing contest. He made a signal with his fingers but remained silent.

"We need to go," Shaw said. "Come."

Alana held out her palm to the two advancing Sinclairs but turned her gaze to Shaw since he was the obvious leader. "No."

Shaw shook his head. "The bairn is too important to leave ye here."

"I will poison her," Alana lied, her voice rising as Shaw stepped closer.

"I will bring ye home once the bairn is delivered to St. Andrews. No one will harm ye, lass," Shaw said, and Alana gasped as one of his men plucked her dagger from her hand, as easily as if it were a daisy taken from a child's grasp.

She twisted back to keep Shaw in her view as he stalked closer. "Well, I will most certainly harm *you*," she said. He was within arm's reach, and she yanked her rose hair spike from the bun holding half her hair on top of her head, aimed for the largest target, his bare chest, and thrust the point forward.

"Fok," one of his men swore as two rushed forward.

Alana stared at Shaw, who had turned at the last second, her hair stick embedded in the flesh of his upper left arm. His face hadn't changed from his determined intensity. Not even a flicker of pain pinched his mouth. The absence of the human reaction shot a cold shiver through her.

He held up his right hand to stop his men from grabbing her. Blood dripped down from around the thin hair spike. Her heart pounded as she tried to keep the panic out of her breathing. She was now completely unarmed, and a Sinclair warrior, who seemed impervious to pain, was determined to steal her away.

With the slightest grunt, he yanked the hair spike out of his flesh, and blood welled out of the hole. Stepping forward, he grabbed her with his good hand. "Ye will sacrifice some of yer smock," he said.

"What?" she whispered, breathless in the face of his granite composure, and then felt a tug as one of his men crouched behind her. The sound of ripping, jagged and stark over the muted sounds of laughter at the distant bonfire, proceeded after the tug. The man ripped a long strip off the bottom of her white smock. Shaw continued to hold her with his right hand while a serious-looking Sinclair with dark hair and a full beard wrapped the wound tightly.

Alana stared, her mind watching as if she weren't part of the world but rather someone viewing a play. Shaw's good arm snaked around her back, and she could no longer feel outside or apart from what was happening. Not with the heat of him pressed against her.

Lord, he was huge, the muscles of his arm mounding upward as he lifted her against him. His skin was hot, and he smelled of leather and campfire. She took a deep breath. "Let me go," she said between her teeth, her anger punching through her fear. His face was right before hers, gazes connected with an intensity that wouldn't release her. It squeezed the breath from her throat.

"I will release ye once I have Girnigoe Castle back," he said. Before she could swallow past the constriction, her feet left the ground. Shaw set her over his left shoulder as if the wound weren't below on his arm, soaking the cloth with his own hot blood.

"Put me down," she yelled. Kicking her boots up behind her and twisting, she slid against the wound and heard him suck in breath. "You bastard! Put me down now!" He gripped her higher, his hand resting against the backs of her upper thighs to stop the momentum of her legs, which were already hindered by her heavy skirts. Without a word, the skull-tattooed Sinclair jumped before her, forcing a rag between her teeth. The linen wicked up any remaining moisture in her mouth, the dryness almost making her choke. The frowning skull-man tied it quickly behind her head while another of the men cursed, grabbing the back of his head as if upset. Remorse? Doubtful.

Alana continued to flex her back, pushing up against Shaw's heavy hold on her, undulating, but the serious one with the full beard wrapped another binding around her wrists. The fool jumped up and down behind him, holding a finger to his lips like a laughing lunatic, his antics almost more terrifying than being held. If Shaw Sinclair hadn't sworn that she'd be safe, she would be certain of her rape and probable dismemberment. She clung to the hope that Shaw had some honor, that his promise on his mother's soul meant something.

With Shaw's hand against her, very close to her arse, her hands and ankles tied, she resembled a dead goose ready to be plucked. Alana struggled against the gag in fury as they strode out into the dark Samhain night, the thickness of Shaw's shoulder pressing into her churning stomach. But her scream only came out as a muffled curse.

• • •

Shaw kept the bairn wrapped in a cloth sling against his chest as he led their silent group riding through the crisp night. The infant had been handed off to him earlier that morning, sleeping in a woven basket cradle, which was now empty and tied to Logan's pack. It wasn't safe enough for the bairn to ride tied within it and strapped to a horse, even if she had come all the way from London that way.

He glanced back at Alana Campbell who sat her own horse. Her entire countenance exuded icy fury. Mungo had easily taken the mare from the tether lines, knowing from watching through the day which one belonged to the woman. The man might act the fool, but he noticed and heard everything. It was as if his silence allowed him to take in much more of the world around him.

Shaw had kept Alana bound and gagged, riding before him on his own stallion, Rìgh, until they'd traveled a mile away from the festival. Her body had remained straight and stiff in frigid anger. When he'd removed the gag, she hadn't screamed, yelled, or cursed, but unhindered hatred sharpened her eyes as she spat toward the ground, hitting his boot.

She rode now directly behind his horse, his men encircling her. If she tried to break away, they would easily catch her, and then she'd have to ride with one of his men.

"Ye know, lass, ye can speak now," Rabbie said, riding next to her. Rabbie was the youngest and the most forgiving of their group. Which made him feel that others should also forgive.

"I. Hate. You," she said succinctly, her words cutting through the silence of the night like a sharpened knife through flesh.

Alistair chuckled. "There are some words for ye, lad."

He could order his men to stop talking to her, but they needed to learn for themselves. Once he'd crossed the line in abducting Alana Campbell, there was no going back. She would hate them all until she died.

"And here I was about to ask if ye would like to ride with one of us so ye can get some sleep," Logan said. Although he was likely trying to help the woman, without knowing his pure intent, Shaw could see how wrongly a lass who'd been trussed up and stolen from her tent could take his suggestion. He scratched his ear, waiting to see if Logan would survive her reply. He hadn't felt another weapon on the lass while carrying her, but she might have one tucked away.

"I would rather swoon from lack of sleep on a moving horse and fall to my death," she said.

Alistair laughed deeply. "Yer viciousness, lass, makes me rather like ye."

"Go to Hell," she said.

Alistair shrugged, his smile dark. "Already live there, lass."

Shaw's jaw tightened, but he kept his gaze trained on the shadows before him. "As soon as we put another mile or two behind us and get to lower ground, we will stop for the night." He halted them at the edge of a forest that slanted downhill toward a valley. With the moon full, when the clouds moved away, it was bright as day on the open moor, making their group easy to spot. The forest would be safer despite it being harder to keep next to the lass.

Alana continued her silence. She was strong in spirit and courage and would likely give them a bloody difficult time through the journey. His right hand came up to adjust the bandage over the stab wound. It ached but had bled freshly enough to wash it clean. Logan was good with a needle and would stitch it when they stopped. Aye, bloody difficult time with a bloody difficult woman.

Alana Campbell, sister of The Campbell of Breadalbane, cousin to Edgar Campbell, the bastard who insisted that the Campbells owned the Sinclair Clan's Girnigoe Castle. If the bairn died on the journey, Shaw would use whatever means to secure his family home once more. Even if that meant making the woman hate him even more, if that were possible. She looked like an angel, but she could despise him like any defeated warrior.

They rode for another hour before he found a dense outcropping of winterberry bramble that could shield them. He signaled to his men to make camp and dismounted, moving carefully with the sleeping bairn against him. She would be hungry when she woke. "We need a fire," he said to Rabbie. "A small one, between boulders to block the light."

He dismounted carefully and walked to Alana who was still seated on her horse. She laid her upper body across her horse's neck, her face turned away from him. He stared for several seconds at the long fall of her hair down the side of her horse. It had come undone, the tie holding the knot of hair on top slipping free while he carried her. He ignored the ache of regret in his middle. "Ye can sleep in a tent that Logan is setting up for ye after ye show me how to make the bairn's pap."

"Why should I help you?" she murmured.

"Ye are helping an innocent bairn."

"Which in turn helps you." She turned her head, laying the opposite cheek on the horse's neck, so she could look at him while still bent forward. "Also, you do not know for certain that I will not poison your charge."

The bairn stirred against him, her small mouth opening. Her closed eyes blinked then squeezed tight as she began to cry.

Alana closed her eyes where she lay on the horse and exhaled with a slight sigh. "Wash out the glove with weak ale," she murmured. "Mix bits of bread with warmed milk until it is thin enough to flow through the hole in the glove."

Damn, she was exhausted. If he didn't have the child strapped to him, he'd lift her down and carry her to the tarp thrown over a tree limb. He and the men would sleep around it while the bairn and Alana slept within, sheltered from the wind. "Come," he said, reaching carefully for her. "I will wake ye if I cannot get the bairn to eat."

She opened her eyes to stare at him as he gently pulled her toward him to help her dismount. Blinking, she managed a glare. "Do not think for even a second that I don't completely despise you because you are acting kind. Because I do...

completely despise you," she said, though she placed her hand in his, their palms clasped together as he helped her slide out of the saddle.

He kept ahold of her, making sure she wouldn't trip as she moved side to side, turning her feet in small circles. "In fact, given the chance, I will slit the throat of every one of you." Her words were soft as if she didn't have the energy to put more volume into them. "Everyone who has a jack," she corrected, apparently not planning to slaughter the bairn after all.

Her hand was small and warm with calluses across the base of her fingers. How would it feel to have her palm slide across his bare skin? The thought was fleeting. He frowned, pushing it away. "Understood."

• • •

Alana barely remembered Shaw looming over her in the tent as he pulled wool blankets up to her chin, a few seconds before sleep swamped her in glorious oblivion. The stress of the day: the flood of hope that her mother might still be alive; the simmering anger at Kerrick for not agreeing to ride immediately with her to the rescue; shock, fear, and fury over being grabbed by Sinclairs; the exhaustion of riding over half the night… It had flattened her as hard as a fever. Dreams were fleeting, leaving her in deep, dark slumber until a vibration shook her. It was low, a tickling kind of sound, deep and thick with warning. It was the warning that gave Alana the impetus to crawl her way up out of the warm comfort of sleep.

She cracked her eyes open, realizing that dawn was already lightening the world outside the tent. But what made her heart pound was the sharp point of a short sword aimed directly toward… "Robert?" she murmured, her voice rough with sleep. She pushed up next to the gray, shaggy body sitting against her, warming her side, his huge bulk taking up what little room was left under the canvas with her and a woven straw basket for the baby. Had her faithful dog tracked her through the night?

He growled, the low note of warning aimed at Shaw, who stared intently at the dog. The look on Shaw's face was restrained brutality. If Robert lunged at him, her friend would be impaled on the blade.

"Do not kill him," Alana said, her voice an urgent whisper in the silent, unmoving battle. "He is only protecting me. He won't harm the babe."

Shaw lowered his sword slowly, his gaze slipping to meet Alana's. "The chances of me killing a loyal beast without provocation are equal to the chances of ye poisoning an innocent bairn."

Her breath rushed out on an exhale, and she clutched the large dog's thick neck, laying her head against him. He smelled of damp dog and grass, and she swallowed hard, squeezing her eyes to stop the tears that threatened. He'd come for her, bringing his love and heat, which had filled the small tent. No wonder she'd slept so deeply.

"The bairn will need to eat before we leave," Shaw said.

"What is her name?" Alana released the dog to peer into the basket where the wee girl was nestled within thick wool blankets. "We cannot just call her babe and bairn through the journey."

Robert lay his bulk down as if believing the threat was gone and yawned, his jaws opening wide, making her wonder how much sleep he'd forfeited to find her. Alana pushed out of her warm blankets, and gently lifted the basket into her lap. Aches, from twisting and bucking so hard against her abductors, made her wince, but she refused to surrender a groan before the man.

"Boudica," he said. "A warrior through and through."

Alana knew all about the legendary Celtic warrior

woman from the first century who had rallied and led troops against the occupying Romans. She frowned. "Something a little softer perhaps. What was her mother's name?"

His eyes sharpened, not falling for her trick at all. "Boudica," he repeated.

Alana rolled her eyes. "I think Violet would suit her better."

"A puny, easily trampled flower?"

Her eyes narrowed. "'Tis my mother's name, and she is the strongest woman I know. Definitely the name of a warrior."

Shaw stared at her for a moment, but then bent his fingers inward in a motion for her to hand over the basket. With a last peek at the sleeping infant, she held it over Robert for the warrior chief to take. "Refresh yourself," Shaw said. "We leave as soon as Boudica eats."

He turned partway and then returned to her gaze. Holding the basket against his hip, he drew something from the belt strapped at the top of his kilt. "If ye stab someone again with it, it will be gone forever." He dropped the steel hair spike that he'd plucked from his arm to the ground before her. So, the scoundrel gave second chances—an interesting characteristic for an abducting villain.

"I am calling her Violet," she said as he walked away, and turned to Robert, whose tongue rolled out of his large mouth. She hugged him, taking in his warmth and strength, for she needed every bit of it she could muster to survive this. And survive she must, for Violet's sake. Both of them.

"Lord help us," she whispered against his shaggy gray coat. She was a captive, stuck nursing a baby on this journey east when she should be... Alana lifted her face from Robert's neck. "On a journey east," she finished the thought out loud. East, toward Edinburgh where her mother was alive. The ruins of St. Andrews Castle, where Shaw said they must take the baby, was just slightly north of Edinburgh, less than a day's ride in between.

Chapter Four

Shaw rode his large bay stallion, Rìgh, at the rear of their small party, his senses alert for anyone who might follow. He had allowed Alana to wear the bairn strapped to her after he'd seen that she was indeed a fine rider now that she wasn't worn out from battle. It would be easier for him to act as protector and guard if he didn't have to worry about harming the infant.

Alana rode in the middle of their group as they worked their way along a windy path down the steep hills at the base of the Grampian mountain range. Like last night, half of her hair sat piled up on top of her head, caught with the weaving of her hair spike, while the rest of her waves swayed down her straight spine with the gait of her horse.

He ignored the ache where she'd stabbed him. Logan's handiwork with a needle had pulled the flesh neatly back together, and it should heal without issue unless she stabbed him there a second time. But he wouldn't have her feeling completely helpless without any type of weapon. He'd felt helpless as a lad, living under the drunken rule of his mother's brother. It could break a person's spirit. Alana Campbell hadn't been harmed physically, but her spirit was surely bruised.

"The sun will be going down soon," Logan called over his shoulder toward Shaw. "We will not make it to a village tonight, and we are almost out of cow's milk."

Shaw scanned the woods behind them, his gaze always looking for threats. "We will stop at the bottom of this hillside. There is a river off to the north."

The bairn had sucked down the warmed milk they had brought from the festival, but they would need to find more soon or broth with crushed millet or oats in it. After feeding her this morning out of his own leather glove since they'd lost the first one back at the festival, Alana requested to wash the bairn. There hadn't been time. Traveling at this rate, it would take them another three days to reach the ruins of St. Andrews Castle on the sea where the bairn must be delivered.

The frosty grass on the side of the hill had melted in the afternoon sun, making the horses step carefully to keep from slipping. Alana kept her hand on the top of the bairn's head or back and held the reins with the other. She bent her head to whisper to the infant or call "good boy" to her hound, who trotted nearby obediently, weaving between the trees. Other than that, she hadn't uttered a word to any of them on the ride. Not that Shaw required or wanted to engage in foolish chatter. However, it was more difficult to read the emotions playing inside the woman without hearing her voice or seeing her face. The swaying of her lush, gold-streaked hair didn't tell him if she was planning to stab him again or break away into a sprint with the bairn when the landscape flattened out.

As if feeling his gaze, she turned in her seat to find him. Her pink lips were pinched tight. "Violet needs to be changed. Now."

"Violet?" Rabbie asked from his horse riding in front of

Alana. "Is that her name?"

Alana ignored the man, keeping her gaze on Shaw. "She has soiled herself and leaving her in it will harm her delicate skin." Against her, the bairn squirmed in the binding, and Shaw could hear her cries.

He looked behind over his shoulder. So far, there had been no sign of pursuit even though the Lowland Scot who had handed the infant off at the festival said that the courier from London reported radicals in pursuit, led by the devilish Major Dixon. Shaw turned forward. "At the base of this hill there is fresh water for her bath."

He caught the gaze of Alistair up ahead and raised his fingers in a forward sweep through the air. Alistair nodded and lay low over his horse's neck, riding faster along the path to reach the bottom first, a scout to draw out any ambush. Shaw continued to scan the terrain, which was covered with brightly colored leaves. No tracks were apparent except for the fresh horse and dog prints. Alistair raised his hand, fingers extended, to indicate that he saw no threats, and they continued. When they reached the bottom, Shaw moved up beside Alana and dismounted. He could hear the river off to the left.

"Take her," she said from up on the horse, unstrapping the bairn. Logan had already dismounted and quickly grabbed the reins from her just in case she thought to break away once the child was handed off. She glared at him.

Shaw easily lifted down the small infant, and a foul smell descended with her, thick and pungent. Alana jumped down and looked toward Rabbie, who was the closest on the other side. "I need warm water to wash her, so a small fire is needed." The lad looked toward Shaw, and he nodded, sending the young warrior off in search of dry twigs.

Mungo jumped down from his horse, performing his usual bends and jumps that he liked to do. Alana just stared at him, and he came closer to her. He hopped from one foot to the next, his hands raking through his hair to make it stand on end. *Damnation*. What was Mungo about? He didn't need to scare the woman any more.

Shaw was about to intervene when Alana stepped before the man, her eyes narrowed. "Why do you do that?" she asked.

"He does not talk," Alistair said from where he took out a package of wrapped bannocks to pass out.

"Not talking does not make one prance around with wild eyes," she said, trying to catch Mungo's gaze. "Have you ever spoken?" she asked him, but he hopped away.

If someone took interest in him, Mungo would act stranger and stranger until the person left him alone in fear for their lives. "Best ignore him," Shaw said.

Alana planted hands on her hips. "Has anyone looked in his mouth? I have known babes to be born with their tongues tethered, stopping them from speaking."

Shaw was too busy with the squirming, stench-exuding bairn to answer, holding the swaddled infant away from his body. "I think there is shite up her back," he said, spying the stains seeping through the swaddling clothes.

Logan and Rabbie made disgusted sounds while Alistair spit on the ground.

"I told you she needed to be cleaned," Alana answered.

He stepped before her with the infant, but she turned to walk toward the fire that Rabbie was blowing under. "Do we have water to warm?" she asked.

"I will get some from the river," Logan said, hurrying away from the smelly bairn. They were near the Tummel River. Streams cut through the countryside, and from the sounds of the burbling water, there was a fast-flowing one nearby.

The lass tsked. "One would think that none of you have

seen a babe. They drink, piss, and shite. That is how they grow. Food and drink in, food and drink out." She looked at the warriors, who stared at Shaw holding the bairn out from his body with straight arms, yet the stench still wafted to him on the breeze. Hopefully it wouldn't stick to him. There were certain odors that just clung: blood, decaying bodies, vomit, and shite.

"None of you have ever been around a babe before, have you?" she asked.

Alistair and Rabbie shook their heads. Mungo just skipped away, leading his horse and Rìgh to find water.

Alana bent to grab some freshly fallen leaves and stomped over to Shaw. "You do not hold her out from you like she is a diseased leper." He gladly let her take the fussing bairn, and she lay the clump of leaves along the bairn's back before cradling her in her arms. "Come along, Violet," she cooed, brushing her lips over her scrunched forehead. "Let us get you clean."

Everything about Alana Campbell softened as she spoke to the bairn. Her frown relaxed into a gentle smile as she loosened the blanket around the wee face. The woman was quite bonny with creamy skin that likely felt like soft doe hide. He remembered her curves in her tight black trousers from the other night, and her dress fit her form well. What would it be like to have her smile at him that way?

Shaw grunted in the back of his throat and grabbed the bags Mungo had taken off of Rìgh's back. Alana would despise him until he was dead and picked apart by ravens for carrying her off the way he had. And…her mother was apparently Violet Campbell. His chest tightened.

"There are more wrappings for the bairn in here," he said, dropping the bag near the fire where Alana had laid out a woolen blanket. Logan came back, setting a small iron pot of river water over the crackling flames of the small fire.

"So, her name is Violet?" Alistair asked. "Violet Campbell?" His eyes opened wide as he stared between Alana and Shaw, but Shaw turned to crouch next to the fire, feeding small twigs into it.

"If anyone asks, yes," she answered.

"I named her Boudica," Shaw said and blew, feeding the flames under the pot. "'Tis a fitting name for a strong lass."

"So is Violet," Alana countered. "And one that she will not hate when she grows up."

He turned his face to meet her gaze. "We will know no more of her after we reach St. Andrews," he said softly. "She will be given her name by people who know her."

"Family, then?" Alana asked. "We are bringing Violet to kin who will love her?" Her hands paused on the ties cinching the bag, waiting for his answer.

"She is being taken away to keep her safe, so regardless of the blood relation, the bairn will be protected."

"And loved?"

"Just because one is raised in a family does not mean one will be loved," Alistair said. Shaw felt his friend's gaze but ignored it. Pity was not something Shaw would ever acknowledge. His own family had been cold, hateful, weak, or drunk. Nay, he wouldn't wish a family on the bairn.

"True," Alana said, looking down at the wee thing on the woolen blanket as she unwrapped her breech cloth. "Perhaps, though, if she will not be loved, she should be raised and loved by someone other than her family."

"Ye cannot keep the bairn," Shaw said.

"I am just saying that for a child to grow to be a strong adult, she or he should be loved and—"

"The bairn will continue on the journey she started. Ye can pray for her to be loved if that would help ye," Shaw said. "And a child does not need to be loved to grow strong." Wasn't he a prime example of that? In fact, he often thought of himself stronger from the pain he'd survived. Even the tightness of the flogging scars across his back reminded him how much he could endure and survive. That knowledge made a man stronger.

Alana didn't look up, but he could see from the tension in the delicate edge of her jaw that she was frowning. Better for her to understand the parameters, so she could guard her heart. Women were sometimes led astray by their hearts, especially when bairns were involved. The love his own mother had carried for him had made her weak and vulnerable to more abuse when he was a small lad.

"Holy God," Alistair said, staring down at the soiled cloth as Alana rolled the infant out of it. Brown, clinging shite had leaked up the bairn's back nearly to her neck.

Logan leaned over her with a grimace. "She is ill. Her shite looks different from before."

Rabbie rushed over, his fingers fanned through his longish hair. "Bloody hell, it was yellow before." He shook his head, his nose scrunched. "What can we do? The bairn is sick."

Alana looked from one to the next, all of them, including Shaw, waiting for her pronouncement. "Will she die, then?" Shaw asked.

Alana huffed, dropping her head forward with the force of her exhale in dramatic annoyance. "If you change what you feed a babe, what comes out of a babe changes, too." She used the cleanest part of the soiled clothes to wipe off most of the brown, stinking mess while the bairn cried. "'Tis perfectly normal for her *cac* to look brown on cow's milk, mashed bread, and broth."

"And stink like the foulness of death?" Rabbie said.

"She does not stink like death," Alana said.

"As bad as a curdled, decaying corpse," Alistair said, and Logan nodded in agreement.

"She does not," Alana said.

"Or like Logan after a night of drinking whisky," Rabbie said, a smile returning to his face.

Shaw dipped a finger into the water sitting in the small fire, which already felt warm to the touch. He brought it over for Alana to use. "We need to keep moving. Get her cleaned up as fast as ye can."

Alana met his gaze with a slight smugness. Her eyes were a glorious shade of green with brown flecks in them. "You think my...Kerrick and the Roses are following? You are worried about them."

My Kerrick? Was the Campbell warrior who had accompanied them to the festival courting Alana? Was he *her* Kerrick? Shaw had seen the man near Alana often but hadn't seen him kiss her or even hold her hand. "They may be following," he answered. "At a slower pace than your dog." Her hound sat next to the blanket, bending its head low to sniff at the soiled wrappings. "I would rather not have to kill your Kerrick if he tries to stop us."

She had returned her attention to the bairn, wiping her with warm water. The shite had spread all up her small back, coating her white skin. Her little limbs looked thin and without the chubbiness that he'd seen in older bairns. Alana sought out all the crevices, even the black stub on the bairn's belly. "She is very young to still have the cord stump," Alana murmured. Robert's big black nose nudged close, sniffing at the bairn until Alana pushed his massive head away. "Go on," she said.

"I saw that black bit when I changed her yesterday. What is it?" Rabbie asked, squatting down to get a better look. "It is hard and rough."

"The vein that attached the babe to the mother on the inside. It is cut when the babe is born and usually falls off within the first three weeks of life," she answered, cleaning around it while the bairn kicked impotently and fussed at the coolness. "She is so young and needs to be with her mother."

"She could die with her mother," Logan said, and Alistair knocked him in the shoulder with a balled fist. "Och," Logan said, rubbing it.

"She needs to be warmed," Shaw said, ignoring the questions in Alana's eyes, and grabbed the satchel to yank out a change of bindings and swaddling clothes that had come with the infant.

"As soon as she is clean and dry," Alana said, wiping down the bairn's legs to her wee little feet, the toes on each one being no bigger than a swollen barley grain.

"Shouldn't ye cover her…" Rabbie said, pointing down to her female anatomy.

Alana glanced up at him. "Or you could walk away so I can get this done quickly."

Alistair shoved Rabbie, and the three men turned to meet Mungo as he led back the two horses. Mungo and Rabbie took the remaining horses for water, the wolfhound trotting after them. Shaw watched Alana work with the bairn in silence.

She kept her eyes turned down as she rinsed out the rag and washed her little back. "I would strike a bargain with you," she said, glancing quickly at him and then back to her task.

"A bargain?" The woman had little with which to bargain.

"Yes," she said, sitting back on her heels. She covered the bairn's naked body, leaving her little feet out to finish. Alana's chin rose slightly, her lush lips pursed. "I happen to need to go east toward St. Andrews, actually to Edinburgh, which is less than a day's journey from where you are forcing me to ride."

"The Campbells were planning to travel this way, too?" he asked.

"Yes, eventually, but I worry that they will be too slow, waiting for my brother to send troops." Her nose wrinkled, and she let out a long exhale as if warring within herself about how much to reveal. When he didn't respond, she lifted her gaze to his. "My mother is a prisoner at Edinburgh Castle. I just found out that she still lives, but I believe her to be failing. She might not survive another winter there, so I am going to free her."

"From a fortified castle?" he asked. "Alone?"

"I plan to petition for her release first, but if it is not granted..." She tipped her nose higher, a look of fierce determination on her delicate features. "Then yes, I will find my way in and free her."

She didn't seem like a lass lost to fantasy, so she must be desperate. "What is your proposed bargain?" he asked, watching her closely.

Her shoulders dropped as if relief had melted away the tension holding her stiff, and she inhaled fully. "I will help keep the babe alive, without you needing to guard me every second and worry about me...slitting your throats or trying to tell the authorities in any town we happen upon..." She sat straighter, her slender neck exposed above her shawl. "And you will take me to Edinburgh as soon as we deliver the babe in St. Andrews."

"So ye can free your mother? Alone?" Alana was exceedingly brave or delusional.

Flustered, her shoulders raised in a shrug and then fell. "If you help me in any way to free her there, then I will convince my brother and the rest of the Campbell clan not to hunt you down and slaughter you in retribution for taking me from the Samhain festival."

They stared at one another for long seconds. The thought of battling Campbells actually filled Shaw with anticipation, not dread, so her veiled threat didn't have the effect for which the lass was hoping. But having her willingly help them instead of the continued stiff silences and glares was enticing. Not that he thought she'd ever forgive him, but if he helped her save her mother, perhaps she wouldn't wish for his painful death with each breath. And just maybe the guilt that had plagued him since the battle outside Stirling would stop eating away at his gut.

"Agreed," he said. "But I speak only for myself. I will not order my men to help, but ye can ask them. Logan has a kindness that makes him want to rescue anyone who needs it. Alistair is always up for a mission that might lead to death, and Mungo usually follows him. Rabbie will likely help if ye smile at him when ye ask."

She blinked, taking in his advice, and finally nodded. "It is agreed, then. I will help you, and you will help me."

She looked back down at the bairn, who was making little circles with her lips as if she just realized that she had dominion over them. Her thin legs kicked out from the blanket, and Alana caught one of her feet to wipe it clean, taking up the second. Rubbing, she paused, leaning in, and scrubbed at the wee toes.

"What is this?" she murmured, inspecting the digit.

Shaw couldn't see what she was looking at. They'd only had the bairn for less than a day before they left the festival. Perhaps she had an odd birthmark?

Alana bent down low, tipping her head to meet Shaw's gaze. She swallowed, her soft-looking lips parting. She held the wee toe as the bairn whimpered. "Shaw," she said. "This babe has been...branded."

• • •

Alana stared up at Shaw, but she didn't see guilt, only anger in the bend of his brows. "The burn is nearly healed," she said, warming the little foot in the palm of her hand. "It must have been done soon after she was born."

For the largeness of the man, Shaw moved with rapid grace as he squatted down, taking up the tiny toe to examine the red circle, coated with dry scabs, on the bottom of it. With slow movements, his fingers pinched, he picked at the wound.

"Do not break it open to bleed," Alana said.

"It is a design," he answered and grabbed the wet rag Alana had used, finding a clean corner. He dipped it in the water and wiped away a bit of the scab that had come loose and looked up to meet Alana's gaze. "It looks like a rose."

A rose? She met his gaze. "Do you know what it stands for?" she asked.

Before Shaw could respond, the Sinclair with the full brown beard, Logan, ran up to them, squatting down as if hiding. "Riders," he said. "Coming across the side of the hill from the south."

"My students." Alana quickly wrapped the babe up in the swaddling clothes and wool blanket.

Logan shook his head, his sword already unsheathed. "They wear red and carry muskets from what Mungo could see." He nodded to the south, where Alana saw Mungo running toward them in a low crouch.

English. She picked up the infant, sliding her snugly into the wrapper that she twined around her own body, so Shaw wouldn't grab the baby away. "The English are coming for their babe," she said. "Perhaps the mother sent them."

Shaw's hands landed heavily on her shoulders as she cradled the infant between them. He bent to look in her eyes as if willing her to believe what he was about to say. His gray eyes came so close that she could see the darker flecks around the centers. "The English are coming to slaughter this bairn, not save her. We need to hide her."

"Why would they want to kill an infant?" she argued, but

the force in his words told her that he believed what he'd just said, believed and was willing to die to keep the child from whoever was coming down the steep hillside.

"Why would a mother secret her newborn bairn away except to hide it?" he asked but didn't wait for her reply. He looked to Logan. "We will move near the river until they pass."

"The fire—" Logan said.

"Scuff it out and hide the soiled clothes. Let's hope they think we have moved on."

"If they do not?" he asked.

"Do not let them cross the river," he answered and grabbed Alana's arm. It was a strong grip but didn't bruise. "We need to go," he said, his deep voice adding to the increased thudding of her heartbeat beneath the baby. There was no burning castle in which to be locked, but angry English soldiers were dangerous on their own. And she had a baby to protect.

To the right, she spotted Alistair and Rabbie crouched down in the undergrowth. Mungo must be with their horses at the river. And Robert? Where was he?

Clutching the baby to her chest, Alana began to run through the deeply colored woods toward the sound of rushing water. Her damn skirts were catching on limbs and slowing her legs. Her gaze swept between the trees.

"Shaw, my dog."

"There's no time. He will follow your scent this way."

She kicked at her skirts as they ran, a few shouts coming from behind them. They'd been seen. She tripped on a tangle of bramble and would have fallen with the child if Shaw's grip weren't under her arm. "Damn skirts," she said in a soft rush of breath. "They tie a woman's legs."

She gasped as Shaw's arm hit the back of her knees. He bent to lift her without breaking his stride, his boots leaping over limbs as he ran. She no longer heard the men behind her. Shaw's dashing through the undergrowth, mixed with the increasing rush of the fast-moving river ahead and the pounding of her own heart, had obliterated all other sounds in the world. She felt the babe squirm and cupped her little head, hopping the jarring wouldn't harm the delicate girl who was already having a very difficult life. Branded, sent away from her mother, and now chased by English devils who may want her dead.

She leaned into Shaw's strong chest, wrapping one arm around his neck to steady them while the other clutched her precious bundle. Up ahead, the river rushed by. "How deep is it?" she asked.

Shaw paused, looking across and along the leaf-covered bank. Far downstream, Alana could see the horses. If she could reach Rainy, she and the baby could ride farther and faster to hide. "The horses," she yelled over the sound of the water. Robert bounded out of a clump of brambles next to them, chasing a pheasant that took flight. "Robert, come," she called.

As soon as the words fell from her lips, a pair of red-coated soldiers rushed up to the horses with muskets. "No!" she yelled as Shaw yanked her around a thick tree trunk so that only their faces could be seen. "Robert," she whispered, watching in horror as her loyal friend ran up to the men, barking. But he didn't attack. He didn't know the darkness in their hearts, the darkness that would make them hunt an innocent baby.

"*Mo chreach*," Shaw said, his jawline hard as his head whipped around, looking for a place to run.

Alana stuck her smallest finger in the babe's mouth to keep her from crying out. Violet sucked on it, her eyes open, watching her face.

Shaw shifted them in his arms, tugging at his kilt, and it

fell into the leaves at his booted feet.

"We are going across the river," he said, lifting her higher in his one arm as he bent to yank his sword from his scabbard that had fallen with his kilt. With a muttered curse, he dropped the sword again and grabbed her more securely with both hands.

"Robert," she said, yanking open her skirt strings at her waist with her free hand.

"He will follow ye to the other side. Meanwhile, he's distracting them with the cunning of a talented jester."

Alana glanced around the tree to see Robert dancing around the two men, his thick, shaggy tail wagging as he tried to make friends. The men were too close to fire at him but threatened him by swinging the weapons in his direction. Robert thought it great fun, like when Alana threw sticks for him.

"Set me down so I can rid myself of these heavy skirts," she said and slowly removed her finger from the babe's mouth.

"Quick, then. Before they notice us."

As soon as she felt the ground beneath her boots, she shook her hips and let her skirts drop, pooling below. She was left in her black woolen trousers with her stays over her long white smock. She gathered the end of the underdress, tying it high in a knot at her waist. The babe whimpered against her.

"Here," he said, handing a *sgian dubh* to her. It was her own dagger, snatched away by Alistair when they were back in the tent at the festival. "Ye may have need of it."

Shoving the blade into the holster in her boot, she glanced at Shaw's bared legs under the long tunic he wore. They were corded with muscle, holding his large frame easily as he waited for her. "Your kilt would weigh you down in the water?" she asked.

His arm caught under her legs, and her breath hitched as he lifted her up. He peered around the tree. "I fight better without it."

Alana had read about the legendary Celts who fought without wearing a stitch of clothing. Did the Sinclair clan follow the same strategy?

"Hold tight," he said, giving her only a heartbeat to draw in air before he plunged out of the tree line, his booted feet taking them directly into the cold river. With barely a splash, he surged forward, holding her and the baby above the waterline. How deep was it? Would they be carried away with the current? Fear, as cold as the water rising up past Shaw's waist, clasped Alana. Over a year ago, Alana had nearly been killed by fire. Now would she die by the cruel, unstoppable water?

"Stop!" one of the English soldiers yelled, and she saw him lift his musket. Shaw pressed against the mighty current, which was so much stronger than what appeared from the bank.

"Good Lord," Alana prayed, her arm clutching the crying child to her. "Save us."

Chapter Five

Had the soldiers already lit their muskets? *Fok*. He needed to get the bairn and Alana to safety before they shot him dead. *Mo chreach*. He'd die without his sword in his hand, something he swore he'd never do. But Shaw hadn't planned on carrying a bairn across Scotland, either.

He plunged forward, the icy river water numbing his legs. But he was a northern Scot and had trained to tolerate winter swims.

"Stop right there!" the bastard Englishman called again. The two of them were running along the bank toward where Alana and he crossed. Alana's huge dog ran with them as if it were a game. They were still too far away, but soon they'd be within firing range.

Shaw threw his weight and muscle against the might of the river as if it were a foe. His boots churned across hidden rocks, their slippery surface making it difficult to keep upright with the two in his arms. As he felt his foot slip, he would lift it, placing his weight against the current and on the other foot to keep himself from falling. Step after step until he felt the bottom tip upward several feet from the other side. But as he carried them out of the water, and the soldiers saw the bairn strapped to Alana, they would shoot all of them dead.

"Can ye swim?" he asked near her ear. They were almost to the other side, but the swift current might plunge Alana downstream if he let go of her.

"Yes, but the babe…"

Damn. He couldn't release them in the water. They could both freeze and drown. "Run when ye reach high ground," he said, and she looked up into his face, terror making her eyes wide. "Run and find a place to hide. My men will find ye and the bairn."

"Where are *you* going?" she asked, but Shaw bent down in the water, his boots balanced on a stable rock.

"I will get ye to the other side. Wrap one arm around the bairn."

"What?"

Running closer, the Englishman yelled, "If you do not stop now, we will shoot!"

Shaw could hear Alana's dog barking over the men. Had the beast figured out who the enemy was yet? "Put your other arm out to catch yourself," he ordered. "So ye do not crush her."

"Again! What?!" Her voice had taken on a hysterical pitch.

"Arm out, lass," he said. She threw her right arm before her, and Shaw sank a little lower into his crouch. With a surge of power up through the muscles of his legs, he straightened, lifting and throwing Alana toward the low bank. He watched as she landed, only then able to draw in breath as she caught herself, the bairn safely clutched and tied, hanging from her chest. Alana's lower legs were the only part of her wet, and she wasted no time in scrambling up the bank to dry ground.

Shaw pushed off the bottom, throwing his body back

toward the bank where the soldiers held muskets. "*Gu buaidh no bàs!*" With the deep war cry burbling up out of his chest, he used his arms, hands cupped to carry the most water he could, to splash the river forward. Fast volleys of water flew at the two English soldiers as Shaw continued to yell, using the Sinclair war cry to give himself extra strength. A musket went off, but Shaw continued to throw a deluge of icy river at the men as he surged back across the river. If he could soak their muskets, they would be useless.

With one more leap, he reached the other bank, heaving up to see a musket trained right at his face. Instinct rather than thought shot his hand around to grab the barrel, yanking the musket from the man's clutches.

"Damn Scot," the soldier yelled as Shaw hurled the wet, useless gun down the river. The huge dog jumped in after it as if it were a branch for him to chase. The current began to pull him downstream.

Without giving the other man time to reload, Shaw propelled himself up the bank, barreling into the two Englishmen. With any luck, they couldn't swim. He grabbed the one who'd lost his gun, swinging the soldier around to throw him headfirst into the roaring mountain water.

Shaw charged past the remaining Englishman to the tree where his sword lay tangled with Alana's skirts and his kilt. Without stopping, he scooped up the sword, the hilt sliding easily into the curve of his palm, right where it belonged. A sense of relief flooded him, loosening his shoulders. With his sword firmly planted where it should be, in his grasp, he turned his entire focus on his foe.

He pivoted to face the Englishman who aimed the musket at him, but Shaw saw the dripping river water where he'd doused the flame. "We have nothing here for ye," Shaw said, giving the man a chance to retreat and live.

"I heard a baby's cry," the man said, throwing his only

chance to live away. "Give it to me. I have come directly from Major Dixon." The Devil himself.

Shaw held out his arms to the sides, his wet tunic plastered to his body. "I have no babe upon me at the moment. Be gone with yer bloody life." He jutted his chin up, indicating the woods leading back the way they came. "There are no bairns here for ye."

The Englishman turned to glance across the river, sealing his doom. "The woman has it." Before the final "t" spat from between his teeth, Shaw leaped forward, swinging his sword around in an arc with the combined power of both arms. The finely sharpened Sinclair war sword sliced all the way through the soldier's neck, his head toppling to the ground as Shaw followed through to land in a crouch.

Straightening, his gaze cut downstream where three Englishmen with muskets forded the river near the horses. The dog was nowhere to be seen. *Damn.* He glanced where his men must be on the other side of a row of boulders, where the sounds of battle warred with the sound of the water behind him. There must be a bloody battalion for his four warriors to allow five English soldiers past. "Foking hell." He swiveled back to the river, watching the enemy climb out on the opposite side. No doubt they had seen Alana, because they tore off in the direction she had run.

· · ·

"It will be well. Shhh..." Alana whispered, clutching the crying baby to her chest. The poor wee thing had been jostled so much, it would be a miracle if she came away from this desperate escape unscathed, even if they weren't shot clean through with musket balls.

Without the hindrance of her skirts, Alana ran, her long legs leaping over low scrub, her body being able to dodge trees in search of a place to hide. But there were no caves or even boulders that she could see. Even with the colorful foliage still clinging to trees and bushes, she felt exposed. And where was poor, sweet Robert? He hadn't even tried to hide. She'd heard a gunshot behind her but didn't dare turn to see if Shaw or Robert were hit or if the soldiers were firing at her and the baby.

There was no doubt now that the English soldiers meant to harm the newborn. But why? Why go to such trouble? Tears in her eyes made the golden forest look warped and watery, and she squeezed them to clear her sight. No time for tears.

Up ahead, a maple tree stood tall and broad, its branches thick, one of them being low enough for Alana to clutch. Its leaves had turned a bright red and still clung, giving a possible place to hide if she could climb it before anyone saw her. Holding the baby girl's little head pressed gently against her breasts, she ran directly for the red tree. It would either be a wonderful hiding place or a bright beacon to draw the enemy. Even though Shaw and his Sinclair posse were the enemy, right now the English soldiers were obviously the greater devils.

Alana released the baby, letting the sashes hold her in place against her while she used both hands to grab the thick limb at the level of her stomach, hoisting herself up by straightening her arms. The rough bark bit into her palms as she turned in the air to balance her backside on the limb, pulling her feet up under her to stand, her gaze going to a higher limb. *Don't look down. Do* not *look. Just climb.*

The crunch of leaves far off from the direction of the river sent more energy into her aching muscles. There was too much noise to be the footfalls of one man. Was Shaw dead? He'd thrown her and the baby to save them and rushed back toward the muskets. The thought caught at her chest, making it harder to draw breath.

Just climb. Higher. She wobbled on a thinner limb, the leaves shaking with her weight, and sucked in a gasp. She panted over the babe's wrapped head, feeling dread and relief at the same time that the wee thing still cried softly. "Shhhh," she whispered, trying to sooth the child. Good lord, please let it be Shaw's men tramping through the woods toward her.

She reached a higher limb where leaves fluttered in the breeze, thick foliage where she could hide. But anyone looking up would likely see some part of her. She wrapped her arms around the thick trunk, careful not to smash the babe against it, and felt her way around toward the back. Facing the river, Alana could watch around the trunk. She rested her backside on a limb and tried to look as thin as possible.

The baby still made little sounds against her. Alana kissed the covered little head and pressed her smallest finger back into her mouth. The babe sucked on the end of the digit, quieting. "I will not let them hurt ye," she whispered. Bracing herself on the limb, she slowly reached for her *sgian dubh*, sliding it out of the thigh holster. And her hair spike was still wedged in the tight twist high on her head.

One finger in the baby's mouth, other hand clutching the blade, she surveyed the forest where heavy boots crunched the crisp fallen leaves. Would they look up? She wiggled her little finger in the baby's mouth, making her suck more. The poor wee thing was quiet, but she might realize soon that no milk came from the digit.

Alana peeked through the swaying leaves, and relief flooded her as Robert ran amongst the trees. He was alive, his sensitive nose plowing through the fallen colors of reds and yellows. But that relief twisted into despair as Robert stopped at the base of her maple tree, his shaggy, expressive face tipping up to find her. He barked, his mouth curving as if in celebration of winning the game.

"*Mo chreach*," she said on the slimmest of breaths and closed her eyes.

"Up there," one of the English soldiers yelled, and Alana heard them running her way.

"The dog found them," another called. "Now aren't you glad you did not shoot the beast, Whitmore?"

Alana clutched her dagger. How many soldiers were there? At least two, and if they had muskets, she and the wee rose-branded babe were dead. Her heart beat hard and fast, matching the thuds of a third soldier running up. One red-coated bastard even plopped his hand on Robert's gray head. "Good boy," he said. "Maybe I will take him back with us."

Damn, she should have trained Robert to rip into people like her brother had advised. But the dog wasn't a war dog, and Alana had known that if she'd trained him to be one, the Campbell warriors would claim him as one of their own because of his massive size. What would happen now to Robert? Once she was dead, would he leave her dead body to rot or stay by her side?

Thoughts shot through her head like flying debris as she watched three soldiers looking up at her from below.

"Where did her skirts go?" one asked. "Those are trousers."

A third solider leered upward. "Maybe do not shoot her quite yet. Look at those long legs."

If the three caught her, would death be a mercy? She glanced down to the ground far below. Would she die if she hurled herself from the tree? Likely she wasn't high enough, and with the baby tied to her, she'd never attempt it.

"Come down, woman," the third man ordered and glanced over his shoulder. "Shite, the Scot got past John and Mathias." He waved his hand. "Just shoot her and the infant."

"No," Alana yelled. "Leave my babe and me or my dog will kill you."

"Just give us the child, and we might let you live."

"She is my babe," Alana lied. "I will never give her away to English devils bent on killing innocent children."

"It is not your babe, and it is not innocent," the soldier who seemed to be in charge yelled back up. "Drop it to the ground, and we will let you stay in your tree."

"How can a babe not be innocent?" she yelled, her eyes wide, fingers squeezing the dagger as she slowly stretched her throwing arm behind her. "A newborn babe is the most innocent creature alive."

"She is a bloody Catholic," the soldier yelled back, spitting on the ground as if the word had tainted his mouth.

There were two muskets. One of them seemed wet from fording the river. The other was dry as if the soldier had been clever and strong enough to hold it over his head as he crossed. He pointed the barrel at her, and Alana's haphazard thoughts came together to focus onto one spot: the man's forehead. With a full breath, she inched back her arm and put all her fear and anger into the forward flick of her wrist as she whipped the blade around to sail through the air.

Thwack! Bang!

The gun discharged as the *sgian dubh* lodged through the soldier's skull right between his eyebrows. Alana felt the burn of the musket bullet skim like a trail of fire across her temple and screamed, pulling back behind the tree. She reached up to her head where blood, warm and red, trickled down like a macabre, soaking rain. A scream, born of panic, flew up her throat and cut through the cold air as she stared at the red smeared across her hand.

• • •

Shaw was in mid-leap over a bramble when the musket fired up at Alana. Her scream tore through him, his arms pumping at his sides as he ran toward her, his sword clutched and thirsty for more English blood. He watched as one soldier slumped forward, face smacking into the leaves and roots of the large maple that the clever lass must have climbed. A second soldier held his musket up at the tree but then threw it down when it wouldn't fire, racing to grab up the musket of his fallen man.

Alana screamed again, a long, fear-filled yell that tore through Shaw. He wouldn't let her die in such panic. *Nay!* He wouldn't let her die at all.

He hurtled over another bramble as the second man quickly reloaded the matchlock musket that had just fired. The soldier was well trained and raised the gun toward Alana, whom Shaw could see hiding behind the trunk up over the man's head.

"*Deamhan die!*" Shaw yelled, his roar making the third soldier turn toward him, sword out.

Alana screamed again, as if she had just refilled her lungs with air, the sound shattering through the trees around them like lightning striking Shaw's entire body. But the soldier with the sword blocked Shaw's path to the one with the musket. He met the man's blade with his own just as the large hound pushed off the trunk of the tree, charging directly toward the soldier holding the gun. His bark changed into a ferocious growl.

Shaw swung at the English soldier before him, his daily training giving him the advantage. It was as if Shaw knew where the man would strike before he swung, easily blocking his advance. His focus slid behind his opponent to the massive dog who had leapt directly onto the soldier with the gun. The man screamed, the dog's jaw locked around his arm as he yanked the man completely off his feet, whipping him around in the leaves with incredible strength.

The soldier fighting Shaw sneered as he came in close,

their swords crossed. "The babe will die either today or on another, but God willing, it will die along with all the blasphemous Catholics."

"Well, God and I had a talk this morn," Shaw said, his words seething, "and He decided that ye will die today instead."

Shaw heard more men running through the woods behind him, but his focus was on the twisted face of the Englishman. With a shove, Shaw jumped back and then thrust forward before the man could react, impaling him through the gut on his long Sinclair sword. The man's face contorted with shock, but Shaw yanked the blade free to turn, ready to meet the next foe.

Mungo, Alistair, and Logan ran toward him from the river. Shaw inhaled fully, and he turned back to run to the tree. Off to one side, Alana's dog continued to whip the man around by the arm while he tried to fight the beast off. One of his Sinclair men would finish the deed if they could get the dog to drop his prize.

Shaw tossed his blood-coated sword at the base of the maple tree and leaped up onto the first branch. "Alana," he called. "Lass." He pulled himself to the next branch and then another until his face came level with her chest, where the bairn was still tied around her, making soft crying noises. Thank God the wee thing was still alive.

"Alana," he said again. He looked up at her face, and his breath caught. *Blood.* Blood everywhere. "*Dia math,*" he whispered, grabbing the limb she leaned against to lift himself onto the same sturdy branch where she'd propped herself.

His hands went to her red-streaked face but hovered. He wasn't sure where to touch without causing pain. Red leaves surrounded her, casting even more color. But the wet shine of fresh blood was no reflection from the foliage. A thick drop of blood dripped off her chin, the sound of it hitting a leaf loud in his ears.

"Ye were shot. Damn, Alana. Where?" His hands seemed too large and rough to touch her, but he must discover from where the blood was flowing. His fingers slid along her hairline, lifting her hair as he peered closer. "I need to stop the bleeding."

"My head," she said, her voice sounding hoarse from the screaming. "Robert?"

He glanced down to see the dog running around the tree, looking up at them. "Wishes he had wings right now to fly to his mistress," Shaw said. Thank God she was conscious.

Her hand, which was completely coated in her own blood, rose to her hairline, where he gently brushed back her hair. "It burns there, near my ear."

Fok. She'd been hit in the head, but the fact that she was alive and talking meant that it must have just grazed her.

"The bairn?" Alistair yelled from below.

"She is alive," Shaw yelled down. "But Alana was shot."

One of his men cursed loudly. "How bad?" Logan called up.

"How bad is it?" Shaw asked, more to himself as he examined the raw cut in her skin that swelled dark with fresh blood.

"Do my words make sense?" Alana asked, her eyes finally rising to meet his. There was pain in her stare, but the fear seemed to be fading. Her rapid inhales were slowing, becoming deeper as if she wished to clear her head. "No slurring?"

He forced an even breath. "Nay, lass." He reached up under his tunic to work the bandage off his stab wound, yanking it out to hold to her head. "I think ye will be fine." He glanced down, nodding fully to Logan. "Be ready to help her. I will lower her and the bairn down."

He pulled her with the bairn forward into his arms. She came willingly. She was warm, the feel of her body soft against him, and he had the ridiculous notion that he wanted to stay up in the tree holding her for a bit. Up there away from the world, shrouded in fall leaves, there was no anger and betrayal, no loss of honor and family pride. Only he and a woman who was brave and skilled as a warrior, intelligent as a scholar, and the most curvy and bonny lass he'd ever met.

"Is Robert whole?" Alana asked, dropping her eyes toward the ground, but the dog was around the other side being rubbed down by Mungo.

Shaw's lips came near her ear. "Robert is the hero of the day, I would say. He is quite vicious once he discovers who the enemy is."

"And yet Robert did not chomp into you the first morning he found me," she said, her brows furrowing the slightest. With the blood smeared across her smooth skin, she looked like his idea of the great warrior woman, Boudica.

His mouth turned up in a grin. "Ye did not scream then." The bairn moved against her, reminding him that it wasn't just Alana and him up in the tree.

"Hmmm…" she said as he helped her turn in the tree to step down to a lower limb. "So, all I need to do is scream now, and Robert will tear you all to bits so the bairn and I can escape."

Shaw bent over so that his face came even with hers as she lowered. It had hardened with the thought of her trying to journey alone. Without his protection, she would be vulnerable to wolves, roughish Scots, and more of Major Dixon's black-hearted assassins. He caught her gaze, his stare serious. "I think ye can see now why riding off alone would be foolish for ye, Alana, with or without the bairn."

"I would have Robert," she said, and he climbed down, keeping one hand wrapped around her arm even though

Logan and Alistair stood below in case she fell.

"Robert might decide to stay with us," he said.

"Never."

He gave a nod toward Mungo who playfully wrestled with the huge dog, the two of them rolling around until Mungo sat up, leaves sticking haphazardly from his frizzy hair. He used both of his hands to scratch the dog's upturned stomach with enthusiasm while Robert kicked playfully in the air. Alana huffed but didn't respond to the portrait of betrayal.

Rabbie ran up, his sword drawn. All of them were soaked through from the river. "There were five more that we took down on the other side. All dispatched here?" the lad asked.

Logan stepped back from Alana when both of her feet touched the ground, his eyes growing wide as he took in her appearance. Shaw jumped from the limb he'd stood upon, landing in a crouch. "Aye," he said, "and the bairn is well."

"I hope so," Alana said. "She was shaken while I ran even though I held her close. A newborn babe should be treated gently."

"Lord Almighty," Alistair said, his eyes round and hand grabbing the back of his neck as he looked at Alana's face, coated in her bright red blood. "Alana Campbell?"

"She was shot in the head," Shaw said, watching her pluck the blanket that encircled the bairn's face.

"In the head?" Logan asked, mouth left open.

"After she skewered that bastard between his eyes," Shaw said, nodding to the English soldier who had first aimed his musket at her.

"Bloody hell," Alistair said, ducking his head to try to see her face better.

"Bet against me again," she murmured, and Shaw heard numbness in her voice.

He stepped up quickly to steady her. "She was grazed. Very fortunate. We need to get her cleaned up before we move on."

He glanced down at the bairn. Clear blue eyes, which looked too large in the bairn's small face, stared up at Alana. Four more heads appeared on the other side, surrounding her as the Sinclairs all looked down, even Mungo.

"Is she truly well?" Alistair whispered, glancing between Alana and the bairn so that it wasn't obvious which female he was asking about.

The bairn blinked, seeming to try to focus on the rough faces staring down at her. Her lips puckered into a tight circle and then stretched into the slightest smile.

"Look," Logan said, bending even closer. "The little lass is smiling at me."

"Nay," Rabbie said. "She is smiling at me." He brought his finger up as if to touch her cheek.

"Clean hands only," Alana said, turning to the side.

"Says the lass with blood all over her," Alistair shot back, a grin on his face as his gaze studied her, making Shaw want to block his view.

She wiped her hands on her trousers, but the blood on her hands had dried. "And she is too young to smile. It is probably intestinal vapors moving through."

Rabbie pointed at the bairn, his young face open with excitement. "She is too smiling, and now it is aimed right at me."

Alana rolled her eyes heavenward, which looked bizarre with her covered in blood. "Well so far, she seems to be whole and hearty without a ruined brain."

She used her hand to shoo the men back, her gaze sliding behind her to Shaw. "Why were those Englishmen trying to kill Rose?"

"Rose? Who is Rose?" Alistair asked.

"The bairn is Boudica," Logan said.

"I thought she was Violet," Rabbie said, still leaning

close and clucking the bairn's wee chin, followed quickly with a raise of his hand to show Alana. "See, clean from the river."

She looked to Shaw. Did she wonder if the rose brand should be revealed to his men? She didn't know them, but Shaw did. He trusted each one with his life. Without looking away, Shaw gave a brief nod to her and spoke. "The bairn was branded on her little toe. 'Tis a rose."

"Branded?" Rabbie asked, his lips pulling back in a grimace. The lad looked like he was ready to throw down his life to see the brander dismembered.

"It is healing," Alana said and turned in a circle, hugging her close, when Shaw began to untie the bindings holding Rose to her. "What are you doing?"

"Ye need to wash the blood from your face and hands, and your wound must be cleaned and checked," he said. She lowered her arms as he took the bairn from her. The wee lass looked well enough, though he supposed it might be hard to tell. He just had to deliver her alive to St. Andrews to fulfill his mission. And winning back Girnigoe Castle was the priority. He frowned as the little bairn smiled up at him, her lips forming another tight circle to match her wide, innocent eyes. He handed the bairn to Rabbie, who was still hanging around, obviously smitten with the little lass.

Alana walked toward the river. Shaw followed, smacking Alistair's arm as he walked by. "No gawking, leering, or even looking," he said, his voice terse.

"Damn hard not to when she is wearing those tight-fitting trousers," Alistair said and smiled. "And the blood... I like my lasses to have a solid stomach."

Shaw pointed to the dead English soldiers scattered around the tree. "Start a hole for them and the ones on the other side of the river."

He jogged to catch up to Alana as she reached the rushing water, her dog running along the bank, following a leaf shooting downstream with the current. Robert still had the soldier's blood all over his muzzle, but it would wash in the river. She leaned over, scrubbing hard at her hands.

"Here," he said, taking the bandage he'd given her away from the wound. He held an end and let it get swept in the fresh current, and then scrubbed it briskly and squeezed it out. "Ye look like ye've taken a bath in blood."

She shook her hands free of water and dried them on her thighs. "The skin of my face and neck feels tight with it. Head wounds bleed profusely."

Turning on his toes, Shaw crouched before her where she sat amongst the damp leaves. He gently dabbed the wet rag to her face, wiping down the side opposite the wound. "We need to get ye cleaned up and make sure the shot is free of taint. If it does not stop bleeding, Logan is talented with a needle and thread."

"I have some salve in my bag," she said, her eyes rolled upward to watch his hand wipe her clean.

He nodded. "We will all cross back over the river and retrieve it as soon as we bury the dead."

Alana met his gaze, her brows drawing closer, which made her grimace, her fingers going up to the cut that seemed to have slowed bleeding.

"You will bury them?"

He continued to wash her face, noticing the light splay of freckles on her nose. "Aye. A warrior deserves a proper burial—else he'd be torn apart by animals. And we do not need anyone to find them right off and blame the Sinclairs."

He pulled away to rinse the cloth clean. Logan and Mungo were already fording the river to drag the English that had attacked on the other side across to bury. It would delay their trip, but it must be done, and he wanted to give Alana time to recover before letting her ride a horse again.

"I think ye should ride with me the rest of the day," he

said, sliding the cloth along her hairline. "I do not want ye falling off your horse." The thought of her snug up against him while they rode lightened his mood immensely.

She huffed. "I am not going to fall off my horse."

"Maybe ye think that our mission is too dangerous and ye should attempt escape," he said, trying to come up with a reason to make her ride with him. He ran the cloth down to her ear and gently stuffed it inside, making her tip her head to her shoulder.

She pulled the rag from his hands and wiped her own ear, looking at the blood coming out on the cloth. "I would not risk Rose by leaving her with men who know much more about dispatching lives than nurturing one."

Green eyes, surrounded by thick lashes, turned to stare at Shaw. "Why did those men want to kill a little babe? Innocent to the world?" She had asked before, but none of them had answered. The cloth rested next to her, and he took it again to rinse the crimson in the water.

"You said that she came from England," Alana continued. "Is she so hated there? And what of her mother? Is she dead?"

The woman wanted answers, and after being attacked today, risking her life to save the bairn, she deserved some. Shaw leaned forward, his fingers brushing aside the wet hair near the streak of raw skin that the bullet had flayed open near Alana's temple. "'Tis possible that Rose's mother does not know for certain that she is alive. Her life is safer that way."

Alana grabbed his sleeve, pulling him down to stare at him. "Whose life is safer, the mother's or Rose's?"

"Both of them."

Alana shook her head. "Who would care so much about a mother and child unless..." She held his gaze, her eyes widening slightly before she looked back where Rabbie was making funny faces at the bairn. Aye, the lass was quick.

Alana turned back to Shaw. "The soldier had called her a bloody Catholic." Her lips hung open for a moment. "She is of royal blood, isn't she? She came north...from London." Alana's palm flattened against her chest. "Good God. Her mother is Queen Mary, wife to King James of England."

Chapter Six

Alana held Rose tied before her and felt the massive form of Shaw Sinclair riding behind her. She was in the middle of wee and helpless and huge and lethal as she sat on Shaw's war stallion. After she'd wobbled several times when washing her face and applying the salve to her head, he'd stopped arguing with her about riding with him and just scooped her and the baby up onto his horse.

Her own horse, Rainy, trailed behind Logan, tethered loosely like four of the English soldiers' horses that followed behind each of the Sinclairs. The regiment had been made up of nine traitors to the king, but they couldn't lead nine extra horses to St. Andrews without pulling a lot of attention to themselves. So, the other five were stripped of their saddles and bridles and left.

"I hate to leave them," Logan said, glancing over his shoulder where the horses grazed.

"There is plenty of water and fresh grasses," Shaw said. "Mungo and ye can head back to Sinclair land along this route. If they haven't been taken in by a lucky farmer nearby, ye can lead them back to Caithness."

Shaw's heat warmed Alana from behind, especially after she'd finally relaxed into him. He threw a blanket over Rose and her to create a nest-like enclosure. "Rest," he whispered near her ear, his voice sending shivers along her. "I will not let ye fall."

It was another kindness. She frowned, then surrendered to a small yawn. She still hated him, but damnation, the man was proving to be more honorable than a scoundrel should be. Not that she was complaining. By now she could have been raped and left for dead had she been captured by true monsters. Yet the Sinclairs had shown real concern for the baby when they thought she was ill and concern for herself when they saw the blood from the shot.

Although that worry could have been about losing a nursemaid for the royal baby. She sighed softly, glancing down where Rose slept against her. Would she still be alive if the Sinclairs hadn't abducted her from the Samhain festival?

Alana slid a finger around the sweet face, feeling the softness of the light hair growing from her head. Hopefully everything inside her skull was well. The baby needed to sleep without moving. Shaw had planned for them to stay in the valley for the night, but after the soldiers had found them, he ordered some distance before stopping.

"Just a bit farther, Rose," Alana whispered and wondered if she should call her Princess Rose.

A princess? Of England, Scotland, and Ireland. King James had taken over the British crown when his brother, Charles II, died. Where Charles was a secretive Catholic while ruling his very Protestant realm, James was much more open about his popish practices, even building a Catholic chapel inside Whitehall Palace for his Italian queen and himself to worship together. The English people, meanwhile, swore beneath their breaths about the king's turn against the

Church of England. The king spoke of religious tolerance, yet his people feared that he would lead the country back to the Pope's religion, persecuting the Protestant masses.

The fear grew from mere whispers into assassination plots. Some said that the five babies Queen Mary had borne, all of them dying, had been killed by those ensuring that the Catholic rule would go no further than James. His very Protestant adult daughter Mary, wife of William of Orange, would follow James in the royal succession if James had no surviving son. Apparently, the assassins weren't taking any chances with him wanting to raise a Catholic daughter, either.

Alana shifted and felt Shaw's strong arms tighten around her, supporting her. Straight and easy in the saddle, he rode with the confidence of a leader. Beside them, Robert trotted onward without complaint. The poor pup must be exhausted.

"Is the bairn well?" Shaw's whispered question startled her. "Sorry. I could tell ye were awake. Does the bairn look to be well?"

She nodded. "She should sleep without being jostled, and we need more milk, but she shows no signs of a rattled brain."

"And ye?" His voice was deep, the rough softness of it sliding along her skin like a caress. "Is your brain rattled?"

Alana cleared her throat. "I...I am well, just tired. A slight headache."

"We will stop soon for the night," he said close to her ear, sending chill bumps up and down her arms. Wrapped up before Shaw, warm and protected, Alana began to wonder about the scoundrel turned protector.

"Do you have children of your own?" she asked.

"Nay, as ye could tell from my ignorance around the bairn," he said. She tipped her face upward and saw him looking down at her. "Do ye?"

"No," she said, leveling her gaze back over the horse's head. "Just pups."

"More like that beast?" he asked nodding downward to where Robert sniffed the ground as he moved along in time with the horses.

"Yes, although Robert has grown the largest." And he had the most endearing smile and a sweet light in his eyes when he looked at her. "He remains mine while I train the others to help the herders keep the wolves and thieves away from their flocks. In time, Robert will sire more litters for me to train."

"A worthy endeavor for ye," he said, and his praise bloomed warmly in her stomach. Och, she must be tired to let him lower her guard and smooth her anger.

Two of Shaw's men rode up next to her. "Your *sgian dubh*," Alistair said, holding her dagger up by its tip. It was clean of the English soldier's blood.

"Thank you," she said. Her stomach had churned too much to claim it as they dragged the dead man toward the hole they'd dug with a few sharp rocks and a pickaxe. "I thought it had been buried with the man," she said softly, reaching an arm out of the blanket to take it. It shook slightly, and she pulled it back to her lap.

Mungo rode on Alistair's outside. She could still see him in the splashes of moonlight that made it down through the leaves. He waved his hand and pointed a finger to his forehead, jabbing it where she'd hit the enemy. He smiled and gave her a nod, the pretense of lunacy gone for the moment.

"He says that your shot was good," Alistair said. "Seems ye can throw even with distractions like someone aiming a lit musket at ye." He gave her a nod, too.

The praise from the men, combined with Shaw's words, brought on a warm feeling inside her chest, filling her there in the chilled darkness of the autumn night. "All Highland Roses are taught to throw with accuracy."

"Taught, aye," Shaw said above her. "But likely they do

not all learn to use it accurately in the heat of battle."

Alana blinked, feeling her face flush. "A discovered talent, which I hone," she said, keeping a coolness to her voice. Pulling the blanket aside, she lifted her skirt to sheath the *sgian dubh* in the scabbard built into her boot and caught Alistair looking at her leg. Dropping her skirt back in place, she spoke with a warning tone. "I can skewer a wandering eye as easily as a forehead."

Alistair grunted a chuckle, his glance shifting from her to Shaw and back to her. "Ye, lass, have too kind a heart to kill a man for taking a peek, but aye, I believe ye could." The man slowed his horse, and he and Mungo fell behind them, leaving Shaw and Alana leading the group.

"I will talk to them, but they know not to touch ye," Shaw said. Anger made his voice sound dangerous, especially in the dark. They rode onward, weaving between trees and shadows.

"Has he never spoken?" she asked Shaw. "Mungo?"

"His mother died young, and he had no father willing to claim him. As far as I know, he has never spoken."

"Was he able to nurse? Has anyone looked inside his mouth?"

"He has a tongue," Shaw said, still sounding sour. "And I have no idea if he nursed."

"But is the tongue attached properly?"

"I do not look in the mouths of my warriors," he said, his large body swaying with the powerful gait of his horse. It was rock hard behind her yet also a soft place to rest. Everything about Shaw Sinclair was a contrast. His shocking abduction of her but his gentleness with Rose. His determination to only help his clan but then his desperate actions to stop the English soldiers from firing on her and the babe.

"Well, I can look in his mouth. A tongue-tie would prevent him from speaking. He would have been born with it."

"Like the one in your group who does not speak?"

"No. Izzy is physically able to speak and used to. The death of her parents has muted her, although we are trying to help her find her voice again."

"We? The Highland Roses School teachers?" he asked, sliding his gaze to her. "They care about her?"

"Not just the teachers but the students as well. We are very close, each one finding her place to help the whole."

"A clan, then."

"I suppose so. Yes."

They rode farther without talking. The babe was sleeping soundly, and Alana's eyes closed and blinked open, her chin nodding forward. Shaw's lips brushed near her ear. "Ye can sleep, lass," he whispered. "I will not let ye fall."

"I know," she whispered back and then sniffed, frowning. That meant she trusted him. No, she argued with herself. She trusted that he wouldn't let her fall with the princess. Leaning back into him, her arms around the sleeping baby, Alana drifted into a warm sleep surrounded by Shaw Campbell.

The darkness surrounding Alana lightened to the glow of firelight. She sat before a hearth, its heat radiating out, sending a tingle through her. But then she realized it wasn't the fire making her tingle, but the large man sitting behind her, holding her to him. Alana tipped her face up to stare into Shaw's face, so rugged and majestic. She reached up a hand to trace the scar sitting like a border along his hairline. "How did you get this?" she asked, her words like a whisper.

"A fire. It burned me."

His words sent fear through her limbs. "But that is not a burn mark," she said. Pain scraped along her head, and she raised her hand to it, feeling the wet heat of blood. She pulled her fingers back, gasping at the sight. Not of blood but of fire, licking up her fingers. Yanking back, she screamed, but there was no escape as the flames surged upward around her.

"Alana? Lass?"

She jerked awake, her eyes flying open to see Shaw's gray eyes staring into her own. His brows were pinched. "Ye let out a small scream."

Lips parted, she sucked in breath, her heart pounding as she lifted her hands, but there was no fire. She turned her head to the side. "Where...?" The side of a canvas tent lay a foot away.

"Ye were asleep when I laid ye in here last night. It is dawn and time to rise." Shaw studied her as he sat back on his heels in the tight confines of the tent. "Alistair rode ahead and said he smelled cook fires. A village perhaps. Somewhere to get the bairn some fresh milk." He glanced outside over his shoulder. "Logan is feeding Rose the last of the milk we had, and Mungo is making sure your beast has a ration of our food."

She cleared her throat. "Yes." She pushed herself up, her hand rising to her head, and she grimaced when she touched the gouge. But her fingers came away without blood.

"It needs to be cleaned, but it will not require stitching. Although ye may end up with a warrior's scar and make young Rabbie jealous." His lips crooked upward on one end in a grin.

Alana raked a hand through her tangled hair on the other side, nodding. She took a deep inhale to clear her mind of the nightmare. Glancing up, her gaze fell on the white mark along his hairline. "How did you get your scar? Battle?"

His grin fell away, leaving a blankness. "Nay. Nothing so glorious." His smile returned, but it lacked happiness. "Acquired when I was a boy." She watched his jaw work as if it was stiff. "We will leave as soon as ye are up and ready." He backed out of the tent, leaving her with more questions than answers.

• • •

Shaw swayed with the gait of his warhorse, Alana riding her own mare next to him as they wove through the dense golden forest. She held the bairn wrapped against her. Without more milk to fill the bairn's belly, Rose had been fitful but finally fell asleep to Alana's gentle singing.

> *Hush, the waves are rolling in, my bairn.*
> *Hush, the winds roar hoarse and deep, my bairn.*
> *Hush, the rain sweeps o'er the knowes, my bairn.*
> *But ye sleep safe in my arms.*

The men remained silent as her sweet melody floated on the crisp morning breeze. Alana's voice wasn't without fault, the notes off at times, but they soothed the bairn. Her voice soothed him as well, and his men from the looks of it as they rode through the quiet trees.

Their group came out of the woods onto a stretch of moor that led to another forest half a league away. A large hawk flew down, its talons outstretched, wings pulled back to swing them forward. The predator snatched a mouse from the ground, soaring upward, never having made a sound. Robert ran forward as if to catch the bird, but the hawk's powerful wings shot it up into the sky, and it disappeared over the tree line. This was the hawk's territory, where he lived and hunted and grew old riding the wind over his land. Envy for a bird. He snorted softly to himself at the hollow feeling.

"Smoke ahead," Alistair said, bringing his horse up to ride level with theirs. He pointed above the trees where a low haze of smoke rose like a fog. "I spotted several homes before I turned back to get the rest of ye."

"A village or even a farm will have milk for the babe," she said. "A wet nurse perhaps."

Shaw shook his head. "Nay. If we ask for a wet nurse, word could get back to anyone interested in following the princess. She will need to be your own bairn."

"'Tis good ye wear a ring," Rabbie said, nodding toward her hand.

Alistair's face snapped around to Alana. "I can be your husband."

"I will be her husband," Shaw said, frowning at his man. Alistair preferred lasses with an edge to them, girls who found his tattoo thrilling and dangerous. Alana was not a lass for him. Alistair's brows rose before he gave a nod in understanding. "In fact," Shaw said, "we should enter alone, a small family acquiring food."

"And lodging," Alana said, motioning to Rose. "With a bath. I need to wash her."

"Logan and Rabbie can find fresh milk and get it to me without attracting notice," Shaw said, meeting their gazes. "And buy bread and meat, as if ye are on your own journey to bring these horses to market. Remove their shoes, with the royal seal on them, outside of town and have the local farrier re-shoe them. Ask if he knows of anyone who would like to buy them."

He turned. "Alistair and Mungo will remain on the outskirts. Hunt if ye can, but I will also purchase more rations for the rest of the journey." The men nodded, all signs of the jester gone from Mungo. Still, with Alistair's skull tattoo and Mungo's usual act, it was best to keep them away from eyes that would remember them. "Be as ordinary as ye can if ye are seen. We will meet tomorrow morning, due east, just outside the edge of town."

Alistair grinned, giving the lass a wink. "Don't know if I have ever been ordinary. Extraordinary is what I am usually called."

Shaw had the strongest desire to punch him.

"We will come in from the north," Logan said. "A different direction from the two of ye and the bairn."

"Leave one horse with Alistair," Alana said. She looked at Shaw. "For my mother to ride home."

Her mother and a horse in exchange for her help saving his clan and castle. It seemed a fair trade. Shaw nodded, signaling for one to be handed off. "Mungo," Shaw said, and the man caught the reins that Rabbie tossed him. A gray mare.

"Thank you," Alana murmured.

A "thank you?" From a captive. He shoved the small seed of hope down inside and cleared his throat. "As a common man and wife, traveling with their newborn bairn, ye should ride in front of me holding the wee one," Shaw said. "Your horse can stay with Alistair, too."

Alana opened her mouth as if to argue.

"If anyone in the town is suspicious of us, and an English troop comes through, they will tell them about everyone stopping in town," Shaw said before she could reply. "We could send Logan and Rabbie in town to buy some milk and supplies, but if ye want to wash and sleep in a bed tonight, we must act the married couple."

"Married couples can ride separately," she said.

After the attack and Alana's injury, Shaw wanted to keep her as close as possible. For the sake of the mission, of course. "Aye, but it would be more convincing if we rode one horse."

Her breath came out long as if surrendering. "How will I act like I am nursing the babe? Will you sneak the milk to me up in the room?"

Shaw nodded. "I will either get fresh cow's milk or find a way to warm it. It will work, and ye can wash the bairn. And yourself if ye wish."

Her beautiful green eyes lifted, a slight smile touching her mouth. "I could wash?"

"If we find lodging with a bathing tub, aye," he said.

Hope lit her features, bringing a slight pink to her cheeks and an alertness to her eyes. If it was possible, Alana became even more beautiful. No one moved, and Shaw glanced at his men, who were all staring at her as if they'd never seen a lass before.

Blast. It had apparently been too long since his men had found ease with a woman, for a simple smile was enthralling them. He frowned, his voice gruff. "Your decision, Alana."

She exhaled in a huff. "Take good care of Rainy," she said, looking to Alistair.

"As if she were my own, milady," he said, bowing his head and holding his fist to his chest like some ridiculous gallant knight of legend. Aye, Shaw definitely wanted to punch him. The man jumped down from his mount, striding toward Alana, obviously planning to lift her free of the saddle.

Without hesitation, Shaw dismounted, his two strides taking him right up to Alana before Alistair could reach her. He raised his hands to her waist and heard a low curse behind him.

Alana had already thrown one leg over her saddle with Rose tied to her chest. Her boot tossed around in the air as if waiting for some mounting post to magically appear beneath it. "I have ye, lass," Shaw said, reaching up to clasp Alana's waist at the gentle curve inward above her hips. "Watch the wee one," he said.

He pulled her back against him, setting her down, and heard her say something. "What was that?" he asked, turning, his gaze meeting the frown on Alistair's face as he took the horse's reins.

"Bloody hell," Alistair murmured just under his breath and looked to the horse.

"I said," she continued as she walked to his horse, "a gentle landing. It is what the babe needs right now." She bent her head to brush her lips against the bairn's covered head. "No more throwing you around if we can help it."

Logan and Rabbie gave a nod and headed north, trailing three horses behind them. Coming to the village to sell them would be a good cover, and they could then use the money to buy food. Mungo and Alistair would stay in the woods with their horses, Alana's horse, and the addition for her mother. They would hunt for game and watch for encroaching English or suspicious activity.

Shaw lifted Alana and Rose up onto Rìgh and left them to walk over to where Alistair stood with the horses. "Alana and the bairn are my responsibility," Shaw said, his voice low.

Alistair turned to stare back, mutiny on his marked face. "She hates ye for taking her. Why not give one of us a chance with the lass?"

The idea of one of his men with Alana tightened Shaw's chest. This was not a place to think about winning the heart of a woman. "I am the chief of the Sinclairs, the one to ensure our clan regains its honor and home. Alana Campbell is for none of us. She hates us all, except for that wee bairn."

"What if she changes her mind about hating us?" Alistair said, his teeth set in a determined line.

Would Shaw order his friend to stay away from Alana, just because the thought of her with any man made his blood race and his fists clench? He had no right to say anything about the woman and where her heart might wander. "Then the lass may choose whomever she wants," he said. Shaw bent so that he was within inches of Alistair. "But for now, ye will keep your distance from the woman. This is not a rowdy Beltane festival; it is a bloody mission."

"That goes for ye, too," Alistair said, his brows rising in challenge. "We are here for our people, our families, and to revenge sweet Reagan."

As if Shaw did not know that. He understood his

responsibilities as chief and thirsted for revenge as much as his men. His fingers curled into tight fists.

"Not to woo a Campbell lass," Alistair continued.

Maybe he should punch Alistair, just to remind him who was the chief. Shaw had kicked his arse when they were young men. Perhaps it was time to knock Alistair back down before his cockiness got him skewered.

"If you two can finish your whispering, Rose has woken and needs milk as soon as possible," Alana said from behind. "We need to get to that village quickly."

Without a word, Shaw turned, striding toward Alana. With an easy lift, his foot in the stirrup, Shaw rose to sit behind her. He nodded to Mungo. "Keep to the woods and tether the dog to stay with ye if ye must."

"Stay with the men," Alana said to Robert, raising her palm toward him in a signal. Mungo hopped down, scratching the dog's head, and tied a rope around Robert's neck. "I sure hope he is strong," she murmured.

Shaw tapped Rìgh with his heels, and the mighty horse walked smoothly forward through the woods. Leaves fell from up high, the wind picking up. He could hear Rose fuss.

"As soon as we reach any sort of home, we need to ask for milk or broth," Alana said.

"Aye, though it would be best for them to not know it is for the bairn, as ye should be nursing her."

"Not every mother produces milk very well," she said. "I have seen new mothers whose milk never comes in."

"Ye have an ample bosom," Shaw said. "People will be suspicious if you are not nursing your bairn."

She tipped her head back to frown at him. "It has nothing to do with the size of a woman's breasts."

If a year ago someone would have told him that he'd be discussing milk production with regards to breast size, while holding a beautiful Campbell lass and a newborn bairn, Shaw would have laughed out loud at the drunk fool. But a year ago, he didn't think he'd have a chance to legally reclaim his clan's seat.

Girnigoe Castle had belonged to the mighty Sinclairs for three hundred years. After Oliver Cromwell's men used it and finally withdrew, his drunken uncle, George Sinclair, sold the castle and lands, and even his earldom to the Campbells of Glenorchy in order to pay his debts to them. George, his mother's brother, had been an abusive fool and drunkard. Shaw had been too young to challenge the bastard at the time, but now that he was a man, he was determined to reclaim all that George squandered away in the name of whisky, foolish endeavors, and cards.

"Some are large, but some are quite small. It is not an indication of milk production." Alana paused as if waiting for his response, but Shaw had absolutely no response in exchange for this new knowledge.

She tipped her head back to look at him, and he returned her frown. "I cede to your knowledge of breasts and everything pertaining to them since I have none."

"Actually, you do."

"I do not."

"Yes, you do. Men have breasts. They are just undeveloped. I read about it in a human anatomy book at our school."

"I do not," he repeated.

"You have nipples," she said. "So, you have breasts."

"Look," he said, never quite so happy to see a house through the trees. He pressed Rìgh into a faster walk, winding through the forest, the trees clearing the closer he got. The narrow path turned out onto a pebbly road with houses beyond.

Thatched cottages lined the road, leading to a center clearing with a well pump and trough. A blacksmith and farrier were working with a horse to the left, and a two-story common house stood several buildings down from it. Shaw felt the stares as they rode up to the well pump in the middle of town.

"Stay on Rìgh," he said to Alana and dismounted. The starkness of the cool morning air against him, where Alana had leaned, pulled his focus. Without her warmth, he'd have never noted the cold, but her heat and then absence was... noticed. He led the horse to the trough, pumping the water into it for him to drink.

"The common house might have lodging," he said, nodding to the second story.

Alana twisted in the seat. "And milk, I hope."

Tying Rìgh to the hitching post by the trough, he reached up to lift her and the bairn down. She slid toward him, her arms out to rest her hands on his shoulders, trusting him to carry her safely to the ground. She trusted him. It should make him content, knowing the mission would be easier, but it gnawed inside him instead.

They walked together across the village square to the common house, Alana holding Rose close as the bairn whimpered, obviously hungry. "We are being watched," she whispered as they stepped up to the door.

"Stay close to me," he replied and pushed through.

"Don't worry, Shaw," she said. "I am armed and will not let anyone hurt you."

He glanced at her, catching her slight grin. It reached her eyes, giving him pause. The corner of his mouth twitch upward. "Glad ye will have my back," he said, stepping before her as they entered. There was little threat with just one patron hunched over a steaming cup in the corner and two women behind the high bar, setting cups out and drying them with their aprons.

"Goodness," one of the women declared, wiping her

hands on her apron. "We have visitors, Fiona." The other woman was already staring at them, a scowl on her face. They looked quite similar, full faces and light brown hair, probably near a score and ten years old.

"I see that," the second woman said. "Welcome to Kinross. I am Fiona Murray, and this is Willa. We run this place."

"Jasper owns it," Willa said, glancing toward the silent man watching from the corner, but Fiona ignored her.

"We are in need of lodging," Shaw said. "Do ye have a room to let?"

"Aye, for three shillings, another if ye be wanting food," Fiona said.

"And a warm bath," Alana added.

Fiona frowned, bending closer to them over the bar. "Ye have blood on your head," she said to Alana. "What is that about?" Her sharp eyes cut to Shaw in obvious assessment.

Alana touched her hairline and smiled. "Foolish me, walked right into a sharp tree limb yesterday. Sliced right through my skin, but I have cleaned it and slathered it with salve. It should heal just fine in another week."

Willa came out from around the bar as if to inspect the gash. She gasped, her face opening into a broad smile. "Look, Fi, they have a little bairn with them. A fresh one at that." She leaned over the bairn's face, inhaling as if sniffing a flower. "I just love the smell of new bairns. How old is it?"

He hadn't noticed anything sweet smelling about their bairn, except for her name. "He is five weeks old," Shaw said. Better for them to think the bairn was a boy since the English were looking for a three-week-old girl.

"So tiny still," Willa said. "Nothing like my Lizzie. She is a bit older, though, almost a full year."

"You are still nursing, then?" Alana asked. "I have had so much trouble with that, perhaps you could nurse little...

George here?"

Both sisters frowned. "I just have enough milk for little Lizzie," Willa said, taking a step back and crossing her arms over her bosom like the bairn might leap across to suckle.

Alana blinked rapidly, and Shaw swore he saw a shine come to her eyes. She nodded, forcing a little smile. "I understand." Her voice wobbled. "I just…I am so worried about h…him. Is there cow's milk nearby so I could feed… George some pap made with it and bread?" She wiped at her eye as if she were trying to stop the tears. "I fear he is not growing fast enough."

Shaw stared, mesmerized by the amazing performance. Both women were instantly at her side. "What a precious little boy," Willa said. "I am sure he will do fine." She glanced at Shaw. "What a strong papa he has."

"We will make certain to get ye some milk, straight away," Fiona said. She turned her narrowed eyes toward the man in the corner. "Jasper," she yelled, making the man, as well as Alana, flinch. "Get off your arse and find some fresh, warm milk for this wee bairn." The man pushed out of his seat, stuffed a hat onto his head, and hurried out the door without a mumble.

"Thank ye, love," Willa called after him and frowned at her sister. She turned a bright smile on Alana. "And I will make ye some lovely nettle and chamomile tea. It will help bring in more of your milk," she said in a lowered voice. Shaw wasn't sure whom she was hiding her comments from. She glanced his way, so he supposed the father wasn't supposed to hear talk of milk-producing tea.

"Have ye had enough stimulus?" Fiona asked, and Willa's eyes widened with another glance toward him. Fiona grabbed her own breast through her apron. "One must rub all around it in circles and then slide your hands…" She glanced at Shaw and shrugged. "Or his hands, down to the nipple to get the milk to come down." She nodded. "Sometimes it starts when the bairn cries."

Alana's mouth opened and closed without answering. Finally, she nodded.

"I can show ye how," Fiona said, making her eyes open wider as she clutched the bairn against her chest almost like a shield.

"My wife is rather private about her...bosom. And feeding our bairn," Shaw said.

Fiona set hands on her ample hips. "'Tis nothing to be embarrassed about, feeding your bairn. A woman should be free to pull out her milk whenever it is needed."

Willa's face was growing pink. "This is one of my sister's favorite topics. It got her banned from the chapel one day when she told the pastor's wife to lower her gown right there to feed their new bairn. People are not used to Fiona's progressive talk." Willa's wide gaze seemed to issue an apology.

"Well, we *should* talk about it," Fiona said. "Anything to help a woman and bairn survive in this harsh world."

She turned sharp eyes on Shaw. "And ye look like a vigorous husband," Fiona said, sliding her gaze up and down Shaw. He didn't move even though he had the strangest desire to guard his jack. "Are ye leaving the lass alone?"

"Alone?" he asked, the single word coming slow.

"Not touching her below the waist for a full two months or longer if it was a ripping kind of birth."

Willa slapped both hands to her cheeks and murmured an apology to Alana.

"I have put three husbands in the ground, so I know a thing or two about randy men," Fiona said, nodding, her chin tipped high. "Do ye take care of yourself like a good husband?" Her sharp eyes fastened onto Shaw's gaze.

"Take care?" he asked.

Fiona looked to Alana. "Does he just repeat everything

ye say back as a question?"

Shaw looked at her, too, and noticed her merry expression. "Not usually," she said. "I think he is just confused."

Fiona turned back to Shaw. "Your jack," she said slowly, pointing to his kilt. "Do ye take care of your needs by yourself?" She made a motion with her hand as if she were stroking a jack. Shaw was dumbfounded. He'd never seen a woman talk so openly about any of this. His jaw unhinged slightly, but no words came out.

Alana snorted softly, covering her mouth. She lowered her hand. "Apologies, Mistress Fiona. My husband is rather private about the care of his…jack, but rest assured that his urges are taken care of, and he is not damaging me in any way."

"Fiona is quite open and vocal about the health and welfare of women," Willa said. "She is the midwife in town and helps any of the lasses if they are being treated roughly."

The lasses of the town were in excellent hands, and Shaw was starting to think that Fiona may have *put* her three husbands in the ground prematurely.

Shaw fished a handful of shillings from his sporran. "I would see my wife and bairn to our room."

Fiona counted the money twice while Willa hurried off. "I will brew the tea." The haggard Jasper ran inside with a small pail. "Fresh from the cow," he said, handing it to Shaw.

"I will find ye a bottle to use," Willa called back from the doorway that must lead to the kitchen.

"Thank ye," Shaw said, handing Jasper a shilling. "Would ye also shelter my horse? He is right out at the water pump." The man hurried off again as if thankful to have a task that kept him out from under his sister-in-law's critical eye.

They followed Fiona up a narrow set of wooden stairs to the second level. With only one entrance, Shaw was glad to see a window in the room. Small, but with a large double bed, the room had a wash stand and a cold hearth. It smelled of cleaning lye.

Fiona let them pass her into the room. "Since ye have a bairn with ye, the peat to burn comes with the room. Don't want the little fellow to go cold."

"And a bathing tub with warm water?" Shaw asked.

"I will send Jasper up with the tub and some buckets of water to heat in the hearth," she said, her gaze critical. "Do not let the bairn be bare in a draft if ye bathe him."

"Thank you," Alana said. "I will take care."

Fiona glanced back and forth between them and made a little snorting sound. Willa's hurried footsteps announced her arrival with tea and a glass bottle. It would make feeding Rose so much easier.

"Try the breast first," Fiona said, pointing to Alana's chest. The woman then pointed at Shaw. "And ye should help her care for your son." She wagged her finger. "I cannot abide a man who thinks he is done helping with a bairn after siring it."

With a parting glare from Fiona and a smile from Willa, the sisters left, closing the door behind them.

After a mutual pause, Shaw and Alana looked at each other. Shaw let a grin grow on his face and rubbed his stubbled jaw. "Are ye needing my help? With your bosom perhaps?"

She threw a hand over her mouth, laughing silently. She slid it off partway. "About as much help as you need with your poor, neglected jack."

He chuckled, meeting her laughing gaze with one of his own. A heat grew in his chest with his smile. It was a feeling he hadn't known in a very long time.

Chapter Seven

"There now," Alana said to the sweet babe over her shoulder. "A full stomach, a burp, warm, and clean. How long has it been since you have been this comfortable? Poor thing." Darkness had descended, and Shaw had gone below to find them a dinner meal while Alana tended Rose. The small brand on the babe's toe seemed nearly healed, leaving the undeniable mark of a rose. Was it done by the queen, so she would be able to find her daughter again? Which would mean that the queen knew Rose was alive. But what mother could burn her own child?

Rose fell quickly to sleep, and Alana lowered her into the woven cradle next to the large bed. There was hardly any room for the basket with the wooden tub before the hearth. Alana had taken a bath with the babe and was wearing a clean smock that she'd bought from Willa while her ripped one dried from a line she rigged out in the hallway.

She knelt beside the tub. If she was quick enough, she could wash her hair before Shaw returned with the food. Tipping her heavy tresses forward over her head, she dropped them in the relatively clean water of the tub. It was definitely cleaner than her poor hair, which was still crusted with blood in spots. Running her fingers through the mass, she soaked it all, kneeling over so far that she could tumble in if she wasn't careful.

The door clicked, and Alana turned her head, her face hovering over the surface.

"I got us two ham pasties, ale, and bannocks." Shaw's words trailed off as he looked at her bent over the tub, but he closed the door and set the dinner on the bed. "Need some help?"

She should ask him to leave, for she was just in a smock that was bound to get wet. "My soap, please, on my bag."

He grabbed up the small bar that was scented with rose hips from the school garden and placed it in her upturned hand. "Thank you." She turned back to stare at the water under her face. Balancing the edge of the tub against her ribs, she rubbed some lather and began to work it into the thick waves of hair. "You can eat. I need to get this blood out of my hair."

Shaw moved to her side. "With the two of us working on it, we will get ye clean to eat in half the time." His big hands reached over her into the water. Her breath caught as she felt his strong fingers work through her strands, parting them and rubbing up through the mass to find her scalp. Scooping some water in his palm, he wet the scalp with the still warm water and began to wind a massaging path along her head.

Alana sighed. She'd never had anyone rub her scalp before. Her mother had been rather rough when brushing out her hair as a child, and none of her friends preferred to fashion hair. Placing her hands over the tub rim, she closed her eyes and held on while Shaw worked the suds through her heavy tresses. "Blessed lord," she murmured. "That feels good." Her words came breathless, and he stopped for a moment before continuing.

He cleared his throat. "I…I think all the blood is worked out. Now to rinse."

She took a breath and pushed forward, submerging her hair into the bathwater as he once again ran his fingers through the floating hair, ridding it of soap.

"A bit more," he said. "Then a little rinse with the water left on the hearth." He picked up the bucket. "Turn around so it falls down the back from your forehead to make sure the soap is clear from the bullet wound."

"Oh…ah, yes," Alana said, pulling a bit higher onto her knees and slowly turning while managing to keep her hair over the tub, the ends long enough to sink to the bottom. Her back was arched backward over the rim. Shaw stood above her, looking down with the bucket in his hands. His gaze swept her, and she felt a warmth rise inside. Not embarrassment but something else, a heat that made her tremble a little.

He gave her a nod and then slowly poured the clean water over her hair, making sure to clean the wound with a gentle touch of his fingers. "It does not look tainted, but we should keep watch of it." He bent forward, studying the gash, and Alana noticed that he'd trimmed his short beard, and his hair looked damp.

"You found a bath, too?" she asked over the sound of the water tumbling down her hair into the tub.

"Aye. The blacksmith let me wash there since there are no public places to get cleaned. He had heard that ye were bathing here with our baby boy. Word gets around quickly in a small town."

"Good thing you said Rose was a boy, then." She slowly straightened out of her bent-back position and took the damp drying sheet from Shaw to wrap around her hair. Standing, with his help under her arm, she glanced down herself. Och, the front of her smock had been wet, making the material almost transparent, and she'd had her breasts thrust forward. She glanced where he was emptying the water from the tub with buckets out the open window. He hadn't said a word about it, so she wouldn't, either. But her cheeks were stained red.

"Rose is sleeping happily," she said.

"Ye should eat and get some sleep, too." He turned from the window and set the bucket down by the hearth. "I will take the floor."

Alana looked at the one-foot path of bare floor around the bed. "Where exactly? Under the bed?"

Shaw opened the door and lifted the tub, carrying it out into the hallway. "Goodnight, Mistress Fiona."

Alana heard the woman grunt in the hall, and he came back in, shutting the door behind him. He pointed to the wall. "Her room I think," he said low.

"Then you need to share this bed with me," she whispered. "In case she has a peephole." Her words were so low that she wondered if he could hear her. He came to sit on the bed next to her, and she dragged her bare toes up under her gown. The heat from the fire was making the room comfortable, even with her damp hair. They shared the food in silence. Only the crackle of the peat in the fire grate and an occasional whisper of wind outside made noise.

A howl sounded far off outside the window. "That might be Robert," Alana whispered. "Alistair won't kill him for keeping him up all night, will he?"

"Not with Mungo there," Shaw said. "The man grew up with a pack of dogs and would fight anyone to the death if they tried to injure one."

"Grew up with a pack of dogs?" she asked. "You said his mother died when he was young, but surely someone took him in."

"My mother looked after him until he was an older lad,

but then my uncle threw him out of the castle when she died."

"The uncle who sold Girnigoe to the Campbells?" Alana asked, biting into the fragrant meat turnover. He nodded and drank from their shared tankard. "How old were you when she died?"

"Eight, almost nine."

Her chest tightened. There was no emotion in his words, and having lived with warriors, she knew he'd hate any pity she might show. "And your father?"

"He died when I was a lad of five, which is why we were living with my mother's brother at Girnigoe Castle."

"And your uncle accrued debt?"

He stood, stretching, his head nearly brushing the sloped ceiling. "He was a drunkard and liked to take his self-pity and rages out on people who were weaker than he. Aye, he accrued debt, and enemies. No one would help him when the Campbells wanted our home. So, he sold it all without thinking about anyone else. The Campbells let us stay in the castle until George died about nine years ago. Then the seat of the mighty Sinclairs was dismantled, but the Campbells still came to take the castle even without furnishings and a complete roof."

Alana watched him bank the fire with more peat, and she let her damp hair out of the bath sheet, sliding her fingers through it. She squatted down near Shaw to splay the tresses out to dry. "My distant cousin, Edgar Campbell."

"Aye, and he has no interest in letting us win or buy the lands back."

Alana sighed. "And somehow, all of this ties to Rose and getting her to St. Andrews?"

Shaw turned his face to hers. The firelight cut across his features, and she felt the prickles of heat on her skin. "It has everything to do with this mission."

"Rose is a babe, not a mission," Alana said softly.

"And Girnigoe is a home and seat of a clan, not just a castle and conquest." She watched his jaw move as if tension ached along it. "I will sleep on the far side, so ye can drape your hair over the bed to dry it close to the fire."

He splayed his hands, stretching them against the ceiling. In the confines of the small room, Shaw Sinclair looked even larger, like a giant captured in a box. One who was gentle enough to keep an infant alive and honorable enough to wash a scandalously clad woman's hair without comment or the hint of a leer.

With a tug, Shaw loosened his belt around his kilt, and it dropped for him to step out of it, leaving him in what looked like a new white tunic. He picked up the length of woven fabric, and Alana tried not to stare at the muscular legs below his tunic. Stretching over the bed, he climbed under the single quilt covered by the wool blanket that they'd had on the horse. With a quick glance at Rose, he settled in, yanking off the tunic to drape it on the end of the bed.

Alana stood there, her mouth dropping open. He was naked, completely naked under the blanket. He wiped a hand over his forehead and looked at her. "It is hot in here, even with the blankets off," he said. "But I can put my tunic back on."

She shook her head. "Not necessary," she whispered, turning to perch on the edge, her back to him. The bed was large. Surely, they wouldn't accidentally touch within it. But what if it wasn't an accident?

Shoving the wayward thought away, she climbed under the quilt, making sure not to lift it too much. A dip of blankets in the middle would serve as a wall, so she pulled some slack. He'd said that he wouldn't harm her, and she believed him. Although he had tossed her over his shoulder back at the festival. *I hate him. Yes, I hate him.* The lie felt hollow inside. For where would little Rose be now without her looking after her? Dead or near dead most likely. Starving, dirty, and jostled until her wee brain was mush.

He lay on his back, hands cupped behind his head, and she was turned toward him, so her hair could tumble out behind her off the edge of the bed. She closed her eyes and lay completely still, her breath shallow as she listened for movement.

"Good night, Alana," he said, his deep voice making her heart skip into a fast beat.

"Good night, Shaw."

"Should I kiss ye?" he asked softly, and her eyes flew open.

"What?" she asked under her breath. Kiss her? He wanted to kiss her?

He came up onto his elbows, the blanket slipping down to his rock-hard stomach. Alana held her breath. The firelight played along the muscles of his chest and shoulders. Good lord, she'd never seen, let alone been close, to a man of such beauty and strength. A warrior with a gentle touch, an honorable heart, and...and stark naked under the same quilt as she.

His mouth bent toward her ear. "In case we are being watched."

"Oh," she said on an exhale and drew in more air. He'd completely thrown off her normal breathing rhythm, and she was feeling a bit dizzy. It was a good thing she was lying down. "Yes. I...I suppose."

"Goodnight, dearest wife," he said, his voice louder in the room, and leaned over her. His face drew near, and she shut her eyes. His lips were soft, almost hovering over her with gentle pressure. She felt him cup her face with his hand, his large body rolling to the middle of the bed as he held her cheek, his thumb stroking it slowly.

She tilted her head, feeling the tantalizing draw of the

kiss. Her fingers came up to clutch his shoulder. Warm skin and smooth muscle. Her heart beat wildly. And then...he pulled back.

Her eyes blinked open to see him staring down at her, a slight shine to his lips where she'd just clung. He frowned, swallowing. "I...uh... Good night."

Her breathing was much too fast, and she rubbed her lips together. "Good night, husband," she said past the thud of her heart. She swallowed as he turned away from her, facing the wall. Alana pulled her knees in and forced her eyes closed. The bed was comfortable with a full tick, and the fire was warm against her hair and back. She'd had a bath, dinner, and was safe for the night. Still, it took long minutes before slow inhales and exhales of her breath were natural again. Her mind drifted into dreams and deeper still.

The forest was snowy, but Alana was warm. She threaded through the trees after a bird until it landed on a limb above her. She smiled up at it, watching it grow into a hawk, its yellow talons clasping the limb. The bird opened its sharp beak. Waaa. Waaa. It cried like a babe. "Rose?" Alana called up to it as the hawk changed into the little girl, perched dangerously on the branch. "Rose!" she yelled, running toward the tree as the babe cried again.

"I have her." Shaw's deep voice penetrated Alana's panic, and he was suddenly holding the babe there on the branch. "Shhhh, little Rose," he crooned.

The scene wavered, growing fuzzy as Alana woke. She blinked in the pre-dawn light filtering into the room but didn't move as her mind latched onto the only thing in her line of view. Shaw's profile, his features strong, even in sleep. He lay on his back, chest bare except for the baby lying flat against it.

Rose slept on her stomach, her little cheek right over Shaw's heart. He held her there with one large hand on her back, the dark lines of the horse's head laying stark on the smooth skin of his upper arm. The design covered the largeness of his bicep in smooth swoops and points. Whoever had marked the pigment into Shaw's skin had been an artist.

Rose cooed, and Alana's gaze moved back to the sleeping babe. Shaw had tucked one of Rose's light blankets all around her over the lace-edged smock that had come in her satchel. The babe made little sucking motions with her lips while she slept, one tiny hand out and curled into a fist to lay against his neck.

She must have woken, and he had calmed her against him. It was the most peaceful and beautiful thing Alana had ever seen. Was this what new parents were afforded every morning when they woke? Clearly not every father spared the mother and tended the baby himself. If they did, she would surely have heard about it. How could a woman not talk about such a perfect vision?

Shaw's inhale lifted Rose upward, and she lowered back down on his exhale like a baby sleeping upon gentle waves in a warm sea. Alana watched them for several minutes, studying the handsome face of her…captor? Partner? She wasn't sure what he was anymore. His nose was straight, his cheeks high. Dark lashes lay under his closed eyes. Her gaze traced the white scar along his hairline. Obtained in his youth? But how? His horrible uncle perhaps. Was he the fiend who had flayed Shaw's back open, the scars still evident?

His lips were slightly parted, surrounded by the neatly cropped facial hair above and below. She remembered the goodnight kiss with clarity, the tickle of his beard, the teasing promise of a wild heat.

"Damn," she whispered.

"Good morn to ye, too," Shaw said without moving, making her gasp softly.

He turned his face toward her without moving the babe,

his gray eyes open and clearly awake.

"I...I did not mean to wake you," she whispered. "Was Rose up during the night?"

"Aye," he said. "But she settled down again." He pointed at his chest. "She likes heartbeats like ye said."

Alana, her cheek still on the pillow, smiled at him. "Thank you for letting me sleep."

He lifted one hand to cup his head, his bare bicep framing that side of his face. "I would have woken ye if this had not worked." He grinned, his body stretching under the covers slowly so he wouldn't dislodge the sleeping infant just yet.

"The horse on your arm, does it mean something?"

"Aye," he said, bringing his arm back down as if to look at it. "A symbol of the might of Clan Sinclair." His smile faded. The haunted look in his eyes told her that there was more to say within him, but he turned his gaze back to Rose.

Alana pushed up in the bed and glanced toward the window. "Time to get moving."

"We cannot leave the town for a few hours," he said, rising into a sitting position, his hands holding Rose securely against him. "The horses are not finished being shoed."

She slid from the warm bed and crouched to stir the fire, adding more peat. The room was cool, and her toes curled under. "I can feed Rose while you check on the horses." She kept her back turned toward him, listening as he moved in the bed. She heard him take up his kilt from the end. "You can pretend you are looking at one to buy."

"Ye can turn around now, lass," he said.

She straightened, the room feeling incredibly small. The space between the bed and the hearth was so narrow that they stood right before each other. He'd set Rose in the warm blankets of the bed and pulled his tunic over his tan, brawny chest, tying it at the neck. "I will send some food up for ye with some milk for the bairn."

She smiled, feeling shy, and edged closer to the window. Was it the small room or the sleeping with a naked man or the goodnight kiss that was making all of this extremely awkward? "I will have us ready as soon as I can." She waited until he finally nodded.

"Very well, then," he said, his words slow. He hesitated but then went out the door.

She exhaled, lowering to sit on the bed that still held their heat. She rested her hand on the sleeping babe and sighed. What would her brother do if he knew that she'd shared a bed with a naked man? And not just any man, but a Sinclair, and not just any Sinclair. *The* Sinclair. "But nothing happened," she whispered to the room, her gaze going to Rose where she began to wiggle and would soon wake, demanding milk.

Alana dressed quickly in her blue dress, pulling on the training trousers underneath for warmth. It was now November, and nights were getting cold.

Rose whimpered. "Let us get you changed and fresh," Alana said. "Then we will hunt for some milk." Laying out the blanket under the blinking babe, she pulled off her wet breech cloth.

Tap. Tap. Tap. The door swung inward. "Morning to ye," Fiona called, pushing into the room.

"I brought more nettle tea for ye," Willa said, following on her sister's heels.

Alana gasped, spinning around.

"Oh my, little George still has his cord stump," Fiona said, peering past her. "That has got to come off soon or it will grow infected."

With such a small space, the sisters were upon them within an exhale, and Alana had no time to grab a clean cloth to cover Rose, and used her hand.

Willa gasped, the cup rattling in the saucer that she held on a tray with some food and a glass bottle of milk. "Little

George is not... I mean... He has no jack," she ended in a whisper.

Fiona's face had hardened with suspicion as she stared at Alana. She reached out, pushing Alana's hand away. "That is because the bairn is a wee lass." She placed hands on her hips, her sharp brows rising.

Alana's mind raced. Why had Shaw made up that lie? Well, she knew why, but now it was going to make the sisters very suspicious of them. Everyone in town would be talking about a little girl now. Worry tightened her face, pulling at the cut on her head.

"I demand to know what is going on," Fiona said, her voice higher.

Chapter Eight

"Shhh," Alana said, stalling while she tried to latch onto a reasonable explanation other than that the infant was the queen's daughter and being hunted by extremists.

"Why must I hush?" Fiona demanded. "Do ye not want that big husband of yours to know ye have a girl instead of a boy?"

"Uh… Yes." Alana nodded vigorously, rounding her eyes even more. She lowered her voice. "He wants a son, not a daughter. I was afraid he would kill the babe if he thought it was a girl." She was painting Shaw in the worst possible light, but it was the first somewhat reasonable explanation that she could use.

Willa gasped, setting the tray down on the hearth and turning in the tight space to shut them all inside the room. "He does not want a sweet little lass?" Willa asked, her question a rushed whisper.

She shook her head and quickly finished tying the new breech cloth into place. "He comes from a warring family and has always said he would only have a son. When my babe was born, I swore the midwife to secrecy and told him that she was a boy. He named him George."

Fiona frowned. "Well, your man is sure to discover the truth."

Alana shook her head. "He never changes the babe. Or bathes her. It is all me."

"But as the bairn grows," Willa said, still speaking in whispers as if he were listening at the door.

"I have hopes that he will die in battle very soon," Alana said. "He is quite brutal and wars constantly. He is sure to be killed before the babe is old enough to be breeched."

Fiona crossed her arms, one hand rising so she could tap her lip in thought. "There are ways to help that along. Then ye will be free of him, and ye can raise your pretty little girl."

"I…I am most appreciative," Alana stammered. Was the woman describing poison of some type?

Fiona nodded, her face softening. "I will make something up for ye before ye leave, just in case he discovers your secret. We cannot have him killing the bairn and ye if he finds out."

Willa shook her head. "He seems like such an honorable and loving husband."

Fiona snorted. "I spotted something was off from the start." She tapped her chest. "A sense I have in my heart."

Alana smiled with what she hoped was something more pleasant than the grimace she hid. Rose began to fuss, and she picked her up, along with the warm bottle. "And thank you for your help with the food and tea."

Willa reached over and squeezed her arm. "Happy to help, love. We women must stick together." Good Lord, how many other women had they helped by killing off their husbands? Hadn't Fiona had three of them before? Willa's husband, Jasper, better be very careful and obedient.

"When you finish feeding little George," Willa said, "come on out in the square. There is a morning wedding happening with a small festival taking place. Lots of delicious treats to brighten your day." She nodded encouragingly. "Gingerbread even."

Rap. Knuckles dropped onto the door, making Willa jump. Shaw opened it and stared at the packed room. "Just checking to see if ye are ready to come below."

Fiona and Willa filed out of the room, a look of fierce judgement pinching Fiona's face. He shut the door behind them. "What was that about?" he asked, frowning.

"They know Rose is a girl," she whispered. She met his gaze and held it. "And whatever you do, do not eat or drink anything that Fiona gives you."

• • •

The bloody morning was wasting away, but the horses weren't ready. Shaw led Alana and the bairn around the village square while the townspeople celebrated the union of a young couple. An old woman had a stand set up with fresh gingerbread biscuits cut in the shape of hearts. "A love token for yer lady," she called out as he and Alana walked by with the wrapped babe in the crook of his arm. "Made with fresh ginger root from the boats docking in Edinburgh."

Alana tugged gently on his sleeve. "Evelyn and Scarlet, the two sisters who started the Highland Roses School, said that jousting knights and their ladies exchanged the spicy biscuits before entering the arena. The spice is exotic and brings heat with it." She smiled. "At least that is what they said. I have never had any."

Heat? Bloody hell, he'd had enough heat already. Shaw was surprised that the entire bed last night hadn't roared into flames with his foolish good-night kiss. What the damnation had he been thinking? That they could be watched? Och. He'd spent an hour trying to cool down, his iron will the only thing keeping him from reaching out to pull the sweet-smelling lass into his arms. Would she have fought him off? The thought made his stomach sour. Of course she would have. He'd abducted her.

He fished two pennies out of his sporran and set it on the lady's table. "A biscuit please."

"Ah," the old woman said. "Young love, and with a healthy bairn already. Ye are fortunate."

Fortunate, his arse. Shaw nodded and handed the gingerbread to Alana. To outward appearances, aye, he was wed to the bonniest lass he'd ever seen, with a healthy bairn tucked between them. Only Fiona and Willa reserved their smiles, Fiona trading hers for glares. But inside Shaw, war raged the closer he came to Alana. The woman was beautiful, intelligent, and brave. And her kiss had been innocent and more alluring than any he'd ever sampled. And he'd sampled many with lasses panting after him back in the north. Women who liked his dangerous look or felt that in time he would be a chief with a castle, and there'd never been a reason to turn them away.

"It is delicious," she said, nibbling at the pointed tip. She handed it to him, and he bit into it, the spice pricking his tongue.

"Aye, there is a heat to it," he said, handing it back. Several men from before the chapel looked their way. Were they discussing the travelers that had come to town?

"Is something wrong?" Alana asked, her voice low.

He slid his gaze to the milling people near the tables that had been set up for a feast. "We should hide away from here before we become a memorable couple to these witnesses."

"Let us head back to the inn," she said. They walked slowly across the square, winding between the tables. A man dressed in bright colors and a pointed hat ran about, reminding Shaw of Mungo's jester act. The man held a pole with a string off the end, dangling a ball of mistletoe and berries. He leaped toward them, and Shaw picked up the pace, nearly dragging Alana and Rose along.

"You are going to draw attention to us," she said out of the side of her mouth, a tightness in her smile.

"Kiss the lass," the jester called, his voice loud. Shaw glanced up and saw him holding the kissing ball over Alana's head. *Mo chreach*. "'Tis tradition at weddings. Go ahead."

Gazes were beginning to turn toward them. If he didn't kiss her, they would surely cause even more of a spectacle.

"A lush one for yer lush wife," the jester demanded. "For giving ye a wee bairn."

"Aye, on the lips," another man said, lifting his mug of ale in a gesture of good health. "*Sláinte!*"

He looked at Alana and saw a gentle blush stained her cheeks. "Kiss me," she whispered.

Och, she was lovely, the sun glinting off her fresh hair and smooth skin as she looked up at him. With the bairn nestled snuggly on his arm, he pulled her close. She pressed her body up against him and tipped her face up to his, her lips slightly parted. Her long lashes lowered to close, her whole countenance open and wanting his kiss, even if it was a complete farce. His hand came up to cup her cool cheek, and he lowered down to meet her lips, kissing her.

A heat roared up within him, making his muscles tighten, his fingers itching to thread through the silky waves of her hair. In those few seconds, oaths melted away under the taste of her, sweetness and gingerbread spice and something more, something completely Alana. Convictions and truths, right and wrong, strategies and intricate plans dissolved away with the feel of her cheek in his palm and the gentle press of her lips on his.

A smattering of applause brought him back, and the kiss ended. Alana remained close, and their foreheads leaned into one another. "Shaw," Alana whispered. He held his breath, waiting for her next words.

A hard bump jarred his arm, and Shaw jerked his head up to see Alistair smiling at him, though his eyes were narrowed. "Pardon me," he said loudly. "Did not see ye." He held a tankard of ale and nodded to them. What the hell was he doing out in the open? Even though he wore a felt hat down over his tattooed forehead, he still had a memorable swagger and caustic tongue.

"Why?" was all Shaw had to say, his voice low. The man, despite his apparent infatuation for Alana, wouldn't ignore Shaw's order to stay out of town without a reason.

Alistair made a small flourish with his tankard and bowed his head to Alana. "Pardon, milady." With his face turned toward the ground, he continued in a whisper, "English soldiers, eight of them with muskets, on the outskirts of town. I didn't get a good look at them."

Damn. Was Major Dixon leading them?

"Pardon accepted," Alana said. "Husband, I need to feed baby George." She bent to kiss the top of Rose's head as if she were fussing.

"I can take the bairn," Alistair said under his breath, but both Alana and Shaw walked away from him toward the inn.

Measured steps, which felt way too slow, brought them finally to the door, and they stepped inside. "Gather the bairn's things upstairs," he said. "I will get the horses, or whichever ones are done. I will act as if I am buying them from Logan if he is there."

"Let's hope they are done, and we can go, else leave them all."

He met her worried eyes. "If questioned, we met at a Hogmanay dance two years ago, married, and had our baby boy five months ago."

"And our clan is Campbell," she said. "In case they have

information about the babe being handed off to Sinclairs."

If Dixon led the soldiers, he would know Shaw and his group of Sinclairs, but it was too much that he didn't want to explain right now. He dipped his chin with a quick nod, their gazes still locked. "Ye are a wise woman, Alana Campbell." A small smile touched her lips, the softness of them imprinted on his memory like a healing scar.

"I will get some milk from the kitchens, too," she said as she turned, arms around the bundled bairn, to hurry up the stairs.

Shaw strode out of the empty inn, his gaze drawn immediately to the soldiers clothed in red who stood at the gingerbread booth, speaking with the old woman. He didn't see Major Dixon, but only four of the eight were there.

He turned to the blacksmith's barn where the farrier would be working on shoeing the three horses that Logan and Rabbie had brought in. Hopefully his two warriors were already there. He hadn't seen them since arriving except to note that their horses were being shoed.

He looked toward the backside of the inn and paused. "*Mo chreach.*" Alistair was standing under their rented room window. Maybe Shaw should have punched him before. He changed directions, his boots crunching in the quiet of the late morning. "What the fok are ye doing out here?" Shaw asked, coming up to the man.

"If Alana climbs down to me with the bairn, I can ride them away. Get a few miles behind us in case ye need to dispatch the English with Rabbie and Logan."

"I will take her and the bairn out of here," Shaw said, his voice gruff. "Or have ye forgotten who is ultimately responsible for the bairn? And who is in charge of your clan?" He stared hard into Alistair's eyes. Shaw had grown up with Alistair, the two of them braced against the cruel world, always working together to reclaim the Sinclair lands.

But since Alistair's father had been killed at the hands of the Campbells last spring, the man had become impatient for an end to Edgar Campbell. Impatience could lead a man to disaster.

Above them, Shaw heard a gasp. Both he and Alistair looked up to find Alana's face in the window. But it was the other face, leaning out over the sill, listening to every word they'd said that tightened his gut. Fiona Murray straightened, lips pursed, her eyes squinted in suspicion.

• • •

"Fiona? What are you doing in my room?" Alana asked, her gaze moving between the woman and the two Sinclairs standing below them. What had they been discussing with the nosy woman listening?

Fiona crossed her arms. "And what are those two arguing over? It sounds like they are arguing over the bairn and ye. Yer husband, or perhaps not?" she said, her voice heavy with questions.

Alana's spinning thoughts had been out of control since Shaw had kissed her outside with such tenderness. A whirling, bordering on panic, that wouldn't slow down. She took a full inhale, hoping the breath would help her to think as she looked out the window. Little Rose had begun to stir and would start to cry for milk soon. There was no time for anything.

"He was my lover," Alana blurted out, pointing to Alistair. Both men stared up at her, Alistair's jaw dropping open. "He followed us here, thinking the babe is his." She leaned slightly over the window sill, holding Rose against her. "Little George is not your babe. Now be gone before my husband runs you through." She made a shooing motion with her hand.

"Ye bastard," Shaw yelled, pulling back his fist and smashing it right into Alistair's face.

"Good God!" Fiona yelled, hand pressed against her bosom as she nearly fell out the window watching the drama unfold.

"Get your arse out of this town before I slice ye open from your gullet to your jack," Shaw continued.

Alistair wiped his lip that bled. "She can choose who she wants, even if the bairn is yours." He held his fists before him as if ready to fight.

Good God, indeed! What were they doing? Alistair should just leave, and Fiona would have a juicy tidbit of gossip to impart to her sister.

"Do you happen to have more milk below?" Alana asked Fiona, trying to distract her from the window, but the woman wasn't taking her gaze from the two men.

Alistair ran at Shaw, but he sidestepped at the last second, tripping Alistair so that he fell as Shaw spun around, waiting for him to rise. He jumped up, running forward to swing at him. Even though Shaw moved his face, Alistair's other fist came up to sock him in the stomach.

Fiona turned from the window, her eyes wide. "Does this lover of yours like girl bairns?"

Did she think that Alana would just leave her husband and run off with her lover even though the babe was not his? Although...she had told the woman that she was hoping her husband would be killed in battle before Little George grew into a girl. And she might even use Fiona's poison on him.

Alana squeezed her eyes shut for a second. What did it matter? It was all a farce. She opened her mouth but didn't know quite what to say. "I...I do not know...how he feels about girl babes."

Fiona looked back out where the two of them were trading punches with realistic enthusiasm. "I mean your husband is the brawnier of the two, and…highly trained in fighting. Oh my," she said, her neck and cheeks growing red with a flush. Alana looked back out the window and saw the muscles in Shaw's arm mounded up, pressing against the seams of his shirt, his massive strength evident. Alistair's tunic had dirt and blood marring it. Shaw held his fist back, waiting for Alistair to rise, which the man did slowly.

Rose had begun to cry. "Stop it," Alana yelled down to them. "Shaw Campbell, I think it is time for us to leave, together. And you," she yelled at Alistair, her voice sharp, but then she hesitated. There was pain and humiliation in the man's eyes. His hat had fallen off, and Fiona was murmuring something about the skull tattoo behind her.

Alana huffed. "And you, my amazing lover. I will forever remember your prowess and mastery of passion, but my allegiance belongs to my husband in the eyes of God. Return to your home on the western sea, sweet man. Find a lass you can love well."

With that she turned from the window sill. Fiona stared at her, her mouth hanging open like a fish. "He will beat ye," she whispered, her eyes wide.

"He will not," Alana whispered back.

Fiona stared, her eyes still wide. "I will get it ready just in case."

"And the milk for the babe?" Alana reminded her. "She is already stirring from all the yelling."

"Aye. I will warm some right up." The woman lifted her skirts and hurried out of the room.

Alana grabbed up the baby's basket and their few articles, including the glass bottle. "Shhh now," she crooned, kissing Rose's head. "I will have your milk ready in a moment." She glanced out the window, but both Shaw and Alistair were gone. What were they thinking, putting on a show like that? The scuffle could have drawn the English soldiers.

She hurried down the steps and froze, her hand clutching the finial at the bottom. Her already running heart began to beat like a thundering drum. For the common room was full of them, their red coats like fire engulfing the space. As if sensing danger, Rose began to wail, and they all turned to look her way. *Good bloody hell.*

Willa stood behind the bar pouring tankards of ale. Her eyes were wide and looked slightly damp as if worry was making her weepy. Technically, the English and Scots were not at war, but anytime they mixed, there was often bloodshed or abuse in one way or another. Neither side respected the other. Respect must be earned, and those carrying muskets usually didn't take the time or have the heart to be kind and considerate.

One man stood out from the rest, the brighter red of his jacket and his gold-edged hat marking him as a commander of some rank. He walked toward her at the base of the stairs. "She sounds hungry," he said, staring at the little head.

"He is a boy, and yes, he is hungry. Excuse me so I can go nurse him," she said, her heart in her throat.

The man's eyes narrowed even though he held his smile. "How old is your...lad here?"

"Five months."

"And yet you are traveling with him? I thought babes were quite fragile when born. New mothers rarely let them out of the house or far from the hearth until they are past a year."

Alana's throat felt tight. The man was obviously trying to figure out if the baby was truly hers. "He...he was born away from home, and we are trying to return. He is quite healthy as you can hear," she said over Rose's squawks.

The man smiled, stepping aside so she could pass. "I am Major Dixon of His Majesty's army. And you are?"

"Mistress Alana Campbell, sir."

He bowed his head, smiling, but the friendliness did not reach his eyes. "If you should need assistance in traveling to St. Andrews, I can be of help."

Alana inhaled slowly, turning back to the man. She pinched her face slightly into a look of mild confusion. "My husband and I are headed to Stirling, but thank you." She turned back around and walked to the bar where the men all stared at her. The heaviness of the major's gaze pressed on her stiff back.

She met Willa's worried eyes and smiled, wishing she could stay with the woman to help her serve. Alone, she was vulnerable, but Alana must get Rose away. Major in the royal army? And he knew they were headed to St. Andrews.

But if he claimed allegiance to the king, why then were they hunting for the king's babe to kill? "Shhh, little love," she whispered and followed the back hallway into the brick-lined kitchen where Fiona rushed around, the woman's hands gesturing wildly.

"A room full of English." She tsked. "A brutish husband. A bleeding lover. Can this day get any stranger?"

Alana certainly hoped not. "Actually, my husband has been quite kind, and I assure you that he would never beat me."

"Yet ye hide that wee George is actually a lass?" she asked, her eyes rising to the door behind Alana.

Her breath hitched.

"Excuse me," Major Dixon said, making the ache in Alana's chest turn to fire, and she drew in a shallow breath. "I wish to rent the room above for the night."

Somehow, she made her feet move forward so that she walked over to Fiona, her gaze traveling around the hot kitchen. Was there another door leading out? None magically revealed themselves.

"Aye," Fiona said. "'Tis a small room with a bed big

enough for two or three."

"Mistress Campbell?" Dixon said, and Alana had to turn to meet his gaze. "Are you in need of assistance against your…husband?"

Blast. Her throat worked hard as she swallowed, but she forced a serene smile on her lips. "No, not at all. Thank you, Major."

His smile was just as false, his sharp gaze moving down to Rose. "So, the babe is a girl?"

Alana's arm squeezed a little tighter around the bundle. Rose was strapped against her, but could the Major somehow cut her free and whisk her away? Or just order them both shot through bound together?

Her lips squeezed together as she frowned. "How now? No. My sweet George is a little lad, Major Dixon. Rest assured that I have provided my husband with a strapping boy to lead our family one day."

Rose was outright crying now, wails of hunger that wouldn't be assuaged with Alana's gentle sway side to side. Fiona brought over the glass bottle filled with warm milk.

"You are not nursing your son, milady?" Dixon asked.

"'Tis a personal matter," Fiona said, chastisement in her voice. "The lady's milk hasn't come in well, and she must feed her son with both breast and bottle. We women do what we must." She wiped her hands on her apron and walked forward. "Now if ye will follow me, I will show ye to your room." Bless Fiona.

Dixon paused in the doorway, looking back over his shoulder. "I would speak further with you, Mistress Campbell, you *and* your husband."

Alana smiled as she held the bottle for Rose to drink even though the poor little thing was still tied against her. She didn't dare loosen her with a murderer of children close, not that the man would admit to such treasonous acts. "Certainly,

Major. We are not planning to leave until late in the day." A lie, she hoped. As soon as she could find Shaw, she would fly from Kinross, with or without him. Even though the major hadn't said he was hunting for the child, saying he was a loyal soldier in the king's army, his keen interest and suspicion marked him as an executioner.

Alana stood in the kitchen, just inside the door as she listened to the sound of Fiona leading Major Dixon up the stairs. She counted five steps before walking into the common room, smiling and nodding to Willa as she headed out the front door. Some of the wedding guests remained in the square talking, and Alana hurried around the corner of the common house. The crunch of pebbles behind her alerted her that at least one of the major's soldiers was following.

Her gaze scanned the woods bordering the back of the common house. Where the hell was Shaw? Or Alistair? She'd even take skipping Mungo, who was a damn good fighter. Battling a soldier would be hard enough but battling one with a babe strapped to her would get them both killed.

Alana's steps increased, but she held herself back from running. Turning left toward the blacksmith's barn, she spotted Shaw with the three horses. Alistair was nowhere in sight. Her gaze on his strong back as he inspected the black mare, with the crunching pace increasing behind her, Alana could hold back no longer. She broke into a run, one arm holding Rose flat against her chest while the other hand, clasping the glass bottle, pumped at her side. "Shaw," she yelled.

He spun around, his gaze meeting hers before lifting to whoever followed behind her. She flew toward him, and he caught her shoulders, pulling her behind him. "Why the hell are ye chasing my wife?" he asked.

Chapter Nine

Shaw's palm itched to pull his sword, but with the soldier holding a musket, and Alana and the bairn behind him, he thought better of it. "Are the king's men ordered to harass good Scottish wives, or are ye just looking to meddle on your own?"

The soldier's gaze cut along his frame as if sizing up an enemy. No, Shaw didn't carry a musket, but his sword and muscle were just as deadly. "Major Dixon wants to talk to the both of you," the soldier said, his dull red coat marking him as an enlisted man. But was he working for or against the crown? Dixon had been supporting King Charles at the Covenanter meeting outside Stirling, but kings had changed, and the courier had mentioned him as one of the assassins hunting the princess.

"What business does he have with us?" Shaw asked.

"That babe you happen to be carrying." The man nodded to where Alana stood behind him.

Shaw kept the enemy in his line of sight. "What would an English soldier want with a Scottish bairn?"

"Nothing, if she is a Scottish bairn," the soldier replied, trying to mimic Shaw's accent. "We are looking for an English princess that traitors abducted from Whitehall Palace." His gaze moved down to Alana. "We would return her to her mother who cries for her stolen daughter."

Clever man. He was playing to Alana's heart as a woman. Would she believe him?

"I have a son," Shaw said. "And he is mine and my wife's. Look for your lost princess elsewhere."

A second man, in brighter reds, strode around the corner to stand beside the first. "Hello," he said, a smirk across his face as he raised his brows. "Chief Sinclair? I did not know that you had married. And a Campbell? How...strategic of you."

The devil himself stood before him. "Major Dixon," Shaw said. "A surprise seeing ye here. On official business?" He kept his tone even.

"Yes," Dixon said. "It would seem Queen Mary's daughter was stolen from Whitehall right after her birth, a dead infant left in her place. Would you happen to know anything about that?"

The bastard was fishing. Shaw would never take the bait. Hopefully Alana wouldn't either. "Nay," Shaw answered. "I do not keep up with English royalty or their lack of security."

Dixon nodded. "Either way, I would take a look to see that this boy of yours is actually a boy and not a girl. Then we will be happy to let you journey on your way."

Shaw knew Dixon had become a player in the radical movement. Yet he still hid behind the power of the crown, wearing the uniform and using their rankings. As he'd seen at the river, those wearing red army uniforms still wanted to kill the innocent bairn. If in fact the queen or king wished for the child to be returned, why didn't they send another message with a royal seal? If the child was taken and killed, the

Sinclair clan would be blamed, losing any hope of regaining their castle and lands.

"Ye want me to strip my bairn down in front of ye?" Shaw asked, his voice thick with disgust.

"It is a simple request," the major said, his teeth set close together under his long, sloped nose.

"And what next?" Alana said, stepping to the side. "Ask me to lift my skirts so you can inspect that I gave birth?" She shook her head. "We are two faithful, God-fearing people, husband and wife with a child between us. Let us on our way."

She spoke with authority and the shaming cadence of a chastising mother. Unfortunately, Dixon didn't seem shocked; in fact his gaze dropped to her skirts for a brief moment. Bloody bastard.

Logan had already paid for the shoeing, and Shaw had come to inspect them as if wanting to purchase one. The blacksmith and farrier had melted away when the soldier had run up after Alana, leaving their fires unattended. No doubt they were close but wished to stay out of a conflict with English soldiers. Because it was growing more likely by the second that there was going to be further conflict. He would relish it if Alana and Rose weren't standing right there. He'd sent Alistair off with a bloody lip, telling him to stay out of sight. Where were Rabbie and Logan? *Foking hell.*

The soldier standing with his commander moved to check that the match was lit on his musket. If it was to be war, then so be it. Shaw stepped before Alana, drawing his sword. "I would think hard on it, soldier," he said, his voice deadly even. "A Scotsman reacts poorly to someone leveling a musket at him."

Before anyone could move, a dagger flew through the air. Alana stood, arm thrust to the side, her *sgian dubh* hitting the soldier's hand, point embedding into his knuckles. He yelped, dropping the musket at the same time Alana turned to run with the bairn. The horses neighed as she caught one of them, hopefully to ride. Shaw jumped forward, his hard boot slamming down on the musket before the major could grab it. It cracked under the force. Damn, they could have used it. Although he was more comfortable with his sword.

The injured soldier turned to run for the other men inside, but Shaw had his attention focused on the major who'd drawn his rapier. Slender but sharp, it reminded him of a thin snake. If they were going to get away, he needed to dispatch Dixon quickly. Without warning, Shaw leaped forward, but the major stopped his advance with a thrust of his own. Swords crossing before them, Dixon gritted his teeth.

"All Catholic heirs, along with anyone protecting them, will die," the major said.

"All innocent bairns, under my protection, will live," he returned, shoving the man away.

Dixon's lips opened as if he had a retort, but Shaw slashed forward, catching the man's cheek, a red slice opening along it. Shock registered momentarily across the man's face as blood trickled down.

"A man gets slow just fighting against newborn bairns," Shaw said.

Before Dixon could raise a hand to his cheek, he lunged forward again. If the man had delayed, he'd have a long sword piercing his gut. Pressed against one another, the major let all his hostility blaze in his eyes.

"You will die for marking an officer," he said.

"Or ye will die for underestimating a Highlander." Shaw dropped his weight, bending his knees, and the major flew over him as Shaw lifted upward. Dixon crashed into one of the ovens, toppling a stack of horseshoes.

"What the hell?"

Shaw spun to see Rabbie standing there. "Grab a horse," he yelled, stepping around the flailing man. With a solid fist around the hilt of his sword, he brought it in a sweep across the back of the man's head. Dixon grunted as he fell unconscious to the stones at the base of the outdoor hearth.

"More are coming," Shaw said, as he grabbed one of the English horses. Rabbie had already risen onto the other. Shaw leaped upward, throwing a leg over the horse, and pulled the bay around, pressing into its sides.

"Stop!" one of the soldiers yelled, but Shaw was already tearing around the back of the smithy behind Rabbie. The lad slowed where his own horse was tethered loosely, bending down to pull the tie as all Sinclairs trained to do after having to escape quickly over the last nine years.

"Alana?" Shaw asked. Rabbie glanced back at him as they started up again, shaking his head. Blast, he didn't know where she was. "East then," he called, hoping she would think to meet them due east of the village.

Crack! Crack!

Fire lit along Shaw's right hip, and he loosened his grip to leap off in case the horse went down under him. The English horse apparently knew what musket fire meant and surged forward unhindered. Shaw leaned over his neck, his hand sliding back to his kilt where a tear from the musket ball stretched from his arse up his hip. Hot and wet, he didn't need to see the blood to know that he'd been hit.

• • •

Alana held Rose against her as she urged the horse to weave carefully between the trees behind the common house, her breath coming in hard gusts. She'd left Shaw to get the babe to safety. *He will be well.*

She wasn't sure which way to go and looked up at the sun directly overhead. From which way had it risen? Holding onto the swift-footed horse, she glanced over her shoulder, then back into the thick woods of colored maples and birch. Gasping softly as she saw two people, she pulled on the reins, and the horse slowed to a stop. Fiona and Alistair.

Tugging the reins, she turned toward them, weaving quickly through the trees. "Alistair," she said. "Shaw needs help. I left him in the smithy with armed soldiers."

Alistair's lip was fat with dried blood, and his eye was bruised with red in the white of it. Had he and Shaw continued to fight after she left the window? He looked back toward the smithy and then to her holding the babe against her. "He would want me to get ye and the bairn to safety."

Fiona's eyes were wide. "What do they want with ye?" she asked, speaking of the English.

"They think my babe is another and want to kill her," she answered. "Can you help us?"

She nodded, lifting a satchel up to Alana on the horse. "It has food and milk with another bottle. After they tore out after ye, I thought ye might need this, which is why I was out here looking for ye and found him." Her thumb jerked toward Alistair.

"Thank you." Alana attached it to the back of the saddle. "Ye are a blessing, Fiona."

Fiona grabbed her hand, squeezing tightly, and lowered her voice to a whisper. "There are some tarts. The one with the currents on top is for your husband if ye think he will beat ye."

She shook her head. "I will not poison anyone, Fiona."

"It is just sleeping powder in the tart, so ye can get away. As much as this town thinks I poisoned my three bastard husbands, I only put them to sleep on occasion." She smiled. "Take it."

Blast! Blast!

Alana twisted in her seat, thankful that Rose was securely tied to her chest. "That was a musket." She looked to Alistair.

"Help him."

But Alistair grabbed her foot out of the stirrup and threw his own in, hoisting himself onto the horse behind her. "I know the way to St. Andrews. I will get the bairn there."

"No!" she yelled, but he grabbed the reins from her.

"I will tell them ye went west toward the isles," Fiona said. "Godspeed."

Alistair yanked the horse, kicking him. He leaped forward, and Alana could only hold tightly to the babe with one hand and the pommel on the saddle with the other while her thighs clutched around the horse. There was no way she could argue with him flying through the trees away from the village. He turned the horse right to skirt around to the west side before heading east. After long minutes, he slowed the horse, and Alana turned, twisting to look up at him. "I am not leaving without Shaw."

Alistair met her gaze, and she stared at his good eye. "Why?"

Why? Her chest squeezed. The man had abducted her. To save a babe. His men had tied her up. But he'd sworn that none would harm her. He'd dragged her away from the festival. Toward her mother and agreed to help free her. He was the enemy. Who had spared Robert. He'd slept next to her without touching her. And his kiss...

"Why do ye care about a man who stole ye away?" Alistair asked, searching her eyes.

She swallowed. "Because...Shaw swore that he would help me free my mother from the Covenanter prison in Edinburgh," she said low. "I will not leave here without him unless..." She wet her suddenly dry lips. "Unless he is dead." The thought felt like a boulder in her chest. Shaw was invincible. At least that was what he'd seemed, tall and broad, his biceps thick with muscle, his body able to move quickly with the prowess of a wolf.

Alistair continued to study her, his eyes narrowed. "Shite," he whispered, and wiped his nose with the back of his hand. The battered side of his lip hitched up, and he broke the gaze, glancing upward. "We will wait a bit then. Up in the trees. See if Shaw or any of them ride this way."

"Thank you." The boulder remained, but she could draw in a full inhale again.

"He has always been a lucky bastard," Alistair said. "I am sure he made it past those musket balls. No matter what comes at him, he manages to survive it somehow."

Lord, she prayed so.

Alistair pulled the horse near a tall oak with thick branches. "Raise up and grab that limb. I will move the horse farther away and run back."

Alana grabbed the satchel that Fiona had packed, thankful the woman had included another glass bottle since she'd dropped the first in the barn. She pushed upright to grab hold of the branch while Alistair steadied her around the waist. The intimate touch made her frown, and she hoisted up quickly. The man held her foot on the branch until she was able to lift to the next, and then he wheeled the horse away. Alana stared out through the woods toward the town and gently rocked Rose against her, hoping the whimpering babe would go back to sleep, but she hadn't gotten much milk before she'd run to the smithy.

"Bloody hell," Alana whispered and kissed the babe's soft head. "We are back in a tree." And she'd lost her *sgian dubh* to stop the soldier from firing at Shaw. At least she still had her hair spike. She rested her chin gently on Rose's head as she stared out toward the village. "Come along, Shaw. Don't you dare be dead." He had to be alive to help her find her mother and…to kiss her again.

• • •

Ducking low over the horse to avoid tree branches, Shaw saw Logan already mounted up ahead. He had Alana's and Alistair's horses with him. He raised his arm, pointing forward, and Logan surged in that direction several trees over. Were the soldiers pursuing? It depended on how close their horses were tied.

Circling from their initial ride west, they moved east, staying well away from the town. Mungo joined them and had somehow retrieved Rìgh from the barn behind the common house where they'd slept. He rode his own horse with Rìgh following. Frowns upon them all, they took off flying as fast as they dared between the trees, the tethered horses slowing them down slightly.

With the rush of leaves and wind, and the hoof beats and leather sliding against leather, Shaw couldn't hear how close the major's men were. He did hear his own heartbeat in his ears, pumping hard, pushing more blood out of the shot in his arse. *Foking hell.* He yanked off the cloth strip he'd torn that morning from one of the bairn's clean cloths in case he needed to wash Alana's gash. Lifting his kilt, he slid the cloth under his leg above the shot. The wound was deep, but it looked like the ball wasn't embedded. He used his leg muscles to steady himself and tied the cloth tightly.

Scanning the brightly colored forest, Shaw whipped his gaze from side to side looking for a rider with long flowing hair. His gut remained tight. Where were Alana and the bairn? Could other English be hiding in the forest away from Dixon? Could they have her bound and gagged, the bairn already slaughtered? His thoughts made him lean over the horse, and it picked up speed with the urgency.

Circumventing the village, they turned east, riding until they reached where Shaw would turn them to ride on the way to St. Andrews. Shaw pulled up on his horse's reins. "Where are they?" he yelled. Before anyone could answer, the sound of a beast running through the leaves made him twist in the saddle.

Robert the wolfhound loped after them, another frayed rope dragging behind him. Mungo signaled, looking relieved.

Shaw bent down. "Where is Alana?" he called to the dog as it leaped around, weaving amongst the horses, nose in the air. The dog tilted his large shaggy head as if to decipher what Shaw was asking. His gaze scanned all of them seated up high. None of them carried anything that smelled of Alana. He glanced down at himself. He'd used his kilt to place a wedge between him and Alana during the night when he couldn't sleep from want, knowing that if she rolled up against him, he might be too drunk with exhaustion to push her away.

Shaw put his weight on his good leg as he dismounted the English horse on the wrong side. He ignored the deep ache of the laceration and tight binding.

"Fok, Shaw," Rabbie said, moving his horse closer. "Ye are shot."

Logan cursed, dismounting, and Mungo spit, jumping down to run over and untie the rope around Robert's neck.

"The ball is not lodged in my leg," Shaw said, walking to Robert, his stride skewed.

Logan ran up to him. "Shite, there's a lot of blood. I need to tighten the binding," he said, flipping up his kilt.

Shaw let him look but gathered the front of his kilt, which was free of blood, in his hand. With his shot leg to the side, he bent his other knee to lower so the dog could thoroughly smell his shirt, where he'd held Alana not even an hour ago as he kissed her in the town square under the jester's kissing ball. "Where is she?" he asked and raised his kilt to the dog's nose, tugging his own shirt forward, too.

"The lass was against your kilt and shirt?" Logan asked, his brows raised.

"And the bairn," Shaw said, a sliver of defensiveness in

his tone.

Mungo started moving his hands with signs. Logan, who understood his signals the best, snorted. "He says, 'no wonder Alistair is in a foul mood.' The poor bastard decided she was the woman for him after she hit that English soldier in the head with her dirk."

"Alana Campbell is for none of us," Shaw said. His fingers curled into the dog's thick coat. "Except for ye," he said, looking into the animal's warm brown eyes. "Find your mistress." He held his shirt and kilt to the dog's moist black nose.

Shaw straightened, grunting as Logan tied the tourniquet tighter on his thigh. "Ye are making my toes go numb."

"That's the bloody idea," Logan said, motioning to Mungo to bring Rìgh closer. "Best ride Rìgh. He will keep ye going even if ye bleed to death on top of him."

"And the ladies think ye are the sensitive one of us," Shaw said, grabbing Rìgh's familiar saddle to pull himself up. "Leave the three English horses. Alana has one that she escaped on."

"There he goes," Rabbie said as Robert, nose to the ground littered with fallen leaves, trotted off farther into the woods. His powerful tail swung back and forth like a flag.

"Follow him," Shaw said, adjusting his numb leg against his faithful mount. Logan was right. Rìgh would take him all the way back to Girnigoe Castle even if he bled out on the way, arriving stone-cold dead. He looked out over the horse's ears, his mind moving past the throbbing of his leg and to the need to find Alana. *Where are ye, lass?*

Robert kept them moving west, farther out from the village, and then turning east nearly a mile out from the town. Was Alistair with her? Or had they left him in the village without a horse? Shite. Despite Shaw's annoyance with the man, he would go back for him. He was a friend, even if he'd foolishly set his heart on a lass he could never have. *Mo chreach.* Shaw rubbed his bristly chin. Was he in danger of doing the same? Nay. He was made of stronger discipline. She was a Campbell, and besides, a part of her would likely hate him forever for taking her in the first place.

He hadn't felt any hate in her kiss last night, nor the one today. Then again, she didn't know him. What he'd done in his past to try and save his clan. What he'd seen when her parents were taken by the English.

Mungo rose up in his saddle, his arms open wide to the sky, waving and then pointing ahead and to the right.

"There," Logan said just as Robert, sensing how close his mistress was, broke into a run. "In the tree."

"With Alistair," Rabbie said.

Damn. Shaw leaned forward, and Rìgh surged ahead, knowing without him even pressing against his sides. They stopped before the thick oak. "Alana," he called up.

"I have her," Alistair said. "And the bairn."

"I have myself," Alana said. "And the bairn." Before Alistair could move, she threw one leg over the branch, her skirts flying over in a blue arc. She lowered onto the bottom one, the bairn still strapped to her chest.

Shaw pushed Rìgh close to the tree so that they were on eye level. "Ye are well?" he asked. "And the bairn?"

She nodded. "I heard musket fire," she whispered, her gaze dropping along his frame. It stopped on his bloody kilt. Her breath hissed through her teeth as she inhaled. "You are shot."

"Grazed," he said, not wanting her to worry over the blood loss.

"I need to tend it," she said.

"We need to get away from Kinross," Alistair said, lowering down. His lip and eye had swollen. Good.

"I knocked out Major Dixon," Shaw said. He should have

skewed him in the back after he hit him, but he wasn't one to kill an unconscious man. And murder was not something he wished tied to the Sinclair name. He exhaled. "But once he wakes, he will follow."

"That bastard is here?" Logan asked, glancing over his shoulder. "Is he leading the search?"

"Aye," Shaw responded, his horse shifting as if he sensed the heaviness of worry that lay about them.

"The woman from the inn said she would tell them we headed west toward the isles," Alistair said, dropping down from the branch to the ground.

"But Major Dixon tried to trick me into admitting that we were traveling to St. Andrews," Alana said, hugging the bairn close. "He knows where we are headed."

Alistair reached up to help Alana down, but Shaw leaned into her where she sat in the tree, pulling her toward him. She came willingly, and he settled her and the bairn before him on Rìgh. Alistair stalked away to reclaim his own horse.

"She might decide to help them," Logan said.

Alistair lifted into his saddle. "She knows the bairn is a girl."

"Or she could be a terrible liar," Rabbie said.

Alana settled in the saddle, the bairn making small noises to show she was awake and hardy. Och, the lass had a smell about her, not exactly flowers, but it reminded him of fresh air and sunshine. She fit right up against his chest as if she belonged there. Damn, she didn't belong there.

"I do not think Fiona will betray us," Alana said, turning to look up into his eyes.

"She wanted to poison me," Shaw said.

Alana's soft lips almost turned into a smile. "She likes me, not you." The glimpse of her smile faded. "And she will not help a man who wants to slaughter a babe."

"Unless Dixon convinces her that he is trying to save the

bairn from us," Shaw said, raising his eyes to his men. "We need to split into groups, separate to better remain unseen. The major and his men have not seen all of ye. Alana and I will ride alone as husband and wife in case we meet any others."

"What if the major finds ye?" Alistair asked. "I doubt ye can convince him now that the bairn is yours."

"Leave Rose with us," Rabbie said. "The soldiers from Kinross will not be looking for her riding with four men, and we will keep her hidden. And if Dixon catches up to ye, ye will not have anything he wants."

"Except my life," Shaw murmured. *Hell.* He regretted not killing the man, honor be damned.

Shaw looked to Alistair. The man had always been his second-in-command and his friend, and that hadn't changed just because the man wanted someone he couldn't have. "Ye are in charge of the mission without me. Lead the bairn safely to St. Andrews, and Alana and I will meet up with ye there."

Alistair nodded, no surprise in the set of his eyes.

Shaw raised his gaze to Rabbie. "Ye are responsible for always looking out for the bairn, keeping her fed, dry, and clean."

"With warm, clean water," Alana added. She'd begun to untie the bindings around her waist. "And warm the milk. Do not let her be jostled if you can help it."

Rabbie nodded, his face serious. "I will protect her with my life and keep her healthy."

"We all will," Logan said. "Her life is the life of Clan Sinclair."

Mungo thudded his fist against his heart and nodded, giving his own oath.

Alistair climbed upon his horse that Logan had brought with Alana's. He moved his horse over to Shaw. "Get that wound sewn up. The lass can take care of it." He nodded to

Alana and then turned.

Alana kissed Rose on the cheek, and Shaw heard her sniff as if tears fell from her eyes. He touched the wee lass's head, a sharp tightness pinching his chest. She lifted the bairn from herself into Rabbie's arms. The lad smiled down at the tiny face peeking up from the warm woolens wrapped around her. Had they all lost a bit of their hearts to the tiny princess?

"We left the basket she came in," Alana said, and Shaw heard a small waver in her voice. "So, you will have to wrap her in blankets next to you to sleep, but do not roll over on her."

Rabbie nodded, holding Rose against him while Logan tied the sashes behind his back, securing the precious package against his chest.

With one last nod, Alistair raised his fist in the air. "*Tiugainn*." The four of them pressed forward, riding off through the woods, her horse tethered to follow behind. Robert trotted after them and stopped to look at Alana, waiting for her.

"He should help protect Rose," Alana said, the heaviness of loss in her voice.

Shaw would spare her another farewell. "There are four of them. Your beast can follow us."

"But he was not with us before in town. If the soldiers find us, they will know someone was keeping him, someone else who then took Rose," Alana said. "Go, Robert." She shooed him with her hand. Logan made a short whistle sound to call him. With one last look, the dog ran after the four men to ride alongside Mungo's horse.

Alana turned in the seat and wiped a hand across her cheeks that were definitely wet. "Let us get you sewn up, and we can head to St. Andrews as fast as possible."

St. Andrews, not Edinburgh? Without the bairn with

them, Alana Campbell was actually free to go on her way, her responsibility to them riding off with his men. Of course she'd want to reclaim her dog. If she'd thought about it, she would have called Robert back to be with her.

"I will still help ye find your mother and escort ye home," he said and turned them due north, adjusting his numb leg, the ache running deep along his thigh.

"I know you will," she said, looking down at his saturated kilt. "But you cannot if you lose all your blood."

There had never been truer words spoken.

Chapter Ten

A cave would be best, back in the forest, preferably without any wolves or vermin inside. Alana's heart thumped as she scanned the trees, feeling the silence around them like a weight. Was Shaw well or was he bleeding too much? His kilt looked soaked. "We need to stop soon," she said and glanced over her shoulder to see if he looked listless and pale. Yet the man continued to show strength in his features.

"We will need to make camp and use the leaves to hide us," he said.

She studied him. Was he delusional? "Leaves?" He nodded, and she turned front. They had ridden several miles from the town in a northward direction, the sun lowering on their left. "We need a stream."

"The River Almond should be just north of here," he said.

He leaned into her slightly, and the horse picked up a faster gait through the woods. Without the babe tied against her, Alana felt the chill of the fall wind. It was freeing not to have the child's weight before her, but it also made her feel rather empty, like an appendage had been severed.

"I miss her," she said.

Shaw's arms came up on either side of Alana. He didn't say anything, but his support was obvious, and she wanted it, needed it. She took a steadying breath as they increased in speed, holding onto Shaw's warhorse as it maneuvered without any outward sign from Shaw through the thick forest.

After nearly an hour, the sound of water rushing caught her ear, and the subtle change of Shaw's leaning made the horse turn right to angle toward it. They slowed and finally stopped near the bank. Brightly colored leaves arched over the fast-moving stream, the setting sun making the water look dark. A stray beam of light danced off the ripples where a leaf shot along like a boat caught in an ocean surge.

"I will climb down first," she said, expecting his no, but he didn't say it. She turned to see a light sheen on his brow. He was in pain. "There now," she said, using the no-nonsense yet encouraging tone she did when helping Cat Campbell back in Killin with her patients. "We will get you down and fix that wound." Lifting her leg to swing forward over the horse's mane, her blasted skirt dragged, momentarily blinding the massive creature. But he didn't move. Maybe Shaw Sinclair did know how to train animals. Alana twisted and pushed off to land on the ground.

Brushing her hands, she looked up where Shaw swung his bad leg over and dismounted on the wrong side. He grabbed the bag on the back of the horse and limped his way to the water's edge, holding the injured leg out as he sat down on his opposite hip. "It hit my arse actually, slid along my hip. Logan tied a tourniquet." The last words came through gritted teeth as he yanked the knot loose.

"Wait," she yelled. "It will bleed again."

"At this point my leg is going to fall off if I do not let some blood flow again."

Alana hurried over. Blood had dried, making his kilt stiff with it. "Damn, it is dried to the wound." She batted his hand away. "This needs to come off," she said, reaching for the belt that held the kilt over his narrow hips.

He was turned away from her but looked back over his shoulder, his eyebrow raised. "Ye know I wear nothing beneath."

"I have seen a man's...arse before." She waved her hand. "And other parts. I assist the healer at Finlarig Castle." It was true she'd seen a man's backside, but only the front in one of the art books that Evelyn had brought from England. The picture of David, who Kirstin said had a small jack, poor man.

Shaw unbuckled, letting the belt fall with the binding of his kilt. His white tunic was also covered in blood from the wound, dried to a darker red now and somewhat stuck. "Lie on your stomach if you can," she said and bent over the stream, wetting another piece of linen she'd ripped from her old smock. *He has a strong constitution.* It was true. He hadn't ended up with a fever from her stab wound. Perhaps he'd heal perfectly fine.

Shuffling back over to him on her knees, she squeezed the water over the dried blood, softening it enough for her to pick the kilt and tunic away. Skin tinged a rusty brown, she lifted the kilt gingerly to see a deep trail cut into the flesh of his hip running three inches down his leg. It still wept, but the flow was slow. "It could use stitches. The musket ball cut a chunk out of you." Her gaze raised to the back of his head as he propped himself up on his elbows where he stretched out on his stomach. The dark waves of his hair looked soft. She swallowed, looking down at the wound. "Less than an inch farther to the left, and the ball would still be lodged in your flesh."

He shifted and she looked up. He gazed back at her over

his shoulder, a slight grin playing along his mouth. "My luck is apparently better than the Englishman's shot."

"Your luck?" A laugh flew out with her exhale. "I have only known you for four days, and you do not have a castle or land, you have been stabbed, saddled with a hungry babe, punched by your friend, and now shot."

"But I am not dead," he said.

She rinsed the cloth in the water, squeezing it over the wound, and wiped the skin around it, repeating the motion until the blood came away. "Why were you and Alistair fighting?" There was a pause where she held her breath.

"An angry husband should battle a persistent old lover."

"Yes, but I think Alistair's face took the brunt of the act."

Shaw grunted, shifting slightly forward so that he lay his chin on his forearms.

Wiping the wound completely clean, Alana tried to ignore the strength in the muscle of his thigh and not look too long at the perfect shape of Shaw's arse. It was an arse after all. Something everyone had. It was used for sitting upon. Surely it was only curiosity that made her want to study him more.

"How does it look?" he asked.

Alana coughed, turning her gaze from his toned backside. "A few stitches are needed."

"I have thread and a needle in my satchel. And whisky to keep it clean."

"You should drink some of it, too," she said, finding the satchel on the back of Shaw's horse. The horse picked at the grasses under the fallen leaves. She opened a flask, sniffing it. Whisky. "Here, best to numb the pain."

"Warriors are accustomed to pain," he said but took a haul of the flask anyway.

A smile pushed up the corners of Alana's lips. "You sound like my father."

"Was he a great warrior?"

She nodded but realized he couldn't see her. "Yes."

"And a Covenanter, someone strongly against the English king's push to unify the country under one liturgy."

"Yes. My father hated the English monarchy and felt that Charles just wanted to restore Catholicism." She shook her head. "He would hate King James even more."

"And the king's children?" Shaw asked, glancing over his shoulder at her.

Alana felt a twist of guilt inside. "I do not know, but a babe is a babe, born innocent, and should not be hated for her father's beliefs."

A small amount of whisky flowed into Alana's palm, and she dunked the threaded needle into it. "Now, brace yourself." Before he could reply, she poured some whisky on the deep gouge that the musket ball had left. Shaw didn't move, but the muscles in his leg contracted. "Try to relax," she said softly. Working quickly, she gently pinched the flesh closed and caught the edge with the needle, pulling the thread through the other side to form a stitch. She added seven more, spaced evenly along the line of angry flesh.

She glanced up after each stitch, but Shaw remained quiet, seeming to stare out at the flowing stream. The salve that she carried in her satchel would help the skin to knit back together, and she wiped some on with the tip of a finger. "I will tie a clean piece of linen around it and wash out the tourniquet to use tomorrow. We need to keep it clean, but it should heal, leaving you a scar for which you may brag."

He snorted lightly. "I have enough about which to brag."

Did he mean the scars on his back? The one on his hairline and small nicks on his face? Or were there others hidden about him?

Alana kneeled before him, placing a clean swatch of linen across the stitches. "The scars on your back look well healed," she said and shook out the long strip to tie it.

"Aye."

He didn't say anything else. "Were you just a boy then?" She paused at the gruesome vision of him, a dark-haired boy, having his back flayed open.

She watched him inhale. "Aye, too weak still to prevent it."

Her heart hurt for the boy who had suffered so. "Who would whip a—"

"My uncle did not like me accusing him of throwing my mother to her death," he said.

Good God. The pressure of tears swelled behind her eyes, but she blinked, refusing to let them fall. He would only see them as pity.

She swallowed hard. "I am glad he is dead, then." She forced her voice into a lighter tone. "And likely in Hell being whipped for his deeds."

Shaw snorted softly where he rested on the river bank.

She lay the clean linen across the stitched wound and paused. Threading it under his naked hip would bring her hand very close to his male parts. Alana took the one end high up on his hip and slid it under his thigh down by his knee.

"Do ye need me to turn?" he asked, not moving at all. His leg was as heavy as stone.

"Just a bit," she said, and he pushed up as she hovered over him, completely uncovering his front. "Oh," she said, dropping her eyes, but not before the size of him was etched into her memory. Kirstin was right; the statue of David was too small to truly represent the jack of a mighty warrior. Heat moved into her cheeks, and she kept her head bent as she worked the binding up, tying it high on his hip.

"There," she said. "You just need to keep it clean and dry to guard against fever. I am nearly out of feverfew. But you managed to avoid a fever from my stabbing you, which you did deserve."

"Aye, I did," he said.

She glanced up, meeting his intense gray eyes. "If you had just asked me, I might have said yes without you having to truss me up like a caught goose. After all, I do need to get to Edinburgh to save my mother. I suppose you didn't know that, and poor Rose was surely to die without a knowledgeable woman to help you."

Lord, she was rambling. It was as if she stood on the outside, listening to the words spill from her mouth in a failing attempt to hide her flustered reaction to seeing him naked. Gathering a full breath, she clamped her mouth shut to stop the flow of words and stood up. Without further utterance, she gathered the supplies into Shaw's satchel and grabbed his clothes to wash at the stream.

"I have another tunic in the other bag tied to Rìgh." His voice was warm, as if there was a hidden smile within it. "And Alana…" He waited, but she was already striding to his horse to collect the covering. She turned to come back to him. He had draped the blanket that he lay upon over his hips and pushed up on his elbow, watching her. "Alana…"

She finally lifted her gaze to his. "Yes?"

"Thank ye. For sewing me back up and for helping me keep the bairn alive."

She nodded and handed him the tunic.

"And," he continued, "for what it is worth, I am truly sorry that we tied ye up to take ye with us. Desperation makes men foolish, and I allowed myself to fall prey to it."

Alana froze at his words, her lips parting as her jaw dropped slightly. She closed her mouth. "Well, I had just stabbed you. You probably did not think I was open to discussing a trip east."

A smile broke across his mouth, relaxing the tightness in his jaw. With his wavy hair haphazard and the threat of laughter in his eyes, Alana's heart squeezed with...what? Forgiveness? Compassion? Want?

"I admit that option hadn't entered my mind," he said.

She felt her lips turn upward into a gentle grin and went to the river to wash the blood out of his kilt and tunic. The cold from the water worked up her arms to cool her heated cheeks and neck. It was a wonder that steam didn't float up from her. She heard the rustle of linen as he pulled the tunic over his head behind her.

"Have ye always been so dangerous with a hair spike?" he asked.

She heard the crunch of pebbles as he stood, and she turned to frown at him. "You should not put weight on the leg so soon. Your muscles could split the stitches."

"I will hobble about, then," he said, meeting her gaze. His head tipped slightly as if he studied her, and his mischievous look slid away. "Have ye had a need in the past to learn the art of war? Or defense? Ye said that ye learned it at your Highland Roses School."

Alana turned back to the water rushing under her hands. It was easier to talk about the fire when a flame's natural enemy was coursing through her fingers. "I understand losing a home," she said. "A castle like Girnigoe even. Finlarig Castle is my home, but those plotting to kill King Charles decided it was a good location for an assassination and used my father's known Covenanter status to throw us out. He was killed, and when we refused to go, the English soldiers involved in the plot set fire to it."

She could feel Shaw's presence behind her there on the bank, but she remained crouched, facing the water. "Ye decided to learn to throw *sgian dubhs* and wield your hair spike to seek revenge?" he asked. She glanced over her shoulder at him. Even in just his boots and a long tunic, he looked formidable. A frown sharpened his gaze, and his fists rested at his sides.

"No." She shook her head, meeting his gaze. "I learned to defend myself so that the next time men picked me up to throw me into a fiery inferno, I would draw their blood."

Without waiting for a response, she stood, walking around him with his dripping clothes to lay out on a boulder upstream. She would hang them on a limb, but if Major Dixon's men rode this way, the clothes would be a flag, calling them over.

A long, sturdy limb sat on the mosaic of leaves, and she picked it up, leaning on it. It might hold Shaw's weight. Thumping with it, she walked back toward him. "You can use this to help you hobble about."

"The English traitors…they threw ye into the burning castle?"

"Yes." She held the limb up straight near his hand so he could take it. "When they found out I was the daughter of the chief, they picked me up and threw me inside, barring the door."

He cursed under his breath, his face hardening into the promise of death. She wondered if he donned it in battle, because it would be quite effective. She moved past him, picking up the woolen blanket he'd laid upon, shaking it of leaves and dirt.

His limp had stolen his stealth, and she heard him thump closer. So, she didn't jump when he clasped her upper arm, gently pulling her to face him. "Were ye burned?"

"My feet and here and there," she said. "A few scars, but nothing horrific, at least not on the outside." She smiled but knew her eyes were sad. Nightmares and bits of memories plagued her. "And now that I know I can at least draw blood, the inside scars are healing some."

"*Mo chreach*," he said, his voice low. "And my men grabbed ye up, under my order."

She smiled. "And you lost blood from it. It is a start." She looked away. "Night will fall soon. I am assuming we will not have a fire, so we better make a shelter. If you tell me what to do, I will build one."

"Alana," he said, his voice heavy with…regret?

She blinked against the ache building again behind her eyes. She didn't let anyone see her tears. "Yes?"

"I would not have allowed them to tie you."

"They did not tie me. They just lifted me up and threw me inside like I was a bundle of kindling to burn."

He shut his eyes for a second, and when they opened, she would have backed away from the death in the fierceness of his face. "I will kill them."

"They are dead," she said, keeping her voice as light as she could.

He exhaled, still holding onto her arm. "And I meant my men. I would not have allowed them to tie ye back at the festival. I would not have thrown ye over my shoulder."

It was her turn to tilt her head, studying him. "Yes, you would have. To save Rose."

Her words made him inhale as if bolstering himself against them. The truth could be a heavy burden to lift. She planted hands on her hips. "Now, how do I build a shelter?"

. . .

Shaw watched Alana lay the blanket under the leaf-covered frame he'd helped her make with fallen limbs. Burns on her feet? Did they still pain her? Were any of the bastards who had thrown her into the inferno still alive? Questions filled his mind as he watched her stretch down on hands and knees to straighten the blanket. The panic in her face when she'd read his intent after his men walked in behind her at the Samhain festival had been the same any woman would show.

Knowing now what she'd gone through before, the fact that she continued to bargain, continued to defend herself instead of just freezing in shock, showed just how much courage Alana Campbell possessed.

Despite her fussing this evening, Shaw had lifted the heavier limbs, laying them down and binding them with strips that they took off the dwindling length of her old smock. The shelter was propped against a rotted tree to cover them with leafy limbs and fallen leaves on three sides. On the fourth side, they had left an opening between the limbs for a hidden door.

Alana backed out of the lean-to, swiping her hands together after laying one of the woolen blankets on the ground. "There, small but snug for the night. And hidden so that anyone passing by should not spot us right away." She looked at Rìgh. "Unless they see a large horse standing by it."

"I will lead him away. I have trained him to lie on the ground when needed. He will not be spotted unless someone trips over him."

"Good Lord. I cannot even get Robert to stay with someone else. If he sees me, he runs over, although he seems to like Mungo," she said, her voice holding a wistful tone.

"I am sure he misses ye."

She smiled slightly at him. "Mungo or Robert?"

Shaw wasn't sure what to do. She was teasing him, even though he'd thrown her over his shoulder and carried her away. Could one truly forgive something like that, especially with her history?

She didn't seem to need an answer and retrieved some mint she carried in her satchel. She walked off to finish cleaning her teeth and freshen up before settling down. He'd do the same when she returned. Shaw looked at the small shelter. Did she plan for him to share it with her or should he be making up a separate bed for himself? He could sleep next to Rìgh. The horse had kept him warm on nights before, camping in the field with nothing more than his kilt to drape over himself. But he didn't like the idea of her being far from him alone.

He must have stood there, undecided for minutes, because Alana walked back around and froze. "Is something wrong?" she whispered, her face whipping left and then right as she peered into the darkness.

"Aye," he said, but then shook his head. "Nay. Just tell me if the shelter is just for ye. I can sleep with Rìgh."

In the darkness, she was a moonlit angel, her hair brushed to one side to lay over her shoulder. She still wore her traveling petticoat, another layer to keep her warm as the temperatures dipped.

"'Tis of no matter," Shaw finally said. "I will bed down with my horse. Just promise to scream if anything disturbs ye in the night." Using the limb as a crutch, he moved toward the stream to wash, grabbing the flask of whisky that he used to wash his teeth.

Her words came soft as he passed. "It would be warmer for me if we share the space. Body heat and only one spare blanket."

His chest tightened with something he'd felt very seldom before. Hope.

Washing quickly, he made his way back to the lean-to where Alana already lay inside the tight quarters. He clicked to Rìgh, and the large warhorse followed him through the darkness fifty yards away, where Shaw tied him with a very long tether. "Sleep well, valiant friend," he spoke close to the horse's ear and made the signal, tugging gently on his halter to get him to lower his bulk down. It wasn't natural for a healthy horse to sleep on the ground, but when hiding from bloody English soldiers, it was necessary.

Shaw approached the lean-to as quietly as the crutch

allowed and lowered to crawl inside. Alana sat up, pulling the woolen blanket aside for him. With his wounded hip, he lay on his left side, facing her. "Thank ye for sharing," he said.

"You make enough heat for two," she said. "Are you comfortable?"

The ache in his hip and arse was nothing compared to the ache forming between his legs, as if his jack hadn't heard that this arrangement was merely practical for keeping warm. "Aye," he lied.

She stared at him in the darkness. Although she was in shadows, the moonlight from beyond the trees cast a bit of silver on the outside of the woven branches, giving them a little light as their eyes adjusted. He held himself on his elbow so that they were level and exhaled, running his hand through his hair. "Lass... I..." His words were slow with the heaviness of remorse, another tightening in his chest that was all too familiar.

When he didn't go on, she leaned slightly forward. "Feel bad that you carried me off against my will? Wish that you legally owned and possessed Girnigoe? Will do anything to get it back? Including bringing Rose to St. Andrews alive and well? Which required you to abduct me? And no matter how thankful you are for me healing your arse, you would do it again? Is that what you want to say?"

The woman was courageous, strong, and highly clever. "I would likely have left off the last part about doing it again," he said.

"But it is true, whether you left it off or not."

He inhaled and exhaled fully. "Aye." He lowered so that his head rested on his nearly empty satchel. "My whole life has centered around retaking the Sinclair castle...from my drunkard uncle and now from your clan."

She stared at him, studying him. "You know something I like about you, Shaw Sinclair?"

"I have not a single guess."

A small laugh came from her. "You are honest," she said. "Which is something I value."

Her words, given sincerely, formed rocks within his gut. *Honest?* He opened his mouth but then closed it again. He should tell her all before they reached Edinburgh, but something stopped him. What would Alana do if she knew the lengths that he had been willing to go to take his castle back?

The distance between them narrowed. Had she moved closer? Their combined heat inside the space created a comfortable nest out of the breeze. It seemed like days ago when he'd given her the gingerbread biscuit in the town square and shared a kiss under the mistletoe ball. Yet it was just that morning.

"Now my turn to tell a truth," she said, her voice lower. She glanced down and rested her head on the rolled-up trousers she'd taken off. Her gaze turned to meet his. "This morning when I heard that musket fire...the thought of you being killed by the major...it made me feel sick."

A slight floral scent came off Alana, and he remembered the soap that she had wrapped in her satchel. *Bloody hell.* His body was reacting to her nearness, her soft words, and her open stare. Blood rushed through him, and his fingers curled inward into fists to stop from reaching for her. She was beautiful and sweet, but she was a Campbell. And she would hate him.

"I am able to take care of myself," he answered.

"But they had muskets and you had a sword. 'Tis not a fair contest."

Shaw slid slightly closer, her siren's voice seeming to lure him in. "Not much in this life is fair, lass. What ye have seen and lived through has surely taught ye that. We just make the best decisions we can in the moment and hope that fate falls in our favor." Was he still talking about Major Dixon in the smithy? Of course not, but she wouldn't know that.

He hovered over her, and she stared up into his eyes. "What decision are you about to make now?" she whispered, her hand raising up to touch his bristled cheek. Her fingers were cool and light, a caress so tentative that if he closed his eyes, he would think it a mere fancy of his imagination. Her fingertips slid to the side where a scar from his uncle's tankard sat along his hairline. Her light touch was more powerful than a fist against him, flooding him with need and desire. He held still, firm discipline his only defense against her.

"Alana," he said, and she moved closer, her lush curves pressing against him. There, alone in the darkness, surrounded by warmth and her sweet scent, it wouldn't have mattered if he'd been shot through with holes; he felt no pain, no aches, only need.

Her cool fingertip moved down his cheek to slide over his bottom lip as she explored the contours of his face. "There is a best decision right here before you," she said, and he detected the slightest tremble in her touch. "And the best answer is…yes."

Chapter Eleven

Alana leaned into Shaw, her heart thumping hard in her chest. She had never tried to seduce a man before and had only experienced two awkward kisses from boys growing up. A part of her, which sounded very much like her mother, asked her what, by the eternal flames of hell, she was doing. But as her lips pressed against Shaw, and his arms came up around her, the wave of passion that had been a persistent but controllable stream all day smothered the little voice.

She sunk against him, drawn by his warmth and strength. His hand slid down her back, sending tingles along her spine, and the pool of heat in her abdomen ached with her stillness, urging her to move against him. The fire that burned within her was the kind she didn't fear; in fact the feel of it pushed all her fears away. In the silent darkness, warmed by their combined body heat, unseen by anyone who might judge her actions, Shaw was not a Sinclair and she was not a Campbell. He was just a man, a brawny, handsome, fierce warrior of a man. She'd been drawn to him ever since he carried her over the river, throwing her and the baby to safety while he charged back across to stop the soldiers from following.

They breathed into one another, their mouths sliding together as she tilted her face to his. Her fingers curled into his tunic as if to hold him there. Shaw Sinclair. Not her enemy, even though he was hated by the Campbells as decreed by his birth. The danger and heroism of his actions had tugged at her heart, but it was the heat that welled up in her as she kissed him that urged her hips forward.

"Alana," he said against her mouth.

"Shaw," she replied, meeting his kiss over and over. Good Lord. He tasted of whisky and sin, and she couldn't get enough.

She worked her fingers down his chest to slide under his tunic and up the fine planes of his stomach, the muscles defined through constant training and warfare. Solid and smooth, his chest was sprinkled with fine hair. With her eyes closed, she felt his hands cup her face as he kissed her with fierceness, the two of them growing wild against each other.

Shifting her leg, she instantly felt his hardness through her petticoat. She remembered the brief view she'd gotten by the stream, and although large before, what she felt now was even larger. Without her trousers and without his kilt, only her skirt and smock stood between them. Pulling one hand out of his shirt, Alana plucked at the knot of her corset, which tied in front. It was a simple matter of moving her shoulders forward and back to bring down the lace edge of her smock, and her breasts swelled out of the top.

Her nipples, peaked and sensitive, slid against Shaw's shirt. He pulled back slightly, and she opened her eyes. The moonlight shining through the leaves of their shelter fell as shards of light cutting into the shadows. Between the two of them, her pale breasts thrust upward.

"*Bòidheach*," he said. "Beautiful." He leaned in to kiss her again as one of his palms dropped to cup her. The rough pad of his thumb strummed against her nipple. The sensation pulled a low moan from her as the heat inside gathered in her pelvis. She rocked against his hardness. Leaning down, his mouth replaced his thumb on her nipple, and Alana gasped at the deliciously hot suction as he laved her, his other hand coming up to cup and plump the second breast.

Alana moaned, thrusting her chest toward his mouth. She lifted a leg to drape over him but stopped as she remembered his stitches. Instead her fingers wound back under his tunic, stroking a path up his chest. As he came away to yank his tunic off over his head, the coolness of the air on her damp nipples made them pearl even more. Never before had she felt anything so exquisite as the fire Shaw was igniting within her, so primal and all consuming. His touch melted away all her concerns, making her feel free and wild. No responsibility, no worry about consequences, her mind and body focusing entirely on the feel of his skin, tongue, and lips against her own.

She looked down his naked length as he threaded fingers through her tumble of hair. Her breath came heavy and fast as she took in the large, jutting jack standing between them. When her gaze rose to meet his, he was watching her, judging her reaction. She wondered what her reaction should be for the space of two breaths before pressing into him.

His hard length lay heavy at the juncture of her legs, making her heart pound with a wild type of want. Her arms wrapped around his neck, making her breasts swell against his naked chest. The fine hair teased her nipples as she dragged herself up level with his face. "Kiss me, Shaw. Make me keep feeling this…this sweet torture," she whispered.

"Aye, lass." His mouth descended to hers. They explored and tasted, her hands beginning to stroke downward, curious to touch the heaviness between them. He kissed a path along her jaw to her ear, the heat of his breath strumming another chord of passion within her, weaving with all the others to drive her mad.

"Alana, lass," he whispered, desire thick in his brogue. "Ye should think well on this...this happening between us."

"Right now, I cannot think of anything," she whispered back and caught the length of him in her hands. It was hot and heavy. A deep groan burbled up from his chest, sounding almost like a growl when she slid her wrapped fingers up and down. "Such smooth skin on such a hard beast," she said against his lips, and the flesh at the juncture of her legs pulsed. No wonder ladies were willing to risk reputation, pregnancy, even inheritances to be with a lover. This primal heat turned all consequences to ash.

His hot mouth returned to her breast, loving first one and then the other, while her hips rubbed against him in time with her stroking hand. Shaw's strong fingers wound a path over the bared, sensitive skin of her neck and chest, stroking and widening the ties of her stays until they completely parted, revealing her lowered smock, the scooped neckline pulled under her bosom. She wore the new smock that she'd bought from the ladies at Kinross, and his fingers slowly rucked up the bottom edge until it balled at her waist. His warm palm stroked the skin of her stomach.

A low moan floated out of her on an exhale. "I want to be completely bare against you."

"Och," he breathed against her mouth as her skirt bunched up at her stomach so that she could press firmly against his hard length, cradling him with her bare body. His hand left her stomach to stroke up her naked leg, lifting and turning them so that she lay sprawled out across him.

"Your stitches," she said.

"I am off of them."

Both of his large hands spanned her naked arse as she rose up over his chest, her hands gripping his shoulders, letting her breasts hang down. Pressed so intimately, she began to rock, and Shaw helped her find a brisk, delicious rhythm, rubbing against him. She leaned her face down to kiss him, ravishing his mouth. Gasping as she felt him touch her entrance, she opened her knees farther.

"I ache there," she whispered.

He groaned but didn't enter. "Och, Alana. There is no going back afterward."

No going back? Did he mean that she wouldn't be a virgin anymore? She knew that, knew that giving herself to a man meant that she wouldn't be pure for her wedding night, but at that moment, none of that mattered. The only thing that mattered was Shaw, his scent, his touch, and the deep ache that yearned for him.

Before she could answer, he shifted again, sliding her back to her side while pulling her leg to lie high over his hip above the stitches. She was spread and naked as his fingers moved to her abdomen and then dipped lower.

She inhaled as he grazed her sensitive spot, as if knowing exactly where to touch her to bring such pleasure. Their kisses were wild, slanting against one another while he delved within, strumming inside and out. Stroke after wild stroke, building the pressure within her.

"Take your pleasure, Alana," he said, his northern brogue thick with passion. "Let go," he whispered at her ear, the velvet roughness of his voice teasing her even higher.

"Yes, Shaw, oh God." The fire inside her erupted, shattering through her like lightning hitting the surface of a frozen lake, shards of pleasure slicing her composure, her muscles clenching as she clung to him, rocking into him. She rode the waves of sensation, a low moan whispering from her lips.

Reaching down his muscular, hot body to his still rock-hard jack, her hands wrapped around him. "I would make you feel as good," she whispered, her breath still fast and shallow.

He kissed her as she moved her hands, groaning softly. "Ye are so beautiful, lass." The passion, thick in his voice, plucked at the satisfied ache within her.

Shaw froze, his hand dropping to her wrists, holding them with gentle pressure to stop their movement. His lips dropped to her ear to whisper, "Listen."

Heart pounding hard, Alana held completely still, though with the rush of blood in her ears she couldn't hear much. She concentrated on slowing her breathing and making it silent. Slowly she drew her hands up between them but made no further movement.

Crack. Snort.

Off toward the stream, a bridle jangled. Rìgh was tethered in the other direction, and from what Shaw had said, the horse was trained not to make a sound. No, there was at least one other horse nearby. Maybe it had wandered away from a farm.

"Should we stop here for the night, Major?" The man's English accent sliced through her passion, cooling her so fast that she shivered. There was no doubt that the major was Dixon.

Her body went rigid. *Mo chreach!* Shaw was naked and injured, and she was nearly naked herself. She hadn't replaced her *sgian dubh*, which she last saw sticking out of the English soldier's hand, and she had no idea where her hair spike had fallen out while rolling around with Shaw. Naked and without weapons, their only chance was to remain hidden.

"Water the horses." Major Dixon's voice confirmed that it was the jackal that had attacked them back at Kinross, demanding to inspect the baby. Thank God they had sent Rose with Rabbie and the Sinclairs. Robert as well. Any noise from either of them would have given them all away.

Shaw held Alana, his hand pressed flat against the small of her back, supporting her, holding her close. Could he feel the panic in her limbs, the wild thump of her heart that made sparks glitter on the edge of her periphery? Was he willing her to remain still? Her heart felt too high in her chest at the thought of what the men would do to Shaw if they found them, and what they might do to her. How would they explain the absence of their babe?

"There has been no fire here," the major said. "And they would need to heat the milk for the baby. No, we will move on. They are likely following this stream east."

"But the woman in the village said they headed west," another man said.

Alana listened to the low *thump* of boots hitting the ground as the soldiers dismounted.

"The woman lied," Major Dixon said. "The tracks led west at first but circled around to the east. They are heading to St. Andrews as we were told."

The water splashed as the horses stepped along the edge to drink.

Shaw's hand came away from her back. With utter silence, he slowly slid her tangled smock down her legs, followed by the light wool fabric of her skirt. He didn't want her naked, either, with eight English soldiers finding places to piss in the dark. She slowly lifted the front of her smock and stays, tucking her breasts back underneath.

A light breeze rustled the leaves overhead, and footfalls walked toward them. She held her breath. If the man saw the leaf-covered structure, hopefully he would just think it was a small berm or covered boulder. Thank God that Shaw's horse was dark in color. Leaves crunching with each step closer, her heart pounded blood through her, readying her to defend herself if found. Lord, it was so loud, it was a wonder the soldiers couldn't hear it.

The steps stopped. She drew an inhale to dispel the sparks in her periphery. Nothing good would come from her swooning. A shifting of cloth was followed by the sound of the man pissing. He cleared his throat and spit. He was no more than four feet from them.

Other footsteps sounded farther back toward the stream. Alana stared at Shaw in the muted silver light. His face was hard, determined, but he kept his gaze centered on her. Slowly, he raised a six-inch *sgian dubh* so that it came up out of shadow before her face, then he lowered it, pressing the handle into the palm of her hand. She grasped the blade, the weight helping her relax enough to draw a slow, full breath.

"Shite," the soldier said. "Fitzwilliam."

"Eh?"

"I swear I saw something move over there, down low to the ground."

Boot steps crunched closer. Alana kept her gaze centered on Shaw's eyes. He would get her through this if they found them. She would do whatever he told her to do.

"An animal?"

Had he seen Rìgh? The large horse was lying on the ground but may have moved its head.

"It was large and dark," the first man said. He lowered his voice. "Maybe a wolf."

"As long as it isn't a babe or foking Scot, leave it. Come on. The major wants to keep riding."

"I hope there is ale and a willing woman at the end of this ride," the first soldier said, and the two of them tramped back through the leaves, stepping a path around the leaf-covered lean-to.

"We will ride on, see if we smell a campfire along this stream," Dixon said, his voice still too close. She strained her ears to hear the soldiers mounting again. It was impossible to count how many were out there by sound alone.

The two of them lay, half perched upright in the dark, listening to the horses walk off through the woods, following the stream. As the last steps faded enough that the breeze covered the sound, she let herself down off her elbow and leaned her head into Shaw's bare chest. She closed her eyes and breathed.

He leaned down, his fingers brushing the hair from her cheek. "They are gone," he whispered right at her ear.

A trembling had taken hold of her, but she nodded, her head brushing his skin. No, there was no fire that the soldiers could throw her into, but they could have done worse to her and could have pocked Shaw full of holes. He gathered her against him, resting his chin on the top of her head. Without a word, she breathed in his smell, his essence, and took strength from his embrace. He stroked her hair. "They will not return. Sleep, lass. Ye are safe."

"They will realize that there are no more tracks along the stream when daylight comes," she whispered.

"Aye. We will ford the stream, head farther north before turning east. It will delay us a bit, but my men will wait for me in St. Andrews with Rose."

"They will not…give her to whomever is waiting for her?"

"Nay. 'Tis my duty as chief to see it finished. They will give me time to arrive unless…the waiting goes on too long." He meant, unless the English had found them and shot them where they lay entwined together. A shudder ran down through her, turning the heat of the passion they had shared into ice. He pulled her against him as if realizing that she needed the feel of his protection and strength. And at that moment, she certainly did.

...

His blasted leg was stiff from the wound, but at least it looked free of taint. So far. Shaw tied his kilt over his hips and tunic. The spot on his kilt that Alana had washed free of blood was still damp, but it wasn't a bother. He looked to the stream where she cupped the clear water into her hands to splash over her bonny face. Dawn had just broken, and they moved rapidly to break camp, just in case Dixon decided to track backward when he couldn't find farther tracks. It left no time for talk.

She stood, drying her face with the edge of her wrinkled petticoat. He could see the black trousers that she had used as a pillow encasing her legs before she dropped the skirt back down. Looking up, she caught his stare. There was pink in her cheeks, but that could be from the brisk water.

Och, how he'd wanted to take her last night. Soft, wet, and willing, her body had beckoned him to the point that he'd almost lost his mind. *She is a Campbell. You abducted her. She might hate you if she finds out the truth.*

The arrival of the soldiers had actually saved him from making a mistake. No matter that the lass had wanted him. He couldn't rut with a virgin under leaves on a forest floor. His mother may have been too weak to protect her young son and herself from abuse, but she had taught him about being honorable.

"Do you think they saw Rìgh last night?" she asked as she walked close, still unwilling to raise her voice much above a whisper.

He patted the noble animal's neck, and Rìgh shook his mane. "Aye. He is likely the only animal out here with a bunch of men clomping around, scaring them off."

"Thank God they did not go closer and find him."

He gently squeezed her upper arm until she met his gaze. "Alana, about what happened last night…before Dixon showed up."

The pink in her cheeks was not from the water now.

"Yes?"

"I did not…I should not have taken liberties," he said. "I would not dishonor ye by taking ye in the dirt and leaves. Ye do not have to worry about—"

"Me seducing you again?" She blinked, and her hands fisted at her sides. "I believe we are both responsible for our actions last night." She didn't look angry, just a bit embarrassed. He opened his mouth but then closed it, not sure how to respond. The lass thought she'd seduced him? Well, everything about her drew him in, but that wasn't her fault. His lapse in discipline was to blame.

Before he could figure out a response that wouldn't negate what she said but reassured her that it wouldn't happen again, she stepped past him to Rìgh. "We should move on. Do you need help climbing on top?"

The vision of him sliding up and over her naked, writhing body filled his disobedient mind, and he coughed into his fist. "What is that, lass?"

"On top," she pointed to Rìgh. "I can help get you up."

Blast, he was already up, and she'd be sure to feel it through his kilt when she nestled against him in the saddle. Och, they should talk, when it was stark daylight, and they weren't wrapped together in a tiny, dark lean-to. But there wasn't time right now. "Nay," he said. "I will…mount first, from the wrong side."

He met her next to the large brown and black horse. "Does the wound pain you?" she asked, a slight frown between her gently arched brows.

He itched to rub a finger over the lines there, soothing them away. "Nothing of consequence."

"I will need to strip you down and wash you when we stop today."

Mo chreach. Was she purposely saying things in a way to bring delicious images of them rutting to mind?

He rubbed a hand down his jawline. "Lass…"

She paused, looking at him expectantly.

What did he want to say? That given time, privacy, and a bed out of the dirt and leaves, he'd gladly let her seduce him again? That he hadn't contemplated using her as a Campbell hostage if the bairn didn't win him back Girnigoe? Nay, for although he may not have told her the truth outright, he would never lie. *Isn't that the same as lying?* Damn his conscience.

"Shaw?"

He braced his legs apart, not caring that the stance made his hip ache. The battle stance prepared him for any outcome; he'd learned that as a boy fighting his way amongst all the other boys trying to grow into men. "Ye do not hate me, then? For…taking ye from the festival?"

Her soft look pinched into annoyance. "I am not in the habit of kissing and…touching men whom I hate. I am not plotting to soften your defenses by falsely acting the willing lass."

"I never thought that," he said to her back as she turned and strode to the front of Rìgh, scratching under his bristly chin. He followed. "I am just… We work better with ye accepting my apology."

"As long as you do not intend to stuff anything further into my mouth, yes, I forgive you. We've been over this. You were trying to keep a babe alive. Rose would likely be dead now if you had not forced my hand in helping. You could not even feed her…"

She was talking, but Shaw had lost track of her words after she'd mentioned stuffing something into her mouth. His jack had gone from hard to twitching granite. Had his blasted jack taken control of his mind, twisting her innocent words into erotic scenarios?

She stared at him as if waiting for a response. He gave her a tight nod before striding the rest of the way around to the other side of Rìgh so he could mount using his good leg. Up in the saddle he gathered his kilt before him, but she would need to be a complete innocent not to notice the hardness nudging the back of her shapely arse. Catching her foot in the opposite stirrup, Alana lifted herself, rucking her skirt up to straddle her legs, settling down before him. Shaw stared straight ahead at the trees as he breathed through the torture of her wiggling and adjusting in the seat.

He grunted, tugging the reins to turn Rìgh toward the stream to cross onto a flat granite rock where it would be nearly impossible to see his tracks once they dried. Alana pressed back into him, and he tried to concentrate on the horse's footing, although Rìgh was certainly capable of crossing the stream that was only two feet deep at most. Blast, this would be easier if she despised him.

Tell her. The words were from his conscience, not his jack. For telling her what he had been willing to do to regain Girnigoe from the Campbells would surely bring about cold hatred from the warm woman who glanced over her shoulder with raised brows. Her gaze dropped to his jack before turning forward.

He opened his mouth, but the words wouldn't come, and he shut it. They were still on a mission, and if she refused to speak to him again and stormed off, he'd follow her instead of going directly to St. Andrews. It wasn't safe alone in the forest. At least he was honest enough with himself to admit that. *Damn it all.*

Checking the location of the lightening sky, he turned them north toward Perth. They would travel on to Dundee where they could hire a boat to take them across the Firth of Tay to St. Andrews. It would add another day of travel, but he'd been certain when he told Alana that his men would keep Rose until he arrived. Saving Girnigoe and reclaiming their lands was the mission of the Sinclair Chief. Even as angry as Alistair was with him, the man wouldn't steal this victory from Shaw, not when he knew how long he'd been working toward this end.

They rode for an hour, the sway of the horse making them rub together until Shaw had the feeling that they were two brittle fire sticks that would ignite at any moment. An occasional ray of sun would break through the cloud cover to shoot down, catching the highlights of red and gold in Alana's brown hair. He knew it was soft, perfect for burying his face. His jack grew harder as he imagined burying his face elsewhere. *Och.* If he didn't distract himself with something, he was likely to stop Rìgh and ask her if she'd be willing to rut around in the leaves with him. He rubbed a hand down his short beard.

"So...the Sinclairs are hated by the Campbells," Shaw said, trying to latch onto a topic that had nothing to do with loving Alana Campbell so well that she'd cry his name out in complete release.

"Not all the Campbells," she answered. There was a smile in her voice. "I have learned that not all Sinclairs are the devil."

Damn, that didn't help.

"Some of them risk their lives to save an innocent babe," she continued.

Now that he knew Rose, he would have ferried the bairn across Scotland to the safety that awaited her in St. Andrews, but that wasn't the reason he'd taken on the mission at the start.

"I hope she is well," she said, her voice dropping.

"She has four burly warriors and a wolf to guard her. Rose will be fine when we reach St. Andrews. Rabbie will make certain the wee lass is clean, fed, and warm."

"But then what? Will she be loved at the end of her journey? Where is that exactly?" She twisted in her seat to look at him, concern in her large, almond-shaped eyes that had taken on the hues of the evergreens around them.

"France," he answered. "Where she will be protected and raised until her royal parents can claim her. I understand that is often the way of princesses and princes. They are raised apart from the monarchy to keep them safe, especially with assassins and plotters threatening King James and his queen."

She turned front. "I suppose, but it seems a lonely life."

One could have a lonely life in their own country, in their own foking castle. But Shaw kept quiet.

They stopped at midday to water Rìgh and check Shaw's bandage. Resting on one side, he flipped up his kilt. Alana's cool fingers brushed his thigh as she tugged the binding loose and slid free the fouled linen. "The stitches are still in place," she said. "The redness has gone down some."

She touched the skin along the gash, and a spark of awareness shot through Shaw's blood. If he thought that he'd taken control of his base reaction around her by forcing himself to mentally go through his battle movements, he was sadly mistaken. He would challenge any man to have Alana Campbell, her deep brown hair with gold highlights, forest-green eyes, and curves that reminded him of the fresh, rolling hills of his beloved Highlands, slide fingers willingly along his skin and not react in a carnal way.

He breathed slowly, willing his jack to calm down before he had to stand. The woman would think he was a randy lad. *Mo chreach*. He'd never had such a reaction around a lass before.

She dabbed on an ointment from a clay jar she kept in her satchel. He concentrated on the slight pinches of pain her ministrations elicited, wishing they hurt worse. She folded a clean piece of linen and laid it over the wound. Pushing his leg up, she weaved the wrapping back under his leg, high up on his hip, while he cupped a hand over himself, so she didn't accidentally graze his ballocks.

He released his breath when she finished tying and leaned back. But he froze when her hand wound around his taut bicep. "Are you in pain?" she asked, leaning over him to meet his gaze. "Your whole body seems tense."

Tense? "Blast it, Alana," he said, the words gritted out between clenched teeth. "Ye lass, are a siren." He rolled forward, tugging his kilt back to cover his hips and arse. He turned to look at her. "I am trying very hard to be a gentleman, but after last night, our riding together all day and then ye...touching me—"

"Tending your gash," she said, interrupting.

"Aye." He buckled the belt at his waist. "All your touches and warm woman's scent..." He shook his head. "Ye should tell me now that ye have no interest, that last night was...a mistake."

"A mistake?" She frowned. "You think kissing me was a mistake?"

"Nay, I mean, aye." He grasped his hands behind his head so that his elbows jutted out to the sides. "Ye are a Campbell, Alana."

"I know very well from what clan I hail." Her eyes narrowed, and he wondered if she were mentally going over where she'd stored his *sgian dubh*.

"And I am a Sinclair. If we... I could bring war to my clan if I were to take your maidenhead."

Her cheeks pinkened. "You seem honorable," she said.

"Aye," he said, thankful that he could finally answer a question without doubt. "My mother raised me for the first years to be an honorable man, and the warriors of the clan continued the lessons."

"Then unless I wish for us to..." She flipped her hand between them. "Then you will not touch me."

He nodded, a frown heavy in his features. If she told him to leave her alone, to never kiss her again, then he would honor it.

Her lips tightened inward before she released them, still frowning. She rubbed a palm across her stomach as she tethered him with her gaze. "What, then..." she said, her words soft. "What if I...do want...something to happen between us?"

Chapter Twelve

Alana concentrated on inhaling slowly through her suddenly dry lips. Shaw looked fierce enough to wrestle a four-hundred-pound wild boar, breaking it in half with muscle alone. She knew he'd never hurt her. No, not since she saw him trying desperately to feed and comfort a newborn baby on the edge of the woods at the festival. Oh, she'd been furious when he'd let his men truss her up, but not afraid. A woman's instincts were her greatest weapon, and hers told her that the honor that Shaw held himself to was unbendable.

"You do not have to answer," she said. "And I am not saying that I do want something to happen. I am just wondering what would happen if I did."

He took a controlled step forward, hands fisted at his sides, so that he stood directly before her. His eyes were so clear, the gray of them flecked with blue, as he stared down into hers. "The fire that has been smoldering between us, lass, would ignite," he said, his voice low and rough as if he struggled with the answer.

"Fire?" Her voice was tiny, something she hated, and she

stood taller. "I am not afraid of that kind of fire."

She held perfectly still as his fingers came up to catch a curl of hers that lay along her shoulder. He still frowned as if he struggled, but he'd softened somewhat. "The fire is not something to fear, Alana, it is the ashes the next morning, what is left afterward." He dropped her curl and shook his head. "For a lass, losing yourself to passion has consequences, permanent ones."

Annoyance calmed her heart from full-out sprint to a rapid run. "Every girl who has ever had a mother, grandmother, or nosy crone next door knows that, Shaw." Her hands propped up on her hips. "An unfair disadvantage for women."

"There are also the consequences that would fall of me being a Sinclair and ye being a Campbell. Two clans at war with each other," he said.

"I am not at war with the Sinclairs," she said, anger sharpening her tone.

"The Sinclairs are at war with the Campbells who have taken over our lands and castle."

"I had nothing to do with your lands and castle," she replied, realizing that they were standing nearly nose to nose.

"Your brother would likely feel differently," he said, his words sounding like a growl.

Her hands dropped from her hips to land palm down on his chest. It was a barrier, but she didn't push against him, shoving him back. In fact, the contact begged her to press into him. Her gaze dropped to her splayed fingers where they sat against the hard muscles of Shaw's chest. She remembered too well the contours that she'd explored in the darkness of their tent, and when she lifted her gaze, she saw that his had followed hers down his chest.

Slowly she curled her fingers inward until two small fists sat against him. She tapped his chest with her knuckles. "You do not strike me as someone who would fear my brother," she whispered, not ready yet to step back. Anger mixed with something much more dangerous to her composure, regret.

His eyes lifted to hers again, sharp with conviction. "I do not fear the Campbells, I fear the destruction of my clan, which is my responsibility. My actions directly affect my people."

She swallowed, feeling a flush rush up her neck as if she'd been caught being selfish, selfish and unimportant. "And my actions only affect me?"

"Ye are the sister of a Campbell chief, Alana. So nay, your actions could also draw your clan into war."

She dropped her hand, not really believing that her brother would go to war over her giving away her maidenhood. Rather, it sounded like an excuse. She turned away. "Let us ride, then. The faster we reach St. Andrews, the faster we can get to my mother in Edinburgh." *So I can release you from my life.*

• • •

Damn. Bloody foking hell. Curses flew through Shaw's mind as he studied the proud woman seated before him on the horse. It had been three hours since their discussion, argument, or whatever one wanted to call the idiotic words that had flown from his mouth. What he'd meant to be a mild warning had slid straight into him reprimanding the lass about being selfish and risking her clan, which was nothing like what he wanted to say. At the beginning, a part of him even wanted her to say she didn't care about the barriers between them, that she wanted him anyway, the hell with her clan and the rest of the world. But that was a fantasy for the foolish. He'd realized it more and more with each word he spoke.

Shaw had his clan to think about. Alana did, too. But she

didn't know about the hell that was the daily living for his people at present. The constant reminders of why he must secure their lands and the safety of their clan by reclaiming Girnigoe Castle. *Because I haven't told her.* Bloody conscience.

They rode in a northern direction, Rìgh weaving in and out of trees at a brisk walk. He was used to traveling for days, riding fast and walking far. He'd been born having to run. It seemed that the Sinclairs had been moving forever, never having a safe, stationary home that wasn't threatened by the Sutherlands to the south or the Campbells riding through Sinclair territory, owning it.

Alana sat before him, her spine stiff, but over the hours, it had sloped slightly. She held onto the pommel with one hand, and he watched as the other slid behind in a fist to rub at the low part of her back.

"Here," he said, holding the reins before her. It took a few seconds for her to take them, and he pressed his splayed hands across her lower and mid back. His thumbs slid along the tight muscles he felt through her thin stays.

She breathed out a sound of relief, rounding forward and then arching as he worked the stiffness there. She wasn't what he'd consider a small woman, but his hands could easily span her back, as if she fit perfectly against him.

After a few minutes, she straightened. "Thank you," she said, her voice soft, and he took the reins back.

They rode past a series of oaks that were losing their golden leaves, so that they rained down upon them. He watched her look up, long hair tumbling down her back to pool into the chasm between them.

She leveled her gaze outward. "We have never had much interaction with the northern Campbells, although my brother, Grey, went with my father and cousins to fight your clan in the north when he was younger."

When exactly had that been? Foking hell, it seemed Campbells had been attacking Girnigoe his whole life, from the first time his uncle took over, bringing his debt with him. They'd ceased for a few years after George Sinclair sold the lands and castle to the Campbells, and Shaw had been too young and preoccupied with learning to become lethal to ask why. Then when his uncle died nine years ago, a new wave of Campbells had burned the village before the castle. It had taken a group of six Campbell bastards to physically throw him out, but not before Shaw had ordered that they ransack their own home so the damn Campbells wouldn't be comfortable in their castle. But even without furniture and tapestries, or even a sound roof, the Campbells had moved in. They took over everything, pushing their own pigs and goats into the corrals and rebuilding huts for the warriors who held the castle.

"How did you lose Girnigoe?" she asked, her question easily picking the lock he held on his anger.

"My mother's brother, George Sinclair, was a drunkard and fool. He was also unfortunately the chief after my father was killed when I was five, becoming the sixth Sinclair Earl of Caithness. He squandered money, so when it ran out, and my mother's money ran out, he sold the castle to the Campbells. We lived there with him. When he died nine years ago, the Campbells came to claim the property, throwing me out by force."

She didn't say anything for a minute. "Your mother and father?" she asked, her words soft. "How did they die?"

"My father died in battle. My mother...died four years later."

"Illness?"

"She fell." It was the most he'd told anyone about his mother's death. Even his men who were as close to him as brothers didn't know the extent of the abuse that had played out under the roof of Girnigoe before Shaw grew muscle and learned to wield a blade.

His uncle was a bully-ruffian, cruel and unyielding, especially when he was drinking whisky. Shaw had learned to develop a tolerance for the spirits when his uncle would force him to keep up with him. As a boy, Shaw would pretend to pass out when his brain grew sluggish. But things had changed after his mother was killed, and George Sinclair learned that if he touched anyone Shaw loved again, the blade that an eleven-year-old held against his wrinkled throat could still be deadly.

Alana twisted in the saddle, and the look across her features was a mix of shock, sorrow, and pity. His gaze raised to look out over the horse's head into the woods of gold and red leaves.

"I am sorry," she said. "Mothers are very important."

He looked back down at her. "Which is why ye are risking yourself to find your own."

She nodded. "My father was returned to us for burial, a blessing I suppose when the English turned their Covenanter meeting into a battle. Only my mother's ring returned with him." She held her finger up before her with the circlet of silver. "We thought her dead, but now I have hope that she is still alive."

His jaw tightened until it hurt. He had thought all the Campbells had died that day when the English attacked the group that had claimed to be a peaceful Covenanter meeting. But everyone knew, including he and his men, that the meeting had been one to discuss dethroning the king who was a secret Catholic and who had forced his approved liturgy on them. Shaw and his loyal men had ridden down to it in hopes to discuss the ownership of Girnigoe with a different Campbell chief, Alana's father.

"I did not see prisoners taken," Shaw said, his voice soft.

She twisted to look up at him. "You were there?"

Tell her. Shaw's muscles contracted as if ready to battle, but he held everything in check. Her eyes were so green, so hopeful, even the questions reflected there were innocent, free of suspicion and hate.

"I came south to speak with your father about supporting us in regaining the castle and lands from his cousin. The English arrived after I spoke with him."

She placed her hand on his arm, the touch sending a tightness to his heart. "I will keep hope that she was taken and is still alive," she said.

"Aye, lass, ye should." She turned back, and he stared at her hair before looking upward into the sky, the leaves framing it. Maybe if Lady Campbell was still alive, she would say the words that Shaw couldn't bring himself to say.

• • •

Alana exhaled, her eyes scanning the forest around them. Although she had kept as far from Shaw as possible while riding between his splayed thighs, his nearness assaulted her senses, and her back still ached. She had held onto her anger from their talk this morning for as long as she could, but the story of his mother dying when he was a boy and him having to live with his horrid uncle had softened her.

Before their argument, she could think of little else than making the powerful man lose control again and the sweet torture his touch ignited within her. She had experienced kisses before, but nothing like the all-consuming ravishing and tasting that she'd learned from him last night alone in their tiny hiding space.

She hadn't cared one whit that he was a Sinclair. They weren't all liars like Kirstin had said. Shaw Sinclair was honorable. Maybe too honorable. She blushed and was glad she faced forward on the horse where he couldn't see her face. Maybe she was too *dis*honorable, risking war between their clans for pleasure.

Blast. Why did everything need to be complicated?

At home in Killin, no one looked at her twice. She grew up as everyone's little sister, blending into the background with her dogs. Even when she grew up, the warriors continued to see her as Grey's untouchable sister or the skinny little girl with wild tresses covered in dog hair from rolling around with whatever pack she was raising. When she'd met Shaw, he'd seen her as something more, someone more. Someone valuable who could help him on his important mission.

"Did you choose me to help you with the babe because I was the sister of a Campbell chief?" She let the words out fast before she could think better of it. Half of her wanted him to say yes, proving he thought that there was something special about her. But the other half very much wanted him to say no, that his abduction was due to needing her help as a woman, not that his plan was calculated and deceptive.

There was a long pause, and the longer it lasted, the tighter her hand gripped the pommel before her. She heard him exhale. "Not at first. At first, I was just impressed by your courage at the throwing contest, and then ye were kind to offer help when ye found me trying to feed the bairn. I knew who ye were, but my mission was to bring the bairn to St. Andrews, not steal away a Campbell."

Her brow furrowed. "And why are you helping to save the king's daughter exactly? Will it help the Sinclair clan?" Alana twisted in the saddle to stare at him. His gaze was already lowered to meet her own.

His features were tense and made even sharper with the growing shadows of the lowering sun. "Aye," he said. The tiny word soaked into her, speaking whole paragraphs.

"The king will give you back your lands and castle if you

save his daughter," she said without question. She pushed aside the initial hurt that he was indeed using her to focus on the information, the needs hidden below the surface of his actions. "That is why Rose must arrive alive to St. Andrews, or the deal is broken."

It wasn't as if his expression changed, but it opened somehow, as if he wished for her to see inside him. "The only thing I have ever wanted my entire life is a family, one that does not have to run and hide or endure constant threats. One that belongs. When my uncle died, I thought circumstances would improve, but they only turned worse until the only course of action was to somehow win back our home through the English. If the Sinclairs have legal ownership again, I can rebuild the mighty Sinclair clan."

"Do you have the money to pay off your uncle's debts?" she asked.

"Not all of it, but we have raised some. A royal decree could see the lands and castle transferred without payment, but I am working to cleanse away his debt anyway."

She nodded, just a little tip of her chin up and down before turning back forward. They rode for long minutes, and she uncorked her flask that held water from another fresh running stream they had passed. As she tipped her head back, Alana felt her hair brush against Shaw. It sent a warm shiver across her chest that she pushed down deep, not wanting to feel when things were so complicated.

"We will stop when we find a suitable site to have a fire." He shifted in the seat behind her.

"The warmth will be good," she murmured.

They rode farther. "Ye do not mind fires, even after being thrown into one?" he asked.

Alana curled her toes in her boots as if the scars on the bottoms of her feet still seared and itched from healing. "No. Not fires. Being trapped in one, that scares me. When the flames are too big to stamp out." She exhaled, a slight sigh coming out with it. "The nightmares I have sometimes are awful. I wish I could banish them. You must have similar nightmares, being thrown out of your home." She kept facing forward.

"I focus on the outcome, what it will look like to win back my home," he said, his voice tinged with the darkness of conviction. "Sleeping in the bed in which I was born, where my father slept before he died and my uncle moved in. I imagine festivals on Sinclair lands with family smiling and laughing together, with warm homes and a solid army of trained warriors to protect them and hunt for food. My sisters…sister wedding and having her own bairns who do not fear men with torches coming in the night. I imagine the respect given to Sinclairs for their strength and honor instead of hearing that we are liars, gamblers, and cheats."

She swallowed. "If you come down from the north more, people will learn that you are not your uncle."

"I have never been able to come down from the north because I am always trying to keep my clan from dying out or losing hope. Right now, they are considered squatters on their own family land. Only a crucial mission made me leave them alone."

"Saving a babe," she whispered.

"Saving my clan."

She remained quiet after the description of his home. Somewhere through their conversation, her anger had begun to change to guilt. Shaw deserved a home, just like Alana did. She knew better than anyone what it felt like to have someone steal one's castle. "Is your hip sore?" She glanced back at him.

"Nay." He didn't say anything else.

"I can make more ointment if we find an apothecary in St. Andrews. I have my own dried herbs back at Finlarig. If you return me there, I can make more."

"After Rose sets sail for the safety of France, and…the Sinclairs are acknowledged for our service, I will take ye wherever ye wish to go." His words were slow and his tone serious and determined.

"To Edinburgh to free my mother, or are you not helping me with that now?"

"Ye gained my promise, and despite what ye have heard, Sinclairs keep their oaths."

"I have not actually heard much about the Sinclairs. The Campbells of Breadalbane are not the same as the Campbells who plague you up north." She did turn then, willing him to see the truth in her eyes.

The connection was strong, like a tether between them, his eyes beautiful and stormy, like they'd seen too much killing in this world, too much heartache. It made her want to cup his bristled cheek, but she didn't despite the fire that still sat in her belly. She watched him inhale, some of the tension leaving his face. "Aye," he said, nothing more, and she finally turned forward again. She wanted to say more, but the words that rose in her mind dispersed like smoke in a strong wind. For up ahead, she caught sight of a tiny structure.

"Shaw?"

"Aye?"

"There is a cottage ahead." Her heartbeat kicked up into a fast patter. Blast her carnal mind, for the first thing that popped into it were his words from early this morning. If the cottage stood empty, they might very well be sleeping up out of the dirt and leaves tonight.

Chapter Thirteen

No smoke came from the tiny, stone-stacked cottage. Grasses grew up through the thatching on the roof, giving it an abandoned look, and colorful leaves rained down over the dwelling. They rode closer in silence.

Shaw's blood thrummed inside. All day, he'd been struggling to put distance between himself and Alana, which was not possible physically, but their discussions had started off erecting barriers.

But nothing about the lass sitting before him was simple. She was brave and lethal with a dagger. Despite being trussed up and thrown into a burning castle, she hadn't cried in panic when his men had grabbed her. She was beautiful with curves and softness to explore. And she was honest. He could tell from her questions and reactions, which she didn't try to hide. But she was a Campbell, the chief's sister, and a virgin. When he'd at first realized that he could use her to bargain for his home if the bairn died, he thought the circumstances were fortunate. Now, though, he couldn't shake the feeling of doom waiting to fall on his head if his discipline gave out against the assault of her softness.

After staring at her multi-hued tresses for hours, he'd counted the red and gold strands woven through the dark, rich brown, following it down to her trim waist. He'd remembered the details of each of her curves in the darkness of their lean-to, the scent of her arousal, the soft mews she made as he stroked her willing body.

He leaned forward, inhaling her unique scent before he remembered to guard against it. His damn jack jerked awake, and he adjusted it, his mouth hovering an inch from the gentle slope of her ear. "I will go inside first, to check that no one is home."

"You are injured," she said, her voice soft.

"Hardly," he said, steering Rìgh around to the side where a small window was cut into the logs and covered by a stretched animal skin. Primitive, it was likely an old hunting cottage, forgotten over the decades. Maybe there would be leaves and dirt inside. *Mo chreach*, he hoped not. *Damnation.* His resolve was already close to dissolving.

"Stay here," he repeated. He leaned into her, willing himself to keep moving instead of pausing to enjoy the contact. He raised his injured leg behind him over Rìgh's rump to dismount and pushed off, landing smoothly but taking most of the impact on his good leg.

"Again," she whispered down at him. "You are injured."

"I am still lethal." He drew his sword, cursing low when he saw her throw her leg over to dismount as well. Creeping toward the closed door, he strained to hear any sign of inhabitance. The wind blew, the gentle rustle above his head, and more leaves floated down as if trying to bury the old cottage until it became one of the fairy mounds his mother used to tell him about.

A crunch of leaves made him pause, glancing back. Alana had unfastened and dropped her skirt, leaving her in the black woolen trousers and her short smock. She had put it back on at dawn after finding her purchased smock dirty with his blood that had seeped past his bandages while they slept against one another. They'd been ripping away at the garment, a strip at a time, until it rested at her perfectly curved hips, looking like a lace-edged tunic. She looped Rìgh's reins over the limb of a thin tree.

Short sword in hand, he grasped the rope pull coated with fuzzy moss and yanked. With a shove of his shoulder against the door, he pushed inward, blinking to bring the dark interior into focus.

Two windows, lit through the watertight skins over them, looked like two eyes, one on either side of the small, sparsely furnished room. There was a stone hearth, a wooden bucket, a shock of dried sticks tied together like a broom, a rickety table, and…a bed, a rather large bed.

He heard Alana come up behind him. "Anyone home?" she whispered, the hush of her voice sounding breathy like the moan against his mouth as he stroked her to climax last night.

"Nay," he said, his voice rough as he struggled to replace the breathless sound of her with the memory of Logan, Mungo, and Alistair stripping down to wash in the lake near Girnigoe. The power that had surged through him at the possible threat inside the abandoned house mixed with the passion that he'd been suppressing all day. It was like the rub of the brittle kindling between them sparked with each of her words and touches. He took a deep breath. "Looks dry, too."

Sword before him and the lass behind him, he pushed into the dark room. She stepped around him, brandishing the *sgian dubh* he'd given her. She circled the room. "Cozy," she said and ducked her head into the hearth, peering up into the chimney. "Hopefully it is all clear up there." She backed up, brushing her hands, and took up the broom. "Just a quick dusting and sweep, and it will be quite nice for a night. Now if only there were a bathing tub." A small frown puckered her lush mouth.

"I will see where the water source lies. Likely a cistern for rainwater or a well if the place was used as a hunting cabin." He watched her whisk the broom around; stopping at the first window, she reached to unlatch the swinging stretch of leather that acted as a shutter. "I saw a lean-to in the back for Rìgh."

She turned around, a slight smile on her mouth. "What a quaint little place. I would like living here."

"In a tiny cottage when ye now live in a grand castle?" he asked. He currently lived in a cottage this size, and although it was snug, it didn't afford him any privacy since his men were also sleeping within it.

"A place of my own," she said with a shrug. "I do not mind if it is small, as long as I am the lady of it."

"Now that I completely agree with. Logan snores and Alistair is always sneaking a lass inside after we are asleep." Her eyes grew round, and he hurried to finish the thought. "As soon as the lass realizes that she'd be tupped with four other men sleeping around her, she leaves pretty quickly."

"I would hope so," she said and began sweeping again in earnest.

He turned to the door. "I will set some traps and bring in some water and anything that will burn in that hearth." He strode out into the growing twilight, which seemed bright after the darkness of the cabin. "Come along," he said to Rìgh, releasing his tether, and the horse followed him to the structure behind the house. A roof, three sides, and a fourth that he could prop over the opening. It wasn't much, but it would keep the animals away from his faithful mount.

The cistern on the side of the house was covered with leaves, but he hefted a square lid next to it, happy to find a chained bucket there. A well, and from the dripping sound coming from it, it was full. Scooping the leaves off the cistern water to reveal what appeared to be fresh rainwater, Shaw brought Rìgh over to drink his fill. The horse grazed on some grasses that he found under the leaves while Shaw unhooked the rest of his tack, setting it in a corner of the barn.

On the outside, he found a wide wooden trough and stared at it for a moment. Aye, it could definitely work as a bathing tub for a lass. He tipped it over to wipe it free of leaves and spiders, a smile breaking through a day of frowning. He would make Alana very happy with a warm bath and a place to wash out her clothes. The work of cleaning the trough out and carrying it inside was very little to pay for the smile she was sure to show.

. . .

"A bath?" Alana's voice pitched high with excitement. Maybe she had been spoiled living at Finlarig with a bath every day, for the idea of getting clean was exhilarating. "In a trough?" She laughed, her smile reaching high to encompass her face. "It will do perfectly." She raised her gaze from the tub sitting before the fire to find him watching her. "Thank you," she said, joy still heavy in her tone. "I have missed being clean."

He looked pleased. "I will help ye haul the water in from the well and ye can set one to boil on the rack in the hearth."

"And then I am washing out my clothes, at least the parts that are stained." Blood, dirt, ash, and odors permeated both her short and long smocks, trousers, skirt, and stays. When she reached Finlarig again, she would need new clothes, for these were being sorely abused. "I can wash some of your clothing as well."

"I will take care of them outside in the cistern. And bathe out there, too, so the cottage is yours until I can catch something for us to eat."

"We still have two bannocks in my satchel and Fiona's sleeping roll," she said and waved her hand. "Do not eat the one with the currants on it." She smiled. "In the morning, I can look for mushrooms and edible berries."

"I set two traps behind the barn earlier. Hopefully the hares around here have gotten used to no human predators."

The thought of hot, roasted rabbit made her mouth water. Her stomach growled, sounding loud and demanding in the quiet. "Now look what you have done," she said, a bit of teasing in the rebuke. "The bannocks will never do after you put the idea of roast rabbit in my head."

A slight smile touched his mouth, the same mouth that had driven her mad last night. He nodded and headed out into the night for her water. She looked at the trough. Was it a truce for his damnably true words this morning?

Shaw carried a bucket inside, lowering it to fill the wooden tub. They both bent at the same time to peer underneath for leaks. Alana huffed in relief when the floor stayed dry. She met his gaze. "I would have still used it even if it leaked. It would have just been a fast bath."

He chuckled and walked back out. He limped, but his hip seemed much improved despite the full day of riding. Perhaps it was as he'd said that he spent most of his days moving, living in the saddle. Hiding and warring. How hard that must be, the strain on him, especially since he was the chief.

She grabbed up the bucket by the hearth. It was made of cast iron and very heavy, but she would be able to sit it right in the flames to heat. Grabbing it to her chest, she rushed outside. Darkness had come on, making the shadows thick. She stepped around the side and ran into a mountain and gasped.

"'Tis me, lass," Shaw said, his hand coming out to steady her. It was warm through the thin linen of her smock. A simple touch to keep her from falling, but the shock of awareness that flew through Alana was not simple at all.

"Sorry," she said.

"I will carry the water, especially in that pot."

The heavy pot strained to fall, and she let it down to the ground between them. With water in it, she wouldn't be able to lift it. "I think that will work better."

He stepped around her to the door. She could hear the splash of the water into the tub, and he returned.

"All a woman's strength seems to be focused on birthing babes. A little more muscle would help in life," she said.

Stopping before her, he picked up the heavy pot like it weighed no more than the other. "I know a woman, a Sinclair, who lifts stones with my men. She is determined to be a mighty warrior, and she is stronger than Rabbie and maybe Alistair."

A tug of jealousy tightened her stomach, and she frowned. "Perhaps I should start lifting stones?" She cringed at the petulance she heard in her voice.

"I am merely saying that determination can make one overcome pretty much anything."

"Even winning back their castle?" she asked, her voice lower.

He leaned in as if telling a secret. "*Especially* winning back one's castle." He nodded slowly as if teasing. He was so close that he could have kissed her, but he slid to the side, turning to continue toward the well. She watched his large frame fade into shadow.

It felt like they were dancing around each other, trying not to collide. Of course he didn't kiss her, wouldn't possibly kiss her after their discussion during their ride. He was determined to cleanse the Sinclair name. Stealing away a chief's sister was bad enough, but returning her without a maidenhead could possibly ruin any type of peace he might win from delivering the king's daughter safely to St. Andrews.

But Shaw didn't realize how unimportant Alana was to the Campbell clan. Yes, she was Grey's sister, but her brother would never ask her to wed for an alliance, and with the English monarchy supporting the Highland Roses School, he didn't need one. Most people ignored her around Killin. Had the Roses even noticed that she was taken from the festival? She snorted, noting the self-pity and ridiculousness of the thought. She strode back into the cottage.

Also, Alana had ridden horses much of her life. She'd heard numerous girls swear that they'd lost their maidenheads in the saddle. She shuttered the windows that she'd opened to air the room and stopped before the snapping flames in the hearth, hands resting on her hips. She should be allowed to choose to whom she gave herself.

She turned when she heard Shaw step inside. His muscles strained against his linen sleeves as he hefted the pot filled to the brim with water, carrying it over to set in the flames.

Yes, there was nothing to stop her from sleeping with a man of her choosing except…the man himself.

• • •

Shaw stood on the outside of the cabin at one of the shuttered windows. The faint sound of splashing water seeped from behind the taut leather seal. By now, the lass must be washing her clothes. He'd given her time to herself while he set two more traps, emptied the first two, skinned the hare he'd caught, and plucked the pheasant that had wandered into the second trap. Then he'd bathed with water from the cistern and washed his own clothes, hanging them to dry in the small barn with Rìgh. He'd given the horse his bannock and plenty of water and let him graze outside the barn for the entire time he was out of the cabin before shutting him in for the night.

He held one of the blankets from the back of his horse loosely around his hips as he walked up to the door. Alana would want to check his wound. He sighed, gritting his teeth. Maybe he should sleep in the barn. Although he'd have to lay on top of his horse, for there wasn't enough space on the ground that wouldn't see him trampled during the night.

I control my actions. Alana is not for the taking. All for the honor of Clan Sinclair. Holding the blanket tighter, he rapped.

"If you are Shaw Sinclair, you may enter," she called through the door.

He opened the door and walked inside. Alana stood before the hearth, wrapped in the second blanket that he'd carried with them. Her bare shoulders and arms were covered by the flow of her damp hair, the tresses already starting to curl with drying.

Holding the blanket before her, Alana threw one arm out. "See, it is cozy." It was only then that Shaw noticed anything other than the near-naked siren smiling at him.

The room was aglow in firelight, and Alana had found two half-burned candles which were lit to sit on the table. The meager contents of her satchel sat with them, their flasks, her ointment, another bandage, and what looked like a pack of playing cards. The room was warm and smelled of flowers and freshness. Her trousers, skirt, stays, and smock hung like a curtain on a rope that she'd fashioned across the room. She had cleaned the dust from the table and the ash from the hearth. It felt rather like a home.

"Much improved," he said and held up his catch. "And I have dinner."

Alana's smile grew until the happiness flooded her eyes. They were dark in the shadows, but the firelight gave them a sparkle. "Thank you, God. I was about to start chewing the leather of my boots," she said.

"It seems this forgotten cabin sits in the middle of easy hunting grounds." He had already spitted both animals and walked across to prop them on the iron grate in the hearth, high enough that they wouldn't burn. He dodged her wet clothes. "Maybe I should hang some of this on the porch. There is a beam by the front door."

She took down her trousers and her shift. "Fresh air will dry these faster if they are under the overhang where the dew will not fall on them."

Tucking the end of his blanket tightly into the edge at his hips, he hung them across the beam and came back inside. She was sitting on the bed and pulled the table up to it, using the bed as a second chair. The one chair in the room sat on the opposite side. "Do you play at cards?" she asked, splaying the painted rectangles out on the surface of the table.

"My mother taught me whist years ago," he said, the pang of her memory like an old scar. He went to the bird and hare, turning them on the grate. It would take an hour or more to thoroughly cook them. When he turned around, his breath caught. Did the lass know that the blanket had slipped just enough to show the top of her cleavage, her breasts propped up on the edge of the table?

"How about cards up? Have you ever heard of that game?" she asked, dealing out five cards to each of them, their faces down on the table. "My friend, Cat, says it is the favorite card game at the London court right now." She smiled, even though her gaze was turned toward the cards as she spread her five out evenly. She gave a little tug up on the blanket, and Shaw's inhale came easier.

"I have never heard of it," he said, standing there. Bloody hell, she must look smooth and lush under that blanket. He scraped a hand through his damp hair.

She gestured toward the chair. "Sit. It will keep our hunger at bay while we wait for our food to cook."

He doubted very much that the hunger that was gnawing at him would be held at bay by sitting across from the beautiful lass who now smelled like flowers more than ever. Pulling the seat out, he nearly flung the puny chair across the room with his pent-up strength. "It may not hold me," he murmured and sat, making it creak under his weight.

"We can switch places?"

He shook his head. "Tell me, lass, do ye always carry flower soap with ye?"

Her brow furrowed. "You do not like the smell?"

Like the smell? Hell, he wanted to roll around in that smell. "Aye, it is bonnie, but I did not know ye had it with ye."

Her frown faded, and she glanced at the remaining clothes. "I washed everything in it after I washed myself."

The stilted silence continued as she gently touched the tops of the painted cards. Memories of those fingertips skimming him made his eye twitch, and he raised his gaze, taking in a full inhale. "My wound is still fine. I cleaned it when I washed and re-bandaged it."

"Good, but I should still put some ointment on it." She moved to stand.

Blast.

"I thought we were playing cards," he said, to delay his torture. "This cards up game that is so popular with the English fops. How do ye play it?"

Her eyes narrowed slightly, but she settled back down. "We take turns flipping our cards. If you flip a black suit, then you must tell me something about you. If you flip a red suit, then you can ask me a question. And the reverse for me."

"A question about anything?" he asked. Did she love anyone back at Finlarig? He didn't think the man who'd escorted Alana and her Roses was anything to her since she hadn't mentioned him. Or he could ask her about her family, what her mother looked like, but that might make her suspicious.

Alana curled her hand into a fist. "Nothing about war or the defenses of the Campbells."

Fok. What was wrong with him that questioning her about Campbell weaknesses hadn't even come to his mind? He grabbed the back of his neck, squeezing it. "Do the numbers mean anything?"

"Yes," she said and pulled a card from the deck, turning it face up. "The higher the number or royal, the more secretive, important, or prying the question or answer should be." She tapped the ten of hearts lying up. "So, if you turned this up, you could ask me a question that was rather…sensitive."

"Such as?" he asked, meeting her gaze.

The glow of candlelight painted her face in gold, but he still saw the slight darkening of a blush. "Such as if I like to be kissed or…" She cleared her throat. "If I enjoyed last night."

"Enjoyed the quiet terror of almost getting pissed on by Dixon's men?"

A small laugh came through with her exhale, her smile returning. "As long as I tell the truth, I might take the question any way I wish."

He nodded. "Ye go first." He stood to turn the hare and pheasant and returned to see a three of spades upright before her. Relief made it easier to sit in the rickety chair.

"Hmmm…" she said, her pretty lips twisting as she thought. "What is your favorite tart flavor?"

"Tart," he said without hesitation.

"Yes, what flavor?"

"Tart flavor. I have no favorite." When was the last time he'd even eaten a tart? Years of squatting and moving about so Campbells didn't catch him hadn't given him time to bake. "I would gobble any tart offered."

"Have you had a honey tart?" she asked.

"That is a question ye can save for the next card." He

smiled at her frown. Baiting her was fun and kept his mind off the memory of her fingers on him. Aye, the night would be one big battle for Shaw.

He flipped up a card. It was a black six. "I have never had a honey tart," he said and smiled.

Her frown deepened. Was the game not going well? He thought it was.

"A six should be something that is a little more personal," she said.

"Personal? Well, I have never had a honey tart because no one has ever made me tarts before, and I have not had a chance to learn how to bake."

"No one?" she asked, her eyes widening. "Not your mother?"

His smile slipped. "The answer is no one."

They stared at each other for a moment, Alana searching his gaze, but she wouldn't find any answers there. She looked down and flipped her second card. A red jack came up, and Shaw leaned back in his chair, crossing his arms.

Alana folded her slender fingers together over the card. "Well." She clicked her tongue in her mouth, and he tried not to think of what else that little tongue could do. She thought herself not very powerful, but she might be able to cripple him with that tongue.

Her gaze lifted. "A jack is pretty high."

And getting harder with each inhale of her flowery scent.

"Well," she repeated. "My secret is that...I am not a virgin."

Chapter Fourteen

The muscles in Shaw's stomach contracted. *Damn it all!* Had the woman been attacked, raped? Was that why she carried so many weapons? She watched him closely, but he kept his features still.

"Ye have been with a man before?" he asked softly. It was another question, but more elaboration was needed, like whether the act was what she wanted or the bastard's name so he could hunt him down and geld him.

"No," she said. "Not a man. A horse."

Shaw's breath caught, making him cough hard into his fist. When he could draw a full breath again, he looked at her. Did she not know what it meant to lose her virginity? "A horse?" he asked, his voice strained.

"Many women lose their maidenhead while riding in the saddle. I grew up riding horses." She nodded. "I am certain that my maidenhead is gone."

It wasn't, at least not from what he'd felt last night. The memory of her hot, wet tightness sent a rush of blood through him below the table. "Being pure from a man's touch is different from losing your maidenhead," he said. "Riding a horse does not make ye less of a virgin."

She frowned. "If being impure because of a man's touch is what makes a woman lose her virginity, then I would say you did that last night."

His palm slid down the side of his face. What could he say? Nothing that wouldn't stir more anger in her. So, he flipped his third card. A black king. *Fok.*

What big secret could he tell her that wouldn't make her hate him? Only one secret came to mind. He looked across to her expectant face, so beautiful and masking a clever mind that would pick up on lies immediately. Best to steer completely away from his past.

She leaned forward, her fingertips wrapped over the edge of the table. "Something true. Something big. A king demands the most." As if he didn't know that. He could call her a cheat, accuse her of laying out the cards she wanted, but purposely making her angry wasn't how he wished to spend their time tonight.

And how do you want to spend the time tonight? His conscience and jack warred within him. *Blast it all.*

He closed his eyes and took a deep breath. "I want nothing more than to love ye here in this cabin all night long." Was that true, though? Didn't he want Girnigoe more? He opened his eyes to see her wide ones staring back at him. "But giving yourself to me could jeopardize my mission to reclaim my clan's lands and castle," he said. "And it could jeopardize your future." He swallowed. "With the man ye wish to wed."

She didn't say anything, didn't even look down when she flipped another card. It was a five of diamonds, but she hadn't seen it. "We will likely not have this opportunity again, Shaw." Her voice was soft but strong, a whisper full of determination and conviction. "I would give myself to the man I want." She shook her head, her unbound hair moving along the skin of her shoulders. "Not to bring two clans together or to do my duty of bringing a babe into the world. I would give myself to one who makes my blood boil with want, my skin tingle, and my body soar. And that man is you."

Her words hit harder than a battle ax, vibrating through his discipline, cracking it open to lay his want bare. His hands fisted on the table before him. "Alana... I am the chief of the clan that your clan has been battling for a decade."

She held up a hand to stop him. "Stop saying that. Tonight, in this cottage, in the deep woods, without men or students or babes or even dogs, we are free of all that. No one need know what conspires between us, what has been consuming our rational thoughts." So, she had felt the pull between them all day, too. "What happens here is just between us," she ended on a whisper.

Sitting higher in her seat on the bed, she inhaled and straightened her shoulders. The golden shades of firelight from the hearth slid over the smooth skin of her collarbone. Slowly her fingers uncurled from the blanket wrapped around her, and she let it loosen, inching down.

His breath stopped as the blanket slid lower, and her beautifully full breasts were bared. Perfectly round and lush, with dusty pink centers around peaked nipples. The skin looked as soft as he remembered feeling last night in the darkness, their size and weight perfect in the palms of his hands. "Och, lass," he murmured but didn't move.

"Something else you should know about me, Shaw," Alana said, rising, her blanket falling to the curve of her hips. "Once I decide on a course of action, whether that is to demand I be allowed to participate in a festival game, kill a man to protect a babe, or seduce an honorable man into showing me what complete passion feels like...Once I decide..." Her hands reached up under the heaviness of her breasts, lifting them, her thumbs strumming against her already pebbled nipples. "It becomes my mission, one that I will see finished."

Mission. See finished. The words surfaced in Shaw's mind like leaves blowing on the wind, but they blackened into ash as the fire within him exploded, lighting his blood. If he had a mind to question what was happening to him, he'd wonder if Alana were a witch. She was certainly a temptress.

His fingers curled around the edge of the table as he stood. He meant to shove it aside, but the light table went flying with the restless energy in his muscles, the cards scattering like the leaves falling on the thatched roof above them in the deserted forest. But his focus didn't leave Alana standing proudly before him as the blanket fell down her legs to her feet.

• • •

The air in the cottage was cool on her bare skin, but the heat in Shaw's stare swamped her with warmth. She shivered anyway, her toes curling against the swept floorboards. The chill in the room was forgotten in the wash of wildness swirling within her. She'd never done anything like this before, had never even been naked before a man. But she'd also never felt anything close to this heat inside her.

The table and cards were tossed away, just like she'd tossed away all Shaw's reasons for leaving her alone and untouched. For she wanted to be touched by him, to feel the magic he'd kindled as they strained together in the darkness last night. She wanted to be felt and seen and remembered by this mountain of a man. When he looked at her, she no longer blended away into nothing, and she wanted something to remember forever when their missions were done.

She stepped forward into the place where the table had

separated them and raised her hand to lay a palm flat over his heart. Shaw truly saw her; the proof was in the wild thumping under his skin. She tipped her head back, feeling the cool brush of her drying curls slide along her bare backside, and met his gaze. Shuddering under the intensity of his stare, she tried to keep her breaths even. "Shaw, I want you. Give yourself to me," she said, changing around the words. "Make the world outside these walls melt away. Just for tonight." She swallowed as she stared up into the darkness of his eyes.

Before she could draw in her next breath, his arms came up around her, pulling her against him. Heat ignited a fire for which she yearned instead of feared. She slid her splayed hands up his thick arms, over the dark lines of the horse etched there. She skimmed them across to the muscular curves of his chest and upward over his broad shoulders. Chill bumps rose on his skin, and his nipples hardened under her touch. He bent over her, kissing her, tasting her, ravishing her mouth as she slid her head to the side, welcoming everything that he gave. She would take it all, every last sensation and detail of the magic coursing between them, locking it all up inside her memories forever.

Breathing against each other, they kissed, and Alana felt the stroke of Shaw's hands down to her naked backside, palming each globe; he lifted her to fit intimately against his hardness, only the blanket wrapped around his hips keeping them apart. She moaned into his mouth and pressed her pelvis against him, the spark of pleasure spreading into a heavy ache there.

With a tug, he pulled the blanket loose, letting it drop. She glanced down to see the length that she'd felt last night. Large and powerful, he stood erect, making the flutter in her stomach twist with a mix of concern and raw want. Shaw didn't give her long to worry, pulling her back in to sweep her away in more kisses. The heat of him pressed against the curve of her stomach, his hands catching her cheeks as they broke apart, both of them breathing hard.

"Alana, lass?" he said. She heard the question and saw it in the small part of his gaze that wasn't totally consumed with their passion.

"Yes, Shaw, yes, I am certain. I want this, and I want you."

His hands slid along her face to cup her head, and she closed her eyes as the warmth of his kiss turned wild. His hands caressed her shoulders and down her arms, as if he were trying to touch every square inch of her naked skin. She raked his back gently with her nails down to his toned backside. He groaned deeply into her mouth, and his hand slid across her collarbone and lower to cup her breast. She moaned with need as he palmed one and then the other, tweaking the raised, sensitive buds.

Shifting, he kicked off his boots and lowered his mouth to one aching nipple. "Yes," she hissed, throwing her head back. His hands held her arched back as he feasted on one taut breast and then the other, loving each with nibbles and hot kisses, sucking them into his mouth until she felt the sensation course down her body to the damp place between her legs.

Alana pressed against his hardness, her fingers curled into the thickness of his massive shoulders. He took two steps, carrying her with him backward until she felt the bed against the bend of her knees. Shaw trailed kisses down between her breasts as he held them, tweaking her nipples which were wet and cool from his mouth, until he was on his knees before her. Feather-light kisses down her stomach and abdomen sent shivers of heat and sensation up and down her.

"Sit, love," he whispered, the endearment sending spirals of tightening through her chest to speed her heart. His large hands captured her hips to urge her down on the edge of the bed. She watched through half-closed eyes as he continued a path of kisses lower, the heat from his mouth matching the heat growing like an out-of-control wildfire within her body.

"Shaw." He was beautiful in a mountainous, powerful way. Like a barbarian of old, full of masculinity and strength, but with the gentleness and honor of a gallant knight.

"Lean back and feel," he said, his northern accent thick, and he lifted each of her legs to rest on his broad shoulders. She was completely spread and bare to his gaze. "So lovely," he said, his gaze moving up to meet her eyes before he bowed his head.

Alana couldn't tear away from the sight of his bent head, the dark brown hair drying in waves, as he lowered, his fingers slipping below, finding her secrets again. She gasped with the heat of his kiss, watching him love her. Sensations spiraled upward, connecting the sweet ache building in her core to the wild beating of her heart, and her eyes flickered closed. Fingers twining in the thin throw that she'd laid upon the bed, her body strained toward the ecstasy she'd climbed to last night. But this was more, more intimate, more intense. He played her with his fingers while loving her with his mouth, his tongue.

"Oh God, Shaw," she breathed, the end of her words bending into a groan. She lay back on the straw-filled tick, arching and clasping her breasts as he moved rapidly below, stroking the fires within her until sparks of light fringed the darkness behind her eyelids.

"Yes, bloody hell, yes," she called, her words filling the small world of the cottage around them. The release of the words and her loud moans built on the rhythm that Shaw had set below, her core pressing upward in time with it until... The peak broke suddenly, sending pleasure shooting off within her writhing body. A high-pitched moan billowed up from her throat, and she let it come, let all of her fall over the edge of reason, her toes curling as her knees bent deeper where they latched onto his shoulders.

He slid up her body, kissing her stomach and breasts until he hovered over her on the bed. Somehow, he'd lifted her to the center. He wiped a hand along his mouth, his gaze fastened to hers. It was fierce and intense and sent another jolt of heat through her, making her core clench again with anticipation. She reached down to capture his hard length, sliding her hand along it.

"*Mo chreach*, Alana," he groaned. He leaned on one elbow as his other hand teased her nipple while lifting her full breast, and he kissed her. Their lips fused together, sliding, giving and taking as he continued to stroke her body until she was again writhing against him. Her hand kept up a rhythm, and his fingers trailed to her heat below. Ready and completely wanting, she spread her knees far apart.

"Please, Shaw," she said against his mouth, her words breathless and needy. Had she ever begged before in her life? No, but she had never felt such sweet fever. She raised her knees, locking her legs around his hips, and pulled the tip of him close to her heat. "See me," she said, her words a breathless whisper. "I want this. I want you."

He leaned over her, his face tense as they locked their gazes. "I will always see ye." His hips surged forward, and she let go as he plunged into her. Large, so incredibly large. A sting of pain shot upward, and she inhaled. He stilled, buried deep inside.

She felt him brush hair back from her temple and realized that she'd squeezed her eyes shut. Apparently, she hadn't lost her virginity in the saddle. "Alana," Shaw said.

"It is no matter," she replied, opening her eyes. "Already fading."

He studied her face as if trying to read the truth. She smiled, her fingers going around his neck to pull him back in. "Kiss me senseless again," she murmured and pressed upward against him.

He sucked in breath. "Good God," he whispered, and slowly withdrew to press into her tight body again. "Ye are like wet fire and heaven mixed together," he said at her ear, his words so full of passion and reverence that she shuddered, moving against him in the slow rhythm he'd started.

"Keep talking," she said, feeling the erotic power of the words.

In and out, he moved, his body strong and sleek with muscle. "Do ye feel me way up inside ye, lass?"

"Oh yes," she breathed, squeezing around him and marveling in his groan.

He leaned into her ear, whispering, his hot breath sending wild pictures through her mind. "I want to take ye from behind," he said. Unable to form words, she nodded vigorously, trusting him to guide her.

She almost cried out in disappointment when he rose, leaving her body, but he turned her around, pulling her up onto her hands and knees. She felt him there again, where she ached, the emptiness feeling hollow. She panted loudly as he slowly pushed back inside her from behind, filling her a different, excruciatingly wonderful way.

Shaw leaned over her, covering her entire back with his chest and stomach as he rocked into her. His fingers wrapped underneath, finding her sensitive spot, strumming it, making her moan and shift against them as she bucked backward. His other hand held tightly to her breast, the roughness of his thumb sliding over her nipple, pinching it to send another shot of passion flying down through her, connecting with her hot core. "Good bloody hell, Shaw," she said, her voice loud and keening.

"Keep talking," he said, and she felt him kiss and nip the back of her neck, his hot breath sending more shivers along her skin.

"Yes," she yelled. "More."

"More what?"

"More…everything."

He picked up the rhythm, thrusting into her open body, playing across her sensitive nub, squeezing her breast. Alana reared backward, feeling him slap against her until the fire built higher and higher. "Shaw," she screamed as she came apart, shattering into a thousand sparks of sensation.

Over her, Shaw growled, thrusting into her as he, too, exploded, his heat filling her. Her body clenched along his length as they continued the rhythm, over and over again with the waves of passion, until her head fell forward to hang between her shoulders.

His hand stroked up her stomach as they slowed. Finally stopping, he pulled her to the side with him, their legs intertwined, his thighs supporting hers from behind. She had never felt so protected, so wanted, so seen before.

She nestled backward into him, watching the shadows and light from the hearth flicker across the walls of the tiny room, loving the feel of him all around her.

As the silence continued, worry began to seep in. She swallowed. Was he regretting the whole thing? "I guess… I was a virgin," she said softly.

He kissed the side of her neck, hugging her, and relief uncoiled a notch in her stomach. He pulled her gently over onto her back, looking down to stare directly into her eyes. A slight smile touched his lips. "I knew, from the feel of ye last night."

"Oh," she said. "But that did not stop you."

His gaze moved above her head and then back to her eyes. "Once ye asked—"

"Demanded," she said and ran her fingers over a wave of his hair that hung around his solid jawline.

He snorted softly. "Aye, once ye demanded, there was no way I could stop." He narrowed his eyes playfully. "Are ye a witch, Alana Campbell?"

She smiled. "Maybe I am. I seem to have quite a bit of power over you," she said, reaching down to find him already growing hard again.

He laughed and passed a leisurely kiss across her lips before rising, his gaze going to the hearth. "Ye have been so full of passion that ye did not notice the hare and pheasant are burning." She turned on her side, watching him step out of their little nest, and reached down to the floor to grab the blanket that she'd dropped. Without Shaw's body against her, the room was cold. She watched him walk across the room, completely naked and comfortable with it, as he crouched before the hearth to turn the spit. The bandage that he'd wrapped around his hip had been torn away. A dab of blood beaded out of one of the stitches, but the thread had held through their madness.

"Well done on one side," he said, seemingly unfazed by his wound.

"I don't mind," she said, mesmerized by the play of light and shadow across his nakedness. The muscles of his shoulders and back contracted and lengthened, showing the long scars across his skin. The white lines where he'd been lashed stood out against his tanned skin, muscles moving under them as he worked the spit around.

"One of your stitches is bleeding," she said, her voice soft.

He stood and her breath caught at the raw beauty of the man as he twisted to look down at the long gash. Toned and full of muscle, the lines and sinew of his body were smooth and full from obvious training with the heavy swords and hammers. He wiped the spot with his thumb. "'Tis nothing. The thread held."

Her gaze traveled over the scars along his back. She didn't say anything, but her heart hurt for the boy Shaw had been. Where she had grown up surrounded by love, he had grown to manhood under the cruel thumb of an abusive man who may have killed his mother.

"They do not bother me." His voice was low and caught at her breath. He was watching her.

"I am sorry," she said, looking away. Sorry that he caught her staring. Sorry that pity showed in her face. And exceedingly sorry that he suffered so much as a boy, and even now, that he had to bear the scars from such brutality.

He walked over, crouching before her, his hand going to her foot. He picked it up, rubbing his knuckle slowly along her scarred arch. Her toes curled as it tickled.

He lifted it to his mouth and kissed the side where the burn scars wrapped up and around. "Ye can look all ye want," he said, meeting her gaze. "Just do not be sorry for me. The marks mean that we survived something fierce and lived to carry the scars. They show how strong we are. 'Tis not something to mourn but a testament to our endurance."

She swallowed past the lump that had formed in her throat and nodded, leaning forward to kiss him gently. "You are a wise man, Shaw Sinclair."

He leaned back, his smile quirking to the side. "Some would argue against that." He stood to go back over to the spit in the hearth. "Including me."

Her gaze dipped to the mounding of muscle in his arm as he turned the meat. The sharp points and swirls of the tattooed horse on his upper arm reminded her of something ancient and magical.

"Is the horse on your skin Rìgh?" she asked.

His arm flexed as he lifted it to look at the tattoo, and her breath hitched a little. Lord, just a simple gesture stirred the fire within her.

"Nay," he said, striding back. "It is the symbol of the Sinclairs from long ago. We have always revered the strength, stamina, and speed in horses." He sat on the edge of the bed, glancing down at his hip as if just checking to see if it still bled. "A century ago, there was a legend that the four sons of Sinclair were the biblical four horsemen of the Apocalypse." He reached forward to slide a knuckle down her cheek.

"Since we are all still here, I guess they were not," she said, though her words came breathless under his light touch. They had just stroked, kissed, and loved each other to shattering peaks, and yet she could feel her blood warming quickly.

He smiled, a real one that reached his eyes. She loved it when he smiled. She hadn't realized how much heaviness he was carrying until he let the frown and tense fierceness drop away from his face, leaving behind a look full of hope and contentment.

"True," he said. "Even if they were not magical warriors sent from God, they revered and trained horses, and our clan has continued to do so." He leaned in, capturing her lips with his own, and all thoughts of horses and legends dissolved under the warm pressure.

She felt the bed dip as he climbed over her, pulling her into him to continue the leisurely kiss. When he pulled back, she opened her eyes to see him watching her, a hunger etched into his features. "We should eat and then sleep," he said.

She shifted, feeling his hard length against her stomach. "That is not what your body suggests."

Swallowing, he slid a hand through her hair to cup her head. "Your body needs time," he said, his voice hoarse with struggle. He was right.

"But," she said, sliding her hand down to find him; a groan rumbled up from his solid chest. "That does not mean we have to just eat and sleep," she said, and pressed her naked, well-loved body up against his, their mouths sealing together for another wild dance. The heat and need blocked out the world beyond the walls of their little forgotten cottage in the woods.

Chapter Fifteen

Bloody hell. What was he doing? He didn't want to let go. *I will never let go.* The traitorous words reverberated in his mind as he held Alana in the bed, the warmth and scent of their bodies joined together. He watched her sleep, her full, sweet lips gently parted, her inhales and exhales flowing smoothly in and out like the waves on the northern beach of Sinclair territory.

It was morning, well past dawn, and he needed to get them up and ready to ride. Yet he remained still, holding her, soaking in every detail of Alana Campbell. She had a light smattering of freckles over her nose and cheeks, intriguing little dots that his gaze followed, connecting them like little stars. Long eyelashes lay flat against her smooth skin. They were full and spread evenly like a lady's fan.

Her long hair was twisted about her, full of wild curl from drying in random fashion while they loved each other through the night. He turned his nose into the pillow that was coated in the length and inhaled the flower scent that would forever remind him of Alana. She shifted, and he looked back to find her eyes open, staring at him. A slow smile spread across her face as she stretched her legs out, her feet sliding along his shins. Her back arched slightly within the confines of his arms. "Good morn," she said, her words barely even a whisper, as if she, too, wished to freeze this time together.

"Good morn," he said, equally quiet.

"It is past dawn." Her gaze flitted to the window over the bed where the sun filtered through the taut leather shutter.

"Aye."

"We should rise then, I suppose," she said but only snuggled closer into him.

He hugged her close, loving the feel of her body wrapped within the shelter of his own, the contrast of her soft skin against his war-hardened form. "Aye," he repeated. They remained that way for several long seconds until he felt her inhale fully as if regret weighed on her chest. Regret about having to rise or regret about their night together? Nay, she couldn't regret their night together. He'd brought her shattering into bliss at least five times. They'd explored, tasted, and pleased each other beyond anything he'd ever experienced before. But loving a man had consequences for a lass.

Giving her a bit of space in the circle of his arms, he met her gaze. "Are ye regretting last night?"

"Is that why you are frowning?" she asked, running a finger over his forehead where lines must be furrowed. She smiled. "No. I only regret that we cannot stay here."

Her words stirred the need to get moving inside him. He had a mission to complete, a quest that began long before he met Alana Campbell. "Aye," he said and released his hold on her. The disappointment on her face probably matched his own. "We need to get to St. Andrews."

She nodded, pushing up in the bed as he stood. "I want to see Rose again."

It would be bad indeed if the bairn was taken away without a goodbye. His chest tightened at the thought, making him frown, but he shook off the feeling. The little princess was just part of his mission to see his lands restored.

"I will ready Rìgh and get my clothes from the barn," he said, crouching to stir the remnants of the fire.

"There will be tea and pheasant when you return," she said.

He looked at her from the door. She was wrapped in the blanket that held their combined warmth and likely the evidence of her maidenhead. Regret tried to take root in him but dissolved with her smile. Damn the consequences. She was happy. He nodded, his gaze intensifying as he felt himself stir. "I have never had tea," he said, "but warm and wet sounds very good."

Her eyes opened slightly at his jest, a small blush working up into her cheeks. Blast, he would roll her back into the bed if they didn't have to leave. Before he completely lost his mind, he threw open the door, letting the chill from the fall morning splash his heated skin. He dodged her hanging clothes and strode naked to the barn where Rìgh shook his mane, eyeing him. Could the horse detect the traitorous sway of his thoughts? Thoughts of a woman, thoughts that tore at Shaw's resolve, thoughts that muted the hunger he'd always had for his land and home?

"Do not look at me like that," he mumbled, yanking his kilt down from the rafter, shaking the stiffness of being washed and dried out of it to wrap the length around his hips. It brushed the scabs on his stitches. He should re-bandage them before they rode. The strain on them last night made them sore, but he didn't care. His night with Alana was well worth any discomfort.

He grabbed his tunic and whipped around toward the door as he heard the distant sound of horses riding through the leaves. *Shite!* Dixon? He'd left his sword in the cabin with Alana. *Alana!* She was alone and *naked*.

Shaw yanked the knot loose on Rìgh's tether and tore off out of the barn in a full run, knowing the horse would follow. Out of the woods ran a wolf, loping up onto the porch. No...a dog. Alana's dog. "Robert?" he yelled, making the dog run down the steps to meet him in the yard.

Robert jumped around him and ran back to the door, scratching and sniffing at the crack underneath. He let out an excited whine. But Shaw's focus was on the horses weaving through the forest toward them, five horses with riders. They weren't his men. They were...women.

Behind him, Alana flung open the door, gasping. "Robert? You came back."

"I need my sword," he said.

"Riders." The word came fast as she dashed inside, coming back with his sword. The handle slid into his hand like a familiar friend. He clenched it, feeling the power in its weight.

He took two steps forward to meet the first rider, recognizing the man from the festival. Kerrick Campbell wore a frown, his gaze taking in the scene before him. Shaw without a shirt, Alana wrapped in a blanket, her shoulders bare and her hair tousled, her stays and trousers hanging over the rail of the porch.

"Kerrick?" Alana called, stepping next to Shaw.

Kerrick pulled up on his horse, stopping before them, the Campbell warrior's look full of shock and fury. The other horses, with Alana's schoolmates seated on them, stopped in a semicircle behind him. Each woman held a dagger ready to throw, and Kerrick pulled his sword.

"Ye bastard," Kerrick said, taking in the obvious freshly-rolled-from-bed appearance of the two of them. Even Alana's skin had a glowing, rosy hue as if her blood were warm from being loved exceedingly well.

Instinctively Shaw stepped before her, shielding her. Kerrick jumped off his horse, striding forward, indignant fury in each step. Damn, he couldn't kill the man for wanting to protect or seek revenge for Alana, so he sheathed his own sword.

"Ye stealing, raping, foking bastard," Kerrick yelled.

"No!" Alana pushed past Shaw, placing herself in front of him. "It is not like that."

Kerrick didn't take his eyes off Shaw. "So, he did not steal ye away from the festival? Him and his Sinclair warriors?" Kerrick glanced quickly behind them but didn't ask where the others were.

"Well...there is a good and honorable reason for it," Alana said. "And he has agreed to help me save my mother."

"And this?" Kerrick yelled, lowering his sword, the point moving between the two of them. "Ye are...ravished."

"It is not how it looks," she said again.

"Ye do look ravished," one of the ladies said from her horse, a grin on her face. The young, mute one in their group sat before her on the horse. She made gestures similar to Mungo's gestures, and another woman nodded.

"Very ravished," the second woman said.

"Son of a whore," Kerrick yelled. He dropped his sword, balling up his fists as he charged forward.

Shaw yanked Alana behind him and met the attack, his fist going straight into Kerrick's fury-pinched face. The man had sought to wrap his arms around his middle, but the impact of the punch caught him off guard, and Shaw easily sidestepped his attack, letting him fall in the dirt.

"Stop it," Alana yelled. "If anyone was seducing and ravishing, it was I who ravished him!"

One woman gasped, but Shaw was focused on the cursing man as he spit on the ground.

"Fok," Kerrick said, coming to his feet. He wiped blood from his nose across the back of his hand. "Alana?" He finally met her angry face.

"I said, *I* ravished *him*." Her words were strong, challenging. "He is honorable and is helping to save a babe from slaughter."

"I knew there was a bairn involved," another woman said. "We found the glove with the milk in one finger on the ground inside our tent." She looked to the one woman who frowned fiercely at him, her hands resting on her hips. "Why else would she have put milk into her glove and poked a hole in the end?" the first asked.

"I hadn't seen a single bairn at the festival," the frowning woman replied.

Shaw's gaze stayed on Kerrick while the ladies bickered. The man wiped his bloodied nose in a rag he yanked from his belt.

"And Shaw has agreed to help me free my mother from the Covenanter prison in Edinburgh before returning us to Finlarig," Alana said. "Without waiting for Grey."

Kerrick's face remained hard, and he looked to Shaw. "In payment for letting him climb atop ye?"

Shaw exploded forward, barreling into him, knocking him and his crass tongue back onto the ground. He planted his boot on Kerrick's chest, holding him there as he leaned down. "Ye will never speak like that to Alana again, or the next thing ye will feel is my blade slicing through your chest."

They stared hard at one another for a long moment, Shaw aware that most of the women had lowered their daggers, though he couldn't see them all.

"Now, ye will apologize to the sister of your chief, the one who is in charge of your group, the one who is currently saving your tongue from being cut from your foul mouth," he said, raising his gaze to take in the ladies around them. When

Kerrick didn't immediately respond, Shaw pressed harder with his boot.

"Aye, aye, alright," Kerrick said, and Shaw stepped back, letting the man rise, but ready to knock him back in the dirt.

"I am sorry, Alana," Kerrick said, and the words sounded sincere. "'Twas a slight at the Sinclair, not ye."

"If she did not want to be…ravished," one of the women called, "she would have stabbed him."

Alana glanced at Shaw, and he knew that she was thinking about the start to their journey. "This is all very complicated," she said, shaking her head. "Let me get dressed, and we will explain while we ride toward St. Andrews."

"I thought we were headed to Edinburgh," one lady with an English accent asked from her horse.

"After we deliver a babe to a ship in St. Andrews," Alana said.

"Is the babe inside?" the lady who had thrown a near-perfect dagger strike at the festival asked.

"I will explain as we ride," Alana repeated, her hand scratching the top of Robert's shaggy head. She smiled at the women sitting proudly on the horses. "But thank you, for coming this way. How did you find me?"

"We tracked you for over a day thanks to Kerrick's abilities," the English lady said.

"A woman in Kinross told us about ye after we told her how worried we were and convinced her we were from your clan."

"Fiona," Alana murmured next to him.

The woman with the easy smile who sat a horse with the mute girl continued, "We followed tracks to a small river." She pointed behind her. "And that is where we found Robert sniffing around. When he jumped the river and started running this way, we followed him."

The mute girl signed, and another woman nodded. "Aye,"

she said looking at Alana fondly. "We knew Robert would not leave ye to be carried away. He disappeared the first night that we found ye gone."

Kerrick cursed under his breath, a fist rubbing against his chest as if it ached. "Bloody hell, Alana, Grey is going to fo..." He started to curse but stopped, glancing to Shaw and then back to Alana. He shot a hand through his hair, scratching his scalp. "By all that is holy, he is going kill me, ye know that." His brows rose high. "Gut me, rip my entrails out, and God willing, quickly slice my head from my shoulders."

Kirstin snorted. "I would worry more about Gram," she said, perhaps referring to Alana's grandmother.

"Lord," Kerrick said, rubbing both hands down the sides of his face. "She is going to bloody poison me."

Alana smiled broadly, her head high even though she stood wrapped in a blanket after proclaiming that she'd ravished a man. "Don't worry, Kerrick. My Roses and I will protect you. Just in case, though, do not eat anything Gram gives you."

• • •

"Where is the bairn?" Kirstin asked as Alana plaited her own hair while walking toward the waiting horses. The Roses and Kerrick had watered them and finished off the pheasant and hare from the night before while Alana washed quickly and dressed.

"Shaw's men took her on a different route because we knew Major Dixon and his men were following us." Martha came closer with Lucy, listening. "If they caught us with the babe, they would kill her," Alana continued. "But they do not know Shaw has four other men with him." Cici and Izzy joined the circle. "The English soldiers will not be looking for Rose to be riding with four hardened Highlanders."

"Rose?" Cici asked. "Her name is Rose?"

"I named her that," Alana said. "She needed a name."

"And ye missed us," Cici finished.

Alana smiled. "Yes, I did, but..." her smile fell. "The wee thing was also branded with the tiny image of a rose on the bottom of one toe."

"Branded with a rose?" Martha said after she gasped. "Who would do such a thing?"

Lucy held her palm flattened over her chest, her eyes wide. "Queen Mary wears a signet ring of a tiny rose."

Alana lowered her voice. "Rose is actually...a princess. Queen Mary's babe."

"He stole a princess?" Kirstin said, eyes wide. Her glance cut to Shaw where he tightened the saddle on Rìgh.

Alana frowned at her. Kirstin had always thought the worst of people, but she was being exceedingly annoying in believing the absolute worst of Shaw because he was the chief of the Sinclairs. "Loyalists in London took the newborn babe at the request of King James. There is a ship waiting in St. Andrews to carry her over to France to keep her safe. Shaw and his men are couriers. Queen Mary has lost five children, and they think now that assassins were responsible."

"Your parents were severe Covenanters, Alana," Kirstin said, hands going to her hips. "Do ye think they would like ye helping the English monarchy?"

Alana stared her friend down. "What was I to do? Let English soldiers slice the throat of a wee babe? Little Rose has no religion right now. She is innocent, and I will always help the innocent."

"And you are certain the soldiers were coming to kill the babe, not take her back to the queen?" Lucy asked, leaning forward. "I would hate to think of how she must feel with her baby taken from her."

Alana remembered the words of Major Dixon's soldier.

We would return her to her mother who cries for her stolen daughter. She shook her head at Lucy. "The soldiers chased me and the babe up into a tree and shot their muskets at us." She touched the partially healed wound on her forehead that she'd already explained. "They would have killed us if Shaw and Robert had not stopped them." Of course that was the first group of English soldiers chasing them. Major Dixon wore the uniform of a high-ranking soldier loyal to the crown. Could he be from a different group looking for the princess? Had the king changed his mind about sending Rose away? No. Alana's instincts told her that dark-haired devil was lying.

"Sinclairs are not innocent," Kirstin said, her voice low. She jutted her chin toward Shaw. "If he is not just lying to ye, he would not help the English king unless there is a good reason that benefitted him," Kirstin said.

True, but he'd already told her about the benefit to his clan, his poor people who'd been thrown out of their home by the northern Campbells. With five sets of eyes, which ranged from wide-eyed interest to dark suspicion, watching her, Alana decided to keep Shaw's motivation to herself.

"We should ride," Shaw called over to them. "Put as many miles behind us as we can before nightfall."

"Alana can ride with me," Kirstin said loudly, reaching out to tug Alana with her toward her mare.

"Alana will ride with me," Shaw said. Alana looked at him, her annoyance with Kirstin transferring to Shaw over his forceful tone. Did he care what she thought? Or about the pressure and questions she was getting from the Roses?

Kerrick mounted his horse, the skin under his eyes already bruising from Shaw's punch. "There is no reason for Al—"

"I was shot with musket fire on my hip, and she stitched it up," Shaw said, overriding Kerrick.

"She cannot tend it while ye are riding," Kerrick said.

Shaw looked directly at him as he hefted his sword, the muscles of his arm bulging against the linen sleeve of his white tunic. "I am not strong enough to hold myself on the horse without her assistance."

Cici snorted, covering her mouth over the absurdity. Even injured, there was nothing weak about Shaw Sinclair, nothing in the least. "I can show ye the stitches," he said, raising the edge of his kilt a bit.

"Aye," Cici called.

"Nay." Kerrick overrode her eagerness.

Shaw turned his gaze on Alana. "I would have ye ride with me." It wasn't a question, but it wasn't a demand, either.

Alana walked over to him, making her decision without uttering a word. She waited until Shaw lifted himself into the saddle from the wrong side of the horse, putting his weight on his good leg. She fitted her boot into the stirrup and rose to sit before him, the place between her legs tender after their long and adventurous night together.

As she seated herself gingerly, her legs straddling the hard saddle, Shaw lifted her, sliding her back enough that her backside was propped onto the juncture of his thick thighs. She twisted in the seat to look at him, frowning. He leaned slightly forward to speak low into her ear, the heat of his breath sending a coil of warmth through her. "To save ye from discomfort having to ride all day after last night."

"But I will hurt your hip. The stitches—"

"Are healing just fine thanks to ye," he said, meeting her gaze with his stormy gray eyes. "I would not have ye cursing my name with every jouncing step." Although he frowned, there was humor in the lines at the corners of his kind eyes.

Her smile crept across her lips. "How very gallant of you."

"I am nothing if not gallant."

Alana sniffed a chuckle and turned forward, enjoying

the warmth of Shaw against her back. He tossed a blanket over her, so it wasn't obvious that they rode up against one another, Alana seated intimately on his lap. He leaned to her ear again. "Ye could even sit sidesaddle if it would feel better. I will hold ye on Rìgh."

She tipped her head back to catch his gaze. "And here I thought that I was holding *you* on your horse."

A wry grin spread across his mouth, a mouth she yearned to taste again. "I have been knocked unconscious before, and this amazing beast kept me on his back as he carried me out of battle. He would never allow me to fall off."

Even though she smiled, her brow furrowed, a mix of feelings adding to the jumble already inside her. "You could have been killed. Where was this?"

Alana watched the line of his brows dip as his gaze shifted over her head to stare out. "At the battle near Stirling."

"You could have been killed, too, just for being there." Alana turned back to see the golden forest under a gray sky, but in her mind she saw Shaw slumped over his horse's neck while English in red and warriors in kilts battled around him.

Shaw had journeyed south to speak with her father and had ended up pulled into the battle. Had he joined the fight to win her father's help against the northern Campbells? Or had Shaw and his men fought to help those like her father and mother who wished to worship without the king's restraint? And yet he was forced now to help a king who was more Catholic even than King Charles.

Questions swarm around in her mind. Maybe he hadn't told her everything. Why would he hold anything back from her? Perhaps it was just Kirstin's prejudice making her question his intent.

"Shaw," Alana started, keeping her eyes forward.

"Aye?"

"Are you a Covenanter?"

Chapter Sixteen

Was he a Covenanter? Bloody hell, Shaw was anything that would win him back his clan's lands, castle, and dignity. "Not at present," he said, making Alana twist to look up at him. Her deep green eyes held questions.

Kerrick rode up next to them, his gaze raking over the blanket, but he didn't say anything about what could be going on under it. It was apparent that he still felt responsible for Alana, even though she didn't see him in that role. "Do ye have a route to follow or are ye just heading east now?" Kerrick asked.

"We will cross another part of the River Tay, and when we spot open water on our right, we will follow the Firth of Tay to Dundee to catch a ferry across to St. Andrews," Shaw said.

"And your men with the bairn are waiting for ye there?" Kerrick asked, some of the anger from earlier subdued, but Shaw wouldn't let his guard down around the man. One never knew what a Campbell might do.

"Aye," Shaw said, glancing down at Alana. It was true

that she was a Campbell, but not like any Campbell he'd ever met before.

"They will wait in hiding with Rose until we get there," Alana said, "because Shaw is the chief."

"Chief without a castle or land," Kirstin said from behind.

Shaw's arms stiffened where they wrapped around Alana. *Mo chreach*, the woman surely had the prejudice of a Campbell. She was friends with Alana, yet so different.

Alana kept facing straight ahead, her voice coming strong. "I think that Grey would agree that it seems to be a rather commonplace problem for chiefs." She spoke of her own castle of Finlarig being taken by English. Did she still resent the English ladies for starting a school there? Even though one had married her brother?

"Finlarig was taken through trickery by English assassins, not in payment for a debt by another Scot's clan," Kirstin said, riding up. She leaned forward over her horse's neck, turning her face to frown across at them. "An honorable clan would pay a debt without crying foul instead of trying to renege on it."

Shaw lifted Alana closer, still cushioning her. He kept himself facing front, his usual mask in place when speaking to denigrating, bastard Campbells. "Until ye live the life of another, ye do not fully understand the circumstances nor motivation for their actions." His voice was even but held the edge of restrained fierceness. Could the woman hear the warning in it?

He turned toward her, their gazes connecting. Kirstin's face was marred by her bitterness. "I am more disciplined than most," Shaw said, "but some of my men, the ones who have watched Campbells slaughter their family members and burn their homes while Campbell warriors yelled obscenities and threats of rape at their mothers and sisters, they will not hesitate to retaliate if ye speak badly of them."

"Some Campbells have lost family members, too," Kirstin said, but the force in her voice had fallen back, and she turned to face forward again.

Under the blanket, Alana's hand slid over to his leg, rubbing there. The gesture was to give comfort. Even though it was light, the support was evident. It twisted inside Shaw. Would she still side with him if she knew the complete truth about his time near Stirling? Fok, he had to tell her what he remembered.

"War between clans only weakens Scotland," Kerrick said on the other side, pulling Shaw's focus back outside of himself and the mess he'd created with the warm woman in his lap.

Kerrick nodded, a dark respect etched there as if Shaw's raw description had influenced his good will. "War between countrymen crumbles honor, making neighbors turn against one another," Shaw said, remorse pressing hard on his chest where Alana leaned.

A long exhale passed through her lips. "As much as I love Evelyn and Scarlet, and their brother who have helped us gain favor with the English king—"

"And Lucy," Kerrick added quickly, looking back at the Englishwoman riding behind him.

Alana glanced back, too. "If the clans united, we would be able to win the rule of our own country."

"Or at least the respect of the English," the woman named Martha said. "At present, they seem more likely to shoot us than to help us."

"Which is terrible," Lucy said. "I do not feel that way at all."

"We know," the woman with the easy smile, named Cici, said, trying to imitate the clipped English dialect. "Ye are an honorary Scot, just with an odd accent."

They continued to ride through the brightly colored

forest, the north wind rattling the boughs so that leaves floated down. The land looked untouched with dense bramble, holly, and thickets around, but Shaw continued to scan the area. Without a scout ahead, an ambush was always a possibility. Dixon should be on the other side of the firth, heading directly to St. Andrews, but there were always bandits about, desperate men. Some of the Sinclair warriors had turned to waylaying rich wagons when times became desperate. His hand fisted to rest on his thigh under the blanket. He wouldn't condemn his clan to another homeless winter. The conviction made his remorse fade even as each inhale of Alana's flower scent tried to bring it back.

She shifted against him. "Do you think that Dixon and his men would harass us if we no longer have the babe with us?"

Rìgh weaved between two large oaks, and Shaw adjusted Alana again on his good thigh.

"I can sit on the saddle," she said, wiggling forward. "It is not that uncomfortable," she whispered.

"Dixon is the type of man who will hunt whoever escaped his grasp," he answered. "He will want to know what happened to the bairn, and unless ye can convince him that ye lost your sweet baby boy and buried him along the way, he will know that we lie. Under his scrutiny, I would not be surprised if he used torture."

"Oh," she said on an exhale.

"And I am comfortable with ye on me or against me, whichever is best for ye," he said, his lips grazing the soft edge of her ear. Once he told her the whole truth of what he had done, or not done, he would likely never have the opportunity to get this close to her again.

Alana slid off his thighs but still leaned her back into his chest. "I hope Rose is well," she whispered.

His chin brushed the top of her head as his hand slid

along her arm under the blanket. "She is. Rabbie is making certain the bairn eats and is clean. Mungo will bring a smile to her wee lips. Alistair and Logan will keep them all safe and moving forward to the coast. They may already be there."

"And they will wait for us?"

She knew the answer he would give but obviously needed to hear it again. "Aye, lass. No one will let her go unless I am there to give the order."

"Within a reasonable amount of time," she added.

"Aye." If Dixon shot Shaw dead, he'd want his men to see the bairn safely to the French ship, fulfilling the duty of the Sinclairs to the crown.

She sighed. "And then what?" She shook her head. "I know it is what the king and queen wish for their daughter, but will she be safe and loved in France?"

"It is not for us to worry over her in France," he said, making Alana's back straighten.

"I do not care if it is my place or not. That little babe is precious, and I worry. What if she is captured in France?"

"Are ye volunteering to sail across with her and make certain she is safe and loved there?" he asked.

"No," she said, drawing out the *O*. "I have to save my mother, get her home to Finlarig, and then probably stop her from trying to throw Evelyn, Scarlet, and their brother, Nathaniel, out of our castle. And then…" She exhaled long. "Everything is so complicated."

Her words couldn't be truer. He brushed his mouth against her ear. "Ye are regretting last night."

Alana bumped his chin as she turned to look at him. They were so close together, their noses mere inches away. "No, I do not regret anything about last night."

He released his breath, blinking as he studied her beautiful skin, the freckles more pronounced after days of riding. "What if ye become with child?" he asked, his words barely a whisper.

Alana wet her lips. "I will love any and all babes that I have now and throughout my life."

What would a wee lass look like with Alana's wavy locks, running through the flowers to hug her, learning to throw a *sgian dubh* like her mother, eating those honey tarts that Alana seemed to love? Or a strapping son with green eyes and a stubborn opinion about everything, running about swinging a wooden sword and learning to ride his first horse? Would Shaw doom a child to grow up without a father like he had done? Would Alana's brother welcome a bastard into his home or would she and the bairn be sent away?

It didn't matter, because Shaw wouldn't turn away from his own child. One way or another, the bairn, his bairn would know he had a father who cared for him.

"Ye will make a wonderful mother," he said. "And ye should know that I would never abandon my own child, so ye must let me know one way or another."

She turned to stare at him, her eyes a bit wider, and nodded.

Aye, one way or another, he would do what was right toward Alana. Not because she was part of his clan, but because he wouldn't doom the child to be fatherless, and...he wouldn't give Alana another reason to hate him.

• • •

"Come stretch," Kirstin said to Alana. "We have been riding all day." Alana walked closer to the fire where the Roses were doing their stretching routine. Evelyn was adamant that they stay bendable for proper self-defense.

Alana reached up high, stretching onto the toes of her boots, and then bent forward. Even without taking off her skirts, she could stretch. She breathed out, feeling the tightness of several days without the familiar exercise. She huffed. "Yes, this feels better."

"Sooo…" Cici drawled as she bent over near Alana. She glanced around to make sure that Kerrick and Shaw were on the far side of the camp they were setting up for the night. "Was last night wonderful?" she whispered. "With him, I mean." Her eyes moved back and forth between Alana and Shaw as if gesturing toward him without using anything but her gaze.

Alana looked around at the Roses; all of them were bent over, but their heads were up to catch her reaction and hear her answer. She pulled herself closer to her shins, her gaze on her skirt. "A lady does not tell about such things."

"Of course they do," Martha said. "Especially to sisters."

Alana looked up to see her smiling. "Sisters?"

"Aye," Cici said. "The Roses are like a clan of warrior sisters."

Kirstin smiled wryly and nodded. Alana frowned at her. "Sisters who condemn one for sleeping with the enemy?"

"Grey slept with Evelyn, and we do not condemn him," Martha said, but Alana kept her gaze on Kirstin.

Kirstin's smile dropped along with her backside as she sat on the ground. "I am worried about ye," she whispered. "I am not condemning ye for having a wonderful time. I just do not want ye hurt."

Izzy started to sign rapidly, and they all stared at her. Her sister, Cat, who had traveled with her new husband down to England, was the person who understood her the best. "Slow down," Martha said. "Oh, aye." She looked to Alana, nodding. "Ye should have seen how frantic Kirstin was when we realized ye were truly gone. Kerrick thought that you had taken off to find your mother all alone, but Robert was still in the camp, so Kirstin insisted you had been taken."

"And I found drops of blood on the ground inside the

tent," Lucy said, also sitting down on the dirt, her legs out to one side like she was seated on a blanket at a picnic.

"I...I stabbed Shaw when I realized he meant to take me to care for the babe."

"Stabbed him where?" Kirstin asked, looking over at him. "Nowhere vital apparently." Her raised eyebrow and smirk pointed to Shaw's jack.

"His upper arm," Alana said. They all turned to look at him as he carried some firewood over to a circle of rocks. "It did not hinder him much."

"I would say not," Cici said, her words sounding a little awed as he dropped the wood and stretched his shoulders, making Alana's mouth go dry. "Let us hear about your wonderful night," Cici whispered without taking her gaze from him. Her hand jutted out to pat Izzy's arm. "Maybe the little one should go help with the fire."

Izzy snatched her arm away, shaking her head. Alana stacked her hands on her hips. "She is fine to stay, because I am not talking about last night, sisters or not." Although, realizing that they felt like sisters, that Kirstin had insisted they leave the next dawn to look for her, warmed her. She smiled, letting her gaze meet each Rose. "This morning was shocking, and we have not had time to talk or I would have already said...thank you, all of you, for coming to find me."

Lucy's eyes widened. "First of all, you are the chief's sister."

"And we would never abandon a Rose," Martha said.

"Or a close friend," Kirstin said.

Their words caught inside Alana, filling her spirit. "Thank you. If I had been in horrible jeopardy, you would have saved my life." She wiped her hands on her skirt. "I better help fry the fish they caught earlier."

Kirstin scrambled up to follow her. "I can help," she said, but as they stepped out of ear's reach of the other Roses, she caught Alana's arm. "Alana. Just one more thing."

The concern in Kirstin's voice stopped Alana more than the grip on her arm. Was she worried about her becoming with child? Or of her plans with Shaw after finding her mother? "What is it?"

Kirstin looked toward Shaw. "Remember when the warriors brought your father back from Stirling?"

Of course she did. The gruesome corpse of the man who had ruled the Campbells of Breadalbane with fairness and honor, a good father and man, her mother's wedding ring tied to his slashed shirt. "Yes," Alana said, her frown sharp over the horrible image. "The English killed him and took my mother."

"Yes, but one of our cousin Donald's men, who brought his body back, said something about damn Sinclairs, as if they did something wrong at Stirling."

"Did what wrong?" Alana asked. She knew that Shaw had been there to gain her father's support.

Kirstin shrugged slightly. "I don't know. Maybe nothing, but the way the man said it and then spit on the ground made me believe everything I had heard of the rough Sinclairs, riding their wild horses, up in the north. Alana..." She touched her arm. "Truly, I have never heard a good thing about the Sinclairs."

Anger tightened her stomach. Kirstin was just trying to help her, but she hadn't gone through the last few days with Shaw, either. "Have you heard how they were thrown out of their castle, that the Campbells burned their homes? Have you heard how they have been forced to move and hide on their ancestral lands, some of them growing ill from the cold and dying? Have you heard me talk about how Shaw saved me and an innocent babe by throwing his own body before a soldier with a musket? Or how he agreed right away to help me free my mother when Kerrick would not help without an army behind him?"

Kirstin released her breath from full cheeks as if resigned. "Those things have been brought to my attention today." She shook her head. "I just do not want ye to get hurt."

"Shaw tries to protect me. He has since that first attack."

"Aye, but I am not talking about you getting physically hurt. I do not want him to break your heart, Alana."

Was her heart in jeopardy? The thought would have been ludicrous a week ago. Of course she had yearned for the type of love she'd seen grow in her brother when he fought and finally began working with Evelyn to make her school a success. But never would she have considered it with a man from a warring clan, especially after he abducted her.

Alana sighed softly, giving Kirstin a sad smile.

"*Mo chreach*," Kirstin murmured, dipping her head to stare hard into her eyes. "Ye are already in love with him, aren't ye?"

"No," Alana said, but the word tasted bitter like a lie. She crossed her arms over her chest. "Although if I was…" She shrugged. "He is brawny, brave, and honorable."

"And poor, homeless, and possibly an outlaw with an English commander wanting him dead."

Alana dropped her arms, frowning. "Because he is trying to save a babe," she whispered.

"He is trying to save his clan, Alana. The babe is just a way to do it."

Alana huffed. "Both are honorable pursuits, but thank you, Kirstin, for your worry," she said, trying to hold onto her charitable thoughts of her meddling friend. The woman had grown up with her. They had always been inseparable, but right now her prejudice against the Sinclairs was shoving a wedge between them.

Kirstin suddenly threw her arms around her, hugging her. "Ye are my only true friend," Kirstin whispered. "I do not want ye hurt, and selfishly, I do not want ye leaving Killin for the very north of Scotland."

Her words, and the heaviness in her tone, filled Alana with a sweet tightness in her chest. "I will just bring you with me," she whispered. Kirstin pulled back, her eyes wide until she saw the teasing in her expression. Her friend's lips turned up slowly into a smile that matched Alana's.

Chapter Seventeen

Damn itching. The stitches where Shaw's wound was healing itched on his arm and on his arse, and he rubbed a fist back against his hip through his kilt.

"Ye best not have given Alana anything that is going to make her arse itch," Kerrick said low where he rode his own horse next to Shaw, Robert trotting ahead of them, and the ladies riding behind.

Shaw's mood was foul to begin with since Alana had decided to ride with her hostile friend, Kirstin, instead of him that morning. He hadn't been able to get close to her alone since the morning after her damn Roses showed up at their cabin. "If she itches from a healing musket or stab wound, then I did not do my duty to protect her and deserve whatever punishment ye think ye could deliver, Campbell."

The cut on Alana's forehead was healing well, Kirstin and the other Roses all washing and caring for the scabs. She would likely carry a scar, showing the world that he hadn't saved her from the Englishman's musket. He'd add the guilt to the boulder of remorse he carried. For his uncle's betrayal in gambling away their home, cold and poverty, and what seemed to press on Shaw more each day...the remorse and guilt in doing whatever it took to regain what was lost.

"The ferry was quicker than I thought," Kerrick said, apparently able to think of something other than hating Shaw. He didn't care what the man thought of him, having learned long ago to ignore scorn. "We should be at St. Andrews by nightfall."

And then what? He would find his men and the bairn, her wee toe branded with a rose. Alana was right. Who would brand a newborn bairn? It could have become tainted and killed her.

Moving about and living in various empty cottages, caves, and the occasional vacant house, the Sinclairs had learned how to signal that they were inside a building. But where should he take his suddenly large group of lasses? They were sure to stand out in the town.

"Ye will take the women to find lodging," Shaw said to Kerrick. "I will find my men and the bairn. On the morrow when it is light, we will find the ship to take the princess." And then the wee one would travel with strangers to a foreign land. Alana's worries pressed on him, worries about love and kindness bestowed upon a girl heir to the English throne. Rose might not find much of either in France.

He exhaled long, his fists squeezing tight with Rìgh's reins in his hands. Not his concern. His priority was making sure that Clan Sinclair was noted for fulfilling their mission to bring the princess safely to St. Andrews. In exchange he was promised documents granting the northern territory of Scotland and Girnigoe Castle back to the Sinclairs, namely to him, Chief Shaw Sinclair, who would win back the title of the seventh Sinclair, Earl of Caithness. Not that the title mattered to him at all, only the land to farm and the homes and pride of his people.

Whatever it takes. I will see it done.

• • •

The sun was dropping fast, and Shaw yearned to ride ahead to find his men before all the daylight had vanished. He raised his fist straight into the air, a silent signal to stop, for he caught the smell of smoke ahead. Hearth fires meant the town was near.

The Roses formed a semicircle around him. Alana gave a whistle, and Robert stopped, trotting back. She rode behind Kirstin and leaned around her friend to look at him.

Shaw's gaze connected with hers but then scanned across the group. "Ye ladies will find lodging in St. Andrews with Kerrick. There should be some place for travelers since St. Andrews is a modest port town."

"Where will you go?" Alana asked.

"To find my men."

"And Rose," she said, frowning. "I will go with you."

He shook his head. "It is safer for ye to remain—"

"I am going to find little Rose," Alana said, interrupting as she swung down off Kirstin's horse. "Kerrick, you are responsible for keeping the Roses safe."

"Ye had to name the bairn Rose?" Kerrick said, shaking his head. "Anything to make things more difficult."

Alana strode over to Rìgh, determination in the quickness of her step. She reached up to the saddle horn, throwing back her skirt to step on Shaw's boot already in the stirrup. Did she worry he wouldn't let her ride with him? The thought was ludicrous, but the silence between them for nearly two days had created a distance.

Perhaps the space was best. That was what he told himself until her warm body settled before him in the saddle, as if she were built to ride in the hollow of his chest. His arms came up on either side of her, and he felt…whole again.

"Let us ride," Alana said.

"The dog will follow if ye come with me," Shaw said and felt her stiffen slightly.

"Robert will be of use if we are attacked."

Or the dog could draw attention to them, although if Dixon was looking for them, he wouldn't expect a huge wolfhound. And there was no arguing with Alana anyway. Truth be told, the thought of her pulling away from him to climb back with Kirstin made his arms tighten instinctively around her, and he frowned over his reaction. He'd never wanted the company of a lass for more than a night or two. There'd been little time to think about anything lasting longer. What, then, was different about Alana Campbell?

With a brush of his heel, Rìgh turned southeast to splash through a narrow stream. "We will meet at the abandoned castle on the coast by sunset tomorrow," Shaw called back over his shoulder. He didn't wait for a reply. If Kerrick had been able to track them until they met up with the dog, he'd certainly be able to find them in St. Andrews. Shaw also wanted to get away from the group before someone else decided that they needed to come along.

Rìgh climbed easily up the low bank and walked swiftly through the trees. The dog weaved his own path, keeping up with his mistress. They moved in the direction that St. Andrews should sit, the tinge of hearth smoke on the breeze. Alana kept her face forward, and he couldn't shake the instinct that in the course of two days with her clan, she'd come to believe the lies about the Sinclairs. He inhaled deeply and realized his folly as her light fragrance filled his breath. *Damn flowers.* He both wanted to rub his face in her glorious hair and pull far enough away that he wouldn't be reminded of it.

"Kirstin said that when the Campbell warriors brought

the body of my father back from Stirling, there were Sinclairs at the battle," Alana said, her words coming abruptly as if her mind was working through information, spitting it out to see how he would respond.

"Aye," Shaw said. "I told ye that we went down to speak with the Campbells of Breadalbane. We wanted help against the Campbells who had invaded us."

"Legally to pay a debt."

The old anger tightened in his gut. "There is a difference between moving onto land and into a castle and chasing down a clan, killing and starving them in hopes that they would die out."

He heard her sigh, and she twisted to look up at him. "Yes, there is." The space around her eyes tightened, her brows lowering, and he looked away. He would meet anger and slander with a steely gaze but not pity. "What is it like there?" she asked. "Having to keep your people ahead of the Campbell chief?"

Edgar Campbell was the devil himself, always holding up the writ of sale before ordering his men to drive the Sinclairs off their own lands as if they were a plague or lepers. "We are always ready to move to another location. We build cabins quickly with stone, logs, and mud, anything to give shelter against the weather, but then Edgar Campbell sends his men to throw us off, saying that the land beneath the shelters belongs to Campbells, and therefore we must leave, even in the icy winter. Children, women, the old. They flee if my men and I are not there to defend them with force." A young, pale face swam up out of his memory for an instant before he shoved it away. *Do not forget Reagan.* He would always remember her, but sometimes he needed to rest away from the pain.

She turned front again, and he felt her melt more into his chest. "And some die?" she asked, her words soft.

"Aye." It was already November. *Och*. "My people at least need to keep their shelters through the winter."

"Have you considered moving the clan south?" she asked.

"Aye, but they are not in favor of giving up land that has always belonged to Sinclairs." He snorted. "If ye had not noticed, we are a stubborn lot, especially those who remember the strength of the mighty Sinclairs and the legends around the masters of the horse from long ago."

"I think stubbornness is in the blood that runs through all Highlanders," she said. She shook her head, and he watched the setting sun glint off a few gold strands. "We need to either get the Campbell Chief to give up the lands and castle or convince your people that it is best to move farther south."

"They will not move," he said, because they could not move the graves of their fallen. "Any move would require war with another clan, and we haven't the men and strength of horse for a successful campaign now."

"Have you saved much to repay your uncle's debt?" she asked.

He exhaled long. "Money is harder to come by than bread. I have a portion but not enough, but if I am successful at this mission, I have been promised the lands and castle for the Sinclair clan."

She turned again to him. "King James will likely not pay the Campbells for the debt. He will just evict them from the land and castle."

"So be it," Shaw said. "Retribution for the lives their harassment has taken."

"What a mess," she murmured.

Everything had been very clear-cut to Shaw before he met Alana. All Campbells were devils, and he would do anything to see them conquered and the Sinclair lands restored. But what he'd learned over the last few days was that not all Campbells deserved the pit of Hell like Edgar

Campbell. Especially not the warm woman in his arms, the smell of flowers still a hint in her hair after washing in the cabin two days ago.

"Alana." He paused.

"Yes?"

He breathed deeply. "I must do everything, everything in my power as a chief, as a Sinclair warrior, and as a man to win back the land of my people. Everything."

She gave a small nod as she stared out over Rìgh's head.

Their time together would end as soon as he helped her find her mother and returned them to Finlarig. He would stay with her to make certain she wasn't with his child. His chest tightened at the thought. What would happen between their clans if they had a bairn together? One with Campbell and Sinclair blood coursing through it? The child would be strong and beautiful, clever, kind, and willing to bend. For the future required some bending, some shades of gray when before there had only been black and white and brittle stubbornness. Something close to hope sparked into Shaw's stomach.

He pulled back on the reins for Rìgh to stop for a moment. For this truth, he wanted to touch her. She turned his way in question, and he lifted his hand to slide across her cheek. "If ye are with my child…" Her eyes opened wider, but she didn't say anything. "If ye are with my child, I will not abandon the two of ye. I have no land or home right now but know that I will do what I can to make the both of ye safe."

She blinked, a smile growing on her soft lips. "Thank you, Shaw." She leaned forward, pressing her lips to his. His world blurred, and his blood rushed forward. He pressed her closer into him, holding her until she finally turned backward in the saddle to face him, their arms going around each other as their mouths began to move hungrily against each other.

"I wish…" She breathed against him, still kissing. "We

had more time in the cottage. Alone."

"Good lord, aye," he said. The rest of the world was a mess, but the one thing he knew, the fact that crashed through him like a battering ram, was that he wanted Alana, bairn or no bairn. He wanted her. "I am yours," he whispered against her and captured her face in his rough hands. He broke the kiss enough for them to stare into each other's eyes. "I am yours, Alana Campbell. Whatever happens from here on out, whether we continue or end this bloody war with your clan, know that I am yours."

She blinked. Her eyes glistened slightly, and she nodded in the confines of his grasp before leaning back into his lips. They kissed for another long moment and broke apart to rest their foreheads against each other.

"I will do whatever I can to help you," she whispered. "You and your clan."

He nodded against her. "Then help me take the bairn to meet the ship to France."

She exhaled, and he felt her breath against his lips. She nodded. "We should go, then."

He helped her turn back around in the saddle, pressing his face against her hair, inhaling the pure smell that he knew was Alana. For riding into St. Andrews, he felt the threat of change. Before they rode into Edinburgh, he would tell her everything, the ugly truths that haunted him. He would see her safely to Finlarig, but he would likely never have the chance to press his face into her fragrant waves again.

• • •

I am yours. What did that mean? It sounded like an oath. Said before God and witnesses, it *was* an oath for marriage. *I am yours*. The words infused a warmth through Alana. He hadn't said "You are mine" as if she didn't have a say in it. He didn't ask for anything in return, just wanted her to know that somehow she'd won his...his what? Loyalty? Love?

The thought flipped through her stomach, making her heart beat faster. If he loved her, did she love him in return? She nearly turned in the seat again to demand he answer her questions, but they rode out of the woods and down between some buildings that marked the edge of St. Andrews.

She felt his breath at her ear, the brush of his lips sending a thrill through her. "Look at each window we pass for sign of my men. A strap of leather, usually a bridle, trapped in the window pane."

"Do you use that when you are hiding from Campbells on your land?"

"Aye." He straightened away from her, and she nearly leaned back into his warmth again, feeling cold without his lips touching her. When had his touch become something she craved all the time?

The street was cobbled with flat rocks, and Rìgh's hooves clopped along them. Robert remained right alongside and garnered his share of glances. Luckily word of a couple riding into town with a large dog wouldn't catch Major Dixon's attention. Hopefully he had given up when he lost their trail and turned west like Fiona had told him that they'd gone.

With the sun sinking behind the two-story structures lining the main thoroughfare, the people along the street hurried by without giving them much notice. Several vendors of puddings and rolls pushed their carts. "Hold Rìgh," Shaw said, dismounting to purchase a few meat pasties, baked turnips, and sweets. He strode back over, putting their food in her satchel tied to the back of the saddle. He climbed up from the wrong side.

"I should check your stitches," she said, although he didn't grimace at all.

"They are healing and itching," he said and leaned to

whisper along the side of her face. "And I bought some tarts. The crone had honey ones."

She twisted in the seat to smile at him. "You can try one, then."

"Aye, I will try one."

"And you will see what you have been missing and find the crone again and buy her whole cart."

He chuckled and took the reins.

"Come, Robert," she said, and they continued along the wide street. Looking down the side streets, she saw other wide streets beyond the rows of houses and shops. "St. Andrews is large."

"I have been here once on my way to Edinburgh to petition for the lands. There is a fair amount of trade here, but it is not as grand as Edinburgh with its mighty castle."

The mention of the huge edifice that they would face to find her mother washed away her smile. Lord, how would they free her if their petitions for her release were ignored or denied?

They continued down the street slower than when they rode through the forest, both of them searching for any sign of Shaw's men. Several horses were tied outside a lodging house. "That is Rainy, my mare," she said, tugging on his sleeve.

He continued past, turning Rìgh down the side street that flanked the structure. "There," he said, and Alana saw the edge of a bridle sticking out of a window on the second story.

"Rose," she whispered, feeling the tightness of missing the little baby in her chest. How could one become so fond of a babe so quickly? Especially when it wasn't her own? *Or a man so quickly?*

A squat barn stood out back with several lads stationed out front of it. One jumped up as Shaw dismounted. "Can ye watch my horse?"

"Aye, for a shilling," the boy said.

Shaw's hands fit snuggly around her waist as he lowered her down from the tall horse. Even through her stays, she could feel the pressure of his hands on her. Lord how she wished that they could have even one more night alone together.

Robert came alongside, dipping his massive head so that her hand would rest upon it. They walked together to the front of the establishment. "Stay, Robert," she said, using her palm-out hand signal to get him to sit by the front door. He obeyed so she wouldn't have to tie him. *Thank goodness.* His largeness wouldn't allow him to be taken by anyone, and he'd shown he preferred to stay near her. He wouldn't wander off unless a child walked by with a sweet.

The murmur of voices spilled into the growing night as Shaw opened the door for her. A quick scan showed no red uniforms. She released the breath she'd been holding. There was a mix of people eating, drinking, and talking. Mostly men, but there were a couple of women sitting near the steps leading upward. They each held a baby, cradling them in their arms. Mothers, their husbands probably amongst the men in the common room.

Shaw made his way to the innkeeper at the long bar and then came back to Alana. "I managed to rent a bed in a shared room above."

"A shared room?"

"Aye, 'tis common in busy towns. I will order Alistair and Mungo to sleep there while we stay with Rose."

"The other Roses will have to find another lodging, then, if that was the only bed."

"There are several places in a town this size, especially with sailors coming into the port to trade," he said, escorting her to the steps.

She nodded to the two mothers. One of them nodded back with a curious gaze, her face young and her shoulders straight. The other frowned, exhaustion seeming to pull at her features. The wooden steps creaked under their weight and were tilted to one side. Shaw's boots thumped upon them as he led the way, holding her hand. He stopped at the top and pulled her up next to him. He pointed to a door at the far end and drew his short sword, so Alana drew the *sgian dubh* he'd given her when Dixon's men nearly found them in the forest.

Knock, knock, pause...knock. Another signal they used?

A moment later there was a knock from inside, just one.

Shaw gave one back quickly, and the door flew inward. "Shaw!" Rabbie ushered them inside a small room with two double-sized beds, one against each wall. "Ye found us."

"Ye were delayed," Alistair said.

"Dixon almost stumbled upon us," Shaw said. "We had to go north and then cross by way of a ferry."

Logan lifted the window to pull the bridle inside. "There is a problem," he said.

"Where's Rose?" Alana asked, and Mungo held up a wrapped bundle. She hurried over to peer into the sleeping face of the wee babe. "She is well?" She met Mungo's gaze over the sweet cherub face. He nodded, though his face looked pinched. She turned to the other Sinclairs. All of them looked tense. Even Rabbie's initial smile had faded.

"What problem?" Shaw asked, shutting the door behind him. The room was full of large warriors, all standing stone still. Only the sound of the patrons below could be heard.

Alana took Rose from Mungo's arms, nestling her head against the inside of her elbow to rock her gently like a cradle.

"We arrived early yesterday," Alistair said, coming over, his gaze on Alana before turning to meet Shaw's fierce stare. His bruises were still stark, but the white of his eye had begun to clear.

"The problem," Shaw said, his voice demanding.

Logan cleared his throat. "We were not the first ones to arrive."

"What the hell are ye talking about?" Shaw asked, coming over to nudge the blanket down that had risen up to cover the babe's little nub of a chin. He turned back to the men who all stood still.

"There are two other bairns," Alistair said. "With wet nurses."

Shock caught Alana's tongue and breath for a moment. She swallowed. "The women below?"

Alistair nodded. "Aye. I talked to their escorts yesterday. They were tasked to bring the bairns from London to St. Andrews to go to France."

Shaw stood silent, waiting for him to finish even though a look of anger mixed with shock on his face.

"Alistair," Alana said. "Who are they?"

The Sinclair warrior kept his gaze directly on Shaw, meeting his look. "They each say...their bairns are Queen Mary's daughters, each a princess to be ferried to France for safekeeping."

Chapter Eighteen

Thunder beat inside Shaw's head. Three princesses? They'd been tricked.

"How can that be?" Alana asked. She pulled the stirring bairn closer to her chest as if to protect her from the foulness of it all.

Logan dropped the bridle on the bed and crossed his arms. "The best that we can determine is that King James planned for three bairns to be sent to France to confuse those hunting the princess. One must be the true princess."

"Are any of them branded?" Shaw asked. "With a rose?"

"None of the escorts or wet nurses mentioned it, and I did not want to ask because that might give away that we have the real princess," Logan said.

Alana nodded, kissing the bairn's forehead. "We must have the real princess. Why else would someone brand a newborn babe?"

Her words helped Shaw draw in more breath. "It does not matter if there are ten bairns bound for France or if we have the real one or not. The mission was to bring the bairn we were given to St. Andrews, alive and safe, in return for our lands and castle. Those two other bairns below change none of that." All his men nodded.

"Will one of the other wet nurses be able to feed Rose on the journey?" Alana asked. "Are they traveling with their charges?"

"Aye, they are," Logan said.

"One is quite bitter," Alistair said. "She takes care of her bairn but does not do much else. The younger lass seems more likely to help, although I did not ask, not wanting to admit that we also had a bairn bound for France."

"Have ye gone down to the castle ruins by the port?" he asked. "To see if there are any foreign ships docked?"

"Aye," Alistair said. "Although there are no flags to distinguish the ship from several others there, I overheard some of the men onboard talking in French. I did not send word that we were here yet. Wanted to give ye a chance to catch up to us."

His men knew this was for the chief to do, completing the mission that would save their clan. The deaths of so many, including Reagan, weighed on his heart, and the guilt of not being able to stop his uncle from gambling their honor away gnawed on his soul. His men knew that Shaw should be the one to bring it to a close, to right the wrongs of his life.

"The women below said that they were told to wait here, so we thought we should stay close," Logan said.

"What can ye tell about the vessel?" he asked.

"Sturdy, large," Rabbie said, staring down at Rose from over Alana's shoulder. "It should be safe to carry the bairn across." He frowned. "Though I hate to see her go, especially without someone assigned to care for her." He glanced up, meeting his gaze. "She eats every three hours. If she does not have a nursemaid for the voyage, I fear she will starve or grow weak and ill. She is just a wee, fragile lass."

"We might pay the younger woman to also care for her," Logan said.

Hell, that wasn't part of the plan. As it was, they had few coins left, and every shilling that Shaw earned was saved to pay his uncle's massive debt in the case he could actually buy back the Sinclair holdings. Although, Edgar Campbell was not the type to agree to that. He took too much pleasure in pushing the Sinclairs away with threats, starvation, and outright attacks.

"If we gain back our lands, then we can use our coin to pay the wet nurse," Alistair said as if reading his mind.

"But we will not know if she truly will care for Rose," Alana said. "Or just pocket the coin and let her waste away." Alana pulled Rose into her chest as if the idea of her being neglected was something she could guard her against.

"We can let whoever is in charge know about the brand," Logan said. "They might find another wet nurse when they realize that Rose is the real princess."

"If she is the real princess," Alana said, determination crossing her face.

They all looked at her. "Of course she is," Rabbie said, frowning.

"What if you get credit for bringing her here?" Alana said. "With whoever is in charge. Sinclairs get the bill of rights to the land in the north and the castle, but then you explain that there is no one to take care of her, saying that likely the real princess is one of the other two babes."

"What are ye planning, Alana?" Shaw asked, but the look on her face said it all.

"I want her," she said. "I will take her, care for her, love her. If she is the real princess, she will be hidden and safe with me surrounded by the walls of Finlarig and students trained in self-defense. If the time comes for her to return to England, I will bring her."

"Alana—" Shaw started.

"The school is already supported by Queen Mary and the Duchess Catherine de Braganza. What better place is there for a possible future queen? We will educate Rose in every discipline from world history and art to French and self-defense. We will teach her not only to be an English queen, but to be an English queen who loves Scotland and her people."

"Taking the bairn will jeopardize our mission," Logan said, his voice rising. "Our only care is to regain our rightful lands and castle."

"*Your* only care," Alana said. "*My* only care is for this innocent babe."

Shaw's frown deepened. Alana had said that she would help him. Had she changed her mind and heart?

Rabbie stood beside Alana, his hands fisted. "We should consider it."

Logan rolled his eyes, grunted, and turned to pace back to the window. He was usually sensitive about all living things, but last winter had been hard on his family, too, with several dying. He had as much desire to reclaim their homes as Shaw.

Rabbie tracked him with a stare. "The bairn will suffer if she gets on that ship without a nursemaid. And it would be good to have a future queen grow up loving Scotland."

"Loving Campbells in Scotland," Logan said with a glare at Rabbie.

"Campbells from Killin in Breadalbane," Alana said. "Not Campbells who have invaded your home." Her slim shoulders lifted and fell. "Or Rose could be raised on Sinclair land, although that might be harder to justify without there being a school to teach her as much or more than she would learn in France." She pressed the bairn up against her chest, cupping Rose's head gently to hold her wee ear against her beating heart. She swayed as if soothing the child. "It could work."

"Maybe ye should go with the bairn on the ship to be her nursemaid," Logan suggested.

"Nay," Shaw said immediately, making his men and Alana look at him. The thought of her sailing away from Scotland made his stomach clench fiercely. "She has her own mission to save her mother from Edinburgh."

"Yes," she said, nodding slowly. "I must free my mother from the prison there and take her home." The sorrow on her face made Shaw wonder. If Alana didn't have a mother to save, would she agree to go with the princess all the way to France?

"We should try," Rabbie said, standing with a stubborn tilt to his chin. "Tell the captain that he would be responsible for the bairn dying on the voyage if he takes her. But that we still fulfilled our mission and require payment with Sinclair lands and castle."

Shaw clasped a hand behind his neck where his head was beginning to throb. "I will walk down to the docks to survey the ships once it is dark. Tomorrow morn, I will see what the captain says when we go down to the castle ruins like instructed."

Rabbie nodded, hope in the tilt of his mouth as he squeezed his hands into tight fists. Logan cursed, and Alistair just looked grim. Alana inhaled, nodding, her gaze thankful. Dammit all, thankful for what? Would he really risk Sinclair lands for this bairn? All those men, women, and children who were headed into another Highland winter. *Fok*. He couldn't. He wouldn't. "I'll secure Rìgh and Robert for the night," he said, turning to leave the room. He couldn't look at Alana holding little Rose any longer with his heart clenching so hard.

• • •

Alana patted Rose's back, bringing up a small burp. "There, wee one," she whispered, carrying the washed and bundled babe over to a nest of blankets that Rabbie had put together. She had laid out the tarts that she'd saved for when Shaw returned from scouting down by the docks. The bun that Fiona had given her sat on the table, too, a little smashed. She'd throw it in the fire if Shaw didn't think it could be used somehow.

Shaw's men had left the room so that Alana could wash herself and the babe. Two would sleep in the shared room, but she wasn't sure where Alistair and Rabbie would sleep. Perhaps in there with them or in the barn.

Rap. Rap.

"Who is it?" she asked, going to the door.

"Alistair."

Alana opened the door. He held some mugs on a tray. "Warm spiced wine for ye," he said.

"Shaw is not back yet?" she asked.

He shook his head. "He is taking his time so not to be seen," Alistair said, brushing off her worry. "Can I speak with ye, lass? For a moment."

"I… Yes," she said, letting him into the room.

Alistair shut the door behind him, and she walked to the dark window. She'd left it cracked for the fresh autumn air and to listen for Shaw's return. She'd been unable to sit still with him out in the shadows by himself. With the fire behind her, she couldn't see much beyond the glass and heaved it upward to look out. But the back courtyard was quiet and heavily in shadows. "When will he be back?" she asked, lowering the window and turning.

She stopped, her lips parted, and she stared at Alistair as he chewed. "Stop," she said, her palm outward as if she signaled Robert. The man swallowed. "Oh no," she murmured.

"I took the smashed one with currants," he said, glancing down. "Shaw hates currants. Were ye saving it?"

Bloody hell. He'd eaten Fiona's special roll. She'd said it would just make Shaw fall asleep, not dead. Alana exhaled. "You might start feeling tired soon."

"What?" Alistair asked, his eyes wide.

"That was Fiona's roll."

"Fok," he said, pushing back from the table, his hands going to his mouth where he scraped at his tongue, spitting onto the floor. "Was it poison?"

"No," she said, hands out, but there was nothing she could help with since he'd swallowed it. "She said it would put Shaw to sleep if he was going to beat me."

"I can puke it up," he said, running to the chamber pot in the corner. He put his finger down his throat but just gagged. "Damn, I cannot do it."

Alana came over. "I think she told me the truth. It will just put you to sleep for the night."

He sat down on the edge of the bed, raking his hands through his hair as he stared at the ground. "I already... feel...tired."

"Perhaps you should go back to your room—"

"But I wanted to tell ye." He glanced up at her from where he perched his head in his hands, elbows propped on his knees. "Has Shaw told ye about the conditions at home?"

"Yes," she said, watching him closely to see if he showed any signs of deadly poison. "He has told me how you are all harassed and chased from your land."

"Did he tell ye about Reagan?"

She frowned. "No?" Did Shaw have a woman back home? The thought curdled Alana's stomach. "He has not mentioned anyone with that name."

"He does not talk about her," Alistair said. "And will likely blacken my other eye for telling ye, if I foking survive tonight." His words sounded slightly slurred as if he'd been drinking whiskey.

Was Shaw married? Or betrothed? "Who is she?" she asked, bending down before the man. He didn't answer, and she caught his shoulder, shaking him slightly. "Alistair. Who is she?"

"Was," Alistair said.

"Was?"

"Shaw's older sister. Died last winter from illness. The Campbell bastards harrying her out into the snow. Grew... weaker."

Alana's hand pressed against her chest. He had mentioned a sister and wishing she could wed and have bairns but not that he had lost one. "He did not say."

"He would not." Alistair exhaled, swaying on the bed. He used his hands to keep him upright. "He still has Bren."

"Bren?"

"His younger sister." Alistair shook his head as if trying to shake off the effects of Fiona's tart. "So, he will not do anything to jeopardize the return of Sinclair lands. His own sister is buried in an unmarked grave on that land, and he will see a stone placed there."

He tried to stand, but his knees gave way. Alana jumped back as the large man fell to the floor, his arms blocking the worst of the fall. She dropped down to kneel beside him. "Alistair?"

His eyes were shut, but he was breathing. He mumbled, and she leaned close. "The life of a wee princess will not stop him," he said. "And neither will ye falling in love with him."

"In love with him?" she asked, her voice higher in pitch.

"Revenge is stronger than love," he murmured. "Shaw has sworn to gain Sinclair lands, and no woman, especially a Campbell, will stop...him. I...will make sure."

"You? What do you mean, *you* will make sure?" Alana

lowered her face opposite his until her cheek rested on the wooden floor. He breathed evenly. She shook his arm. "Alistair?"

"Like…at…Stirling," he mumbled. His mouth fell open, and he breathed as if falling into a deep sleep.

"Dammit, Alistair," she said, sitting back on her heels, hands on her hips. "Like what at Stirling?" She already asked Shaw about the battle at Stirling. Alana frowned at the closed door. If she didn't have a babe to guard and now a fallen man for whom she felt responsible, she'd go out to find him. She looked at the dark window. A gnawing sensation sat in her chest, a feeling Shaw would recognize. The hollow of missing someone.

Did Shaw have secrets? Things that would change her mind about the honorable man for whom she'd begun to care? She was a Campbell, and he was the chief of the Sinclairs; she'd known that from the start. *Like at Stirling.* Alistair's words prickled along the skin at the back of her neck. She rubbed it and exhaled long. No matter what happened tomorrow or the day after, she knew that deep down Shaw Sinclair was an honorable man, trying to save his remaining sister and clan.

She glanced at Alistair sprawled out on the floor. A deep snore came from his open mouth. Apparently, he wasn't going to die.

She walked over to look down at the sleeping face of the infant nestled within the soft blanket. Rose's tiny lips moved in and out as if she dreamed of nursing. Alana crouched down and inhaled the sweet baby scent, sighing. Alistair was wrong. Love was stronger than everything. Even the darkness of hate and betrayal, and even revenge.

• • •

"No," the English commander, Colonel Commandant Wendall, said in a clipped tone. "Bring the infant in the morning. All three must climb aboard the *Queen's Song* to sail for Calais."

"*Oui*," the French captain said, nodding. "The second wet nurse, she will care for *la petite fille*. There are to be *trois bébés*, eh?" he asked, looking at Wendall.

Even with the darkness of the deep shadows, Shaw could see the frown on the man's face. "Three, yes, not two."

"The bairn I bring may not survive the crossing without her own wet nurse or someone to care for her," Shaw said, but it was the same argument that he'd already made. "You will deliver a dead princess to your contact in Calais."

The Frenchman shrugged. "If she dies on board, she dies. 'Tis the way of infants."

The man had likely never been a father, and even if he had a bastard in every port, he hadn't watched the bairn sleep in his arms or blow bubbles with the milk on her lip. Nay, there would be no arguing with them.

The Colonel shifted where he stood. "If you do not bring the baby to the dock to sail tomorrow and place her on the ship, I will not hand over the royal letter for you to regain Sinclair lands and Girnigoe Castle. That was the bargain." If the man had brought the letter with him, would Shaw have been tempted to kill them both and take the letter? Surely word would get back to London that Shaw hadn't delivered the bairn like he'd promised.

"Aye," he said, his voice low. "I will bring the bairn. She is healthy and strong right now, as promised."

"Very well," Wendall said, the man's intense look making Shaw wonder if he knew that Rose was indeed the true princess.

With a nod to them both, he turned away, Robert trotting beside him. The dog wouldn't remain behind with Shaw walking into town. And his hulking form had made it less necessary for him to guard against desperate thieves in the shadows.

Shaw listened to the crunch of his boots as he walked the vacant street. It was nearly midnight, and most were tucked into bed. Was Alana sleeping soundly or up feeding Rose? Robert's head slid under his hand, raising it for a quick pet. "Aye," Shaw murmured. "Let us find your mistress."

Two of his men were sleeping in a shared room and two more were bedding down with all their horses. Shaw would sleep in the room with Alana, although they would have a bairn with them. *And a secret between you.* No matter what scenario Shaw played out in his head or what words he planned to use, the outcome was always the same. "She is going to hate me," he said, sliding his hand along the dog's bony head. If not for sending Rose to France, then once he helped her free her mother, a Campbell, who would not only remember him, but who might wish to kill him if given the chance.

Walking to the front of the inn, Shaw drew his short sword as the shadow at the corner moved. Logan stepped around, apparently waiting for his return. "Did ye find the captain?" he asked.

"Aye," Shaw said, still holding the weapon.

"What did he say about the three bairns? And whether the lass can keep ours?"

"Two bairns are decoys apparently, but the colonel and the captain at the ship either don't know who the true princess is or are not telling. And all three bairns must ride to France. The other two couriers bringing bairns will also gain back land or money for fulfilling their bargains, although the colonel would not divulge any details."

"I know the younger woman is a Maclean from the western isles," Logan said. "The other will not give up any information, but from her accent she hails from the lowlands near the English border."

Shaw nodded. "To gain our lands and Girnigoe, we have to put Rose on that damn ship." He frowned, hating the idea of the little lass sailing without someone assigned to feed her.

"Which is our mission," Logan said. "It is almost done."

"I know our mission."

"Aye." He shook his head. "And yet a Campbell lass convinced ye to ask if we can keep the bairn. We are just so close. If we help the king save his daughter, we win back everything."

Shaw rubbed at the ache at the back of his head. If he didn't have the weight of being chief to a desperate people, he wouldn't help the blasted English with anything.

Logan reached out, his hand heavy on Shaw's shoulder. "We are so damn close. Just like at Stirling."

Usually it was Alistair who thought to remind him about his duty. Shaw leaned forward, his gaze like a sword as he stared at Logan. "I know our mission. I planned it. And this is nothing like Stirling." He turned and strode into the quiet common room, Robert following him.

The innkeeper slept slumped over on a bench as if awaiting more patrons. "Stay," Shaw said to Robert, using the signal Alana had taught the dog. He brought him over to the warm hearth and made the motion. Tongue hanging out from his jog back up the dark streets, Robert turned in a circle and laid down. "Stay," Shaw said again and glanced at the innkeeper who snored.

The steps were dark, and Shaw used a light foot, treading carefully to the third door to the right. Damn Logan. Did he really think he had forgotten their mission? That after a lifetime of praying for and working to become strong enough to help his clan, he would just give it up because a lass asked?

He paused before the door to her room. Alana wasn't just

some woman who ignited his blood more than any other. She was more. Courageous and clever, unafraid of hard work and able to persevere without complaint. Her inherent kindness had forgiven him when he'd abducted her. But would she be able to forgive him for putting his clan first?

The latch gave easily under the pressure of his thumb, and he pushed inside. Alana gasped, whirling around to face him. In the light of the fire, he saw the bulk of a man lying at her feet, his knees showing from under a Sinclair kilt. *Alistair?*

Shock numbed Shaw's tongue. The lass had taken down Alistair Sinclair? What the bloody hell had he done to make her have to defend herself? The muscles in his arms contracted with his fists tightening.

"Shaw," she said, hand at her chest as if keeping her heart inside. "I can explain."

Before any word could make it to his tongue, the vibrating thunder of a snore came from the mass on the floor. He met Alana's wide-eyed stare. Perhaps she hadn't had to gut the man. "Ye put Alistair to sleep? On our floor?"

She nodded. "He ate Fiona's tart." Her nod turned quickly to a shake of her head. "I did not give it to him." Another deep snore came from the floor. "I think he took the smashed tart, thinking to leave us the fresh ones."

Shaw walked forward and squatted to look at Alistair. The man's mouth had fallen open wide, his chest rising and falling. He glanced sideways at her. She stood with her hands pressed together before her lips, long hair tumbling down around her shoulders. She still wore her gown, though her feet were bare. Worry was all over her face.

"So," he said, starting slow as he rose to stand. "He finally irritated ye enough to poison him."

"No, I—"

"We need to buy more of Fiona's tarts," he said. "Save us Alistair's tongue all the way home. I can tie him to his horse."

Alana stared at him, and slowly her wide eyes relaxed and a small smile grew on her lips.

"Should we just let him sleep here?" she asked, her arms going out.

"Nay," he answered, his eyes going to the baby in the nest that Rabbie had made for her in the corner. "I would..." He looked back to her standing there. Och, if only they were just two people who had met away from war and lies and sacrifice. "If ye would..."

"You are having a hard time finishing your thought," she said, her voice low.

"If we could be alone tonight. To...talk." Shaw didn't want to talk. He wanted to touch her, kiss every sweet inch of her.

Her smile faded. "Before he fell unconscious, Alistair told me to ask you about the Covenanter Battle outside Stirling again, and that your thirst for revenge would make you give Rose up without a fight."

Bloody damn Alistair. "Alana," Shaw said, reaching up to rub the back of his neck. He brought them down between them. "We should talk."

"I know," she said, nodding. "We should." Her voice grew tiny. "Why do I feel like after all is said, things will not be the same?"

Because they would not. She would know that he'd been willing to help the English when Dixon came to Stirling. The guilt sat like a rock in his chest. "We could...talk tomorrow. On the way to Edinburgh," he said.

Between them, Alistair snored loudly, but Shaw kept his gaze on Alana, trying to decipher her. She watched him, her breathing shallow, eyes dark in the shadows. Her fingers curled into the sides of her skirt. Did she want him as much as he wanted her?

His breath stopped as he caught the slight bob of her

head forward in the firelight. "Tomorrow," she whispered. "In the light of day, when clan names mean something again. When the Highland Roses find us, and Kirstin cannot hide her prejudice. When Kerrick tries to convince you that he will help me free my mother so you can go home with your royal document. When I am awash with sorrow as the little princess is carried onto the ship."

He heard her take a deep breath and saw her chest rise and fall. "Let us wait to talk tomorrow."

A loud snore stopped Shaw from reaching for her. His gaze dropped to his friend who continued to be a thorn in his side. "I will carry him out." He glanced at the bundle in the corner. "And ask Rabbie to keep the lass with him so...ye can sleep well tonight." Before she could object, Shaw reached down to grab Alistair's two limp arms. He grunted as he lifted the man up slowly, pulling him to lie over one shoulder. Dead weight.

Alana made a little noise and yanked Alistair's kilt down to cover his arse and ran around him to open the door. With a quick stride, he walked down the hall to the room Rabbie and Logan were sharing, giving the signal knock.

Rabbie opened it, his brows rising when he saw Alistair. "He ate a sleeping tart."

"Sleeping tart?" Rabbie asked. Shaw pushed past him, lowering Alistair on the floor by the hearth. Logan wasn't upstairs yet. Good. He didn't want the man questioning his loyalties. Punching him in the face would delay him returning to Alana.

"And I am bringing ye wee Rose to watch tonight," Shaw said.

Rabbie opened his mouth, but Shaw spoke over his question. "Alana needs to sleep undisturbed."

"And being alone in a room with ye will allow her to get a good night's sleep?" Rabbie asked.

Shaw ignored him, stepping into the hall to stride back to his room. Inside, Alana held the sleeping bairn wrapped in the blankets. She leaned in, kissing her face, and Shaw's chest squeezed. With her hair falling around them, the firelight giving her beautiful face a golden hue, she looked like a goddess and loving mother all wrapped into one beguiling woman. Och. What he wouldn't give to have that in his life. *Would you give up Girnigoe?* He smashed the thought down before it could take root.

"She is still sleeping," she whispered and lay Rose into his arms. He nodded, and their gazes met over the sleeping bairn. If only they could stay like this, together as a family. Impossible.

Shaw turned, his feet propelling him out the door and down the hall to Rabbie, who leaned out of his room.

"Are ye sure Alistair will be well?" he asked.

"If he doesn't wake in the morn, let me know," Shaw said. He kissed the top of Rose's soft head and handed her off to the young warrior.

Rabbie's eyes were wide, but he nodded. "Sleep well," he said, the side of his mouth hitching upward despite the warning frown Shaw gave him. He traipsed back down to Alana's room, this time his steps a little slower.

Perhaps the lass had changed her mind. She could send him away, and he'd sleep in the barn with Rìgh. Or perhaps she had decided that they should talk tonight, lay all the truths out before each other. *Damn.* He ran his hand through his hair, feeling more nervous than an untried lad.

The door was still open, a splash of firelight coming from within. With a fortifying breath, he stepped inside, his gaze circling the empty room. "Alana?"

"I will be out in a moment," she said from behind the privacy screen set in one tight corner.

"If ye... I can sleep out in the barn," he said before the

sight of her stopped his tongue.

She stepped out from behind, wearing only her long smock. "Then who will I...not talk about anything with tonight."

Lord help him, she was beautiful. Like an angel in white, the firelight casting her in gold. She glided up to him, and his gaze traveled along the softness of her skin and fullness of her lips. Her eyes were so expressive, and right now they stared into his eyes, into his very soul. Could she see the need there, his need for her?

"Alana—"

"Give me tonight." She reached onto her toes and threaded her fingers through the back of his hair, pressing up while pulling his head down to brush a kiss against his lips. "Give us tonight."

His hand came up to capture the softness of her cheek. Her face was tilted up to him. "Aye, Alana lass. We will have tonight." His lips came down to slant against her already open mouth in a molten kiss, filled with desperation and the tattered vestiges of hope.

Chapter Nineteen

"She is fed, clean, and wrapped warmly," Alana said, lifting Rose against her shoulder. The room was filled with Sinclairs, except for the one she wanted. Alistair sat on her bed, his head heavy in his hands, apparently having survived the night. Shaw had left earlier to locate Kerrick and the Highland Rose students. He'd given Alana time to wash and say goodbye to baby Rose in private. Although, no amount of time would be enough.

Shaw had told her what the English colonel and the French captain had said at the docks the night before. Her plan to keep Rose looked rather hopeless. Perhaps the princess would be just fine, living like royalty in France. She kissed the sweet infant's forehead, her big blue eyes staring up at her. Her eyelashes seemed to have unfurled overnight.

"I have packed her two bottles and some fresh milk and pap made up," Rabbie said. "Extra warm blankets and enough cloths to keep all three bairns clean. But we need to talk with the wet nurse to make sure she will be able to feed Rose after the milk runs out."

She knew all this, but Rabbie seemed to need to say it again. She nodded, giving him an understanding smile. "Let us go find her."

They filed out of the room, Alistair rising slowly to walk to the door while she gathered Rose's blanket better around her. He turned in the doorway, blocking her. "Did ye ask Shaw about Stirling?" he said, his voice low.

Alana hadn't let Shaw talk about anything last night. Only whispered encouragement and soft moans of pleasure hovered in the heated darkness around them. Both of them had clung to each other with desperation, exploring and tasting as if committing each other to memory. On the surface, it looked quite possible for them to remain together after rescuing her mother from Edinburgh, but Alana's instincts, tangled up with Alistair's cryptic questions, nurtured dread within her. Only the fire between Shaw and her last night had kept the worry away.

"He came in late and left early this morn," she said. "There was no time to discuss." She studied the man who said he was Shaw's friend. He looked haggard, his eyes red and face still heavy with the sleeping drug. "Why don't *you* tell me about the battle near Stirling? I know it is his tale to tell, but you seem quite anxious for it to be out." Maybe if she knew a few of the details, whatever Shaw told her wouldn't seem so troublesome. For despite them agreeing to put off their worries until later that day, she could tell something weighed heavily upon him.

Alistair looked over his shoulder where the other Sinclairs had descended into the common room and then back at Alana. "We have met Major Dixon before. He was at the battle outside Stirling, following King Charles's orders to squash out the rebel Covenanters."

"Is that why the major was so suspicious of us with Rose?" she asked.

"Likely," he said, his gaze shifting behind him as if he was afraid to be overheard.

"And yet, Major Dixon wants to kill the princess? He switched loyalties, then?"

Alistair nodded. "He was loyal to King Charles, not his brother, King James, who sits on the throne now. Many military and political players hope for James's daughter, Mary, to come quickly to power with her husband William, both of them staunch Protestants."

"King James is Catholic," she said, understanding. "Whereas his brother Charles was not openly so."

Alistair shifted from foot to foot.

"And why are you telling me this?" she asked. "While looking nervous and worried about being overheard?" Rose began to fuss, and Alana began to sway.

Alistair stopped shifting, his face pinched. He opened his mouth and then closed it before finally speaking. "We had made a bargain before at the battle, well, Shaw did, made a bargain that is, to save our lands and castle from Edgar Campbell."

"Alistair, what is taken ye so long?" Logan's head appeared at the bottom of the stairs.

"Nothing," Alistair answered. "The bairn was fussing."

With one last look at Alistair, Alana turned to bring Rose downstairs, her mind repeating his words. Shaw had made a bargain to help his clan. With whom? Her father but then he was killed?

The common room was full of her friends and Shaw's men. Kerrick and Kirstin kept their frowns as they stared at the Sinclairs. Cici smiled at Logan, Martha smiled at Rabbie, and Izzy tipped her head while watching Mungo make hand signals to Logan. For a room so full, the only sound was the innkeeper wiping the bar down, his eyes wide.

"The bairn," Kirstin said, weaving between the tables in

her skirt to Alana. Her frown faded as she peered down into the babe's sweet face. "So pretty," Kirstin whispered. "Pink cheeks, blue eyes, the cutest little nose." Kirstin looked at Alana. "If her eyes turn green, she will look like ye."

Her words were kind, but they twisted inside Alana. She managed a sad smile. "I would miss her that much more."

Kirstin leaned toward her ear. "If she is a princess, maybe we should keep her."

Alana stared numbly at her. "I fear that is a hopeless notion. If we keep her, the Sinclairs fail to retrieve their lands and castle."

Kirstin met her gaze with an unblinking one. "Something we care nothing about. If anything, we want the lands and Girnigoe to stay in Campbell hands."

"You do not understand what they have been through these past nine years," Alana said, shaking her head and raising her gaze to the large warriors who stood near the door. "The Sinclairs should get it all back, their lands, castle, and honor. I wonder if my father would have agreed if he were still alive. He did stop helping Edgar after the first push to take the castle."

Kirstin said something back, but Alana didn't pick up the words. Her eyes had gone to the door where Shaw walked in, surveying the room as if it were a battlefield. She supposed that it had the potential to be one.

"It seems St. Andrews is overflowing with Campbell lasses," Alistair said to Shaw.

"And MacInneses," Cici said.

"I am a MacPherson, to be exact," Kirstin said.

"And I am a Kellington from London," Lucy said. "And Kerrick is definitely not a lass."

Robert ran in past Shaw's legs and trotted from person to person, his powerful tail swatting skirts and thumping table legs. He didn't care who was a Campbell, Sinclair, English, or Scot. Alana sighed, wishing that the world ran according to canines.

"These are the students from the Highland Roses school and their escort," Shaw said.

"A large group will draw eyes," Logan said, looking sideways at Cici, who had sidled up next to him as if she'd been there the whole time.

"We will stay back from your dealings," Kerrick said. "I am here to make certain Alana gets safely to Edinburgh, where we will free her mother." His gaze slid to Shaw. "After today, ye can return to your lands. Violet Campbell is our responsibility."

Alana's stomach tightened. "No. Shaw said that he would help me. 'Tis why I went along easily with them. It was an exchange." She hugged Rose closer, inhaling her sweet baby scent. Could she stand losing both Rose and Shaw on the same day?

Shaw walked across to her, his gaze going from the babe to Alana's eyes. She smiled sadly. "Did you notice," she said, "Rose's eyelashes have unfurled. Look how long and perfect they are." He bent over the babe, peering in her face. Rose blinked as Shaw laid his hand over the wee one's chest. Her little hand lifted, and thin fingers wrapped around Shaw's thumb. He made a sound in the back of his throat. "She has a strong grip. A warrior to be sure."

Kirstin came close. "Aye, look how tightly she squeezes."

Alana's gaze was fastened on Shaw's waves of dark hair, so she met his gaze when he lifted his face. "It is as if she wants to hold on and not let go," Alana whispered.

The gentle look on Shaw's face hardened, and he slowly pulled his thumb from the babe's grip. "We need to go. I can take the bairn down to the docks."

"I will carry her," Alana said. "We need to talk to the wet nurse to make certain she knows that she is responsible for Rose."

"Aye," Rabbie said, jumping forward to go with them.

"Kerrick, keep the Highland Roses back here and be ready to ride once we are back," Alana said, her voice strong even though her legs wobbled.

"We will gather some supplies," Kerrick said. "Although we should make Edinburgh by nightfall if we leave right away."

Alana walked out into the brisk, fall morning. The tang of low tide made her sniff, her nose wrinkling. She tucked Rose's little hand back into the blanket and hurried beside Shaw and Rabbie toward the docks, their steps rapid. Logan, Alistair, and Mungo followed behind, no doubt watching for anything suspicious. Robert, loving the interesting smells, trotted along, his nose bobbing between the pebble-packed road and the breeze off the water.

Shaw's arm brushed Alana's as they walked. "I will still help ye free your mother," he said. "And escort ye back to Killin in Breadalbane."

She glanced up at him. "Are you certain? Do you not need to get home with your royal papers to make Edgar quit your castle?"

She felt his tug on her arm and looked up as he slowed his pace. His eyes seemed to search hers. "I would know before I leave if ye are with child," he whispered. "I will not abandon my bairn or the mother of him or her."

Her heart squeezed, and she managed a nod. Shaw caught under her elbow, steadying her as they resumed their pace. Her gaze fell on a man standing before a storefront, his eyes following them. Alana made her gaze turn forward as if she hadn't noticed him. The press in her heart changed to a wild thumping. "That man by the milliner is one of Dixon's soldiers," she said, her voice low.

Shaw didn't change his stride but turned them down one

of the narrow, vacant streets.

"What is it?" Rabbie asked, the other Sinclairs coming up behind him.

"Dixon is about. Alana saw one of his men."

"Yet he hasn't tried to stop the French ship?" she asked.

"The commander who has our papers outranks him. Dixon likely wants to kill the bairn before she gets on the ship," Alistair said, his gaze going between them.

Alana hugged Rose closer, as if her love and body could shelter her from musket balls.

"Shaw," Alistair said, drawing out his name. "Ye don't think the bastard has been tricking us from the start, setting up Clan Sinclair to be the murderers of the king's infant bairn?"

"From the start?" she asked. "From the battle at Stirling? Has he been chasing you since then?"

Shaw's gaze snapped to her, but then it turned on his friend with a deep, seething fury spreading across his face. "What the bloody hell have ye been talking to Alana about?"

"Shaw," Logan called from the corner of the street. "There are more English." He jogged back toward them. "They are not dressed in their reds, though. Common clothes."

"If they get the bairn before we deliver her to the ship, Dixon will blame us for her death," Alistair said, grabbing Shaw's arm. "All we have to do is get the bairn to the French captain. Then we will have done our part to help the king. Take the document with the royal seal, and we will have our lands back."

Shaw's hands curled into tight fists. Alistair let go and took a step toward Alana, his arms out. "I will take the bairn. Dixon will be looking for the two of ye."

"Nay," Shaw said, shoving him back. "We will take the bairn."

"Shite," Alistair said, righting himself. He threw his arm

out. "Then go. We will guard your backs."

Alana hugged Rose and strode quickly away down the narrow street with Shaw, the others behind them moving slower, keeping watch.

"What is going on between you two?" Alana asked.

"Later," Shaw answered, his gaze surveying the buildings as they passed as if someone might fire down upon them with muskets.

Alana angled closer to one side, under the eaves, so she only had to look up at one set of windows. The street sloped down toward the bay. Her legs moved fast in her trousers, hitting her skirt with her long, urgent strides. Her heart thudded with worry and the race as she held the baby against her. Robert followed, his tail down as if he could tell something sinister was afoot. A low growl grumbled up from his chest.

Alana wanted to demand to know everything, the questions and odd glances between him and Alistair reaching a tipping point. Last night she'd wanted to hide in the dark warmth of ignorance, but not now. Now, she needed to be the leader of the Highland Roses and do whatever she could to keep the babe safe.

Rounding a corner, Shaw gripped her arm to lead her down another short path to the water. Dock workers heaved barrels and pallets, hooking them up to thick hooks to lift onto their ships. Their voices were brusque, peppered with crass curses. An occasional bark of laughter mixed with the caws from the seabirds, and the wooden planks squeaked as the water shifted beneath.

They ducked out from the buildings to hurry across the narrow dock. But instead of stopping there, Shaw ushered her toward the rocky ruins of what could only be St. Andrews Castle way at the far end and up a short grassy knoll. As they neared, Alana saw one of the hired wet nurses from the common room, the younger woman who said her name was Bess. Bess held her charge and talked with a man in military dress in the shadows before the stone walls of the main keep. Off to the side, two men crept closer to them. Dixon's men.

"*Mo chreach,*" Shaw cursed, and they broke into a run toward the castle, Alana cradling Rose's little head against her. "Traitors at arms," Shaw called out, and Bess jumped, pulling away from the man in red dress to disappear into the castle grounds while the man drew his sword.

With the baby before her, Alana couldn't fight, but she could protect. Her hair stick was in her hair, and she wore the *sgian dubh* in her boot beneath her skirt. "I will hide in the castle," she said to Shaw as they neared.

He drew his sword. "Keep Robert with ye."

"Come," Alana said, patting her leg to get the large wolfhound to follow her as she broke into a run toward the interior of the castle. Time and weather had broken through the main wall, and she hopped over it instead of seeking a door. Where had Bess gone? They should stay together.

She stuck close to the wall, hearing the clash of swords and curses from the men behind her. As she ran into the exposed courtyard she stopped, her eyes riveted on another woman standing opposite Bess and the baby. The other woman had a blade in her hand.

Breath frozen, Alana took several seconds before her mind could find the word. "*Màthair?*" For there in the ruins of St. Andrews Castle, standing with determination and what seemed like vigorous health, was Violet Campbell. Hair long and dark and worn in her usual braid, Violet whipped around, confusion and shock in the lines of her face. Robert went prancing into the center, sniffing at her mother's shoes. He hadn't been born before she left Finlarig.

"Alana? What are ye doing here?" she asked, her eyes locking onto her face. She shied away from the huge dog, and

Bess ran toward the far side of the ruins, disappearing inside the half-deteriorated walls.

"*Màthair*," Alana cried out again as emotion tumbled inside her. To see her mother strong and alive. "You have sight," she said, running toward her.

She grabbed her mother to her with one hand, still holding Rose between them. Her mother was stiff, breaking the awkward hug to touch Alana's face. "Why are ye here?" Violet asked, her gaze dropping to Rose in her arms.

"I was on my way to save you in Edinburgh," she said. "I only just found out that you were there, that you were even alive. We thought you dead when they brought Da's body home. Grey is the chief now. He is married and has his own son and daughter."

Her mother's eyes swelled with tears. She blinked and one fell out to cut a path down her cheek. "Ye should not be here, Alana. 'Tis dangerous."

"Why are you not in Edinburgh?" she asked, her hand resting on top of Robert's head as he came to sit next to her. "Did you escape on your own?"

Violet looked over her shoulder toward the main part of the ruins. "I am still earning my freedom."

"And you are not blind? A man told me at the Samhain Festival that you were alive but blind, and I came right away. Grey does not even know yet. Kerrick sent word."

Violet turned back, her face pinched. "No one cares what a blind woman is up to. It was easy enough to act after one of my fevers that first winter."

Lord, what had she gone through over the last two years? Alana's stomach clenched with guilt.

Her mother's gaze shifted to Rose. "Is that one of the three babes James is sneaking away to France?"

Alana's mind went blank for several seconds. Instinct to protect made her twist away as her mother grabbed for Rose.

"What are you doing?" she gasped as Major Dixon, wearing hose and short trousers, jogged into the courtyard from the side facing the sea. She tucked Rose against her and felt the babe squirm. Robert stood, growling low. "We need to go," she said to her mother. "He wants to kill her."

"Give it to me," her mother repeated.

"*Màthair*, we need to run." Alana's face turned back and forth between Dixon and her mother. She swallowed over the hard *thud* of her heart and wrapped both of her arms around Rose, sheltering her with her body. Her mother reached out and grabbed her arm, anchoring her there in the beaten grass.

"What are you doing?" Alana asked as the weight of horror dropped down upon her.

"I am freeing myself," her mother said, her words spitting from her clenched teeth. "Now give it to me." The silver edge of a *sgian dubh* slid free of her mother's skirt, and she held the dagger, her knuckles turning white with the force. "The babe must die."

Chapter Twenty

Shaw yanked his sword free of the Englishman's gut, and the man crumpled to the rocky path. He twisted to see Alistair yank his own sword from the soldier who had attacked him. Apparently almost getting skewered had shaken off the last of the effects of Fiona's tart. Shaw nodded and spun around to shove the Englishman fighting against Logan, throwing the man off-kilter so that Logan could easily finish him. The two soldiers who had held muskets at them had been the first to fall under Shaw's blade, their weapons awkward and slow up close.

Shaw heard Robert's barks inside the ruins. *Nay!* He ran in the direction of the dog. Where were Alana and Rose? Were there more of Dixon's soldiers hiding around the half-toppled walls and along the shoreline? There might be even more traitors against King James, willing to doom their own souls by killing innocent bairns. They could have met up with Dixon, adding to his numbers. Where the hell was Colonel Wendall? His men could help.

"Alana," he yelled, running into the dark interior of the

main keep, his bloody sword before him. "Alana!" An image of her lying across the rocks, bleeding from musket balls or slashes from a blade, sickened his stomach, his leg muscles contracting to push him even faster.

Out into the courtyard beyond the keep, Shaw saw Dixon tugging her through the broken back wall. "Shite." He ran across the rough weeds, leaping over fallen blocks of granite from the toppled walls. Where was the dog? "Dixon!"

Jumping down through the opening, he dodged, crouching down, as musket fire chipped the wall next to his head. *Damnation!* Dixon had a lit musket with him. But he'd just fired, which gave Shaw a good thirty seconds before he could reload, and that was if he didn't have to fight with a stubborn Highland lass protecting her bairn.

They disappeared from sight, and Shaw threw himself forward, grabbing the edge of a wall as he pulled himself around it. A deep cut in the bank plunged to the sea where the boulders dumped directly into the freezing depths. Farther to the right, the boulders gave way to a slip of sand where the French ship was anchored at the dock closest to the ruins. Horses were being led aboard, and men stood on the deck. None were within firing range, even if they thought to help save the bairn and Alana.

On the rocks, Shaw spotted Robert as he lunged at one of Dixon's men. The man screamed as the dog's large maw clamped down on his arm that held a musket. Shaw cut his gaze to the right where Dixon threw Alana onto the sand. He set his musket end down to reload the ball. A second woman ran over to Alana, grabbing her arm to help her stand. She wasn't one of the wet nurses.

"Hold on, lass," Shaw murmured as he watched Dixon raise the gun level. As soon as the he saw the tiniest twitch in Dixon's hand, Shaw dropped to the ground before he even heard the shot. The bullet hit somewhere behind him, shattering rock, and Shaw jumped up, hurling himself the rest of the way down to the beach, his feet churning up the sand as his legs and arm pumped, his bloody sword held ready in his other hand.

He kept his focus on Dixon but saw Alana struggle to pull away from the woman, shouting at her. Realizing that he wouldn't get the musket loaded in time, Dixon dropped the weapon and pulled his sword. Along the ridge above, Shaw saw several other soldiers running toward the castle, but Shaw's men and...

What the bloody hell? Alana's students and Kerrick were also there, plunging into the fight to keep the Englishmen from running down onto the beach to help their commander. Behind him, Robert barked and growled, perhaps at more English traitors creeping out onto the rocks.

"The infant needs to die, Sinclair," Dixon yelled, holding out his sword. "The one you have is the real princess, is she not?"

But Shaw wasn't going to be baited into discussion and swung his blade, the vibration singing through the air. *Clang!* Dixon met his attack, barely redirecting the force past him.

"James and his popish witch will raise the baby Catholic, especially in France," Dixon said, his teeth clenched as he stared at Shaw from between crossed steel before their noses.

Shaw shoved him back, bringing his sword around. "Leave the bairn and Alana, as well as the other innocent bairns, and I will spare your bloody life," he said.

"They are not innocent, Sinclair," Dixon yelled back. "They are all Catholic, sent by Catholic families to support the continuance of James's religious line."

"Sinclair?" Shaw heard the woman behind Dixon yell. Dread slammed into Shaw as her face came into focus. *Fok.* It was Violet Campbell, the Campbell chief's wife from Stirling, Alana's mother. He hadn't placed her face in all the commotion. She wasn't a prisoner in Edinburgh? And her round, angry eyes did not look sightless.

Dixon spun, his razor-sharp blade coming around. Shaw jumped back, his instincts propelling his legs to keep him in one piece. All the training he'd done to meet Edgar Campbell's attacks would save his life against the obviously skilled English swordsman.

"Lady Campbell?" he heard Kerrick yell from the top ridge. The Campbell warrior ran down the boulders flanking the beach. This was a catastrophic mess. Was his English contact even still here with the royal seal on the papers to give the Sinclairs back their lands? By now, the local magistrate would have been notified of a sword fight, especially one involving warring women. Which side of the royal and religious debate the local law fell on would either help Shaw or find them all tossed in the gaol. He needed to finish this quickly.

"James will never honor his promise to give you back your lands," Dixon said as he deflected Shaw's blow. "He did not when you turned against your own countrymen at Stirling, joining me to stamp out the Covenanters, and he will not after you have helped his daughter flee the country."

The words, loud with force, slammed into Shaw's chest. Alana had to have heard the bastard. He glanced toward her, and his heart clenched. Her lips were open, her face numb with shock. There was no time to utter a single true word to refute Dixon's statement. He must continue with his mission and hope that Colonel-Commandant Wendall would uphold his end of the deal when they brought James's daughter to the French ship. There was no other way to save his people this winter, to save Bren and set Reagan's headstone.

He pressed his sword against Dixon's, level between them. "Turn with me, Sinclair," the English major hissed, spittle coming from between his yellowed teeth. "We will overthrow the Catholic throne, and I will help convince the government to give back Sinclair lands."

"Lies are bitter on the tongue," Shaw said. "Like the ones ye told at Stirling that none of the Covenanters would be harmed. Do not expect me to ever believe a foking liar and turncoat ready to spill the blood of three innocent bairns."

Dixon's eyes narrowed. "You will die today along with the babes, then, and I will report to the king that it was you who did the deed, turning against him. Thanks to your uncle, Sinclairs are known miscreants. James will believe me, his loyal major who led the attack at Stirling." Dixon grinned wickedly. "Sinclairs will never have a home again."

Fury tried to sink its claws into Shaw, but he kept his focus. Dixon was talented with a sword and was purposely trying to bait him into a vengeful attack to tire him. When emotions raged within, they clouded his judgment, and right now, even a small mistake would be lethal. With the practiced discipline of a man raised on the knife's edge of violence under his uncle's brutal reign, Shaw inhaled, waiting, using his patience to prepare for Dixon's next move.

Dixon's grin pulled back into a snarl, and he shoved hard at Shaw. But Shaw had anticipated it and yanked back his sword to throw him off balance. He slid his short dagger free with his other hand and thrust it into Dixon's side, the force throwing the man to the rocky beach. The major's eyes went wide, his mouth opening. Shaw slammed his boot down on the handle, jamming the dagger completely into his middle until the hilt stopped it. A gurgling groan came from the evil man. "Sinclairs…will never…have a home…"

Shaw pivoted on his heel, bending in his stride to grab the hilt of his family sword. Standing a few feet away was Alana, holding the bairn against her. From the pain on her face, the tears streaming down her cheeks, he knew that she'd heard Dixon's words.

"Alana," Shaw said, coming forward.

"Do not touch my daughter with your dirty Sinclair hands," her mother yelled while Kerrick held the woman around the waist.

Alana shook her head, her lips opening to pull in a ragged breath. She closed her eyes for the first few words. "My mother was working for Dixon to win her freedom from Edinburgh prison. Rose is not safe here. Let us get her to the French ship."

Alistair ran down the slope, jogging up to them. "Dixon's men have been thrown over the other side. We best hide the major's body before the authorities get here and the lass's Highland Roses become outlaws with us."

"Alana," Shaw said again, but she wouldn't look at him. He tried to take her arm, and she turned away. "Lass, I need to explain. I would have last night."

Her gaze swung around to his, and in the evergreen eyes he saw such sadness, such pain, that it physically pierced through his chest. He nearly looked down to see if someone had stabbed him through. "We have had a week together," she said. "Do not blame me because I wanted one more night."

"I do not blame ye for anything," he said.

"One more night? Ye slept with him?" her mother screeched, twisting with Kerrick's lock around her waist. Fortunately, the woman seemed weaker than Alana's dog, and Kerrick managed to hold onto her.

"Lady Campbell, please," Kerrick said. "Calm down."

Logan and Mungo ran up to grasp Dixon's arms, dragging him toward the far side of the ruins. Robert ran with them, barking at the fallen man.

"Ye slept with the man who ordered his clan to help the English kill your father and imprison your mother," Violet Campbell yelled, her wild eyes making her look like someone afflicted with the insanity of grief and fury.

Shaw knew that look. Had seen it before in his own reflection after he found his mother pale and sightless in a puddle of blood at the base of the castle walk. There would be nothing said that was strong enough to break through Violet Campbell's hate. Did Alana share it?

She was already walking toward the ridge where her Roses stood. Kirstin ran partway down to help her and the bairn up the slope. Her friend whispered in her ear, glancing back at Shaw. Was she poisoning Alana with more...what? Truth?

Foking hell. He scraped a hand down his face and strode after her. Let Kerrick deal with her irate mother. He'd known that Alana would hate him, he just thought he'd have another day before reaching Edinburgh. Another day to tell her what had happened at Stirling, even if the memories were muddled for him.

With two more powerful strides, he was next to her. He sheathed his blood-soaked sword, something he would never think of doing before that day. "Alana, stop." He caught her arm, and she halted but didn't look at him.

"Let her go, Sinclair," Kirstin said, but he ignored her.

"We need to get Rose to the ship, so you can get credit for bringing her safely there," she said, her words just above a whisper.

"Dammit. I would have the truth out now before the partial truth can poison ye more against me." He didn't wait for a reply he wouldn't get and didn't care that her friend stood glaring at him while he talked. "I led my men down south that winter to..." He swallowed his pride. "To beg your father, the chief of the Campbells of Breadalbane, to help me reason with or defeat Edgar Campbell. Over the nine years since my uncle died and Edgar Campbell kicked us off Sinclair land, I had tried every avenue I could think of, but my petitions to the king were never returned. Even if your father would not convince Edgar to give us back our lands, my hope was to have your father convince him to let us live on the edge of the lands to the south. So many had already died, my own sister, and we were in the beginnings of another cruel winter." Shaw paused, watching her tuck the soft blanket under Rose's little chin, the bairn staring up at her face.

He took a deep breath. "When your father refused to help, I was furious, desperate." His eyes shut as he remembered the turmoil shooting through him, the anger making him curse to his trusted men. "And then Major Dixon arrived with his troops. He realized that he was outnumbered by the Covenanters and said that in exchange for our help breaking up the Covenanter meeting, he would personally take my petition straight to King Charles."

Kerrick walked past them, dragging Alana's mother. Both of them watched, but he didn't allow Lady Campbell to stop.

"I should have trusted my instincts and left or stayed to help the Scots. It was obviously not a religious gathering, Alana. Ye need to know that. Before the English showed up, they were discussing how some Englishmen who were sympathetic to their cause had broken into the king's circle and were drawing him out."

She looked at him, her expression pinched as if she wanted to ask a question, but it stayed inside her tightly shut lips.

"Shaw," Alistair yelled from the bluff.

"We need to go," Alana said but didn't try to pull away.

"Dixon told me he only planned to break up the meeting, send them home." He shook his head. "I would not have helped him slaughter Scots, even if they were Campbells."

"And yet you stayed," she said.

He released a breath. "I was…knocked unconscious on top of Rìgh. The horse led me out of the valley. Alistair found me after it was over. He said that they had begun to carry out my original order to help the English but had ridden away when they could not find me."

"How does a man over six feet tall, riding a huge warhorse, get knocked unconscious?" The narrowing of her eyes was like daggers hitting his already clenched chest. She didn't believe him.

He shook his head. "I had a lump on the back of my head with dried blood. A rock thrown most likely."

Alistair ran down the slope. "Ye two will have to finish this discussion later," he yelled.

Shaw turned to him, his hand itching to grab him by the throat, but he was right. He caught Alana's chin in his two fingers, looking down into her hard gaze. "We will talk more."

"After today, you will have what you came for," she said. "Victory for the Sinclairs. There is nothing more to say." She turned her face toward the docks, her chin slipping from his light grasp, and walked away as if he'd vanished from her thoughts.

• • •

He is lying. Could a man lie so well while staring someone straight in the eyes? *Da was plotting to kill the king.* Had her father given the assassins the idea to use Finlarig as a place to lure the king? *Ma was willing to kill a babe to escape.* Had she gone insane while imprisoned? *Shaw.* Shaw. *How could he have not told me? How can I trust him?*

Alana's thoughts twirled around her, making her both dizzy and perilously close to vomiting. Feeling her wobble, Kirstin kept a tight grip on her arm as they hurried with Rose down the path to the waiting ship. Robert caught up, his large body right next to Alana, giving her the strength of his presence. Several men stood on the dock, most of them in the red uniforms of the English. At this point, Alana didn't know who to trust with Rose.

"A bit of a battle down there?" the English officer asked Shaw, who was right behind her. He eyed Robert, whose large head swung back and forth as if trying to decipher who was the enemy.

"There are those within your ranks, Colonel Wendall, who would kill the princess along with any decoys," Shaw said, looking back to the beach. "I had no choice but to defend the princess with force."

"You killed Major Iain Dixon?" Wendall asked, his brows slightly raised, as if something humored him.

"Aye, he was attacking the bairn. Like I told ye last night, the bastard has been following us for days."

"His body is over there?"

"My men dragged him and his men inside the ruins," Shaw said.

The commander nodded. "We will take his body to King James, but right now it is time to get the last of these babies on your ship, Captain LeFevre."

Alana looked at the ship where the other two wet nurses stood on the deck holding their charges. "I must speak with Bess, to make sure she can care for R...for this babe, too. Otherwise she will die during the voyage."

"I will personally make certain that *la petite fille* will be cared for," the French captain said, his smile almost bored. He snapped his fingers, and one of his men came forward, arms outstretched for Rose.

Alana's heart squeezed, and she couldn't stop the tears from swelling out of her eyes. Maybe she should go with her. Her mother was free, and Kerrick would take her back to Finlarig. The Highland Roses would continue to learn without her. Her mother could continue to hate her for sleeping with the enemy, and Shaw could return to Girnigoe victorious with his royal papers.

Alana dodged the French sailor's reach, making Robert growl, showing his teeth. "I will go with her," Alana yelled. "I will make sure she is cared for and reaches France safely. I can even stay to see all three babes settled."

"What?" Kirstin snapped.

"Nay," Shaw said at the same time.

Alana stood tall without looking at any of them. She nodded to emphasize her words. "Take us aboard, Captain," she said, determination in the tension of her face. She clutched Rose to her chest and turned to Kerrick. "You will have to keep Robert here."

Colonel Wendall waved his hand. "You will be paid the same amount as the other wet nurses. Take them aboard."

"The papers for the Sinclair clan," Alana said, her face turned away so that she didn't have to look at Shaw or his men. She sunk down, her one hand supporting Rose, as she brushed her forehead against Robert's shaggy head, kissing him before standing back up to meet Colonel Wendall's gaze. "You will give them back their lands and castle?"

"That was the agreement," Colonel Wendall said, pulling a large sheaf of parchment from his military coat. "Signed and sealed by King James for the safe delivery of his daughter to the ship."

"Alana, no," Shaw said.

Out of the corner of her eye, she saw Alistair take the agreement from Colonel Wendall's hands even though Shaw was the one who'd fought for nearly ten years to win back his home for his people. Kerrick grabbed a rope coiled along the dock and looped it around Robert's thick neck. "Alana..." Kerrick said, shaking his head. She held her hand palm up at him to stop him from saying anything else. Yes, Grey would be angry, but maybe now that he had children of his own, he might understand her need to protect the little girl that had taken up space in her heart.

"Let Grey know that I will return when I know she is safe and loved," Alana said and waited for Kerrick's nod.

Shaw jumped in front of her. "'Tis not safe. Ye cannot go."

"If it is not safe for me, it sure as Hell is not safe for Rose. God willing, Captain LeFevre will get us to Calais, and then the French government will escort us safely to Paris, where I can make certain she is well cared for and…loved." The word "love" stuck in her throat, almost choking her. Because she knew, knew now as her heart broke looking at Shaw, that she had given up her heart to him. But he had not told her the truth, had not trusted her enough. How could he love her in return if he could not trust her? *He never said that he loved me.*

Tears filled her eyes again, and she turned toward the ship, exiling him like he had told her to do to Robert back at the festival. It seemed so long ago. Alana forced her legs to step forward, and a flutter of people surrounded her.

"Ye cannot go," Martha said, tears in her own eyes.

Izzy gestured frantically, her face drawn tight. Kirstin grabbed Alana's arm. "Do not go, Alana. Your brother will… Well, I don't know what he will do, but we will all suffer. And…" She shook her head, her own eyes looking wet. "I cannot… Ye are like my sister. I love ye." She stepped closer. "What if ye die, drown, get caught up in France by killers? Nay, Alana, I need ye."

"Surely you must reconsider," Lucy said. "You have only just now found your mother."

"Evelyn and Scarlet will go after ye," Cici said, her face more serious than Alana had ever seen before. "We all will." She glanced at the French captain. "Can I go, too?"

"Me, too," Kirstin said right away.

"We all will," Margaret yelled, Izzy nodding viciously

and pulling her hair stick out to hold like a dagger at the captain.

"Absolutely not," Kerrick said, but everyone, including Alana, ignored him. He threw his hands in the air, grabbed the end of the leash, and strode back to her mother who squatted on the ground, her arms clenched about her knees. Robert sat down next to her, his usual joyful face appearing sad.

Captain LeFevre looked amused. "As much as I would like to take such lovely *mademoiselles* on our voyage, I have only enough room and provisions for one woman with a *bébé*. Only *Mademoiselle* may come aboard," he said, holding out his hand toward Alana. One of his men yelled something down to him that she didn't understand. "We must go," the captain said.

Alana had started learning some French from Scarlet but hadn't gotten very far. She huffed, knowing that she would have to learn quickly. Everything was happening so fast that there wasn't time to think things through. But that also meant there wasn't time to think about Shaw, how he hadn't told her that he'd met her mother before, that he'd supported Major Dixon at Stirling, at least for a bit.

I must do everything, everything in my power as a chief, as a Sinclair warrior, and as a man to win back the land of my people. Everything. His words came back, haunting her. He had warned her that his clan was his priority but then had given her his oath right afterward.

She paused on her way to the ship and turned back to look at Shaw. "You said…" She wet her dry lip. "You said that you were mine, no matter what happened." Shaw stood there, and Alistair grasped his shoulder as if holding him back. Logan had the other arm. Alana shook her head. "I release you from your oath. I…I do not want you to be mine." It was the biggest lie by far floating in the air with all the other lies and foul truths that had been revealed.

I do not want you to be mine. I do not want you. I do not want Shaw. Alana clung to the lies as hard as she clung to the warm bundle strapped to her front and climbed the gangplank up to the ship's deck. Bess and the other wet nurse nodded to her but didn't leave their station at the rail. Alana kept walking to where large coils of rope were being thrown about and leaned her back against the thick mast. Only then did her face crumble inward, and she raised a shaking palm to her face, tears bleeding out of her to soak her hand.

Chapter Twenty-One

"A word," Captain Wendall said beside Shaw, but Shaw kept his gaze on Alana's soft form, watching her walk away to disappear on deck. "Chief Sinclair," he said, his tone stern and loud.

Shaw glanced to the gruff older man. "Ye have your princess safely aboard, and we have our papers." Shaw's words came even and low, a far different sound than the warrior yell resounding inside his brain.

Wendall nodded and leaned into him, lowering his voice. "I will let King James know of Sinclair loyalty when I bring back Dixon's body. Without my words and support, James could easily turn against the Sinclairs, yanking back all your lands, titles, and castle, making every last Sinclair an outlaw. Do you understand?"

Shaw's eyes narrowed with his increasing frown. "I understand ye are threatening me."

Wendall's mouth turned up into a half smile, his nostrils flaring as he inhaled. "Good. Remember that." The man pivoted and strode to mount his horse, and Shaw turned back to the ship, the man's cryptic threat already replaced by the pain of loss. It bored into his chest as if intent on hollowing him out.

By now, after a lifetime of loss, he should be used to pain that carved through him, leaving emptiness, an emptiness that nothing could fill. Not revenge, not whisky, not war, not even peace and friends. Alana had walked away. She'd taken Rose and climbed aboard a ship, and he couldn't even go get her back because he knew Alana wouldn't leave Rose. And Colonel Wendall had just made it very clear that his support required Rose to go to France.

He stood in a battle stance, his hands fisted at his sides as he watched the crew prep the ship to sail.

"Tell him," Logan said behind Shaw. "Damnit, look at him. He looks worse than when Reagan died."

"Let's get the fok out of here," Alistair said. "We have the documents with the royal seal. The mission is complete."

"Tell him what?" Rabbie asked. Somewhere behind Shaw at least two of Alana's friends sobbed. Kerrick cursed, and Alana's mother remained silent. Did she care so little about Alana that she could just let her sail away? Or had Alana's surrender in Shaw's bed driven the mother to apathy?

Shaw moved to the edge of the dock, looking for a glimpse of Alana. All he could see were the French captain's horses being led below on a ramp on deck and barrels of trade stacked in orderly rows. The gangplank was still down. What if he barged up it and grabbed Alana and Rose away? Alistair had the bloody papers, but would they mean anything if Wendall painted the Sinclairs as traitors to King James?

Damn it all! If the wet nurse could just assure Alana that she would take care of Rose. Not that he wanted the bairn to sail away, but if she was a princess, she would be taken well care of in France. "Alana," Shaw yelled, but no one paid him any attention.

"Fok Alistair, he thinks losing Alana is all his fault," Logan said and cursed again. Bloody hell, I will tell him." Logan strode closer, but Shaw didn't care about anything anyone wanted to tell him, unless it involved a way for him to get Alana off that ship or him to France. Could she ever forgive him for not stopping the slaughter of her father and capture of her mother?

Logan grabbed his shoulder, giving him a shake. "Shaw, ye were going to help Alana's parents once ye saw Dixon give the order to attack the group. Ye need to tell her that."

Alistair grabbed Logan's arm, yanking it off Shaw's shoulder. "Leave it be, man. We have the papers. Let us ride."

"Look at him," Logan yelled at Alistair. "He looks...like the day he found his ma bloody and broken under the castle walk. Tell him the truth."

His men's words began to penetrate Shaw's plans to chase after Alana and Rose. He looked at Alistair. "Tell me what truth?"

Alistair's face was red, his jaw clenched. His free hand gripped the back of his own neck, and he rolled his shoulders. "Ye were going to jeopardize what ye had worked so hard for. Dixon was a high-ranking English officer who would petition King Charles for our lands."

"That would be the same Dixon who was going to kill three innocent bairns and is right now bleeding out in the incoming tide over there," Logan said, pointing with a jabbing motion.

"Why else do ye think that Shaw was contacted for this mission?" Alistair countered, throwing his hands out. "King James just thought..." He sharpened his normal brogue into a skewed version of a royal English accent. "'Aye, I will ask that annoying laird up north to take my daughter to St. Andrews.' Nay, Dixon gave him your name and got that other colonel to bring these papers."

"Dixon was going to kill the bairns and blame the killings on the Sinclairs," Logan yelled back.

"I did not know he would do that, and if Shaw had backed out of helping Dixon at Stirling, I would not be standing here holding these papers," Alistair said.

Shaw turned to look at the two angry men. He knew that they had hot tempers and definite opinions about how they should rectify the loss of Sinclair holdings. But their blazing stares and clenched fists told him that this was something more than counter-opinions.

Shaw looked directly at Alistair. "What did ye do at Stirling?"

Alistair lowered the papers down, and Logan snatched them away from him. "I do not want ye bleeding all over them when Shaw hears what ye did," Logan said.

"Fok," Alistair said and raised his fists to his forehead, rubbing hard. He inhaled fully before meeting Shaw's gaze. "Ye were going to tell Dixon we would not help, that Sinclairs would defend the Covenanters if he turned the confrontation into a battle." He shook his head. "I could not let ye do it."

Shaw's jaw clenched as he waited to hear the words, but he remembered clearly how angry Alistair had been when he said he was going to ride down to stop Dixon. "Ye hit me in the head," Shaw said, watching him closely.

Alistair's gaze slipped away as if he couldn't look Shaw in the eye. "I was the only one close enough to reach ye."

"And stupid enough to try it," Rabbie said, hate for his cousin thick in his tone.

"He hit the back of your head with a rock," Logan said. "Knocked ye unconscious, and ye fell forward over your horse's neck. The beast led ye out of the mess."

"While Logan and I helped Dixon and secured his favor by riding down with them," Alistair finished.

Shaw stared at Alistair, his eyes moving to Logan, who

was nearly as guilty for keeping this from him. He reached forward, taking the thick roll of papers from Logan and handing them to Rabbie. The lad tucked them inside his sash across his heart and backed away.

"Bloody hell," Logan murmured, both hands sliding down his face as he realized that he, too, would soon bleed all over the papers.

Shaw shook his head. "Traitorous bastard," he said, staring at Alistair.

"But it worked," Alistair said, pointing to Rabbie's chest. "The end justifies the means," he said, quoting from one of the books Shaw's mother used to teach them to read as lads.

"Because we did not help the chief of the Campbells of Breadalbane, he is dead and his wife will order all Campbells to destroy the Sinclair clan," Shaw said. "We have won back our castle and lands, but we will be besieged by the thousands of Campbells across Scotland. Did ye think of that?"

Alistair glanced at Violet Campbell, who now stood, watching the French ship as if looking for a sign of her daughter.

"Or are ye now planning to murder her?" Shaw asked. "And now all the Highland Roses who overheard?"

Alistair's face tightened, paling. "Nay."

Shaw looked at Logan. "The two of ye may have started a war that will never end until the last drop of Sinclair blood soaks the earth."

Logan's mouth dropped open, his brows raised. He pointed at Alistair. "He did that. I told him not to, but once ye were unconscious he was the acting chief. I...followed his...orders..." Logan's words faded off, his face growing red.

The anger at his two friends should have erupted an inferno within Shaw, making him dole out immediate punishment and declare banishment. Rabbie and Mungo stood near as if waiting for it. But Shaw only felt sick, sick of the betrayal, the secrets, and the darkness that had plagued his life since his father died.

The only light had come from Alana, and she was sailing away from him. He turned toward the ship, the gang plank already raised. The French sailors scurried around the decks, coiling up ropes and loosening sails. Long poles pushed against the pylons holding up the dock, to encourage the ship to move out into open water.

"I am going to France," he said.

"What?" Logan spit the word out.

Shaw turned to him, his gaze taking in all of them. "And ye will oust Edgar Campbell, defeat any Campbells that Alana's mother sends, without killing any of Alana's family, and prepare Girnigoe Castle for our return."

"*Our* return?" Alistair asked, his face and tone wary.

"Aye. When I bring Alana back from France, if she forgives me, she will be the lady of Girnigoe Castle." He stepped forward, grabbing Alistair's shirt at the neck, his fist curled under the man's chin. He leaned in to stare hard into his wide eyes. "Are my orders clear?"

Shaw felt his hand tightening, his arm lifting Alistair up so that the man stood on the toes of his boots. How easy it would be to slip his grip up to Alistair's bristled, dirty neck, squeezing the bastard until his windpipe collapsed. He knew no one would stop him. From the look on Alistair's face, he knew that, too.

"Aye, Shaw," Alistair stammered out. Shaw could feel his Adam's apple rise and fall with his hard swallow.

"Bloody hell!" Kerrick yelled.

Shaw's gaze snapped up to where the Campbell warrior stood staring down the dock. He pointed, and Shaw turned, dropping Alistair with a shove. The man sputtered, his hands resting on his knees.

Shaw spun to see a line of men standing with Colonel

Wendall. Wendall's arm was extended as his men fired at the ship with muskets at the same time at least ten of them shot arrows blazing with fire. They hit the ship's sails, catching quickly as if the arrows dripped with fiery resin. Too far from the dock for men to jump to safety, the crew who weren't shot with musket fire scrambled to put out the growing flames. Shaw ran to the dock, looking to the Englishmen.

Wendall's gaze fell directly on him, and he gave a nod. *Without my words and support, James could easily turn against the Sinclairs, pulling back all your lands, titles, and castle, making every last Sinclair an outlaw.*

The man wanted the princess dead, too, but would put the blame on Dixon and remain in King James's favor. Wendall turned, issuing orders for another round of lit arrows to be released, and then mounted his horse, disappearing with his band of men as townspeople ran to the edge to see the growing inferno in the bay.

"Wendall?" Logan yelled.

"Already gone," Alistair said, and Shaw realized they'd run up next to him, but his focus turned back to the ship where Alana and Rose and the other innocent bairns were.

Kirstin grabbed his tunic, yanking it back and forth. "Wendall just paid ye off to let the bairns die in that fire, but Alana's on there." She looked to the ship. "And she is...oh God, she is terrified of fire." Tears streamed down Kirstin's face.

Blast. Would Alana be able to think straight with the fire growing around her? Shaw drew his sword, an instant reaction to threat that could do nothing against fire.

"What do we do?" Alistair asked, his voice filled with so much remorse.

Shaw didn't answer, just threw his sword on the ground and kicked off his boots.

• • •

"Oh my God," Alana whispered, her breaths shallow and fast as her heart pounded beneath Rose and the wrappings holding her to her chest. She crouched low by the barrels, her gaze riveted to the fire licking up the sails. It crackled and flared in the breeze, racing higher and dropping bits of flaming sailcloth to rain down on the deck. Its sinister hunger and the breeze made it catch on the wooden crates surrounding them.

She was paralyzed. Memories of the walls of Finlarig covered with fire as it ate up the tapestries made tears swell out of her eyes. Smoke. Panicked yelling. Desperate stomping and slapping. Closing her eyes, she was once again trapped within Finlarig Castle after the English had thrown her inside to burn with her family.

Someone ran past her, stepping on her foot, but the pain was nothing compared to the squeezing of her heart. She sucked in a breath, coughing on the smoke. Rose cried, and Alana opened her eyes to see the babe's gaze on her, watching her with wide blue orbs. Was the smoke clogging her little lungs? Alana caught her one little hand that had wiggled free of the blanket. Rose's long, slow-moving fingers wrapped around Alana's thumb, squeezing. The trust in her gaze broke through the haze of panic as abruptly as a slap.

Alana blinked, forcing several even breaths, coughing with the smoke. She used her legs to push up out of her crouch and unhooked her heavy skirt. *I am not trapped. I am outside.* She looked up at the sky through the smoke. Granted, she was on a boat that had pulled away from the dock, the water was frigid, and she had a newborn babe to keep warm. "But I am not trapped," she told herself out loud. She gasped, jumping back, her hands over Rose's head, as a large section of sail dropped, showering sparks of burning cloth on them. She lowered her lips to the baby's covered head, kissing it through the blanket. "I will get you out of here, Rose."

Shaw. The name pressed through her mind like a prayer. *Shaw.* If he were with her, he could help. They could work together again to save Rose. Had he left the docks when she boarded? Would she never have a chance to accept his apology, because she knew he would apologize again? For what? For doing whatever he could to save his remaining sister and clan? He'd told her that from the beginning. Maybe he *had* been knocked unconscious when he decided not to help the English. The desperate need to hear his story reverberated through Alana. To look into his beautiful gray eyes, to feel the stroke of his finger over her cheek. She didn't want to die not knowing the truth...or telling Shaw that... none of it mattered. "I love you," she whispered. She didn't want to die without telling him that.

Alana's gaze jerked left and then right. From the quick destruction of the flames, she could tell that there was no saving the ship. She tucked Rose's little hand back inside the blanket. "We have to get off," Alana whispered, her arms hugging around the baby as she ran down the narrow path made by the barrels. The smoke made it difficult to see, but then the wind reached in dispersing it but also feeding the growing flames.

Darting around the end of the barrels, she tried to run for the rail closest to the docks. She dodged two men running by and heard the cry of one of the wet nurses farther down the rail. "Help!" the woman called. "Help us!"

Alana ran to her where she cradled her charge who was crying. "Where is the other babe?" Alana asked.

"Here!" called the older woman, running up, thankfully with her baby with her. The woman's eyes were wild, her hair singed, making Alana wonder if part of the sail had fallen on her. "We will die if we do not get off," she said, desperation in her face making Alana think she might jump into the freezing water.

Alana grabbed her arm. "The babe will not survive it." For a second, she thought the woman might just drop the babe and leap over the edge, but she nodded quickly, like a nervous bird.

Beside them two sailors climbed over the rail, the splash of their descent sending spray upward. Alana looked over the rail, and her breath caught.

The two sailors were swimming the twenty feet to the dock, but passing them on the way over was Shaw. His powerful arms cut through the freezing water as if he were born to the sea. Head down, bare feet kicking, his strokes pulled him across the distance. On the dock behind him, Alana saw Alistair dive in, followed by Mungo and Logan. Kirstin jumped up and down, ripping her skirt away to dive in after the men, her legs encased in the wool trousers. Kerrick waved his hands at Rabbie and then followed Kirstin, all six of them in the dark, frigid water between the dock and the ship.

Tears flooded Alana's burning eyes, and she caught Bess's sleeve, shaking her arm. "They are coming to help us." She ran over to a coil of rope that had held the vessel to the dock, the end being tied to the ship. Squatting down to lift with her legs, she heaved. "Help me get this over the rail," she yelled, and the other two women ran over, the three of them struggling, babies tied to them, to lift and drop the thick rope over the side.

Crash! Alana spun to see one of the heavy sails having dropped down from up high, its flames dancing across the wooden barrels. The relief from seeing Shaw squeezed into panic again in her chest, and she struggled to draw breath. She turned back to the rail, her fingers curling into the polished wood. Another man jumped overboard next to them.

"Isn't there a little boat off the side somewhere?" Bess asked.

Alana leaned over, looking left and right. "Where is it?" Above her, Captain LeFevre yelled orders in French, soot and fury making him look like an avenging demon, as his arms worked to send his remaining men scurrying with buckets that they'd hauled up from the bay. But he must be able to tell that the wind and dry cargo was too much for the crew to battle.

Shaw climbed the rope that they had dropped. Alana watched him pull his dripping body up from the water, hand over hand.

"Shaw," she called. He didn't look, but his climb grew faster, and he used his bare toes to catch the edges of the portholes, propelling himself to the top. She backed up as he threw a leg over, jumping aboard.

He spun toward her, his face red, water dripping from his hair into his face. He'd never looked so beautiful. "I love you," she yelled, the knot inside her unfurling. "Even if I die, you know," she said. "I love you." Relief at getting the words out made her feel weak.

He grabbed her to him, careful of Rose between. "Ye are absolutely *not* dying today," he said, his words sharp, but he reached to cup her cheek, sliding a cold thumb across her skin. It gave her strength.

She nodded. "Then let us get off this boat."

"Blasted hell," Alistair cursed as Mungo, who'd just climbed aboard, helped him over the side. "The whole bloody shore is swimming to a burning ship."

Logan climbed over the rail then, his bare feet hitting the boards hard. "The horses. They were loading horses below."

"*Mo chreach*," Shaw cursed. "Go on." Logan and Mungo ran into the smoke, toward the hull full of trapped horses.

"We can swim the women over, lower them down,"

Alistair said, gesturing to the rope.

"The babes cannot withstand such cold water," Alana yelled, shaking her head. "There must be a boat."

"Find it," Shaw ordered, and Alistair dodged men through the shifting smoke to the far side of the boat.

"Look out," came a shout from the smoke, and large bodies ran up from the decks below, snorting. "Lower the gangplank so they can jump in," Logan yelled. Shaw and Mungo threw open the gate so that the side was open, backing up. The horses wouldn't jump in until there was no other choice.

Alistair emerged from the chaos. "There is a rowboat off the port quarter," he said.

Shaw grabbed Alana's arm. "Wait," she yelled. "Kirstin."

He tipped his head toward the side. "Kerrick caught her," he said, and a glance showed the two of them drenched and watching from the dock with the rest of the Roses and her mother. A sob threatened Alana, but she turned away. Her mother hated her, but she didn't know everything, didn't know what Alana had realized when she thought she'd die. She loved Shaw Sinclair. And love was stronger than revenge and hate.

His hand was warm around her own as he led her through the maze of smoke-filled paths, dodging burning crates. "Wendall gave LeFevre crates of dry hay instead of goods," Shaw yelled back to her as they jumped over one barrel that had broken open to show the hay. "So it would burn quickly."

Colonel Wendall? He was responsible for the ship catching on fire? She glanced behind her where Alistair helped the other two women follow, both clutching their babies. Racing to the far end, Shaw let go of her to grab one of the two crew members who was climbing into the small boat to be lowered. "The ladies and bairns get the boat," he said.

The one he grabbed threw up his hands, eyes wide. "I no swim," he said in broken English.

Idiots! Sailors who never learned to swim. "Fool," he said and motioned to the boat. "Ye will make room for the women and bairns." The man nodded vigorously, and he turned to the second sailor. "And ye?" The sailor held up two fingers pinched together and rattled off something in French. She didn't know if Shaw understood him, but he cursed again. "The two of ye will row them to shore," he said, pointing to the land. They both nodded like chickens pecking on scattered corn.

Shaw helped Alana climb aboard the raised rowboat, his strong arm under hers as she lifted her leg over the gunwale. "I will lower ye down slowly," he said.

Alana rubbed Rose's back. She'd grown quiet in all the commotion, and Alana hoped she was well. "Then you will follow?" she asked, scooting over as Alistair helped the other two ladies into the boat, the Frenchman taking up the oars and nodding.

Shaw met her gaze as he and Alistair began to lower the boat to the choppy water of the bay below them. Her fingers clutched the side of the little boat. "Shaw?"

"Aye," he yelled down, bracing his legs. "I will follow. I have a need to hear what ye said when I boarded without flames roaring around ye."

She kept her gaze on him as they lowered, the muscles of his arms bulging as he slowly gave the rope out little by little. A cold spray of water misted off the bay, but it was the fire roaring up like a furious, greedy monster behind him that made a shudder spread through her. With the ship packed full of hay and made entirely of wood, it would go quickly.

The older woman was praying loudly opposite her while Bess just stared at Alana. "Will it explode when the fire reaches the gunpowder below?" she asked.

Alana's gaze snapped back up to Shaw, and she waved her hand, almost rising out of her seat. "Jump in!"

Chapter Twenty-Two

"Shaw!" Alistair yelled.

Shaw turned away from Alana to where Alistair pointed down alongside the ship toward the bow, which faced the other ships along the dock. "Wendall's waiting for them."

Bastard. The colonel was standing on shore, farther down, watching the boat burn. He had three armed men with him, each one willing to give up his soul for shooting a wee bairn. If he couldn't burn them or drown them, he'd just shoot them.

"He does not see the rowboat yet," Shaw said.

"He will," Alistair said.

Shaw shoved his arm. "Help Logan and Mungo with the horses and get off this thing before the gunpowder blows." Without another word or thought, Shaw threw himself out over the gunwale, pointing his hands overhead to dive, cleaving into the bay next to the rowboat. The shock of cold water radiated along his muscles, but years of swimming in icy lochs made the minor cramping familiar. Turning upward, he broke the surface and easily cut through the water to the side of the rowboat.

"Wendall is waiting to shoot ye," he yelled up at Alana. "We need to hide behind this burning beast." He spit the salty water from his mouth. "And then row to the castle ruins." His legs churned against the water under him. How long could he last in the cold North Sea before numbness took him under?

Alana reached over the side to grab his hands. "We need to get you in here."

He shook his head. "It will capsize."

"Here," Bess cried, throwing a small barrel over the side. "It floats."

Shaw swam to it, avoiding the one Frenchman's oar. "Turn around," he yelled up at him, pointing out into the bay to head north toward the shore of the castle ruins.

"*Quoi*?" he asked, shaking his head.

"You need to row that way," Alana said, pointing toward the ruins of St. Andrews.

"*Non*," the other crewmember said, and started to push his oar through the water.

"*Mousquet*," Shaw yelled, pointing toward the bow. His mother had long ago started teaching him French, but he knew very little. He'd never regretted avoiding his mother's French lessons more than right that very moment.

The man still shook his head, determined to row the shortest way to the dock. Shaw, kicking hard, surged upward and grabbed the man's oar, yanking it out of his hands to throw in the water. The sailor started yelling obvious curses while the other started rowing again in Wendall's direction.

The cold was penetrating Shaw's muscles, making it harder for him to work, and the small barrel had floated away when he let go to grab the oar. One of the women above him in the boat gasped, and he heard Alana's words slice through the sounds of chaos around them.

"He said row that way," she said, her words punctuated

and full of deadly determination. He glanced above to see her holding her *sgian dubh* in her throwing hand aimed at the rowing crewmember.

With the bairn still tied to her chest, Alana was the powerful image of a warrior mother, saving her child. In her other hand, she clutched her hair stick, its deadly point lodged at the back of the first sailor's neck. One shove upward and she'd pierce his brain. Something he apparently realized as he started to yell at the other man who bobbed his head. His oar pulled to the side, turning the nose of the little boat around.

Alana threw a rope over the side toward Shaw, and he grabbed it. He needed to swim to keep the blood flowing through his numbing body. Sliding on top of the water, he began to slice through the small waves, concentrating on keeping his legs moving toward the ruins.

She yelled something to him, but he couldn't hear her over the water flooding his ears. *Keep swimming. Keep going.* He didn't care how numb he grew, he would keep swimming, for he needed to hear the words Alana had said on the ship.

I love you. Had she meant them, or had fear, panic, and then relief that he'd come to help pushed the words onto her tongue? Damn if he'd die not knowing. The hope that there might be forgiveness within Alana kept his legs kicking, his arms swinging overhead to cut through the choppy, icy water. He'd seen men die in the cold ocean off of Sinclair land, even in the summer, their strokes slowing until they sank, falling into the sleep of death in the ocean depths.

Bloody hell. Not me. Not when Alana had said she loved him. *I love you. I love you.* The three simple words began to take on the cadence of his strokes as he pushed himself to keep up with the rowboat. Its zigzag pattern, due to the single oar, slowed its progress across to the rocks tumbling at the base of the castle.

The water cleared his ear as he tipped his face to gulp

another breath, and Alana's voice sang to him. "Keep going." He stroked, right, left, tipping up again. "Almost there."

He looked through the water swamping his eyes to see the rocky coastline. God, let Wendall's men have already taken Dixon's body. Or would they be there, ready to shoot them anyway?

But with the cold slowing him, there was no other option but to climb out of the brutal waters. His bare foot hit something, but the numbness made it impossible to distinguish. Rocks or sand, he didn't care and let his legs drop to walk out of the bay. He looked up to see Alistair standing there, his arms outstretched to haul him up onto the rocks. Logan, soot on his face and hair singed, held a blanket.

"Dammit, Shaw! Take my hand," Alistair yelled. "We both know I was foking wrong."

The rowboat lodged up against the shore, and the Roses surged forward to help Alana and the others out. He turned back to Alistair and grabbed his hand, letting him pull him out of the North Sea's grip. "Wendall?" Shaw asked.

"I knew ye would be coming over here," Alistair said as Logan came up to throw the blanket over Shaw. "So, we ran over here and dragged Dixon and his men up to the front of the castle. Wendall's men already collected them."

Shaw watched Alana hand Rose to Rabbie and run toward him, the Roses following right behind her.

"I told him I saw the ladies and babes die in the flames when I went down to get the horses," Logan said, yanking a hand through his blackened hair. Guilt still sat heavy in the lines around his eyes. He carried Shaw's discarded boots and Sinclair sword. "I used enough curses that I think he believed me." He set the items on the ground, the cleaned sword and scabbard balanced on the boots.

"And we all started screaming and crying," the usually-smiling student, Cici MacInnes, said. Kirstin and Kerrick were wet, blankets around them, and Violet Campbell stood close by, her hands clasped, tears running down her cheeks. Robert, the end of his leash dragging behind him, circled them.

Alana reached for Shaw, her hands warm against his cheeks. "You are freezing."

"And ye are warm," he said, his hand catching one of hers.

Her green eyes were full of worry. "We need to get you dry, give you feverfew just in case."

He leaned in closer. "And then we need to talk. No running away. No climbing on a ship to France." His words were low, gruff.

Boom! Shaw felt the impact through the ground as the ship exploded out in the bay. Alana jumped toward him, and he caught her in his arms as she craned her neck behind her to see the burning debris rain down. Shaw ached to pull her completely in, surrounding her so that nothing could hurt or scare her again. He breathed deeply, his gaze covering her from the tight curls about her face where the ocean spray beaded to the strength in her stance. Every detail about Alana Campbell dug into him, tethering him to her.

"Colonel Wendall did this?" she asked, turning back to face him.

He nodded. "The English monarchy is going to tumble soon if one of James's Colonel-Commandants is killing his heirs."

There was no sign of Wendall or his men, apparently eager to leave the traitorous scene. No doubt, he would tell the king and queen that their daughter had perished in the fire. Hopefully he would keep his word about the Sinclairs dutifully bringing her to the ship.

Rabbie cradled Rose against him, trying to calm her after the blast. Within his kilt were the papers granting the lands and castle back to the Sinclairs. Aye, they had the papers, but at what cost? He no longer trusted his two closest men. They had almost been killed, leaving their clan without leaders and their best warriors. And Alana's mother hated them. But Alana was holding onto him, and they'd saved three innocent bairns. Och, he was suddenly weary. Very weary.

The two French crewmen started to walk off. "Does anyone speak French?" Shaw called out, motioning to Mungo who raced after them, stopping them with his sword out. The men paused, looking back in alarm.

One of the Rose students held up her hand: Lucy Kellington the Englishwoman. "I do."

"Tell them not to speak of the women and infants," Shaw said. "If asked, they are to say they died in the fire. Otherwise..." Shaw turned his lethal stare on the men. "I will hunt them down, and they will never speak another word again."

Shaw kept his features hard as stone while the woman spoke to the men in a rolling cadence. They each bobbed their head. Only then did Mungo lower his sword, and they hurried toward the docks where soggy men stood, gesturing wildly at the burning remains of the *Queen's Song*, and dripping horses shook their manes. LeFevre was nowhere to be seen. Had the French captain been on board when the gunpowder exploded? He'd also trusted Colonel Wendall.

The other two wet nurses hurried over to them. Bess held her baby close. "This child is my widowed sister's. She lives in the country and doesn't talk to anyone. I would take her home and help to raise her safely. No one will know she lived."

The older of the two had tears in her eyes. "I am Alyce. I have no home, nowhere to go. I was promised a comfortable life in France for me and my baby, but that is impossible now."

There were so many issues, details to consider, people to help. 'Twas the burden of being the Sinclair chief, but helping people was also a gift. He hadn't been able to help his mother or his sister, but he could help his countrymen, women, and their bairns.

Alana squeezed his hand and turned outward next to him, as if they were one. "You have both been exceedingly brave, and we will make certain that the best possible outcome be awarded you." Alana sounded like a queen or a Highland chief's wife. The thought flared through him.

More tears flowed out of Alyce's eyes, and the two ladies nodded, clinging to one another. Rose's cry brought Rabbie closer. "She will not calm. I think she is hungry," he said.

"Too much going on around her," Kirstin said, peeking over his shoulder as she clutched the wool blanket at her chin. She wiped a finger under her eye and smiled at Alana, coming forward to hug her. "I know how she feels."

"You are wet," Alana said.

"I jumped in to swim to the boat when the fire started," Kirstin said and glanced at Shaw. "Just in case the brawny Highland warrior needed some help." Her lips tipped upward in something of a wry smile. A truce perhaps?

"I had to pull her back to shore," Kerrick said, shaking his head, his hair spreading water about.

Rose continued to fuss. Alana opened her arms to take her, but before Rabbie could give her the bairn, Violet Campbell threw herself into the middle of them. Shaw stepped back as the two wrapped their arms around each other.

Alana's mother openly sobbed. "I thought…I thought ye would die." She pulled back, her cracked, dry hands cupping her daughter's cheeks. "I am so sorry. I…I thought all had forgotten me. I was desperate to get home. Major Dixon saw through my blind woman act and said that if I did not help him get rid of the Catholic heir that he would reveal me. But if I helped him, he would see me free to return to Finlarig."

"Shhhh…" Alana said, pulling her mother close again. "It is well now. I am so sorry that we did not know. We would have come right away." She held her hand out with the ring on it. "They sent your wedding band back with Da. We thought that meant you were dead, too." Violet looked at her hand where the ring sat and clasped Alana in another hug.

Waaaaa! Rose would not settle. "Bring her here," Shaw said and held his arms out for the wee bairn. She was likely wet and hungry, and nothing but Alana would help.

"There now, lass," Shaw said as he took the bairn up. His deep voice seemed to catch Rose's attention. "Your ma cannot hold ye right now. I will have to do," he said, holding his thumb under the bairn's tiny fingers. They curled around him as her big blue eyes stared upward, her cries softening. A wave of warmth ran through him as he looked at the sweet bairn, so strong even at one month old.

"Your ma?" Alana asked, having turned to him, eyes questioning.

A smile touched his mouth. "Aye. Rose, our bairn."

"Our?" she asked, her eyes swelling with tears.

He shook his head. "I will not take back my oath, Alana," he said. "I am yours, and I will protect this bairn as my own." He swallowed, hope nearly choking him. Everyone stood around them, staring in silence, but his gaze only rested on the beautiful woman before him. The one who had continually showed her courage, compassion, and strength in the face of every challenge. The squeeze of Rose's wee fingers on his thumb helped him to find his own words.

"If we live apart, it will be difficult for me to protect her," he said. He exhaled, trying to find the words. "And I do not think I have the strength to watch ye walk away from me again."

Alana's breath sucked in quickly, and she wet her lips. "Do you mean...you are going to carry me off over your shoulder again?" she whispered.

He kept his distance, letting her make her own decisions.

Everyone held their tongue, even baby Rose. He slowly shook his head, keeping his gaze connected with the bonniest green eyes he'd ever seen.

"Nay. I mean, Alana Campbell, will ye wed me? Become the mistress of Girnigoe Castle where we can raise wee Rose and all the other bairns we are blessed with?"

Her hand rose to her mouth as a small sob came out. Shaw took a step toward her, but he couldn't hold her with the bairn in his arms. And he must know her answer if he was ever going to breathe again. He must hear it from her lips, here before her family.

Rabbie stepped up to Rose, but Violet Campbell reached for the bairn first. "Come to your grandmother, little Rose. I think we started off all wrong." Violet met Shaw's eyes and gave him a small nod. After a pause, he slowly let the woman take the bairn. She smiled down at the little face, swaying as the other Highland Roses gathered around her.

Shaw turned back to Alana, his arms dropping to his sides. He couldn't force her into them, couldn't lure her somewhere she might not want to be. He met her watery gaze. "Alana Campbell, will ye marry me?"

She sucked in a trembling breath. "Yes," she said. The word tore through him with the power and razor edge of a blade. He stepped forward, his arms open, and she threw herself against him.

"*Tha gaol agam ort.* I love ye," he said, cupping her cheek with one hand as he pulled her tightly into the circle of his body.

"I love you, Shaw Sinclair." She reached up to pull his mouth down to hers, sealing her oath with a kiss that filled him with a surge of happiness and strength. He lifted her off the ground, swinging her around as she laughed, only to set her back down and kiss her again, and again, and again.

Epilogue

"Time to walk," Grey Campbell said, looking down at Alana. He smiled, his brows lowered. "Unless ye want to run away screaming. I can slaughter Shaw and his party."

Alana smiled up at her big brother. "The only direction I am running is north," she said. "But I appreciate your offer." Although she doubted even her mighty brother could beat her brawny betrothed.

He squeezed her arm. "And we will be going north with ye after this," Grey said. "To make certain Edgar Campbell clears out of Girnigoe and leaves Sinclair land."

"I just hope he will leave peacefully with the money that Shaw has been saving to repay his uncle's debt," she said.

Grey leaned his face closer to her. "I will pay the remainder of the Sinclair debt that Shaw cannot."

Alana's eyes grew wide. He nodded. "'Tis your dowry payment, and Evelyn has plans for ye to start a school for lasses at Girnigoe Castle, a second Highland Roses School." He stood up tall but cut his gaze back to her. "And if Shaw ever leaves ye or ye get tired and kick his arse out, the castle and lands are yours. He knows. I made him sign a document in blood."

Alana couldn't tell if her brother was teasing or not but grabbed him in a hug. "Thank you, Grey."

"Aye now," he said after a moment and pushed her gently back from him. "Do not muss the updo that Mistress Jane wove in your hair else she will stick me with one of her needle rings that Cat told us about."

She laughed softly, pulling away to peek around the stone arch in Finlarig Castle, her smile fading when she didn't see Shaw. The great hall was filled with the Campbells of Breadalbane. Alana's mother sat at the front beside Gram. Having returned to find Finlarig in the hands of more English, Violet was just starting to find her place at the school with her mother-in-law.

Gram held one of Grey's twins while Evelyn sat next to her, holding the other. Scarlet and Aiden sat beside Evelyn, Aiden holding their newborn babe over his large shoulder, patting their little boy with a slow tap. Even Cat and Nathaniel were back from closing down his estate in England, all of them rushing to Finlarig when word reached Grey about their mother being alive and then about Alana being abducted.

Kerrick sat next to Lucy Kellington, the two of them inseparable since returning home. He probably would be holding her hand if he wasn't putting his muscle into keeping Robert on his tether next to him, the wolfhound determined to run amok greeting everyone.

The Highland Rose students and instructors all sat flanking the holly-bedecked aisle with Kirstin waiting up at the front to stand beside Alana as she took her vows. Kirstin had been her best friend from childhood and was even now planning to stay by her side as she journeyed to her new home at Girnigoe Castle.

"Did you tie Shaw up and leave him to rot somewhere?"

Alana asked, looking at her frowning brother.

His brows rose. "Now that idea has merit."

"Grey," she warned, but he tipped his head toward the front of the hall, making her turn.

Behind the elderly Protestant minister, Shaw Sinclair strode inside the keep. Alana's chest squeezed, and a smile bloomed on her face. Strength and dignity commanded his every step. He wore a cleaned Sinclair tartan kilt, the sash flowing down over one of his broad shoulders, his chest covered in a bright white tunic of fine linen that Grey had given him. His sword hung in the scabbard at his side, and his boots were polished. Shaw's beard was trimmed short, leaving his cheeks smooth, and his waves of dark hair had been cropped above the chin.

His gaze raked across the crowd, but she knew he couldn't see her hidden in the shadows of the arch. Did he worry that she'd taken Grey up on his offer to run? She almost laughed at the ridiculousness of the idea. For the only person she wanted to be with, besides the little infant girl being carried by Rabbie behind Shaw, was the man that she'd grown to respect and love. Not just for his bravery and fierceness, but for his gentle touch, golden soul, and compassion.

The other Sinclairs followed behind, all cleaned up, trimmed, and wearing borrowed tunics with their cleaned kilts. Even Alistair and Logan, remorseful and quiet since returning, walked with them. Rose was dressed in white lace and bundled in a green blanket to match Alana's dress.

"Ready?" Grey asked as everyone stood, looking toward the alcove where they hid in shadows.

Alana straightened the long folds of the green silk mantua around her, a gift from the Worthington sisters, and adjusted the crown of matching mistletoe woven amongst ribbons of red and white in her curls.

Alana took a deep breath. "With my whole heart," she

said, bringing a smile to Grey's usually stern face.

He leaned in to kiss her cheek. "Ye are lovely, little sister."

She beamed, turning to face front, and they stepped out from the alcove, pausing for Izzy to fix the long, embroidered train behind her. Izzy came around the full gown smiling, touched her heart with her hand, and hurried up front with the other Rose students.

Alana held Grey's arm as the musicians started a pretty tune with a slow cadence. She focused completely on Shaw waiting for her, his face even more handsome, reflecting hope and his love for her. The aisle, with everyone standing, watching on either side, seemed so long. Yet the trip down it was over before Alana could even notice the effect that Scarlet had championed. Everyone held a fragrant sprig of evergreen or holly, giving the room the feel of a winter forest with white ribbons and swaths of fabric swooping like snow under the rafters and across the mantel and windows set in the granite blocks. Candles lit and the fire cheery, the room was warm and full of smiles.

Alana stopped opposite Shaw, meeting his happy gray eyes. The minister leaned toward him. "Who does the bairn belong to?" he asked, confusion pinching his brows.

Shaw kept his gaze on Alana. "She is our daughter, Rose Sinclair," he answered.

The minister clucked his tongue. "Well then, ye should have been saying these vows months ago. Best get on about this."

Alana stifled the laugh that threatened, keeping her lips pinched tight. But the happiness shone in her eyes to match the bright joy across Shaw's entire face.

"Robert, no. Sit." Kerrick's loud whisper rose in pitch as the large dog broke away, pulling the poor man over to the ground before his chair. The beast galloped across to stand next to Alana, the rope hanging from his neck. She laughed.

"And this is our other child, Robert." She made the sitting signal with her hand, and Robert's back end plopped down on the floor right next to her as if he had decided to take the role of witness from Kirstin. Alana's hand rested on the curly hair on his head.

The minister frowned, but with one look at the dog, he knew that it would cause more trouble to try to move the beast than it was worth. The minister lowered his arm, and all the people joined Robert in sitting about the crowded great hall of Finlarig.

The elderly clergy cleared his throat. "Who stands with this woman as her family today?"

Grey came to the outside of Alana, reaching around Robert who happily looked up at them, his tongue rolling out. "I do," Grey said.

There was a rustling of petticoats. "We do, too."

Alana glanced behind her to see the Highland Roses standing up from their seats all along the aisle, broad smiles on their faces. Kirstin, Martha, Izzy, Cici, and even Lucy stood. They moved closer to form a line, their hands clasped.

"We do, too," Evelyn, Grey's wife and headmistress of the Highland Roses School, said, standing with her daughter over her shoulder. Her sister, Scarlet, stood, too, as well as the other Rose students and instructors: Cat, Fiona, Jacqueline, Mouse, Michaela, Francis, and Molly. Each one of them smiling in support.

"I did not mean all of her family," the minister said. "Just the…" he indicated Grey, "the closest family." He threw his hand out to the room in exasperation. "Because most of ye are Campbells."

Kirstin met Alana's gaze. "But we are the Highland Roses, even closer than blood. We all stand up for ye and your happiness."

Alana felt tears of joy break from her eyes as she smiled

back before looking to Shaw. Grey placed her hand in Shaw's palm. She stepped around Robert to stand directly before her mountainous Highland warrior.

"Very well," the minister said, shaking his head, and proceeded to collect the oaths, said before *all* of her family and God.

As Alana turned toward Shaw, holding both of his hands, they stared into each other's eyes, repeating their vows to love, cherish, and be faithful always.

He pulled her closer, his arms sliding around her back. "*Buin mo chridhe dhuit*," he said as he looked down into her face.

She reached up to touch his cheek with one hand. "My heart belongs to you, too. I love you, Shaw."

He leaned down with promises of a lifetime in his eyes. "I love ye, Alana." The words warmed her, but it was the pure joy in his gaze and smile that caught her breath. He lowered his face, and she lost herself in the heat of his kiss. The room around them erupted in cheers. She had never before felt so loved, by the man of her heart and by her very huge and loud family.

A Bit of History

The Sinclair clan was established in Scotland in 1057 when Sir William St. Clair of Rosin near Edinburgh married Isabella, daughter and heiress of Malise, Earl of Caithness. The castle of Girnigoe, situated on the east coast of northern Scotland, was built around 1480 by William Sinclair, the Second Earl of Caithness as a tower house defensive structure. Another part to the castle was built in 1606 and connected to the original tower by a drawbridge over a ravine.

George Sinclair, the Sixth Earl of Caithness, had accumulated a huge debt with the Campbells of Glenorchy. To pay the debt, the Campbells claimed the earldom and lands from George Sinclair. He died in 1676. In 1679 the castle was besieged and captured by George Sinclair of Keiss, who claimed the earldom from the Campbells. The ensuing battle over the earldom and lands was at Altimarlach, where the Sinclairs were "slaughtered in such numbers that the Campbells reportedly could cross the river without getting their feet wet."

In 1681, the Privy Council of Scotland settled the feud by

giving the Sinclairs back the earldom, while the Campbells were made Earls of Breadalbane (where Finlarig Castle sits). Girnigoe was so damaged by Sinclairs, who had been making it uninhabitable for the Campbells in 1680, that it was never reused.

After being owned by several families through the centuries, it was sold back to the Sinclairs in 1950 and now sits in a historical trust. Today the castle ruins are open to visitors, although the cliffs and structure can be dangerous. I plan to visit it in 2020!

In my next historical romance series, Sons of Sinclair, we will journey to Girnigoe Castle back in the late sixteenth century when clashes with the other northern Highland clans were part of the rich history of these brawny Highlanders.

Acknowledgments

A huge thank you goes out to all of you wonderful readers! Your support of historical romance and the authors, who work for months to create these adventures, is as rich and valuable as gold. I love receiving messages and notes from you. Writing can be a solitary pursuit but knowing that you are rooting for another book to read makes the hours typing worth it. *Slàinte!*

Also...

At the end of each of my books, I ask that you, my awesome readers, please remind yourselves of the whispered symptoms of ovarian cancer. I am now a seven-year survivor, one of the lucky ones. Please don't rely on luck. If you experience any of these symptoms consistently for three weeks or more, go see your GYN.

·Bloating
·Eating less and feeling full faster
·Abdominal pain
·Trouble with your bladder

Other symptoms may include: indigestion, back pain, pain with intercourse, constipation, fatigue, and menstrual irregularities.

About the Author

Heather McCollum is an award-winning historical romance writer. She is a member of Romance Writers of America and the Ruby Slippered Sisterhood of Golden Heart finalists. She has over twenty romance novels published and is a 2015 Readers' Crown Winner and Amazon Best Seller.

The ancient magic and lush beauty of Great Britain entrances Ms. McCollum's heart and imagination every time she visits. The country's history and landscape have been a backdrop for her writing ever since her first journey across the pond.

When she is not creating vibrant characters and magical adventures on the page, she is roaring her own battle cry in the war against ovarian cancer. Ms. McCollum slew the cancer beast and resides with her very own Highland hero, a rescued golden retriever, and three kids in the wilds of suburbia on the mid-Atlantic coast. For more information about Ms. McCollum, please visit www.HeatherMcCollum.com.

URL and Social Media links:

Facebook: www.facebook.com/HeatherMcCollumAuthor

Twitter: https://twitter.com/HMcCollumAuthor

Pinterest: https://www.pinterest.com/hmccollumauthor/

Instagram: www.instagram.com/heathermccollumauthor/

Discover more Amara titles...

HIS REBELLIOUS LASS
a *Scottish Hearts* novel by Callie Hutton

When Lord Campbell inherits a Scottish beauty as his ward, it's his job to marry her off. Easy. Lady Bridget will have plenty of suitors. But Bridget has plans for that fortune and she refuses to help her handsome guardian find her a husband. Bridget and Cam are on opposite sides of a war that neither one plans to lose. Even if neither can deny that they set each other's heart afire. And then Cam makes a bold proposal...

TO TAME A SCANDALOUS LADY
a *Once Upon a Scandal* novel by Liana De la Rosa

Christian Andrews, Marquess of Amstead, notices his assistant trainer has a special way with the horses. But once he realizes *he* is a *she*...and a very beautiful, spirited *she*...he should sack her before scandal breaks. Headstrong Lady Flora Campbell embraces her dream of working with racehorses and disguises herself as a lad to learn as much as she can from premiere expert, Christian Andrews. Although she develops a tendre for the dashing marquess, she can never let on she's not only a woman, but the daughter of a duke...

What a Scot Wants

a novel by Amalie Howard and Angie Morgan

Highlander Ronan Maclaren is in no hurry to marry. And he hasn't found the right woman. Lady Imogen has avoided wedlock for years. Determined to remain independent, she makes herself unattractive to all suitors. When a betrothal contract is signed—unbeknownst to Ronan or Imogen—it's loathing at first sight. They each vow to make the other cry off—by any means necessary. But what starts out as a battle of wits... quickly dissolves into a battle of wills.

Highland Salvation

a *Highland Pride* novel by Lori Ann Bailey

Finlay Cameron weds stunning Blair Macnab to ensure her clan's loyalty. She's everything he's ever wanted, but she may be plotting his murder. Always considered nothing but a pretty face, Blair Macnab refuses to be used as a political pawn, but when confronted by a blackmailer, she marries the brawny Finlay Cameron to escape. But her blackmailer is hot on her trail and her secrets could soon be exposed...

Made in the USA
Las Vegas, NV
02 September 2023

76951023R00198